Also by Helen Elaine Lee

THE SERPENT'S GIFT

Water Marked

A NOVEL

Helen Elaine Lee

Scribner Paperback Fiction
Published by Simon & Schuster
New York   London   Toronto   Sydney   Singapore

Lee

SCRIBNER PAPERBACK FICTION
Simon & Schuster, Inc.
Rockefeller Center
1230 Avenue of the Americas
New York, NY 10020

First Scribner Paperback Fiction edition 2001

SCRIBNER PAPERBACK FICTION and design are trademarks of Macmillan Library Reference USA, Inc., used under license by Simon & Schuster, the publisher of this work.

For information regarding special discounts for bulk purchases, please contact Simon & Schuster Special Sales at 1-800-456-6798 or _business@simonandschuster.com_

DESIGNED BY ERICH HOBBING

Set in Granjon

Manufactured in the United States of America

1 3 5 7 9 10 8 6 4 2

The Library of Congress has cataloged the Scribner edition as follows:
Lee, Helen Elaine.
Water marked : a novel / Helen Elaine Lee.
p. cm.
1. Afro-Americans—Fiction. I. Title.
PS3562.E3535W38   1999
813'.54—dc21   98-32204
CIP

ISBN 0-684-83843-5
0-684-86573-4 (Pbk)

"The River's Invitation" by Percy Mayfield. Copyright © 1952 Sony/ATV Songs LLC (Renewed). All rights administered by Sony/ATV Music Publishing, 8 Music Square West, Nashville, TN 37203. All rights reserved. Used by permission.
James Wright "Trying to Pray" from _Above the River: The Complete Poems_ © 1990 by Anne Wright, Wesleyan University Press, by permission of University Press of New England.
From the book _She Had Some Horses_ by Joy Harjo. Copyright © 1983 by Thunder's Mouth Press. Appears by permission of the publisher, Thunder's Mouth Press.

For those of my line:
the ancestors, whose stories guide;
the living, whose voices nurture and inspire;
and the one newly arrived, whose heartbeat uplifts.

The river flowed both ways. The current moved from north to south, but the wind usually came from the south, rippling the bronze-green water in the opposite direction.

from *The Diviners*
by MARGARET LAURENCE

It is almost too dark
                    for vision
these ebony mornings
but there is still memory,
the other-sight
and still I see.

from "Skeleton of Winter"
by JOY HARJO

I

THERE HAD BEEN NO WORDS for naming when she was born.

She was "Girl Owens" on the stamped paper that certified her birth, and at home, she had just been "Sister," that was all. When asked to decide, at five, what she would be called, she had chosen "Sunday," time of voices, lifted in praise.

She climbed aboard the morning train with a small suitcase and the note which had summoned her home. "Three days I'll stay," she mumbled as the train pulled away, "three days." For the first time in five years, Sunday Owens was bound for the small, damp town that had formed her, determined to recover the parts of her story she had tried to refuse. She had set off for Chicago half her life before, trying to take with her only what had been resolved and chosen, deciding to leave Girl Owens and Sister behind.

Squinting through the train window's scratches and smudges, she looked for the landmarks that would tell her she was drawing close to home. After wiping the glass with her scarf, she recognized a wall of interlocking fieldstones which ran along the tracks and then digressed to mark as separate two neighboring farms. Alone in a vast field, harvested of corn and soybeans, stood the tiny, clapboard building whose sign boasted "Smallest Church in the Whole Midwest." The naked field became a reservoir, and then a parking lot, and in the distance Sunday saw the aged windmill, its four arms still in motion like a resolute and weary Hindu god.

The train crossed the landscape as if pushing through memory, flashing the past to Sunday's left and to her right. It was the territory between home and home, witnessed from her many standpoints of departure and return.

At the end-point of her train ride waited Delta, last of her blood kin, the sister who was five years older and had never left home. And with her were the dead, their treasures and their crimes half-buried, their secret lives untold. All that Sunday had forsaken lay behind and before her, and she was sure of only a few things. She realized that she had to go back and somehow discover the father whose absence had defined her life. And she knew that in order to find him, she would have to be a sister first.

Folding and refolding her Café Car napkin until the creases broke its smooth paper weave, Sunday looked out at a trail of flimsy new buildings, identical in their design and their early decay, and wondered if the land remembered the trees and crops that had given way to asphalt and brick. Home to discount shopping centers and dwellings with low-ceilinged rooms, did the soil mourn its former life?

As the train pulled away from the platform of the final stop before home, the graffitied embankment of boulders slid past her window, announcing, "Tyrone was here," "Rita Loves Wayne."

"Three days," Sunday repeated to herself as she opened her bag and found Delta's note, staring at the postmark for "LYNCHBURG, IL." The black residents of the town had refused to call it by that name, opting instead for the county title, Sault, assigned for the leaping rapids of its river. Even then, they spelled and called it "Salt," despite the dictionary's pronunciation, "Soo."

When the note had arrived, two months before, Reed had brought it to the kitchen that was also her painting studio. He had tried to assess the stage of her work before entering the room, and she looked to be finished working, in the midst of cleaning up. "There's word from your sister," he had said, and she had reached for it without cleaning her fingers, smearing the envelope with paint. Instead of the usual Hallmark card, she had found a sheet of white paper, folded once and unsigned.

She had stared at Delta's words until they ran together, and then she had handed it to Reed and stumbled to the living room couch as her sister's words filled her chest, ballooning out and contracting as if the rounded letters themselves were breathing. Pressing her face into the couch cushions, she tried to stop it, to sort it, to place herself within the spin.

Reed found, as he held the note, that the looped script was overlaid with Sunday's thumbprints, left in paint. Through a screen of smudges and tiny, cobalt cyclones, he read its message: "He's been alive. He died last week."

Awaiting Sunday's arrival, Delta Owens stepped out onto the front porch. She waved at Exie Claybourne, who was on the ground with her flowers, pulling up the fence of frail, white wire humps that lined the beds in summer, covering freshly entombed bulbs with mulch. Delta wished she could get down on her knees and invest in spring, but she just let the bulbs planted years and years ago keep surfacing. The April before, plenty of leaves had driven through and up, shifting the thawing soil with their green, determined length, but there had been only four or five blooms all season. Delta brushed the fallen autumn leaves from the top step and sat down, turning away from her neighbor, whose industry and joy in her planting seemed a reproach.

Delta hoped she would be able to find the right way to talk to Sunday after so long. Since that night of grieving, five years before, when the friction that had gathered for decades erupted in accusations and insults, the only words exchanged had been written ones.

Delta had tried to demonstrate a persistent bond, depending on the ornate script and polished rhyme of Hallmark cards to express what she had never been able to say. Each one she had signed "Always, Delta" before addressing the envelope carefully and mailing it off to Chicago. She had heard back irregularly, receiving wood-block prints or splashes of paint on wefts of heavy paper with ragged edges or on see-through skins. She had turned these creations round and round, looking for right side up with the help of the signatures. Each one she had saved. Though she hadn't known what, specifically, to make of any of them, she knew their appearance said something about the habit of love.

Glancing at her watch, she thought how strange it was not to be at work. When Sunday called, she had decided to take some of the leave time she had accrued and never used. She imagined the train Sunday was riding as it closed the gap between Chicago and Salt County. Maybe she was sitting next to some stranger right then, sipping on a drink from the dining car, sharing her excitement and good memories of home. "Maybe not," Delta said aloud, imagining instead that Sunday had been as anxious as she was ever since her brief and awkward phone call. After all, it had taken her two months after getting the note to decide to come.

Sunday had always been clear on how she felt about Salt County. "I'm in a little box," she had complained while growing up, trying to express to Delta how different she felt, how she came from Salt County, but would never be able to stay. And Delta, who early on had fought anyone who criticized her sister, had listened and comforted her, but hadn't really comprehended. Sunday was the one from whom she felt different.

Delta pushed the night of conflict from her mind, hoping that this visit might help them leave behind their troubled history. Closing her eyes against the recollection of spilled whiskey and insults, she encountered, instead, the memory of those brown shoes, left side by side at the edge of the swift, churning river. "No," she said, "oh no," and rejecting that, too, she groped for the private language of chosen memory.

She invoked the blue bowl, bringing it up, up through the past.

She found it within her memory, resting on the counter. Traveling across the smooth, glazed furrows on the sides and then over the lip and down to the curve of the bottom, her hands remembered the iron-gray cracks that were like stray hairs escaped from Nana's tamed and coiled plait. She could hear the rhythm of her wooden spoon against it. Even, like a heartbeat. And the chorus of women working together, making bread. Delta cupped her hands, imagining the bowl, and it filled her open palms. She could see its azure, its hints of purple bleeding out from blue.

She put it aside where she could reach it, and called up the next thing: the placket down the front of her mother's worn, yellow housecoat. For this she had to reach further back, and when it rose from recollection it smelled of milk-warm skin. The fabric's tiny flowers were faded almost to white. Anchored with bumps of thread, the pale buttons were streaked and flecked with reminders of their former lives as bone. Their chipped edges worn smooth from daily fingering, they made a steady line: a trail of buttons marking the way home, like fairytale bread crumbs through the woods.

Once she had the bowl and the placket of buttons in the now, she searched amid the unrest of her life for her third thing, trying to picture the navy blue metal chalk box, its top open, rust spreading at the seams. As soon as she could see it, she retrieved the box from the outside window ledge where she had left it, when she was twelve years old, as the house slept. Raising it to her face, she smelled the rainwater she had collected in the secret envelope of night. If she tried, she could see, through the water, a leaf, new and yellow-green, that had found its way to the bottom. And she could see the other cherished things she had hidden: bits and pieces of colored glass and stone, and a clay fish, flecked with green and red, which she had made.

Delta was lifting these things past silence, past the lovers' wildfire that had nearly consumed her two years before. Past a pair of scuffed, abandoned shoes.

When she heard the kettle from the kitchen, Delta released her conjured things: the blue bowl, the button road, the rainwater with its sunken world of colored glass and fish. She returned them to their buried places, knowing she would need them again.

As the train slowed, Sunday leaned toward the glass and saw the terrain through the faint reflection of her own tired and anxious face. Suddenly she could smell the burnt, sweet odor of the paper mill that sprawled across the edge of town, and as the train got closer, the past became present in all she saw. She could hear her grandmother's, Nana's, voice and she felt herself entering the greens and reds and browns of her own paintings, pulling aside her brush strokes as if they were curtains and stepping through. There were autumn trees on fire everywhere, and as the train approached the river, she moved beyond the surface of color and texture into the layers of the past, from which she had learned to speak her life with paint.

After avoiding it as long as she was able, she had called Delta two days before boarding the train to say that she was coming home. As she slipped the note from the envelope, she focused on her unintentional signature of thumbprints, a veil of color over Delta's writing that had darkened and settled into the paper's grain, leaving "alive" the only word unmarked.

Note in hand, Reed had followed her to the couch she had streaked with cobalt and russet and perched on the cushion's edge, in the bend of her waist. Sinking his fingers into her springy hair, he had massaged her scalp, smelling paint and linseed oil, wishing he knew what to say to the ardent and trying woman who moved in and out of reach. He had brought her a cloth and turpentine to clean her hands and waited several hours, offering tea and food, pillows and blankets, until she could speak about Delta's words.

Reed hadn't had to wonder who the "He" in the note might be. Mercury Owens, ever-present in his absence, had managed to leave her again.

"Whatever there is to find out, I don't want, I don't need to know," Sunday had said, remembering the unrest of her last trip home and the even more shameful silence that had followed. Delta, she thought angrily, master of passive influence, hadn't come right out and asked her to return, but had provided the single fact that had the power to draw her home.

She had submerged the note at the bottom of a cardboard box filled with old letters and cards, and sealed it with packing tape. But it was the first thing she thought of on waking and it stayed with her, just below the surface of activity, throughout each day. "Where was he?" "Who was he?" haunted her until she was separate from everything, including art. Never before had she been unable to express herself with paint, for her work was where she had turned in times of crisis and danger. She had even used it as a refuge against lovers and friends. But her hands had fallen silent, and then, in spurts, she had been able to work, using every color but one.

After two months of intermittent painting and exile from blue, Sunday had torn open the taped-up box in the middle of a sleepless night, finding Delta's note and two mementos, a coaster and a belt buckle, which she had taken with her from home eighteen years before. That night she had accepted the fact that she had to go back and recover Mercury Owens, no matter how much he had wanted to be lost.

Returning the note to its envelope, Sunday looked out at Salt County and tried to picture what her sister was doing as she awaited her train. Her nervous hands would be busy with a cigarette, unless she, too, had struggled to quit. She would be reading the paper for local news, drinking coffee, checking her horoscope. Maybe she was playing the piano again.

Sunday wondered how Delta had changed. She knew from the return addresses on her Hallmark cards that she still lived in the family house. But did she have a lover and a circle of friends? Did she still work at the tiny, two-room post office, and go to lunch across the street at Frank and Etta's every day? Did she look forty, and have the same bags beneath her eyes that Sunday had? Had her hourglass figure surrendered to gravity, or spread?

The top of the mill came into view, its chimneys belching the smoke that settled over Salt County like a weight, and the train edged its way through trash-strewn tracks where discarded and rusted railroad cars had been put to rest, approaching the iron bridge.

She watched from now and from before as the train left behind hollow storage buildings to cross the swift, ocher river that had carried Mercury away. And then it passed through the part of town in which she had grown up, where the people were dark and the comforts slim. As the aged stood waiting for late-running buses and young men gathered on corners to fool away time, compact frame houses huddled in the October chill. Exhausted buildings leaned.

Sunday revisited Salt County as native and exile, woman and child. She saw it as Girl Owens and Sister had known it, and as Sunday, who was coming to claim her story as she had taken her name.

Delta turned off the flame beneath the teakettle and busied herself with arranging a sunburst pattern of cookies on a china plate while she listened for the telephone. At the same time that she was anxious to see her sister, she wondered how they would shed their troubled past and manage to use words to reach, and not wound, each other. She kept returning to the night of Nana's funeral, when they had tried to drink away their grief. In the expansive post-funeral quiet, after the visitors had gone, they had uttered indelible things. Sunday had damned Salt County, and Delta had taken it to heart.

"This place clutches you," Sunday had argued urgently, slamming her glass on the table so that the bourbon spilled over the sides and wet her hand. "It sleeps and shelters you, but safety's not the same as health." And Delta knew that just like the town, she was insular, settled and ordinary to most anyone's eyes. Yet she felt just like its yellow-brown river, fitful with secrets and undercurrents, churning, rolling, but bound by the place where it had cut its glacier path from rock and clay.

Delta had responded by calling her "arrogant," a "misfit" who thought she was better than the folks she'd left behind. But it was Delta's recognition of her own rancor, as much as the substance of what they said, that had staggered and disgraced her. She hadn't even realized all the things for which she couldn't forgive Sunday, hadn't known her own smallness, until she found herself attacking her sister out loud.

As Sunday got off the train and secured her bag to the luggage cart, she heard the coaster and the belt buckle clack against each other in her coat pocket and patted her other side to make sure she had the earrings she had bought for Delta as a gift. She jerked her cart over the places where expanding tree roots had buckled the sidewalk, remembering that Delta had asked her to call when she arrived, since that train was sometimes late. "Oh damn," she mumbled, feeling guilty for not calling . . . for leaving eighteen years before . . . for the things she had said and done the last time around.

Arrogant . . . misfit . . . Delta had gone for her most vulnerable spot. She hadn't meant to condemn her sister; she had been trying to encourage greater reach. It had all started when Delta grilled her about why she had to leave so soon. "Just when the going gets tough," she had said, gulping at her glass of bourbon, "leaving is what you seem to do best." Sunday had sought to justify her departure, and offended Delta, instead. As so often seemed to happen, the words had come out wrong.

And just before the heavy-bottomed whiskey glass had left Delta's hand, Sunday had cried, "What would you know about me or this place? You don't see because you can't see. You can't see me or my painting, or even yourself. You won't even make music, because it might hurt." She, too, had aimed for the tenderest place.

Intoxicated with expressing long-held feelings, they had spoken without restraint or care, and then the rush of words had ended when the drink hit the wall, scattering ice and glass across the floor, leaving the area above the baseboard dented and stained. Both of them stunned, neither sure for a moment who had done it, they had silently cleaned up the mess and gone upstairs without repairing their other trespasses. Sunday had gathered and packed her things in a wild, tearful stupor of regret and relief, while Delta had climbed into bed fully dressed and wept, both bitter and remorseful at the crude and unruly scene she had helped cause.

"It was the bourbon talking," they had both declared the next morning, knowing as they said it that it was neither true, nor enough.

* * *

As her cart caught on a sidewalk juncture, Sunday was jolted into the present. She bent down to free the wheels, wiped her sweaty face with her scarf, and began to walk more slowly and to look around.

She decided to take a short detour to the river that had remained such a force in memory. Standing across the street from its slope, she saw a man in a wet suit at the water's edge. He was moving a large piece of machinery from a boat to the riverbank. What was his purpose? she wondered, as she watched. She was tempted to call out to him or cross the bridge and find out, but she knew Delta would be waiting, and she moved on.

She followed the route she had taken from school to her afternoon job: past the post office and the drugstore, then past Salt County's one Chinese restaurant, the Rice Bowl, the Social Security office, and the Y, and then into the black part of town she had seen minutes before from the train. When she got there, on familiar ground, a young man paused from trimming his hedges to nod and say "Mornin'," and she greeted him and smiled back.

When she reached the house, Sunday stood at the front steps and stated firmly, "Three days." Looking up at the second story, she pictured herself sneaking out of her bedroom window at night and climbing to the roof or down the adjacent tree to look at the stars or explore the neighborhood undetected.

Often she had stretched out on the roof and breathed deeply, becoming a part, it seemed, of the open sky. She hurt to think of how, in those teenage years of soreness and yearning, she had felt herself constricted and apart, but until some time around the age of eight or nine, she had looked up to her big sister, depending on her to guide and protect, and Delta had shared her secrets and let her tag along beside her. For a while, they had been each other's refuge. They had been an alliance of two.

All that had long since changed by the time she left for Chicago, just after Dolora died. But there had been fleeting occasions of closeness, Sunday thought as she recalled climbing up there with Delta on a starlit, April night.

Sunday looked the house over, seeing that the paint had faded and thinned in patches, noticing the bare flower beds and the unruly boxwood hedges. Chains hung where the porch swing used to be, and all the blinds were drawn. She imagined the sound of Nana singing and the image of Delta seated at the piano, accepting the force of their grandmother's song.

When Delta heard the groaning of the wide porch floorboards, she came to the door.

Sunday paused, surrounded by saffron and flame-red leaves, and stepped in.

2

DELTA MOVED ASIDE as Sunday came through the doorway, and in an instant, they felt their manifold heritage of silence and remorse, and the pull of common history and blood.

Sunday called her sister's name, and Delta's hands began to reach for her, before pausing and returning to her sides. She offered a determined smile, and then, seeing Sunday seeing her, she smoothed down her hair, oiled and halved by a careful part.

As Sunday looked at her, Delta nodded, reminded of her sister's aptitude for sight, and wondered if she could sense the toll of misbegotten love. She felt a sudden kinship with a tree she had once known, lightning-struck and fired from the inside out, a few singed spots the only clues, but changed, unmistakably changed. Her roomy, flowered shirtwaist offered no cover at all as she seemed to thicken, further, under Sunday's gaze, and she crossed her arms over the fullness of her waist and breasts and fumbled toward speech.

"Well . . ." she said, damning herself as she spoke for her ineptitude in launching their reunion with that word that was all-purpose and meant nothing, asking herself why she could never find the right way to begin, the right thing to say, even to her own sister, and there she was groping, idiotically groping as she heard her own voice trail off, her alarm at the impending silence and her own impotence spreading, and again, "Well," this time as if it were a statement, the completion of what she had started.

Each one took a step forward, and then Sunday reached for Delta, smelling Ivory soap and Kool Milds, and Delta felt herself enfolded in the soft, loose weave of her baby sister's clothes. She tightened her balled-up hands and inhaled the woody musk, the train, the oil paint in her neck, identifying them all in a tumbled rush of memory as the thin, gold music of Sunday's earrings quieted against her face and hair. She hadn't been held for so long, and here were Sunday's wiry arms around her and her fingers spread wide across her back.

"Wing stumps," Sunday whispered as she touched her sister's shoulder blades, giving her own childhood explanation for the protrusions of bone. Delta laughed as she remembered how Sunday had once drawn herself holding a set of folded wings, prepared for flight.

Delta freed her hands from her pockets and patted her sister stiffly as she eased herself away, noticing as Sunday moved to the center of the living room how tall she seemed beneath the layers of overlapping aubergine cloth. Her hair was unstraightened and unconfined, and she was so tall, so purple, so much, she seemed to fill the room.

"I know I was supposed to call, but I forgot, and it seemed easier just to come. That way I got to walk through the neighborhood."

Delta stepped back from her and focused on the different textures of cloth, some nubby and fibrous and some watery smooth, and what was that she had on, anyhow, she wondered silently, unable to tell if it was pants or a skirt, and where the top ended and the bottom began, and standing out from those waves of purple, from the corkscrews of bark-red hennaed hair and strings of beads that rang together as she moved, were her eyes, unquiet and night-black, taking in the details of sister and house.

Sunday saw the green and rust that had appeared again and again on her own canvases, and the familiar symmetry of the room, where crystal candlesticks stood like sentries on the ends of the mantel and lamps of bulbous, tarnished brass sat beside the easy chairs that flanked the window. Little was changed, aside from the new afghan of alternating brown and white crocheted squares that Delta had recently made, folded neatly at the end of the couch.

Following Sunday's gaze, Delta looked around and saw threads escaping the bound edges of the sculptured pea green carpet, the dark, beetle-shaped cigarette burns climbing up the threadbare arms of her chair, the fingermarks around the switchplates on the walls. She saw that the brown oak leaf pattern on the drapes had faded, the curtain rod sagged in the center, and she would have to get the side cords unknotted. Everything was in its place at least, but she hadn't realized how shabby some aspects of the house had grown. She need not feel embarrassed, she told herself as she looked at the room crowded with furniture and knickknacks, for they had both grown up there.

Sunday's beads sounded against each other as she turned in a circle and then stopped, caught by the ribboned light coming through the half-opened venetian blinds. Feeling for the edge of something she couldn't place, just a feeling, maybe, a color or a shape that might be, for her, like a first word, like the start of speech, she stepped into the banded light.

Delta watched her. Nate had walked right into that light, too, she thought, recalling that his arms, bare and muscular, had been briefly tattooed with stripes as he extended them, offering plenty. She found that he visited her in sudden alarming flashes: She would see a customer at the post office who waited tensely, flexing his jaw as Nate had done, and it would freeze her fast until she could recover and return to the present moment. Why, she asked herself, did mistakes have to stalk you, no matter how hard you tried to right them and forget? She didn't seem to be able to lose Nate Hunter, and here he was now, walking, uninvited, into her living room light. She shook the memory off and went to the kitchen to restart the kettle, watching the blue fire of the burner leap into a mesmerizing ring.

Absorbed in her study of the room, Sunday didn't realize Delta had left. She felt a pang of guilt at her scrutiny, hearing the voices of those who had told her it wasn't gracious to look so hard at things. Countless times she had tried to defend herself, to say that looking was her job. She approached each object hungrily, seeking something without even knowing what: some clue that would bring understanding, some key thing that she might find in the landscape if she read it closely enough.

She recalled the cloudy rings on the coffee table and its veneer rising up along the edges, exposing warped and naked wood. The mosaic tabletops and trays that Dolora had made were still displayed around the room, overlapping spirals of color and glyphs of private and ancient languages. She could see the few survivor plates and ceramic figurines behind the glass doors of the china closet, and tiny pieces of glazed tile and stones were scattered on the shelves like bits of excavated treasure.

The missing leg of the phone caddy had been replaced with three of the secondhand encyclopedias Dolora had purchased over a five-year indenture: Q through S. Sunday stared at it and thought about the bound, compiled world of facts in the hall bookcase, the gold letters on the spines harder and harder to make out, missing an entire chunk of information two-thirds of the way through, missing quartz ... rhinoceros ... scarab ... She reached out to straighten one of her first paintings, hanging where it had been placed fifteen years ago, recalling that as Nana was putting it up, Delta had said that she liked the texture, but wanted to know what, exactly, it was supposed to be. The plaster had crumbled above in places, leaving a fine grainy film on the picture glass.

The walls and furniture were still marked with horizontal lines from years of flooding, when rain burst the river and filled their home. She remembered sitting on the stair landing, watching wastebaskets, colored pencils, and even chairs float, and recalled the dank smell that remained when the water receded and left its dark, wavy line across their lives.

She could still detect it, she thought, sniffing, just a trace. Either that wetness or a recollection, surfacing.

Their lives had always seemed open to water. Loose, rattling windows and their ill-fitting frames accepted heavy rain into the house, into the ceiling that every now and then grew distended like a swollen belly. There was always a saucepan or that blue bread bowl of Nana's sitting in the middle of a floor upstairs to catch some drip from the roof that failed them again and again. The border of the oak floor was scarred with dark blots around the arching ribs of radiators that hissed and knocked and leaked.

She looked around the cramped, moist house she had been desperate to leave. Although she had never managed to lose it in her work, she had returned annually after leaving for school, and not once in the past five years. After Dolora and then Nana died, she had wondered if the present could exist for her in that house.

There was Nana's photo across the room. That last time, when they were supposed to be comforting each other, she thought, they had given in to a kind of smallness that had made Sunday feel disgraced before Nana's memory. It all came back to her as she passed through the hallway: the airborne tumbler of bourbon, the arsenals of words and tears, the resentments, grown thick and malignant, fed by absence and discontent. But the thing she had never been able to forget or forgive, the thing that came to her at night, just before sleep, was how she had heard Delta come softly to her bedroom door.

Sunday had heard her in the hallway, and had chosen to stand on the other side, separated from her sister by a piece of hinged and hollow wood, so close that she could almost hear her inhale and exhale. Not knocking, Delta had stood there for a full minute and then left, and Sunday had neither spoken, nor opened the door.

Blinking away the image of that door, she saw the piano resting in the corner, its closed keyboard piled high with library detective novels, magazines or horoscopes, mail order catalogs. So many things in the house made her want to either flee or weep. The try at cheerful domesticity of Delta's ruffle-edged apron brought tears to her eyes, and the crowded dining room with its crocheted doilies and centerpiece of plastic lilies reawakened the cornered sense of longing she had felt as a girl.

But there had been touches of beauty, she thought, while her mother was alive. Her mosaics had always given the house a distinctive quality, as had jelly glasses and coffee cans filled with fresh flowers. Mason jars of vibrant canned fruit and preserves had stood on open shelves in the kitchen. And in the daytime, the venetian blinds Sunday had always hated were raised; there had been light.

Overwhelmed with remembering, she went into the bathroom and sat on the chenille-covered toilet seat, collecting herself. I have never left this house behind, she thought, touching the dusty crocheted doll, no doubt bought from one of Delta's post office co-workers, whose skirt concealed an extra roll of toilet paper. Standing, she looked at her face between the abstract shapes where the mirror's silver backing of paint had cracked and flaked off, and pulled the mass of unruly ringlets from her face to force it into one of the elastics she had around her wrist.

She followed the ridged path of the yellowed plastic runner across the carpet, listening for the *rrrrrrh* her shoes made. When she entered the kitchen she remembered the women who had regularly inhabited that room, Nana's voice leading the others, and she could almost hear their wooden spoons and smell the flour and sharp yeast. Standing in the doorway behind her, Sunday watched Delta straighten the quilted rooster-shaped toaster cover and raise her fingers to the half-moon stainless steel handles of the white metal cabinets and drawers. With her sturdy, flat-heeled shoes and her broadened hips rising under the pastel cabbage roses of her dress, she looked upholstered from the back.

Glancing away, Sunday could see the dent above the baseboard and a dark trace of splashed whiskey. How would she meet this woman who was her sister across the chasm, not only of their past but of their adult lives? She sat at the round oak table and took out the gift she had brought as Delta turned around, retied the bow on her apron, and flattened her palms along its fading green and yellow fruit. She took her cigarettes and plastic lighter from the counter and placed them on the table as she sat down.

"A peace offering," Sunday said as she pushed the foil-wrapped box a few inches toward Delta with her fingertips. She hoped the gift wasn't too extravagant, recalling how Nana had told her you had to be careful what you gave middle-class black folks, for if you brought jams or wine to dinner, they might be insulted, construing the gesture as a declaration that they couldn't afford, or didn't know enough, to get such things for themselves.

Delta opened the box slowly, anxious that she wouldn't know how to respond or might not understand its importance or its use. It might be some artsy thing she had never heard of, or some cosmopolitan gadget that was all the rage. And she was embarrassed that she had not thought to get Sunday a gift.

When she saw the dangling, pewter fish earrings, crafted into hinged and moving pieces, she smiled carefully. Sunday knew immediately that again she had chosen something discordant with her sister's quiet taste; she had chosen the gift she herself would like to receive. And she also knew that Delta would try to like them, and would wear them, at least once, before she left.

"They're . . . dramatic," Delta said, pulling one out of the box. She went to the hall mirror to put them on, and returning to the kitchen, unable to think of what to say, she began to apologize for not having a gift.

Sunday interrupted the repentance with a wave of her hand, and they both focused on the tabletop.

"It was definitely him, then?" Sunday asked, raising her head. "You're sure it was him?"

Delta nodded as she reached into her apron pocket to pull out an engraved gold locket the size of a half-dollar. She placed it on the table between them.

"What I'd like to know," said Sunday, staring at the dented face of the locket, the letters of their mother's monogram looped together in a continuous line, "is how. How, I ask you, did he manage to die twice?"

*   *   *

The locket lay between them on the table as they looked at each other. "It came in the mail, along with what you might call a note," Delta explained. "He had kept it all these years."

Sunday's mouth went dry. She wanted to ask for every detail and then devour Delta's answers, but she couldn't seem to pose even the first questions: Where was the locket mailed from and what did the note say? She didn't understand why Delta was silent, why she didn't say everything then, right then. She looked up and saw herself in her sister's face. She had her skin, her oval face, her hairline. And unlike their mother's mouth, lean and carefully governed, theirs were liable to transform suddenly into reckless smiles.

Although Delta's hair was pressed straight and divided into the two dark curtains that Sunday remembered, its smooth surface had been invaded by recalcitrant white hairs that stood up at the temples and along the part. They had both sat on the edges of their beds while growing up and rolled the ends of their hair with pink foam-rubber curlers, but she had long ago abandoned that ritual. Delta's was turned under, as it had been for twenty years, in an even pageboy. Her deep-set eyes were sheltered by heavy brows, which she had plucked back to narrow pointed arches as a teenager, until Nana had convinced her to let them be. She still had the habit of smoothing them down with her fingertips, first the right one and then the left.

She seemed different to Sunday, but it wasn't her roundness, or her graying hair. As Delta raised her gaze from the table, Sunday sensed a change within the restive eyes. She searched the striated browns of her sister's irises, seeing behind the folded shutter of russet and seal brown and weathered grass something scorched and too quiet. The aftermath of fire.

She watched as Delta moved from taming her eyebrows, to turning her spoon over and over and over, to circling the gilt edge of the saucer with her fingertips. Delta took out a cigarette and tapped the filtered end against the table, and Sunday remembered how her fidgeting had unsettled Dolora, who had impatiently told her, "Be still . . . be *still*." Only Nana had been able to quiet her. "Be *here*," Nana had urged in her hoarse and gentle voice.

Delta jumped up to escape the discomfort of her sister's eye and emptied the coffee grounds from the pleated filter. As she rinsed the pot she also searched for a way to start the talking, glancing sideways at the locket in Sunday's rough, discolored hands, the nails cut close and straight across, the cuticles bearing traces of brown and yellow paint. Sunday examined the gold wafer intently, as if her touch and concentration could make it surrender its story, and Delta noticed the lines, like Nana's, that appeared in her forehead as she focused.

Reaching into the bag she had dropped next to her chair, Sunday rummaged through pens and sketchbook, lipsticks and barrettes, and the collection of found stones she carried with her. She unearthed her eyeglasses and put them on to inspect the details of the gold engraving that she had been taking in with her hands, and pried open the gold disk with her blunt fingernail.

Inside she found a faded picture of Dolora at fifteen or sixteen, her hair free of the French roll they had always seen her wear, her face plump and unworried, lovely in its innocent excitement at the just-opening world. Although Delta had looked at it when it arrived, she wiped her hands on her apron and came closer, bending over Sunday's shoulder to peer at the photograph that was cracked and water-warped. Together, they thought how different the young girl was from the mother they had known.

They had opened the locket, but they would have to work their way toward what it meant. They sat at the table chatting about local news. Then Sunday pulled the beaded brass chain that hung between them, flooding the room with soft, warm light.

"Remember Mama's jewelry box?" Sunday said as she eased her glasses up onto her forehead, where they stayed, like a second pair of eyes. "How when you slid the little brass button on the front the flat catch popped up, and each of us wanted to be the one to open it. Remember the embossed pink leather . . ."

"I think it was brown . . ."

"Pink. And it was darker, with the gold embossing fainter along the middle edge from all of our fingers touching it and pulling it open. And we would beg to go through it, getting her to tell us the lineage of each little thing in its velvet-lined division, always asking for more information. Unsatisfied, no matter what she told."

"You would want to try it all on and we'd pretend it was rediscovered treasure and make up our own tales about those things. Then we'd sneak into her closet when she was gone and play make-believe with her purses and shoes. I remember the little necklace with the dangling purple stones. 'Those are tourmalines,' Mama used to say, whenever I touched it, as if it were important to her that the stones were authentic, and she could call their name."

"She never said where it came from," Sunday remembered. "She had costume stuff, too, the bracelet of shiny birthstones that must have been fake, and matching pin. But it was all super-real . . . magical, to us. And when you held it or put it on, you were transformed. It was the way into a fantasy."

"And there were the colored plastic bangles that probably came from the five-and-ten, and the one that boy had made her in his ninth-grade shop class from twisted metal." A symbol of love that had never had a chance to fail.

Delta also remembered the everyday, unremarkable things that were in there with the jewelry, and had thereby acquired a magic of their own: tiny safety pins and keys to forgotten or changed locks; buttons, lone ones Dolora must have been meaning to sew back on, and special, cherished ones made of rhinestones or cast brass that she had cut from clothes before giving them away, threaded into clusters with tangled wire.

"Grandpa's watch was in there, too," Delta added. "It's upstairs now. And a ring that was missing its stones. I used to imagine it complete, faceted sapphires intact. And there was a silver belt buckle, I vaguely recall."

Sunday stirred and cleared her throat, but decided to say nothing yet about the buckle she had brought in her coat pocket.

Delta lifted the chain and let the locket swing back and forth before she put it down. "Well, it seems like I've seen this locket, but clearly, it was never there after he left. Maybe she showed it to me beforehand, but maybe not. Probably she created it for us in the telling, 'cause when it came, I knew immediately what it was. What I hadn't known was that he took it with him when he left."

They had heard about the locket again and again, as Dolora made and remade her tale. Always it began in the same way, with her pointing to the empty velvet depression where it had been housed. She recounted her sitting for the photograph, and its presentation as a gift from her father, when she turned "sweet sixteen." As she described its intricate monogram and delicate chain, she looked into the distance and they could tell she was seeing it, repeating chosen pieces of the chronicle with embellishments, until it was a myth with a life of its own. As explanation of its absence, she had said only that it was "lost."

"Tell me . . . tell me the whole story," Sunday said, reaching across the table to take Delta's wrist and to feel the pulse beneath her fingertips, helpless at how little she understood, wondering what it would mean to have the whole story about anything, anything at all.

"Tell me," she said, "about the suicide that wasn't death."

Daunted by the hunger in her sister's voice and the rough hand that encircled her wrist, Delta looked away.

As Sunday watched her, she relived her recent impasse with paint. She wanted to be able to tell how she had gone each morning to her kitchen studio to stare at the blank and half-done canvases that filled the room, reminded of tombstones, and then turned their faces to the wall. Riding the El to the end of the line and back, she had walked the city streets, searching for something, a face, a storefront, a window that would move her from silence. She had even found herself standing at church doorways, attracted, yet hesitant to enter for the first time since she had left home, except in requiem. She had walked the lakeshore, trying to think of the water that stretched before her as ocean, but unable to lose the feeling that she was landlocked.

She had tried charcoal and pencil drawing, collage and modeling clay, never getting past concept to give her beginnings life. She had collected paper scraps and photographs and fabrics, but had been unable to turn them into anything. Her relentless, vague anxiety seeded and took root as she stretched canvases and mixed colors, and then flourished into panic when she tried to begin. She couldn't even focus on the rote drafting projects that were her steady source of income.

And then, after retrieving Delta's note from the box, she had drawn and painted furiously for close to a week. What came to her were shadowy figures bent into fetal question marks and disembodied limbs and hands, floating, buried, rising, layered. Again and again she painted the world from above, patchworks of city and field joined by branching rivers that fractured into overlapping pieces, like shattered trees. But she would come to a stop while painting, as if full sight just closed up, and then her palette began to narrow down.

Reed had walked in one day to find her stuck, trying to make a mark, a stroke, in any kind of blue, but lost. She couldn't seem to choose it, just as she couldn't seem to fully choose him. She knew she was trying his patience, but how could she explain something she didn't even understand?

She wanted to tell Delta how it had been. Fingers still around her wrist, she could only say, "I need it. I need all of what I am."

Except for the moth wings that homed in and trembled on the lightbulb's yellow curve, the room was still. And then Delta pulled away and tightened her pocketed hands into fists. "You see," she answered, "there isn't much I know." Tears filled her eyes and she felt as if she had failed her sister, once again. "We weren't a family that talked about what was gone." She looked at Sunday, apologizing silently for every time she had come up short.

"You know a hell of a lot more than I do," Sunday answered. "You had him for five years, so you've got your memory, for one thing. And by the time I came along, everyone had decided to just keep quiet about his leaving and everything else that had to do with him. I don't even know the smallest things about him, like whether he wore cologne . . . what he liked to eat . . . how he moved his hands. You and I scarcely even talked about him. Maybe everyone was protecting me, but in the end, I was left with my imagination, and a gaping hole."

She leaned into the circle of light. "Delta, this didn't only happen to you; it's both of ours. I know you can't give me what you haven't got, but let's remember together. Tell me, anyway, what little bit you know."

Delta paused. At least she was sure what the beginning was, for it came to her all the time, despite her resistance, as if occupying its own tier of the recessed past. She placed her palms flat on the table.

"Shoes," she said. "What I remember most is that pair of shoes."

Delta could see them. From the witnessing or the telling, or both, they were there, worn through brown to gray and dirty at the squared-off tips from work and daily travel. Laces tucked inside. Heels run-down and placed neatly side by side.

"Yes," Sunday responded. "I heard about the shoes. It's practically the only concrete thing about his disappearance that I do remember hearing. Describe them for me, so that I can see them, too."

She did describe their run-down heels, one eroded to a sharper slant than the other, and they both savored that clue to his walk, imagining him moving along, favoring one leg. She told about the places where the dark brown, dusty leather was strained and bunion-cracked on the sides. The twisted laces and elongated tongues. The mud-encrusted toes. And then they wondered what had happened to them, and Delta said, "Maybe Mama threw them out."

As Delta stared out the back window, seeming to fade farther and farther away, it occurred to Sunday that they might not be able to begin with Mercury's disappearance, which had never, in all their years of growing up, been discussed. Would they have to start to remember him as a person, to make him real, first? "You know," she said, "I wonder what Mama did with the rest of his stuff. There must be something, up in the attic, maybe. Something of him she kept."

"Well, I never heard anyone talk about his belongings, and I can't even recollect what all he had."

"But . . . but you must have kept something of him, then, if not a possession then a memory, some little thing he liked or used to do?"

Delta thought for a while, her hands in motion, turning and tipping the edge of her coffee cup and lighter. What came to her suddenly, despite attempts at forgetting, were his restless and uneven footsteps as he paced the upstairs hallway late at night, reaching one loose and groaning floorboard again and again. She willed away the sound and recounted other things.

"I know. He had a beautiful gray fedora that he always wore when he left the house. Sometimes he would take it off and let me feel the soft, pressed felt and the raised lines in its wide, grosgrain ribbon band, where a couple of feathers were tucked before the hat broke out in a cold-blooded brim. I think he felt really fly in that hat, even if he was just going to the plant. I'm sure Grandpa thought that was ridiculous, but he loved that hat, was proud of it, and when he came home he brushed it and placed it just so on the closet shelf . . . I can see him come through the door and do just that . . . but the clearest thing is me looking up at it, from my little-girl height, as it rested, tilted on his head, surrounding his frowning face with a dark oval that blocked out everything else."

After a pause, she went on, "I remember him playing cards at the dining room table, by himself. He liked to listen to the news while he played, and I can see those cards being turned over, building and shrinking and building in overlapping columns, and then his sudden curse and a hand scooping the mass of them together and cracking the edge on the table, evening them up, before starting again. I was entranced by the ceremony of it, and the mirrored, noble pictures on the cards, the bright red and black and the faces turned, secretively, to the side, as if they knew things they would never tell. But I was afraid of the curse and the sound of them hitting the table, and even more afraid to ask if I could play."

She spoke faster and faster. "And you know what else, Sunday? He used to bring a whole bagful of Mary Jane candies when he got home late. We both loved the thick, chewy molasses taste, and he would take one out and hide it in one hand, and ask me to guess which one. Whichever one I chose, he gave it to me, and we both laughed as we ate them together.

"I hadn't thought of that in a long time. It's small, but it's a good thing, isn't it?

"Mostly . . . he seemed ill at ease with me, like he didn't quite know how to relate to a child or a girl child, anyway. Those Mary Janes were something we shared."

Sunday looked at her expectantly, pushing for more. "So what else?"

Delta continued, "He liked fine things. Champagne taste and beer money, Grandpa used to say. And Nana told me how he bought that belt buckle, which he had engraved, along with a pair of inlaid silver cuff links, and a shirt to go with it, and Grandpa chided him with the uselessness of that. 'French cuffs,' he would say, and suck his teeth. It had turned into a big fight, because Nana had defended him, unable to bear the way he got on Mercury at the slightest provocation, telling Grandpa 'a body's got to have a little something nice, just for himself.'

"Grandpa didn't budge, I guess, even though he had his own weaknesses. He sure loved getting all decked out for Mason meetings, and his ring was so important to him that he made Nana promise to bury him in it. Being a Thirty-second-Degree Mason, the secret rites, the ring, all of that was major, along with the gold pocket watch that he cherished so. But in Mercury, he just couldn't tolerate it. Nana said Grandpa thought a person had to work their way up, to pay their dues before they got nice possessions and respect, and that attitude seemed to make Mercury even more withdrawn. Nana said he had one pair of really good shoes that he changed into after he got home and showered, and they were impractical for the life he led. Thin soles and fine leather . . . and she thought he would change into them to try and mark off the separate parts of his life. It was as if he was saying: This isn't all I am. I am also a man who appreciates the distinctions between things."

Sunday wondered at Delta keeping such details to herself for all those years, and at the slight smile in her eyes as she told them, as if they made her proud. She knew plenty of people like that, who found certain indulgences necessary, whatever their means. As she had studied the belt buckle over the past weeks, she had been struck by its extravagance, and she knew she had that taste for special things in her, too. Reed was forever reminding her of the time she had decided to have a pair of antique fountain pens repaired, when they'd scarcely been able to put together rent money.

Delta went on, "He would shower as soon as he got home and put on that shirt and those shoes and take a walk around town before dinner. The ones he left by the river weren't those; they were his other pair."

"You mean that when he left, he went wherever it was he went barefoot?"

"Well . . . I guess he did."

"I wonder what he did about that?" Sunday pressed. "I mean, how long could he have crossed fields and roads without shoes? I wonder if he stole some or what. Are you sure he didn't take those good shoes, too?"

"Nana said he left the good ones home, of that I'm sure. But the hat, the hat went with him. It was never found."

"The fedora?"

"That's right." She frowned in concentration and then went on, "You know, Nana would sometimes talk to me about him, as if she was trying to give me something of him to hold, and I often wondered if it was her own imagination talking, like she was forming an outlook that she could pass on to me. I remember those times by her gentle voice and her clove smell.

"She told me he had worked delivering papers and groceries and whatever else he could manage, from the time he was nine or ten, and then he had landed that job at the paper mill his junior year, most likely with Grandpa's help. At first he worked part-time, and then, after graduating, he had a regular shift. They still had segregated bathrooms, by unstated policy, though, and the black men used to have to warm their lunches on the radiators outside the makeshift 'colored' washroom, which wasn't much more than a closet with one toilet for the dozens of men, and that had filled Mercury with rage. She said he was a prideful man, who liked words. He read the dictionary sometimes and he liked to work crosswords during his breaks at the plant . . . and, what else . . . I know, he used to say all the time that his white supervisor didn't even know the word 'quandary.' It used to burn him, Nana said, and he would repeat it over and over again, 'Quandary,' and shake his head, as if it summed up everything about the unfairness of the world.

"Nana said he used to walk the river early in the morning, a big branch of oak like a staff in his hand. Looked like he was pretending to be someone in an adventure story, striking out for new ground."

Sunday asked, "But what was he thinking about while he walked? And on his last day here, did he pass the corner store and the little triangular park? Did he nod hello, and good-bye, as it turned out, to those he knew, and stop to chat at the barbershop, with its rippled iron grate and Mr. Odell out front, closing up?"

"I wonder. Maybe he saw that lilac tree downtown as you round that corner near the river, and scent floated up over the curb to greet him."

Sunday thought about that. "Somehow I don't think so. Even if he passed it, he likely didn't really see it. At least for me, that tree, with its tender perfume and cones of star-shaped blooms, might just make me able to deal with things. Really seeing that tree might just make me want to live."

"Well, everyone's different, Sunday," Delta said with irritation as she lit a cigarette. "Seeing . . . seeing a tree might not make some folks want to live. Some folks who might feel unlovely could have a *harder* time going on, with lovely things like lilacs around. People . . . individuals, I mean, see different things in things. Some people might even look up and see a tree as a potential place to hang."

Sunday stared at Delta and then picked up her glasses and began to clean them again. She was taken aback by the despair and resistance in her sister's words, and at the fury with which they had rushed out. Damn, Sunday thought, focusing on getting one lens completely free of lint, you can count on family to be there for you, in the same awful way they always were. And all you have to do to inspire their antipathy is be yourself. I wonder how soon I can get a train.

"I'm sorry," Delta said to the table.

"No," Sunday responded, putting the glasses on, "I wouldn't want to deny you a chance to express a grievance. It's quite okay."

Delta sighed. "Anyhow, I overheard someone say that he left for the paper bag plant that morning, showing no more than his usual dislike for his job. He had been talking in the weeks before, though, about his new assignment of pulling the bags out of the folding machines, where they had been turned from flat sheets into rectangular sleeves, one after another, on, on, and on."

They were silent for a long time, both pondering the embalming force of mechanical routine, from which Sunday had always been escaping and about which Delta knew so much.

Sunday pointed at the locket and finally asked, "How did it get here? When did it come?"

Delta went to the hallway and returned with the shoe box Sunday recognized as the family photo archive. Placing it on the table, she explained how she had been at the post office on sorting detail when it arrived in a small padded envelope, made out to "The Owens Girls" at Nana and Grandpa's obsolete address. She had turned it over and shaken it as she tried to think of whom she knew in Clare County, all the way across the state, and after prying open the stapled end, she had reached in and pulled the contents out: the locket, a long piece of lined, yellow paper folded into a tiny square, and a store-bought sympathy card. As she read the card she heard herself shout, "He was alive," and then she looked around and realized, from the uninterrupted flow of events around her, that no sound had emerged from her mouth.

Delta lifted the gray cardboard top of the shoe box, its edges worn soft, its corners split, and removed the brown padded envelope that held the note and card.

"Well," she said, and then cursed herself silently: There you go again, with that pathetic floundering. Unable to find the words to go on, she placed her fingertips on the envelope and slid it across the table.

Sunday began to sweat as she opened the card from the stranger. The words seemed to wave across the page until she placed it on the table and anchored it with both of her hands, recalling the sight of her thumbprints on Delta's note. She finished reading, put it back in the envelope, and got up for more coffee, her cup rattling against the saucer in her unsteady hold. She would have to do this in two stages, she realized, and she was not yet ready to confront her one and only message from a man who had been dead her entire life. Reaching out to touch the kettle without a pot holder, she felt nothing at first, and then a sharp white heat pierced her numbness and she jerked her hand away. Instead of running cold water on her fingers, she took solace in waking to the throbbing burn.

The card, whose printed message read "With the Deepest Sympathy" in embossed silver script, had a handwritten message inside. It said,

> *Your father he asked me to send this along. He was brother to me these last years. And he was sorry.*
>
> *Sincerely, Clement Woods*

She came back to the table and picked up the folded yellow paper, smelling the chemicals in it and detecting the minuscule fibers within its smooth surface. Aware, suddenly, of the fingers that held the paper, she noticed the dryness of their skin, the paint deep in the cuticles, and the scars the fingers bore. She could hear her heart beating, the air moving through her lungs, and the thunder of the paper unfolding as it grew from a two-inch square to full size.

When she got the creased paper open she found the same leaning, elongated scrawl she had studied on the back of the snapshot she had found. Five words: "I remembered and I paid."

Questions erupted in Sunday's chest, and with them a lightning flash of outrage.

Remembered, remembered and paid? she said to herself. *And that's your offering to me who never even knew you never even saw you and I hope you did pay in fact I'm counting on it and what does that mean anyway that you paid and what does it mean that you were brother and never forgot and were sorry yes sorry you surely were and does it mean you married again and had another family you did not feel the need to leave?*

It was too little, and far too much.

She wanted to know if he had recalled the 704 of Nana's address, and whether he had ever phoned their number and hung up when someone answered, or let his imagination run wild as he let it ring. Whether he had taken anything besides the locket that he had kept all those years, and wondered, wondered, what his fatherless children had grown up into, how they had turned out, if she looked anything like him? Delta, he had a chance at remembering, but what about her? The baby who was not yet born? What about her?

She heard tearing paper and before she understood what she had done, she had ripped the note in half and Delta was crying, "No!" and snatching it from her, running to the hall closet for Scotch tape. There she was again, Delta thought in panic and rage: Sunday, taking everything for her own.

"I'm . . . I'm sorry . . . I didn't realize . . ." Sunday stammered as she stood holding the envelope, aware that once again, she had just made Delta the victim, and had given her something else to hold against her.

Delta leaned over the table, carefully matching up and rejoining the halves of paper, while Sunday tried to find different, more meaningful words than "sorry" to express her regret.

"Do you want me to fix it?" she ventured, reaching out to touch her sister's hand.

"I think I'm capable of doing it," Delta replied as she pulled away.

"I didn't mean . . ."

"Oh damn, I almost had it lined up. Why don't you make some coffee or do something useful?"

Okay, I feel really shitty, Sunday thought as she looked at the paper, bisected with a shiny, Scotch-tape scar, and while I'm at it I'd like to apologize for every wrong I've ever done to you. She knew she had acted impulsively, "before thinking," as Dolora had always told her was her biggest flaw. And selfishly.

Delta smoothed the paper and added tape to the back to reinforce the mend, while Sunday, returning to the padded envelope's postmark in the heavy silence, considered whether she might be able to cope with finding Clement Woods.

They both jumped at the teakettle's shriek. "I figure," Sunday said, after rushing to turn it off, "Mama must have been puzzled by him taking that one thing. Lord knows she had a whole story about that locket that was very important to her."

What had his selection of that one possession meant? they pondered. Had it crushed her and comforted her both, that he had left behind the ring, which had stood for a promise that bound, keeping instead the smooth, gold disk that held a timeless memory of the girl she had been, before the demands of life began. Was it a talisman he had selected for his afterlife, rejecting commitment and choosing love?

While they considered Dolora's feelings about the locket, Sunday reached into the shoe box and started spreading the contents out on the kitchen table. When she came to a photo of her own art school graduation, she stopped. There they all were: she in her cap and gown, waving her diploma in the air; Delta, matronly at twenty-seven, hands folded and pageboy intact; Nana dressed in a navy suit and hat and gloves, head held high; and five of the bread-making ladies from church surrounding them, dignified and proud. The Bread Ladies had arrived on commencement morning by train and returned that same night, trusting neither the cleanliness nor the hospitality of white, city hotels.

There was a picture of Dolora's younger brother, Wilborn, who had gone to the East Coast after college and married Anna, from a prominent black family, who loved to say their people were never slaves. At each family death, she and Wilborn had flown in the morning of the funeral and left that night, only visiting once that Sunday could remember for longer than that. "I know he's embarrassed by me," Delta had overheard Dolora declare tearfully to Nana one night.

Sunday and Delta remembered enduring holiday phone calls placed by Wilborn and his family to Nana and Grandpa, following the arrival of extravagant checks. Everyone was forced to take a turn on the line, composing pleasant summaries of school and health and prosperity. "We're having a really good quarter," Wilborn would always begin, and then he would tell about the earnings of his latest sales line and the gifts he had given that year. Dolora was always reduced to icy withdrawal by what she called Wilborn's "all-out bragging" and Anna's "digs." "Isn't family great?" Sunday and Delta used to say, after hanging up.

Wilborn and Anna sent a yearly form letter detailing family accomplishments, and an annual Christmas photo taken in front of their hearth, in which they wore matching holiday outfits, and even the dog had on a red and green sweater. Sunday found many of these in the box and arranged them chronologically on the counter to observe the changes the years had wrought. She found that although the children grew taller and their parents' faces and bodies aged, the photos were amazingly uniform. They showed the same poses and expressions, the same dark hair, and only slight variations on the outfit theme. And then for three years in a row, they presented forced smiles and hints of discord. Wilborn and Anna had moved apart, to the sides of the fireplace instead of its middle. Her arms were folded tightly in a posture of defense, and she looked tired, unamused with her part. Aha, Sunday thought, there was trouble in paradise. What was it, Wilborn, an affair, unbearably average children, declining revenue? Yet after those three pictures, they resumed their presentation of triumphant harmony. The pictures stopped the year before Nana's death.

Beneath those holiday photos, in the shoe box, was a collection of picture postcards that Nana's cousin, Boykin, had sent from all over the country. They remembered how he had come through town as a traveling salesman, bringing the jokes and tall tales he had picked up on the road, jigsaw puzzles and hand mirrors and folding fans with silky red tassels. They had loved it when he showed up, unannounced, spreading mischief and laughter.

They put Boykin's cards aside and took a brown and white photograph of their grandfather from the box. He had died of a heart attack when she was only four, so that most of what Sunday knew was what she had heard. Delta picked up the photo and noticed right away how it had captured his unyielding, unforgiving gaze, and the resolution and pride in the set of his jaw.

"He was a reserved kind of man," Delta said, "and he took everything he did seriously, never missing a Masons' event and revealing nothing, even to Nana, about those sacrosanct meetings or the lodge. He wore a stiff collar and a coat and tie to work at the store, and kept it on even at home while he sat in his easy chair and read the paper as Nana cooked their evening meal. I always wanted to be in the kitchen with her, and I think he scared me. He seemed to need adulthood from me, when I was just a little girl."

She went on to say that his most unforgettable habit was directing an inventory of questions to Nana or Dolora, about the way some chore had been performed. And after the inquisition, during which his respondent had grown more and more vexed, he would demand with quiet force, "Since we now understand each other, tell me. Tell me that you love me now."

That feeling behind "Tell me that you love me" was what Sunday remembered about him. She felt uncomfortable just thinking about it, and she still responded to compelled affection with flight.

"He wanted things to be done in a certain manner," Delta said, "the way he had seen those he called 'important white folks' do them at various points in his life." She told how Grandpa had also been religious about "upholding the race." Although he was a man of few words, one topic he went on at great length about was "the betterment of the Negro." He had worked since he was seven, first farming soybeans and wheat with his family and then, anywhere he could earn something extra. For many years he had had two or three jobs, and he had always taken on something extra, like picking up people's clothes for the white cleaners downtown or delivering groceries. His experience working for a fancy country club, during the one year of college for which he had managed to pay, left him bitter at white folks and determined to emulate them, too.

He took pride in knowing that he was one of the most hardworking and prosperous men in Salt County, and he had a corner drugstore and several pieces of property to show for it. He always wore a suit to work behind the counter at his store, and he felt his people had to show both white folks, and themselves, that Negroes knew how to do right, that they were capable and responsible. And what disturbed him about Mercury Owens were his inklings that he had neither tenacity nor rectitude.

Delta remembered him checking with her to see that she had done her homework. "Always follow through, child," he had told her, stabbing at the air with his forefinger. "Always follow through."

Delta remembered being perplexed by the difference between Nana and him. In contrast to his distant formality, she was warm and fluid, but one piece of common ground Delta had been able to discern was the church, where he was an alderman and Nana was forever organizing some activity, baking for benefits, and singing in the choir. The other quality they shared was a kind of dignity, expressed in different ways.

"Did you ever hear anything about how he and Nana got together?" Delta asked. "Because I don't believe I did. I don't even know what year they married, or exactly how old they were at the time. Well, I have to think about who else would know, about their getting together, I mean. Opus Green knows, if anyone does."

There were no pictures of Mercury's family in the shoe box, but Delta knew that according to Nana, after his father had been killed in a sawmill accident, when he was three, his mother had tried for a year to feed and clothe them. She told Sunday what she knew about how they had often gone hungry, and how his mother was sick with consumption. She had been forced to leave him with her sister, Edna, who thought it best to try to raise him as her own and to speak of his mother as little as possible. He had been a handful growing up, restless and inattentive in school, a loner who had trouble making friends, and his mother died soon after his aunt Edna took him in.

Delta had seen Edna regularly at church. She had brought them birthday and Christmas gifts, but had never stayed long at the house and had never been there for a holiday meal. Delta recalled Nana commenting that Edna and Mercury seemed to make each other so defensive and ill at ease that her visits were dreaded by everyone, and then, after his disappearance, she rarely came. She had brought food for Dolora and sat with the children several times right afterward, and then she had faded from their lives, moving, a year or so later, to another town.

Sunday made a mental note to see what she could do about contacting Edna, or any of her family who might still be alive.

They put aside the photo of Grandpa and uncovered the last things in the box: two pictures of Mercury, one a yearbook photo and one a riverside snapshot with Dolora, that they had both memorized. They had retrieved the meager bequest from Dolora's closet often when they were growing up, determined to read his expression and posture, to know him through his dimpled chin and folded hands. "Who are you?" they had both puzzled, inspecting the figure in the yearbook pose and the youth at the riverside. "Who are you and how are you mine?" Sunday remembered looking at the second snapshot and imagining what everyday essentials and treasured possessions he had carried in his bulging pockets.

Studying the snapshot with a magnifying glass, Delta had speculated on what things had been withheld and professed. She noticed how their shoulders barely touched and the attention her mother's tilted head revealed, and imagined the charged aftermath or prospect of touch on their impatient, adolescent skin. Surely they were dreaming, she thought, of the life they would make together, of the home and family they would one day have. Or had he just told her about some aspect of her beauty, "You have the longest lashes I have ever seen," or "Your waist is perfect for my hand"? Maybe they had laughed a private laugh.

They both imagined the people their parents had, at that moment, been. And then, as there was nothing else for the shoe box to yield up to them, Sunday went to her coat and took out the mosaic coaster, its tiles set within a brass frame. "Oh, that one I remember," Delta said. "In fact, I can picture her making it, for the church sale, and then deciding she didn't want to part with it, because she had gotten the colors just right, and almost hidden in the pattern was a scarab she just couldn't bear to let go."

As she handed Mercury's monogrammed belt buckle to her sister, Sunday thought she saw Delta's face stiffen with resentment while she smoothed her eyebrows, right then left. "So you had the buckle," she whispered. "He wore it only on special occasions, not to work, and he always placed it in a dish on his dresser, where I was told never to go. It was off-limits, you see, to my touch. He used to polish it with a piece of flannel, I remember that."

Sunday explained hurriedly that she had forgotten packing the coaster and the buckle when she left for college, only to find them before she came home.

She didn't tell how, halfway through that night when she hadn't been able to sleep or work, she had opened her taped-up box, cutting the packing tape with her matte knife to retrieve the note. Before she got to it, she read every other piece of correspondence she had saved, arranging Nana's letters and Delta's greeting cards by date, combing through her other boxes for the things she had brought with her from Salt County. Unsure of what she was seeking, but driven, she had unearthed her high school yearbook; her drawing contest awards from elementary school; her first set of markers, now shrunken and dried; and the ticket stub from the first train she had taken to Chicago. Amid the other contents of the box, she had found the coaster and the buckle, which as a child, she had liked to use for bouncing moonlight at the window, pretending it was a signal to contact airplanes and helicopters as they passed high above Salt County.

"Well," Delta said, before she could stop herself, "I'm surprised you found anything from here worth keeping." She placed the photo on the table and stood up to clear the plates. It was quieter than ever, and Sunday's bitterness at her sister's long-standing martyrdom flared. Two small mementos seemed little enough to take, when Delta had every other possession that had been left them right there with her. But nothing between them was free of the past, and Sunday guessed that the paucity of things selected, as well as the taking, itself, had provoked her sister.

She looked at the things on the table, stung silent by Delta's comment, and disappointed, too, that she hadn't been more excited about the items she had found. It made her even more reticent to reveal the bigger yearnings she had in mind, for Delta would surely think her maniacal for deciding to track down the man Mercury Owens had become.

For her part, Delta couldn't believe how sharp her own tongue sometimes got. This was no way to begin a reunion, she thought, and yet Sunday just seemed to get under her skin like no one else. She didn't understand where it came from, when she hadn't even been aware that all that ugly history was still so alive. She suggested that they put the pictures and the shoe box aside and they made lunch, relieved to have a concrete task.

To the background of the clock's steady meter, they made and ate their sandwiches, saying little except to comment on the train ride and the condition of the neighborhood. And then, settling back at the table and taking out a cigarette, Delta told the detail, overheard and never shared, which had caused her untold pain: In the laces of one shoe, Mercury Owens had tied his wedding band.

Once she had added that piece of information, the surviving image of his departure became, for both of them, those side-by-side work shoes. Run-down unevenly at the heels and holding a slim ring of gold.

3

THE OWENS GIRLS had grown up with Salt County's commentary, receiving its compassion and its pity, too. And that inheritance was with them, still, as they sat in the kitchen and confronted the shifting story of their father's absence and death.

When they were children, people had watched them with curiosity as they walked to school or to the library, as they entered the dime store or the Y. "Those poor girls," they had more than once overheard on their way into church, or standing in line at the store. Folks glanced furtively to see how they were turning out and inquired after their mother's and grandmother's health. Looking forward a couple of pews to see them sharing their opened hymnal, with Delta stooping to equalize their heights, the congregation's hearts went out to Dolora's solemn and polite brown girls.

People felt for them and they hoped for them, measuring the distance between the family's misfortunes and their own lives. And the women, at least, were thankful that despite their own troubles, their lovers and husbands continued to come home most nights.

When word first got out that Mercury was missing, the townspeople had focused on believing that he would eventually show up. "Maybe it's just an accident," women said as they came by the house with smothered chicken and banana pudding, "and he's somewhere with a broken leg or something, waiting to be found." They told Dolora they were sure he was about to return, and that all would be okay. "Pray on it," they said as they left.

The Bread Ladies took turns sitting with Dolora while their husbands went out to look for signs of Mercury, and Nana packed her toiletries and a change of clothes so she could "do for her" and be there when she got some news. When Grandpa heard that Mercury was missing, he shook his head and snapped open the evening paper as Nana left the house, muttering from behind his screen of newsprint that he always knew the boy would come to no good.

The only sign of Mercury was the pair of abandoned shoes. When two days passed and he didn't reappear, Dolora realized that the shoes and the ring amounted to a suicide note.

After proclaiming in church that he was a good and misguided young man who had finally found relief from untold pain, the folks of Salt County wrestled with Mercury's choice, trying to understand what might have driven him to the point of such despair. They fashioned the explanations which were bearable, the ones which dovetailed with their visions of themselves, and some decided that he had gone over the edge of sanity, that he was "not in his right mind."

A few were certain that despite her ladylike appearance, Dolora had done something to him beyond imagining, and stoking the compassion of many was a long-standing rancor toward Grandpa, known to them as Mr. Blount. Some were convinced that his disdain and avarice could make even a righteous man welcome death. And a couple of holdouts, like the bread-baking Valentine Cross, maintained that he hadn't died at all. "I'm acquainted with his kind," she said repeatedly, "I knew me one who was capable of that." She never stopped asserting his survival, but in the end she wasn't certain which was worse, the desertion of one's family, or suicide.

A few refused to even consider motivation; he was a scoundrel, pure and simple, nothing left to say. "So low, you can't get under it," Mr. Odell was known on more than one occasion to state, from behind his barber chair. But most declared that he had had it "god-awful hard," and the tale of woe grew and grew, with folks supplying details of his tribulation, even when they had to make them up. "I heard tell," said a man to the others in Mr. Odell's shop, "that Mercury Owens was what you call an escaped felon, running from the chain gang." "Debt," said another, as he leaned back for a shave, "I'm absolutely certain it was debt what made him run." At times it became a collective story, for after all, they had been through war and deprivation together, and they had endured the flood that had sent them to their rooftops for rescue. They understood the kinship of shared trouble.

Yes, they stated, things had been hard for Mercury Owens. But in the backs of their minds, the black folks of Salt County knew that life had been rough for each and every one of their people.

Minnie James thought of the trouble her family alone had seen. There was her aunt Sara's husband, beaten by police, who had died when no hospital would agree to treat him, and Sara, who had share-cropped cotton until the day she died. And her own white grandfather, who had "snuck around, regular, practicing 'nighttime integration,'" she said, in order to enjoy her grandma, had passed his half-black daughter on the street and looked right through her, as if he didn't know she breathed.

Toots Williams thought of how hard his parents had worked to end up living on beans in a trailer park, and how his sister had set off for the city and raised her children in a tenement. And before he came to Salt County, the Klan had burned his house down, with his daughter inside.

Addison Crown had failed grandly in his personal contest with whiskey. He was living with the fact that he had used his fists against his wife, and his kids up in Detroit were trying to forgive him, stay employed, and live their lives without putting needles in their arms.

After they closed their eyes at night, divested of demands from the day completed and the day to come, the black residents of Salt County wondered if they, or those lying next to them, were capable of a desolation that would make them choose that way. Each one struggled with Mercury's suicide, wondering, also, who was fit to judge him, after all. To whom were any of them owing, they asked, and wasn't death the one thing a body got to choose? Many of them knew about the grave-yard of the Atlantic Ocean, about those million gone who had chosen drowning over bondage, and what about them, they wondered, how did Mercury's death compare with theirs? Where was the line, each one wondered, that would make me opt for death?

Their losses followed them, generation to generation, into the present, and they couldn't afford to forget the very things that broke their hearts as they remembered. The hardest parts of their stories somehow survived and were carried into each day, and now and then, they were transformed into things sacred and fine.

They thought of the insults and hungers they had learned to bear, and the ways they managed, daily, against reductions and exclusions, against thankless work and meager pay. They tried to imagine Mercury's misery and comprehend him, but they thought about all the burdens and the dangers that were part of life. And they thought about that sweet, brown girl and her newborn sister he had left behind. After all, they wondered, what did it mean to unchoose your life?

They wrestled with Mercury's story, and in that borderline between waking and sleeping, they had to admit that they didn't, they didn't really understand.

While Sunday took her suitcase to her room, Delta sat at the kitchen table, reliving the moment when she first found out that her father had chosen death.

One morning Delta had come upon a chattering group of nine- and ten-year-old girls after Sunday school and heard them fall silent. She had stood outside the group, shifting from one foot to the other. And then a girl had leaned into the knot of girls and casually made a comment that had rent her world. She had looked directly at Delta and said, "Her daddy kilt hisself."

Delta had focused on the floor and counted the squares in the church basement linoleum until she reached the stairs that led outside. Twenty-three. Twenty-three squares.

When he had first gone missing, Delta had asked, "Where's Daddy?" and Dolora had answered, for an entire month, "He is away." When she persisted with her question, asking where away was, Nana had explained that he had "passed on to the next life," and when her classmates talked about their fathers, she had been happy to have something to say about hers. Although she had failed to comprehend its meaning, beyond picturing a shadowy world of pastels inhabited by slow-motion angels and pillowy clouds, she had been able to say, "Mine's in the next life. He's passed on."

Suddenly, she had a staggering piece of information, and her twenty-three squares. She had sat through the church service imagining the pattern on the linoleum, counting it in her head again and taking comfort from her mother's nearness and perfume. Closing her eyes, she had leaned against her mother's arm and thigh, listening to Nana's voice as it led the choir, and when they finally reached home, she had gotten up her courage to ask Dolora what it meant. "What that girl said, Mama, is it true?"

Dolora had wrung her hands and said, "Oh dear, oh dear," answering as she turned to go upstairs, "Your father's in heaven and that's what matters. That's what you tell those heartless girls."

She had gone then to Nana, who had held her close to her breast and said, "Yes, my dear child. These things you are far too young to understand, but as you get older, meaning will be revealed."

Delta had looked up into her worried face and asked, "Do you?"

"Do I what, child?"

"Do you understand?"

Nana had had to admit that she did not, but that what she was able to figure was that "his hurt was just too deep."

"So," Delta had inquired, "did Grandpa kill himself?" and Nana had said, "No, he didn't. His heart gave out."

Delta nodded, but she wasn't really certain what the difference was. Meaning will be revealed, she repeated to herself, for she trusted Nana, anyway, to tell her the truth.

Delta never brought it up again, but took to hanging around the Bread Ladies and anyone else who was imparting information, in order to gather the little knowledge she could about her father's death. And a few years later, she put her arm around Sunday's shoulder and told her what she had been able to piece together.

While Delta was in the kitchen remembering, Sunday sat on the edge of her girlhood bed and started at her suitcase. No need to unpack, she thought, since I'm staying such a short time. She believed that Delta looked even more wounded than the last time she had seen her, and she seemed to have retreated even further beneath the protective shield of her hair. "Hell, we're both wounded," she said aloud.

Since a young age, Sunday had been aware that her family was a living metaphor, through which the folks of Salt County tried to imagine the end-point of hopelessness. Although she had always felt a vague sense of it, the moment when she had really grasped that role had come when she was thirteen and buying kitchen shelf paper for her mother in early June.

As she rummaged for her change purse, the dime-store clerk watched her through narrowed eyes with a combination of fascination and pity. Sunday felt the young clerk's green-shadowed eyes studying her, as if she were a specimen under glass that might somehow, through concentration, be made to reveal an essential key to the workings of sorrow.

"You're one of the Owens girls, aren't you?" she said. "The younger, I bet."

Sunday had nodded, counting out her coins.

"Well, I've never met you, but I sure have heard about you-all." She tilted her head sympathetically and said, "I guess it's a hard time for you, Father's Day this weekend and all."

Sunday's cheeks burned. She felt as though she had been turned inside out, and all her stitches and seams, her torn and raveled places, were open to view. She gripped the edge of the counter while the clerk rang up her purchase, and then, as she held out her hand for her change and received the bagged shelf paper, she realized she had left her sweaty fingerprints along the rim of counter glass.

"Try to have a nice weekend, anyway," the clerk said, as if it were a lost cause. She took out a cloth and a bottle of cleaner and began to wipe the smudges and prints away.

Sunday stood outside the store, looking in at the salesgirl. And in that moment, she was afraid that she would never get to be more than Girl Owens, would never get to raise her voice, with its own desire and elation and grief. In Salt County, anyway, she would always be a story others needed and told.

She grew to resent Delta's willingness to accept that distinction, for in allowing herself to be cast as the left-behind, Sunday argued to her sister, she was settling. "Even if I mess up," she told her as she made her urgent, late-night case for going to school in Chicago, years later, "even if I find out that I'm no good at painting, or can't find a way to make ends meet . . . even if I trust the wrong people or get in a jam, I don't want to be someone things happen to. I want to make my life take place."

As she thought back to those times of realization and argument, Sunday considered her mother.

She doubted that Dolora had ever been free of the label of "abandoned wife, raising children on her own," and Sunday thought she showed that identity in her weighted shoulders and incarcerated smile. Did she carry that designation always, or had there been some way to incorporate it into things? Had there been some means of naming it so that it was just one part of the story, rather than its major theme? She pictured Dolora working on her mosaics and thought that maybe she cast off that role when she was making things. And maybe it was only in working from that past that she found freedom from it.

Sunday came downstairs and cleared the table. She and Delta were silently reliving how it had felt to state that their father was dead, and by his own choice. Disgraced by their own abandonment, they had grown up knowing that their needy mouths and curious hands had not been reasons enough to make him pull through, whatever that required, and they reflected on what definition of parent their father fulfilled. They had grown up ashamed, among black people who had borne unspeakable things, and uneasy at being the tale other people told. But with their new information, Mercury Owens had become a benchmark for how far folks could sink.

Sunday mulled over those memories as they washed the dishes and cleaned up the kitchen. She was wondering what the day of Mercury's apparent suicide had been like for Dolora.

"What do you think," she asked, "Mama was doing on the day he disappeared?"

Delta was still trying to leave behind the residue of her conflict with Sunday over the torn note. She fought to turn her thoughts to that day, and found that she couldn't remember anything coherent or whole. All she could pull up were impressions and remnants of feeling and fact. She responded with another question: "Was she worried, you know, because he had gone missing, or was it a complete surprise?"

"What did she do when she found out, Delta?"

"Yes. And who delivered the news?"

Neither one had any answers. "I've always wondered," Sunday said, "what kind of memorial they had, and how Mama grieved." She turned to Delta and asked if she had been present at the funeral. Delta shook her head and told her that they hadn't allowed her to go.

What she remembered of the day when they realized Mercury was gone was playing with the paper dolls Nana had given her, alone on the bedroom floor. She had been told to go upstairs and "occupy herself," and later heard the screen door slam and her mother's heavy footsteps leave the porch. She recalled trying to lose herself in cutting out new outfits for her dolls from discarded magazines, reassuring herself that her mother would soon return.

"And there was Nana," Delta said, "a little later, calling upstairs to see if I was okay."

After playing paper dolls, she lay on Dolora's feather comforter, pretending it was a pond that would float her until their return. She was given cream soda pop, which she was rarely allowed to have, when she got up. Without being told, she had understood that something very bad had taken place, and that it had either happened to her father, or had been caused by him. She remembered raised voices and crying and things breaking later that night, but that was patchy and vague.

"Do you remember how Mama was, after the funeral was over?"

"Well . . . pregnant. Slow-moving and enormously pregnant with you."

"Yeah, but what else? Do you have any recollections of what was going on with her? Did she cry or shout a lot, or was she absent and depressed? In disbelief? Maybe she was all those things. I guess I would be."

Delta flipped her lighter over and over in her hand and shook her head. "Well . . . I remember some commotion . . . things breaking in the middle of the night, but I'm not sure when or why. I just recall waking to the sound. But otherwise, from then on, the feeling I remember is tightness."

"Tightness?"

"That's it. The house was airtight and quiet. I can picture Mama making dinner and then the two of us sitting at the table without speaking and everything kind of winding up. The air growing so . . . so tense . . . as I tried to think of something to make it better, but I couldn't, and I was afraid to anyhow, so I just concentrated on eating while my ears felt like they might just pop. And then as soon as we were finished eating she would heave up out of her chair and begin clearing and washing dishes, so that she could go upstairs, which she did carefully, one by one, at eight months pregnant, to lie down.

"And I just remember that she had been mine, but now she was gone, and I waited and hoped she would come back."

"I wonder what was going through her mind as she was lying up there with me, unavoidable, growing and moving inside of her, and him gone?" Sunday said.

"I don't know what it was like up there, but it felt dry and empty downstairs and it was clear that I was to tend to myself as much as possible. I was too afraid of her reactions to say or ask for much because she was so tightly strung. Nana came over most nights, either with food or after dinner to sit with us, and when she opened the door and came in, the pressure would, I guess, ease up. It was like she let some of the built-up air out, whoosh," Delta said, pushing her hands out from her chest, "by coming through the door."

More and more questions were forming, and then Sunday thought of a way to find some answers. "What about the Bread Ladies?" she ventured. "We could see what they know."

Delta's eyes flickered and she compressed her hand into a fist around the lighter. She felt peculiar about the way she regularly conjured up those women who had made bread on Saturday afternoons in Nana's kitchen, and she wasn't sure she wanted to forfeit the marvel of her envisioning by either talking about or to them. Maybe there was something not quite right about the way she pictured objects from the past, and she didn't want Sunday to know about her inside vocabulary of things.

"Are Opus Green and Laveen Walker still alive? They must be almost eighty by now."

"Yes and they're still here. Valentine Cross did pass away last year, but she was always so grouchy that we tended to avoid her anyway."

"Well, I bet Opus would remember things she might be willing to tell."

"You go, then," Delta said, getting up and leaving the room. Sunday could hear her last words from the stairway, "I'll take care of matters here."

Sunday didn't know what matters there were which needed taking care of, but her sister's diffidence wasn't new. She thought how strange absolutely everyone was, and went to the phone book to call Opus Green, who had always been her favorite of Nana's friends.

Opus answered the phone with a tired voice, but when she found out it was Sunday calling, she said, "Give me half an hour and come on over. I'll put some tea on."

When she got to the house, Sunday was so nervous she considered turning back. "Maybe I shouldn't start this," she muttered, afraid of what she would open up by extending her search beyond Delta, by asking questions whose answers might be more painful than what she already knew.

Opus unlocked the door before Sunday could change her mind. She was dressed for company, in stockings, pumps, and a shift, and she had a polished walnut cane in her hand. She wore lipstick and two round spots of rouge, and her hair was neatly pulled-back and hair-netted, as it had always been. Sunday felt she had been transported back in time and she almost expected Nana and the others to be inside, singing and talking and making bread. "Miz Green," she said, kissing her cheek lightly and handing her a bouquet of flowers, "it's so good to see you, and I've been so bad about keeping in touch."

As Sunday entered the living room, she noticed the powdery tea rose smell that Nana's house had also held, and the crocheted doilies and antimacassars that had been there as far back as she could recall. Above the baseboards, she saw a faint waterline, recording bygone floods. Opus's plants still spread their webbing of green over the front windows, and her curio cabinet displayed the glass and ceramic bells Sunday had loved to take out and ring as a child, and the little porcelain replicas of slippers and high-heeled ladies' shoes that had delighted her. "How could anyone walk in these?" she used to ask as a girl, and Opus would answer, "I guess some ladies don't have to do any walking, and in any case, these are for looking, so you don't have to worry about getting around in them."

Sunday helped her get the china teapot and cups, and a plate of sugar crystal–studded butter cookies, and once they were settled in the winged-back chairs, they began to talk. "I sure do miss your Nana J.," Opus said, nodding her head. "It's truth. It nearly killed me when she passed."

"You're not the only one, Miz Green. Nana was the family glue."

Opus nodded, thinking of how she sometimes picked up the phone to call her, before realizing she was gone. She and Sunday talked about Nana's gentleness, and the honest and penetrating nature of her voice, whatever kind of music she chose to sing. And then they caught up on Salt County happenings and Opus's family. Her husband of fifty years had died just before Nana, and Opus was still adjusting, she said, to facing the rest of her life alone.

"I sure do remember Mr. Green, with his Wrigley's chewing gum and the limericks he used to recite to make me and Delta laugh."

52

"I miss him in every minute that I breathe. There's all the little things I'd like to be able to talk to him about," she remarked, leaning out of her chair toward Sunday. "Who said or did what thing that was perfectly in character, what I witnessed outside and read in the paper, or what those conservatives have been up to. As you know, Wilson was a devoted follower of politics, and the Republicans, not the party of Lincoln, mind you, but the new ones, drove him mad. You know, Sunday, he loved watching birds come to the feeder we put out back when he was sick and housebound, and I wanted so to be able to tell him the other day about the cardinal I saw in our evergreen tree."

"I guess you could still talk to him," Sunday said. "For a while I did that with Mama, though the funny thing about that was that we hardly talked at all in life."

Opus nodded. "I do talk to myself now and then. There's so much I'll never get to say to Wilson now." She thought how she also mourned his touch. At night she still reached out for him, and the bed seemed far too big for one. "What often brings me to tears," she said, "is the littlest matter: not feeling his breath against the nape of my neck at night. It's truth."

Sunday felt awkward with Opus's intimate revelation, and there was silence until she asked, "Miz Green, do you still make bread?"

"Every Saturday, though it's mostly for myself, now. I've got some pumpernickel in the kitchen if you'd like some. Yes, I keep the bread thing going; it seems to give form to my week, and every now and then I convince Laveen Walker to come over and make it with me, when she's not globe-trotting to Senegal, or Hong Kong, or wherever her latest trip has taken her, and then the two of us just get lost in memories and end up laughing and crying and puttin' a hurtin' on my Hennessy. The morning after Laveen's last visit I had a headache that was way bigger than this room. I always make more bread than I can eat, so I give it to my next-door neighbors, or those birds get it, since my mouth can't seem to keep pace with what my hands get going.

"Now that's enough on me. Tell me, do you have a young man, and if so, why don't you bring him home?"

"I do, but, I don't know . . ." she stumbled, ". . . it would seem weird to have him here. I'm afraid he belongs to another part of my life, and anyway, I'm afraid Delta wouldn't like him much."

Opus was puzzled. "Well, has she met him? How can she not like him if she doesn't know him?"

"I hear you, Miz Green." Sunday shifted in her chair. "It's just that I'm not sure he's her idea of the right kind of man. I never really had a boyfriend when I was living here, but you know, Delta always liked those hunks . . . muscle-bound, sweet-talking guys. Reed is kind of quiet and bookish, gentle, you know. And he's got . . . unconventional hair."

Opus stared at Sunday, her cup stalled midway to her mouth.

Sunday doubted that Opus would approve either, but she could only guess what she was imagining. "Dreadlocks, long. He wears them back, in a ponytail or a French braid."

"Oh, like that fellow on the stories."

"Yes."

Opus had to admit to herself that she didn't understand such hair, but she said, "I see. Well, nobody here is wearing it that way, but we all get *Ebony* and *Jet*. They probably even do it at that new shop here in town that Delta's friend Dinah started. They do every style you can imagine, and I've started going there to get mine done, during the special for ladies of my set. I imagine Delta would honor your young man's choice, if you gave her a chance, and as for her views on men, if you had met that Nate fellow she took off with, you would know that her definition needs revising. That one was smooth and handsome, all right, but a starving little boy if ever I saw one. Eyes big as saucers and a hungry-seeming smile, he ate a whole loaf of my bread in one sitting, with butter and honey, and I don't know where he put it, thin as he was. He looked like he'd never get enough."

Sunday nodded and tried not to betray that she knew nothing about this Nate. Maybe he had something to do with the changes she had seen in Delta's face. She wondered how long it would take her sister to tell her about him, if she ever did.

"Of course it's not his hair or his looks, Miz Green. It's just that Delta never understood any of the choices I made. Maybe I should give her and Reed a chance, but he and I have our own problems to work out. And so do Delta and I."

"But remember, Sunday, Delta may not have ever understood you, and she may not even like certain things about you sometimes, but she has always loved you. All families have these problems; they can't stand each other and they care, both."

Sunday knew that was truth. She and Delta felt so much for each other, and still, they couldn't seem to get it right.

Opus decided to tell Sunday part of her own story, to show her what she meant. "My brother and I got along something terrible, fussing and criticizing each other every chance we got, but when Wilson died, he came over every single evening for a year, and we sat together and talked about the news and watched TV and played Scrabble or gin rummy. Half the time we argued, and each night when he went home I was glad to see him leave, but he took to heart what my mother taught him about our duties to each other, and he was simply coming through in the way he knew how.

"There are things that tie people together, and blood's only one of them, it's truth. But that tie is there with sisters and brothers, and if you want it, if you don't undo it and altogether toss it away like your uncle Wilborn did, it can be pulled . . . twisted . . . tested, you know, and it stretches, but it seldom breaks.

"Is Delta the reason you stayed away?" Opus asked, taking off her gold-rimmed eyeglasses and tilting her head down to look at her with the no-nonsense attitude Sunday had always appreciated. "What you see is what you get with Opus Green," Nana had always said. "She's got no side at all."

Sunday laughed and said, "You always did get right to the point." Clearing her throat, she looked away. "Well, there's been a silence between us. Since Nana's death."

"A five-year silence, with your sister?" she asked, communicating her criticism with the emphasis she placed on the last word.

Sunday felt even smaller than she had when they were talking about Reed, but she tried to express how complicated it was, how what had happened after Nana's funeral was an expression of things that had long been there. "I guess it wouldn't have drawn on so long if Nana had been alive," she said.

Opus set down her teacup. She had no intention of supporting Sunday in such a lame excuse. "Well, she's not alive. So I guess it's on the two of you."

Sunday's face flushed and she felt her chest cramping as an image came to her of Delta standing at her bedroom door trying to bring herself to knock, and she, motionless and mute on the other side.

Opus refilled her cup and went on, "Well, you have come home, so what has brought you? What is it that's troubling you now?"

She dropped her teacup when Sunday told her about the locket and the package with its note from Mercury Owens. As she rescued the teacup, Sunday returned to the arrival of Delta's note and Opus excused herself to get a bottle of Hennessy.

My goodness, she thought, I do wish I could have a word with Valentine. She always suspected this was true.

As Opus poured them both a drink, Sunday framed her request. "Miz Green, there are things I need to ask you, things I need to understand. I hope you won't think it's wrong, somehow, to discuss them," she said slowly, "that they're secrets or that you'll be upsetting me if you do, because, you see, I think these are subjects that Nana would want me to know about."

"Ask, Sunday. You know I'll tell you straightaways if I object. It's truth."

"Okay," she answered, and she began by asking about Dolora on the day Sunday's father disappeared.

On the way home Sunday thought of what she had told Opus about Reed and Delta. It hadn't occurred to her that her sister might be hurt by the fact that she hadn't brought him with her. Maybe she thought that, like their uncle Wilborn, she was ashamed of her family, but she just couldn't envision the past and present of her life meeting up, and she didn't want Reed to see what might be the least lovable parts of her. She didn't want him to see her through her sister's eyes.

When she reached the house she told Delta she had a headache, and would report on her visit to Opus after she rested. Too tired to talk and full of everything the day had held, she stretched out on the bed and asked herself how she would ever digest all the things that were rising. Once she had decided to return to Salt County, she had wanted to think that the trip home, however difficult, would dispose of her questions. Instead, what was unsettled seemed to multiply. She had thought it was chiefly Mercury whom she was after, but she was beginning to realize, after less than a day, that her mother's life was encrypted, too, and within the conundrums of her naming and Mercury's leaving, there seemed to be a hundred other unknowns.

She had just begun her search, yet the facts she had discovered were leading to wider questions that had no simple or conclusive answers. She had hoped that she would hit on some piece of information which would function as a keystone, making sense of everything tangential, everything else. But who were they, Mercury, Dolora, Grandpa, and Nana? She couldn't even say that she understood Opus . . . and perhaps she grasped Delta least of all. It was hard enough to know the living, without fathoming the dead.

Whether she had been painting figures, or nature, or abstract pigment and form, she had always aimed in her work to reveal something of the mystery of being alive. Most recently, when she had sought to capture city-dwellers through their windows, she had tried to unmask both the compression and the far reaches of their lives, venturing, with images, to burn off the dispensable, to bare some animate core. It took a kind of knowing, she thought, to be able to see and to name what mattered, what endured, and it was plugged-in living, along with the vantage point of exile, that made that knowing possible.

Yet the characters in her painting, even those drawn from her life, were of her own invention. They lived on canvas and in her head, and her main responsibility to them was disclosure of the marrow. Many of them she sensed at a distance, from the other side of the window, across the aisle of the El train or down the street, and she had always handled people better in the abstract. But these inhabitants of her homeplace, kin and neighbor, led their own lives, messy and shifting, and those lives were intertwined with hers.

Each person she sought to understand was an intricate puzzle of desire and need, and Sunday was asking something monumental of herself in coming home. She was striving for the vision to perceive and decipher them, through the voices of survivors. By way of the objects in which histories are housed. Via the myriad reverberations of their acts. That kind of knowing seemed impossible, she thought, like holding on to breath, or light. Like stalking echoes and afterimages.

She closed her eyes and tried to stop sorting and analyzing, aware that although she had offered it as an excuse, her head did, in fact, ache with the story that was taking shape.

4

SUNDAY STRETCHED OUT on the bed and tried to relax. Reed was always talking about the beauty of napping, but the problem, as she told him, was that she could not shut off her head. She worked at drifting off, despite his suggestion that sleep was something you had to let happen, not something you could force. She even tried to fool her body into it, distinguishing it from nighttime sleep by lying, "in reverse," with her head at the foot of the bed.

After getting in reverse and covering herself with one of Delta's afghans, this one in alternating black and white squares, she willed blankness and sleep to come.

Reed teased her that she needed to find a way to simply be in her body sometimes. "You can't be plugged in all the time," he argued, "even lamps take a break." To be still, or merely to move, without creating or thinking, that was the challenge, he said. Recently, when he had seen that she was unable to focus anywhere but on the torment of her stalled work, he had tried to get her to let it go, and take nourishment somewhere else. "Fuck art, let's dance," he would say as he took her in his arms, hoping that he could at least provoke a laugh.

If only I were able to ease up, to surrender to dance or unconsciousness, but I even dance and sleep and have sex intensely, she thought. There seems to be no escape at all from me. As she tried to quiet the throbbing of her head, the pieces of Opus's story came back. She could envision her direct eye and smell the rose perfume of her house. She kept returning to Opus's implicit condemnation of the separation she had abided with the only blood she knew. *With your sister . . . your sister . . . your sister?* Opening her eyes, she flipped over, getting the afghan tangled beneath her so that her legs were bound, and when she heard Delta beneath her in the kitchen, she gave up.

As she descended the stairs she could hear her banging around at the sink, unnecessarily loudly, it seemed. She knew she probably should have told her what she had learned from Opus right away, but it hadn't felt possible. She had needed to sit with it for a while and begin to sort the information she had gathered. She entered the kitchen as Delta was putting a casserole in the oven and picked up a potato and a peeler to help with the casserole that Delta was finishing up.

"I'll have to make you a nice dinner one night, Delta. I've learned how to cook a few special things."

The atmosphere was strained and Delta was peeling and chopping potatoes furiously. When Sunday saw that her face was fixed into a concentrated frown, she knew her comment had been misunderstood. Had Delta thought she meant to imply that her casserole and roast were predictable and plain, not a special dinner? Was she angry that she had shown up when the preparations were nearly done? She tried to redeem her remark. "This sure will be a treat. I haven't had Nana's cheese potatoes in I don't know when."

Delta nodded and began to slice the potatoes with sharp thwacks on the cutting board.

Sunday's peeler slipped and she gouged one of her fingers.

"Oh shit," she said, dropping peeler and potato.

"Forget it," Delta said, picking up the half-peeled potato that trailed a curling ribbon of skin, "I've got enough."

Sunday's search for a Band-Aid took her upstairs to the bathroom, where she opened the mirrored medicine cabinet and found herself fascinated with the array of supplies that were there. Although Reed told her it was "invasive," she always looked in people's medicine cabinets when she visited their homes. She couldn't resist access to the hidden accumulations of practical and personal things, the clues to people's lives. "Would you like it if someone did that to you?" he asked, and she would shrug, imagining that most people would do it whether she liked it or not, and then tell him what she had seen.

Delta had a whole shelf of bottled nail polish, different brands of deep red. Maybe she used it on her toenails, Sunday thought, for she couldn't picture her wearing it on her close-cut fingernails. She didn't seem the kind of person to indulge herself with red toenails, but who knew, she thought, maybe she'd taken it up recently, or maybe she had a vampy side. On the next shelf were prescription drugs, some Nana's and some Delta's, all between five and ten years old. Surely she didn't have any intention of taking medicine that old, Sunday thought, restraining the impulse to throw them away. There were safety pins of different sizes and alcohol and cotton balls. Lipsticks in various stages of use, all Sunset Orange. Medicine for headaches and cramps and stomachaches and gas. There was a big blue bottle of Vicks VapoRub, which evoked the memory of Dolora's massaging hands when she unscrewed the top. When we got sick, Sunday thought, were the rare times we got to feel her touch.

When she came to a pair of condoms, Sunday stopped, suddenly embarrassed. Did Delta have a lover, or were they preparation for possible fleeting nights with strangers? Were they left over from the Nate character Opus Green had mentioned? Since condoms came in packs of at least three, one must have been used. She stared at them, uncomfortable with the concrete expression of her sister's sexual activity. She found a Band-Aid, closed the cabinet, and firmly decided not to think about Delta's intimate life.

When she got back to the kitchen Sunday recalled that, as a girl, Delta was always urging Dolora to set the table on weekends and holidays so that they could sit down together and eat, unhurried, passing serving plates and bowls around. Sunday suggested that they eat on the good china in the dining room, thinking it would make things special, but Delta said it would be too much trouble and the whole room needed dusting before they could use it. She put plates and cutlery on the counter and when the food was ready they helped themselves from the stove and sat down at the table.

Sunday asked Delta how it was going at the post office, and Delta asked Sunday how her artwork was coming along. Neither posed a question to which the other could not choose to answer "Fine." They ate quietly, Sunday commenting again and again on how good the food was and Delta responding each time with a nod and a thin smile.

After dinner Sunday convinced Delta to walk through town with her. The smell of the paper mill grew stronger as they approached the river. After crossing to the middle of the bridge, they stood and looked down through half-round iron rails at the rusted stilt-legs sunk to their knees in murky water. Once on the other side, they tried to ignore the sharpened smell of the paper mill, the beer cans and tires and cigarette butts discarded in the weeds along the river's edge, and sat on a group of rocks, pulling their coats around them against the autumn chill.

Sunday had read once that beneath most of the region's soil lay underground reservoirs, and it awed her to recall that water was all around her, both below and aboveground.

She had heard about the time, in the early fifties, when Salt County's river had far exceeded its typical flooding. Although most houses in town had been marked in some way by the spillover of river water, she had never seen it rise above thigh-high. But that time, people had taken refuge on their roofs, as bicycles and even cars were swept away. "The town became a big lake, dotted with little building-islands, and you could see cows and horses swimming," Nana had said. "It was quite a sight from where we sat, clinging to the shingles of our one-story house, waiting for help to come." Nana had laughed as she remembered that in her panic over what to salvage, she had grabbed a rolling pin and taken it up to the roof.

Despite the damage it visited and the uncertainty it brought to their lives, people never did leave the floodplain for good. Maybe it was some kind of amnesia, Sunday thought, like women often said erased the pain of childbirth, or maybe they just couldn't avoid the river's force. They couldn't seem to separate themselves from it, and had incorporated it into their lives. Nana had sworn that she knew someone named "Floodina," born in the middle of one of the worst floods in Salt County's history.

Sunday visualized those people who had been stranded atop their shelters, holding the one or two cherished or practical belongings they had thought to grab. And she tried to picture what she and Delta looked like at that moment from above, at the edge of the water and not far from their house and block, their county, state, and middle chunk of continent that produced and reclaimed them, no matter how far away they got.

She wished she could see the river from above, via airplane or hot air balloon, or from even higher up, by way of satellite or rocket. Sitting at its edge, you could know only a small piece of the river, and she wanted to see what else it was: origin and destination, winding route.

If she could look down on its branching veins, the whole of it would be revealed, and she would know its passage from ocher into green and back again, from green into blue. She wanted to see the source, and the place where river met ocean.

Had Mercury followed the river's course, she wondered, directly to Clement Woods? Where had he been over all those years? Maybe the water had governed him, so that even when he left it, it always called him back.

Delta threw rocks she had found amid the weeds and refuse, and watched them slip into the surface of the water, which glinted in tinfoil patches from accumulated grime and end-of-the-day light. She stared into the water as it closed over the rocks and echoed with concentric circles, and then noticed a familiar figure coming down the riverbank across from them.

"There he is again," Sunday said, pointing across the river, "the man I saw this morning when I got here."

Delta smiled, realizing how mysterious the man must seem without the story that explained his campaign. "That's Mr. Harris, our local diver. He's been exploring the bottom of the river, to see what he can find."

The man had noticed the two women as he approached the water. No one came to watch his progress anymore, especially with autumn's chill setting in. He wondered what the two of them were doing there, in that barren spot, sitting so far apart from each other.

Oh well, he thought, there's no end to human difficulty, and he knew that from life as well as books. He turned back to his work, bending his tired back once more, and thought how he would soon have to suspend his search for the river's story until things thawed in the spring. Or maybe he would consider this river known, and move on to another one.

He had got the idea from reading about all the things that were revealed when a local quarry was drained. Although he knew his project was strange and pointless to most, he hadn't been able to give it up until he felt he knew something. An isolated man, whose only love had left him before their life together even got started, he knew people through novels, and through his work. He was not a man who could go out into the world and strike up conversations or socialize, and he would never be able to come right out and ask people what had mattered to them. Even if he had been capable of asking, he wasn't sure that he would trust the responses, for people showed what mattered through their actions even better than they told. He had his ways of being an explorer and a witness. He had his ways of finding out.

He had needed to see what was at the bottom of the river that had shaped Salt County's life, to find out what people relinquished and what they lost. The riverbed had showed him some of what was taken by the overflowing water, and what might be returned.

Delta lit a cigarette and Sunday said, "Let me have one of those," reaching for the Kools and then changing her mind. "No, don't. Don't let me have one, not unless I beg."

"Did you quit, or not?"

"I quit. Or maybe I didn't. In any case, I still allow myself two a day. I've already had one, and it's too early for my evening hit."

Delta hated the kind of virtuous restraint that enabled a person to have only two cigarettes. In fact, she thought it was more irritating than completely quitting. "Okay then," she said, exhaling pointedly, "no cigarettes for you." She moved the pack to her other side.

"So, our scuba diver, Harris something or other, his name is, he started out fishing in the river for lost things. I saw him sitting in a boat, the first week or so that he was at it. I was coming from the library on a weekend morning, and there he was, the strangest-looking sort of man. He had on these overalls with things attached all over them with jumbo safety pins."

"Things attached? What kinds of things?"

"I don't know, charms. Things like bright-colored and brass beads, like you rope around Christmas trees . . . and coins, dimes I think, like I've heard folks wear down South to ward off evil spirits. And some of the objects he had fastened on looked like found things, like a thimble or an iron handle, or a button hook. Odd things, all of them. But it was his face that was strange, too, because even at a distance, it seemed to just give off a kind of . . . of heaviness, or . . . what was that word Nana used that would amuse us? Woe.

"He had a long, sturdy cable he reeled out with a big hook on the end, and he was pulling up all kinds of stuff with it: a boot, a broken umbrella, a little kid's wagon gone from red to rust. But some things were too big, too stuck in the muck and in whatever was growing down there. I found it amazing that anything could grow down there, but he said there were these different kinds of river weeds surviving in that dark, awful water polluted from the paper mill. Strange to think the river was once clean."

They watched Mr. Harris as he waded into the water to attach his hook to something and then return to his truck to reel it out and up. It looked like a car engine, dripping with slime and weeds.

He was lost in his task, no longer aware of the two women on the opposite side. He was thinking of who had owned the engine, and in what car. Where had it taken its owner, he wondered, to what disappointments and delights? And how had it come to be abandoned to the river, after all?

Delta and Sunday sighed with relief as the engine was landed on the truck. "Anyway, he decided to get diving gear and go at it that way, in order to get the big, stuck things. The county decided it was a good way to get the river cleaned up, and it agreed to pay him to bring up large pieces of trash and abandoned stuff. But *I* think they were hoping that missing guns had been thrown in there, and if he found them, they could close the books on a bunch of old crimes."

"Delta, I think you've been reading too many mystery novels. There haven't been but a couple of murders here in the last fifty years."

"Yeah, okay"—she flicked her cigarette and rolled her eyes—"I guess you're the authority on that, since there must be a murder in Chicago every day, or every hour. Even the crime is better there."

Sunday chuckled, unwilling to enter that argument. "I'm not taking that bait, Delta, there's no future in it."

As for Delta, even if Sunday didn't believe her, she was happy to have an unusual story to tell about Salt County. "Anyway," she went on, "the county gave him this crane that he could attach to things he found underwater, things that were too heavy to bring up by himself.

"'Crazy' is what lots of people called him. And nobody understood why he was doing it. But he said he was a historian, and it was one way of doing his work. This river was a tributary of the Mississippi, and it had helped bring who knows how many of his people 'out of bondage,' he said. Those were the words he used, when the local news did a story on the whole thing. He had read lots of stuff on slavery, and he went on and on giving all kinds of facts. Some people called him negative for focusing on such a horrible period that was so far back in the past, and some laughed at him. But tons of people stood by watching, to see what he would find.

"He said he had read about great rivers like the Niger and the Amazon and the Ganges all his life, because I guess as a 'historian,' he had studied about a whole range of things. I'm not much on reading history myself. All I can remember about history in school is being bored. It seems like I pick up a history book and my eyes close. Most of the time I can't see myself in what they're saying, not in any way that's good, at least.

"But this Harris, he had a different take on things. 'What makes a river great?' he asked the reporter, and I have to admit, I think he lost that reporter and the rest of us when he started talking that way. And then he said, all passionately, 'I want to know what's down there and I'm willing to find out.' I guess he's kind of wacky, for getting all worked up like that."

What makes a river great? Sunday turned the question over in her mind as she observed Mr. Harris wrapping his cable around what looked like a piece of a building or a gravestone, flat and curved at the top. If magnetic pull was the standard, then their river was a contender for greatness. It had never seemed to let anyone in Salt County leave it behind.

Mr. Harris was watching the stone slab rise on his hook and cable and then descend to the bed of the truck, where he put it down. Now how did that get in there, he wondered, a burial marker, buried itself. He would have to see if its inscription was readable, if he could clean it up.

"First," Delta continued, "he followed the river out of town, stalking it and getting to know its bends and its flow, which, as you know, can shift from north to south and back again. Since he couldn't dive the whole thing, he decided to focus right here, on the downtown part of Salt County. And it seemed like everyone had lost something to the river.

"Mrs. Jenkins, you know, who worked at the Sears before it closed up, well, she had thrown her wedding ring in there in a fit of anger, which was followed closely by alarm, and probably by Mr. Jenkins hitting the roof. She bought another one on layaway, paid for it herself, but all those years later, she wanted that one back. I don't know how she thought this guy was going to find something as tiny as a wedding ring, but she was hoping.

"And this little white girl from the east side said she had lost her favorite doll the spring before, and she kept saying that it had slipped right from her fingers as she crossed the bridge.

"Some people seemed to be hoping that buried treasure or something really valuable would be down there, even though they wouldn't have had any personal claim to it, you know. It was a big deal, but some people came just to watch and make fun of him for being crazy, and it kind of gave some folks something to do. Two retired men in their seventies, who used to work at the auto parts shop, came down to the edge of the river every afternoon with lawn chairs and thermoses, full of ice and Wild Turkey, no doubt, and sat down to watch what Mr. Harris raised.

"I came a bunch of times on my lunch hour, just to see. All these people were down here, watching him and thinking of something the river had taken from them . . . of, you know, some way it had affected their lives."

After loading a mangled automobile grille onto his truck, Mr. Harris started the motor and began to drive away. Delta paused from her story as they watched him go.

"He would strap an air tank onto his wet suit, and get this searchlight kind of thing set up, and he looked like some type of alien, for real, and then, when he disappeared into the water, all of us would kind of hold our breath."

"So what's been down there? What all has he found?"

"A lot of it's been garbage, like bottles and tin drums and odd machine parts, like the one we just saw him put in the truck. But other things came up, too, and whenever he broke the surface with something new, those two retired men would applaud. An old-fashioned baby carriage and spoked wheels came up, and a frying pan one day that I was there. I always wondered what the story behind that was."

Sunday said, "It makes perfect sense to me. I'd like to toss every one of my pots and pans into Lake Michigan. There just seems to be no way to free yourself from the bondage of cooking, except to flat-out refuse. Once you show that you know how to turn on the stove, even the best man in the world knows he's got you. It's all over from then on."

Delta smiled. "Well, so much for you making me dinner."

"Yeah, on second thought," Sunday said, laughing, "my offer is withdrawn."

"Well, Mr. Harris found a bunch of other household items, like washboards and teakettles. Maybe you're right and fed-up women had thrown them out, or maybe they had drifted over to the river during the floods, and been sucked into its current as the waters fell. And he found things that he said were from our slave past. He found a cutlass and some broken leg irons."

They were both quiet as they thought about those things. "And what were you hoping he would find?" Sunday asked.

Delta suddenly felt embarrassed. "I know what you're thinking. It's not that I really thought Harris would find *him*, Mercury, down there. By then, he would have been just random, disconnected bones. Although if he'd disappeared more recently, there might be some trace of him left, 'cause I heard that when that plane went down near Long Island, they couldn't find one man's body, but they found his credit card. You never know, I thought there might have been evidence of some kind." She looked at Sunday. "I thought Harris's efforts might have something to do with me."

Sunday saw that she had tears in her eyes, and moved closer to take her hand. "I understand the thing about searching for clues. I think I've always been doing it, looking for information. Looking for meaning in anything to do with him. I've always had the feeling that somehow I just wasn't piercing the silence about him in the right way. As if . . . as if I wasn't locating the right opening, and that if I did, my questions would lead me to him." Sunday paused and then continued in a hushed voice, "Now I realize that we didn't even ask each other. I at least had you."

Delta had to fight the urge to cry, pull her hand from Sunday's and retreat. Here she was just trying to tell a quirky local tale, unaware that it would lead to this. Before Sunday's arrival that morning, no one but Dinah at the beauty shop had touched her for a year, and that was while doing her hair. No one had held her hand.

Feeling her discomfort, Sunday gave Delta's fingers a squeeze and then let go, acting as though she needed to button up her coat.

"One thing I always thought of as a clue, though I don't really know to what, was his name. Mercury Owens," Sunday said, "it's quite a tag. Mama loved all that classical, ancient stuff, loved that long-past world better than her own, I guess. I remember reading in her mythology books about those Roman gods, and finding that Mercury was a messenger, riding that line between this world and the next. I got to thinking how his name might have been what drew her to him, at the start."

"I wonder who thought of it," Delta responded. "Even though there's a lot of freedom in naming with our people, it's not exactly common."

"You know black folk," Sunday said, laughing, for she had chosen a unique one for herself, and whenever she told it to people, they said it back to her, like a question. In school, kids had teased her by calling her other days, instead: Come here, Saturday, and tell me what you know good. She said, "What I wonder is, what it was like to have been given a definite, uncommon name like that, but to have chosen to be without any people of your own, separate from those who provided it. Was it like a tether, being 'Mercury Owens,' I mean, was it a thing he could call on, that was just his, or something to get away from?" Sunday picked up a rock and loosened the earth from its edges as she talked. "Was it a name that was given after he appeared, that seemed just made for him? And later, what I wonder even more was whether, in some small way, that name played a role in the man he became."

Sunday tossed the rock and they watched the river roll, revealing now and then something half-hidden, the corner of a stick rising like an elbow and then gone, a bleach bottle tumbling up and under, up and under, pulled along by the flow.

Until now, they had wondered what had made him need to leave them, for need it must have been. What had made him choose the swallowing river and probable blankness, over what was known? Pain must have fueled that need, they had always thought, pain that had been big enough to block out the three of them. Like a lunar eclipse.

Mercury had defected, that was still true. But now they were facing the fact that he had not selected the blank release of death, and the worst part about the whole thing was the fear that they would never get the story from his side.

As they sat on the riverbank, Sunday disclosed the things she had learned from Opus Green about Nana and Dolora. She knew that they were second- and thirdhand, that they had passed through other people's understandings and had been shaped by their words, so that the tellers' truths were in the story, too.

Before she got started talking, Opus had said that Dolora sometimes came to unburden herself to her. She would show up without
notice and ask to come in and talk, apologizing as she began. "She
seemed to have decided I was safe to tell the things she couldn't expose
to her own mother," Opus commented. "She trusted me and knew I
wouldn't judge her hard, and I guess it's easier to tell your story where
you haven't got as much to lose."

Opus said that soon before he disappeared, Mercury had taken to
walking through every part of town, black and white, center, outskirts,
and riverside. She said there had been a "powerful wanting" in him,
that often, when he was spotted walking, he was so wrapped up in
whatever he was after, or wherever he was imagining himself, that he
didn't even speak.

Sunday told how Opus had removed her glasses and looked intently
at her as she leaned out of her winged-back chair. "Now listen," she had
said, "wanting itself isn't wrong. Wanting can be a good thing, it can
make people reach. But the other thing about wanting is that it can take
you, like fire, from the inside out. Depends on what it is you're wanting,
and how you go about getting that thing."

Delta nodded fiercely and said, "I've got to give Opus an amen on
that."

Sunday noted how Opus's statement had struck home. What was
it, she wondered, that Delta had wanted like that? Nate? Was that it?
She waited for a moment, and then went on with what Opus had said.

When he had failed to return from work that day, Dolora had worried,
but his absence had also provided a relief from tension. Hugely pregnant
and tired past gauging, she had gone to bed routinely angry and disgusted, and it wasn't until the next morning that she felt something was
really wrong, for he had never stayed away throughout the night. When
a neighbor returned from the day shift at the plant to say that Mercury
had never showed up for the 7 A.M. shift start, she was certain of disaster.

As Opus was talking, Sunday had realized that Mercury must have
reached the river before daybreak, and she pictured the sight of the
water at night, reflecting the stars, the bridge, her father's young and
troubled face. Since the one fact she had grown up with had been his
drowning, she had always pictured him in the water, immersed and
maybe fighting, in spite of himself, for air. But now she didn't know if
he had ever entered its current at all. Had he waded along its banks or

maybe run alongside it, shoeless, the surface registering his flight with a streak of movement and color?

Nana had told Opus how her daughter had appeared suddenly at her door. It had taken her a long time to get her to say that he was missing, and then Nana found out that she had just left Delta at home in her room, stepping off the porch and heading toward her, with barely a word to her five-year-old child. She sent her home, packed some things, and followed. For two days, Nana and Opus waited with Dolora, while neighbors and churchgoers searched for any sign of Mercury Owens at all.

When Tyler Ruffin from across the street found the shoes beside the river and brought them to Dolora, Opus said she had taken them and stared at the ring tied in the laces, speechless.

Without a body, there had been no funeral, but they had arranged a memorial service at the church. The congregation had filed past the family with mournful eyes, shaking their heads at the loss, holding and patting their hands as they murmured condolences and bewildered sympathy. Many loaves of bread were offered, as if that token of sustenance would fill what was missing with its grainy weight.

Opus said people brought food to the house and tried to say positive and comforting things, and then they went home and started reconciling what had happened with what they knew about the workings of the world. After the shoes were found, Dolora had been nearly silent. She had spoken only of preparations for a memorial, never crying or openly expressing her grief. Although Nana was worried, she figured her daughter was numb with shock, and would come around, and she prayed the baby would be okay. Grandpa was unable to offer anything besides his physical presence at the church, and the money for the flowers and program. Nana told Opus that she knew what he was thinking as he sat there smugly in his crisp, tailored suit. She knew he was condemning his son-in-law for breaching his dearest code: Above all, Mercury Owens had failed to follow through.

That evening, after the service, Nana, who had come to stay with them, awakened suddenly to a crash. After closing Delta's door she descended the stairs to find Dolora in the kitchen, smashing her china and crystal, piece by piece. Nana stood stunned, looking from the counters piled with loaves of bread to the wreckage on the floor, afraid to wrench her daughter from her mute rage.

Oblivious to Nana's presence, Dolora stood barefoot, the growing life within turning her white nightgown into a white curve lit by moonlight, and cracked a dinner plate across the sharp edge of the table before throwing it to the floor. She had finished the cups and was halfway through the glasses and plates. Iridescent wedges painted with delicate lilies and creamy ivory fragments banded with gold surrounded her on the kitchen floor.

When Nana saw blood, beaded in a garnet string across the broken white and pastel porcelain, she gasped and stepped, barefoot, too, into the broken china field, reaching for her daughter, uncertain if its source was baby, hands, or feet. She didn't reason it through, didn't think at all, just went in for her, without feeling the shards that cut into her own flesh. Dolora stepped back and grabbed another plate, smearing its floating pastel flowers with red, and Nana, seeing that the blood came from Dolora's hands, grabbed her arm and took the plate. She held Dolora by the arms and shoulders until she surrendered to her embrace.

Nana could feel the child who would one day name herself moving against their two skins. Dolora's silent sobs shook their bodies and drops of blood fell and bloomed like tiny roses in the white cotton weave of their gowns as Nana walked her carefully through the splintered porcelain and faceted glass.

Once in the bathroom, Nana lifted her daughter's gown to check for cuts and felt along the taut membrane of her abdomen, one hand on each side of the darkened middle line, assuring herself that the baby was safe. She eased around the skin with her nine and a half fingers, one segment having been claimed by the mill decades before, and held them there in quiet reassurance of the life within the brown vault. "What an entrance," she declared. "What an entrance to this world."

After she had washed and bandaged the cuts on Dolora's fingers and feet, she got her to bed, rocking her as Dolora said, over and over, "How could he do this, Mama? How could he do this to me?" And then Nana tended to her own callused soles, too hard for most of the china to penetrate. Easing open Delta's door, she found that she appeared to be asleep, and returned to the kitchen with the broom. She swept up the broken pieces and sifted through them: wedding plates given to Dolora, the last two gold-rimmed goblets from a set that had been Nana's, and the lace-edged dessert plates hand-painted with water lilies that had been Dolora's favorites. There was even a serving plate Nana had decorated herself while working for a white woman who had taught china painting many, many years before. They had hardly ever used those things, saving them for company to keep them safe, and although she wasn't sure why, she could not throw them away. She placed the fragments in a box and carried it up to the attic.

Years later, after she had taken a class in mosaics at the Y, Dolora found that box. After breaking up the larger pieces further with a cloth-covered hammer, she had incorporated them, over the years, into most of the things she made.

"I guess that was the breaking I remember," Delta said, "and just a fuzzy sense of Nana's presence in my room."

Although Delta had heard the crashing, she had been too afraid to go downstairs and find out what it was. Later, she had noticed the missing plates and cups she had loved to examine through the window of the china cabinet, wondering when a time special enough to use them would come. She had recognized the pieces when they reappeared in Dolora's creations, but she had never asked about them.

Adding to Opus's story, Sunday said, "For me, it was a private game to study the compositions for traces of a rose or leaf, or for a distinctive line of faded gold. And when I first asked Nana about the fragments I could tell were china, you know, pieces that had the curve of a cup, or a turned handle that looked like part of a question mark, she told me Dolora tried to add them to whatever she was making, and pointed out how that end table in the living room was the first thing Mama made with them. Nana said, 'That table's got everything in it: anger, grief, and pride. It's got the story, that there.'"

Dolora had told Opus that when Delta and Sunday asked about their father, she hadn't known how to respond. She had never told her daughters what she felt about Mercury's disappearance, how she dreamt about him leaping an arc through the air, leaving them behind to wage the struggles of the living, how she thought she saw him sometimes, pausing to stare in at them in ordinary moments, through little rectangles of window glass. Looking in, looking in at them.

Since the first time he had spoken to her, after history class, she had never been the same. Although she hadn't had a plan for her future, Dolora had been a deliberate and obedient girl, conscientious to fulfill her father's expectations, be helpful to her mother, study hard, and make good grades. And because her father was firmly opposed to her dating, she had never had a boyfriend. From behind her books she had watched

Mercury Owens shyly, uncertain what to make of his alternation between easygoing bravado and solitary restraint. And then, one day she had spoken up in class about the ancients, raising her hand in unaccustomed self-possession to tell what she knew about the Roman gods.

She had felt his eyes on her as she spoke, and from the doorway he had watched her gather her textbooks and pencils, touching her arm and asking if he could escort her to her next class as she left the room. Her arm had burned from his touch, and as she undressed that night, she felt it still.

The weeks and months that followed were a tumble of risk and awakening desire. Although she had concealed their walks and meetings, careful to appear as though nothing had changed, within she felt her life upended, as though she had boarded a dizzying carnival ride whose rhythm and duration were independent of her will. Dazzling language flowed from Mercury and she felt the rules she had never questioned dissolve. Like her, he felt alone, but he had giant dreams and wants in which no one else had dared invest. He had chosen her to share them, and the least, the very least she could do was believe.

Before she knew it, she was pregnant, and the reeling carnival ride careened to a halt.

Dolora had heard Nana argue against her father's unbending decision to enforce their marriage, but what had the options been in those days? She couldn't shame the family. She had to follow through. Maybe Nana thought Mercury would live up to the adult role he had backed himself into, that responsibility would bring out the best in him.

At first, Dolora had also felt trapped, but maybe, Opus said, she hadn't sought so much more than that. She had passed three months of sleepless nights, horrified at her thickening torso and swelling breasts, when all the things that had seemed to justify the risks they had taken were fuzzy to recall, and she could already see the sullen and controlling silence that would become more and more dominant in Mercury as the years wore on.

Once they had been pushed swiftly into marriage by her father, she had settled in to bear her fate, and turned her attention to providing for her child, perceiving that the only way to do it, to survive with the extreme and frustrated man to whom she had become tied, was to submit. So she had tried to bury her resistance, to shrink the modest dreams she had for herself and work at making her family last.

She tried to build Mercury up by asking him about his longings and dreams, and by believing in them all. But she suspected that he was lost in the yawning gap between fantasy and life, and she knew enough about him to sense his belief that if the grand dream was not within reach, then what he had was dust.

She cooked what he liked, tried to keep herself looking nice, left him alone if that's what he wanted. She tried not to make him mad; she tried to disappear. With little idea of how to span the growing distance between them, the small pleasures and excitements they had shared had seemed to waste away. He no longer wanted to take her hair down and brush it, or tell her the new words he had learned. He turned toward the edge of the bed and went to sleep without their ritual kiss, and began to leave the house earlier and earlier in the morning, without the morning "coffee moment" they had at first shared.

His periods of silence lasted longer and longer, and she paused in the middle of a task to find him staring at her like a hostile exile. If she went to stroke him once they were in bed, he remained impassive and remote, leaving her embarrassed by her own longing. After their infrequent bouts of passion he was resentful and nervous, and she was helpless to right it, or to even understand.

And then she had felt promise with her second pregnancy, hoping the excitement of a new life would narrow the gulf between them and bind him to her anew. That part of her future was, again, undeniable, and as she felt her baby move, she prayed for the boy she hoped would inspire a deeper connection in Mercury. But she had sensed, as he looked over at her in the night, that he was sure he couldn't do it, that he felt as though, instead of her, he was carrying the weight of their unborn child. The silence and tension crowded out everything else, and when he chose leaving, amid the grief and rage and sadness, she had felt relief.

Once he was gone, she vowed to herself that she would speak of him as little as possible, and for her own, internal story line, she focused on several things that would let her accept his suicide. Her dream life refused to submit, but in her waking story, Mercury Owens was simply too passionate, too proud, and too wounded by the unfairness of the world. At the time of her own death, she called her girls to her hospital bedside and repeated those three things about the father who had left. "And remember," she said, "remember only what you choose."

*   *   *

Whatever their mother had advised, Mercury would continue to clamor for attention with his dramatic farewell. His act of complete, unexplained abdication had made a hole in his daughters' lives that was as wide as their imaginations, and they not only recalled every detail they were given but tried to surmise his suffering. It was "Remember me" that he seemed to say from every place they turned.

Perpetually grieving, they looked for him in the two photographs they had been left. "Remember . . . Remember me," he said from the confines of those black-and-white squares, and his daughters tried to know the courting almost-man by the riverbank, and the youth who raised his chin with studied sobriety in his yearbook pose.

Inventing explanations other than death, they had imagined him taken by force, kidnapped or waylaid on his way from work. Compelled to flee persecution, to protect them from harm. Or afflicted with amnesia, he had spent days searching for wife and daughters, clueless as to who they even were. Maybe he would inch his way back across desert, over craggy mountains, through dense forest that held only filtered, temporary light. Whatever shape their daydreams took, each of them privately kept one question open: Could he somehow return?

Delta and Sunday remembered him, but not in the way he had been there. It was his exit, and his absence, that had filled their lives.

Adding him to the family stories told by Nana and Dolora, they had filled in his part, if only to place him in the shadows, in the corner, looking on. They had listened for him in the spaces between words, sifting through spoken language for what might have been withheld.

When they shopped at the corner store, they pictured the hands they had seen in their two cherished photos, pulling and folding brown paper bags like those that held their purchases. "Remember," the snapped-open, stand-up bags seemed to say, and they saw him in the notched half-moons that were cut from the top.

Over time he grew from man into symbol. He was everyone who had ever left.

Unavoidable, he had straddled every aspect of their lives, and there was no measuring what Mercury Owens had set in motion, with his departure which was dying, and not death.

5

CONSTELLATIONS ANNOUNCED THEMSELVES, as hints of blue bled through the ceiling's chalky white. Propped with pillows against the narrow French Provincial–style headboard of her girlhood, Sunday looked up and saw the dark, cracked veins that showed the house's strain and shift over time, and the bloated corners and plaster welts left by trapped water and patched-up leaks. Amid that record, she could distinguish Ursa Minor and Cassiopeia in the sky map she had made.

At fifteen, she had locked the door and stood on the dresser with the wide, thick-bristled brushes she had found in the basement and the slim, fine-pointed ones used for artwork, covering the ceiling with lapis lazuli blue. Working her way from a corner outward. Leaving white star-holes that seemed to have been punched out from the background night.

Dolora had been furious when she found out, and had made her paint it over with primer and white paint, explaining that each thing in life should be kept to its proper place and time.

Before she had put up those stars, she had lain on her back staring at the blank ceiling and pretended she was filling large squares of empty paper or cloth with color and shape. She had envisioned murals that would unbound and expand Salt County with museums and buildings and parks, and imagined painting her family into completeness, stepping away and looking, from the outside in, at a living whole. She had pictured herself layering paint on her ceiling, making and remaking a private world.

She thought about the layered, relief-map thickness of the canvases that were propped against the walls of her rooms back home, along with her unfinished work. Months before, when she was first shut off from blue, she had kept the piece she was working on in the middle of the floor, so that she and Reed found themselves walking around it in order to move about the room. He had patiently respected its placement until, unable to finish, she decided to move it and begin again.

Reed is probably lost in a book right now, she thought, or he's finally dozed off with it spread across his chest, and in the coming night she would miss the way they seemed to sleep the same sleep, rousing together and reaching out blindly for each other's skin. She thought of the places on him, private and familiar, that she protectively sought. The spine her fingers traveled like a rosary to the tender, twin depressions at its base. The hollow at his throat, unguarded between the armored curve of collarbones, and the hinge of inner thigh and torso, soft and untanned, where the pulse surfaced and she could see it pound.

She had neglected to call him, she realized, and it was almost midnight. She hesitated to pull him suddenly out of his hard-won sleep, from which he rose panicked if awakened prematurely, lost and unable to rejoin its calm.

Instead, she picked up the cigarette she had slipped from Delta's pack and then put it back in her pocket, feeling satisfaction at her hidden maneuver, but resisting the indulgence that would ruin her achievement of three years with only two cigarettes a day. She was fighting hard for discipline, but "there is something about this house," she whispered, "that makes you want to sneak and break the rules."

Shaking her box of wooden matches and looking around, she realized that apart from the emergence of assertive blue, the room was just as she had left it when she boarded the train that led to art school, three months after her high school graduation. Although there were no recent possessions to be found, the faint smell of cigarette smoke and rumpled pillows told her that Delta had not long ago spent time in the room they had shared growing up. Both of their books and high school mementos remained on the two-by-four shelves they had hung, and a mound of stuffed animals covered one of the twin beds. The dresser top still held a hot pink papier-mâché bank in the shape of a frog, a music box housing an armless ballerina, and a bottle of Wind Song perfume, saved so long for special occasions that it had ages before gone dark and thick.

Getting up, she glanced at her suitcase, which she had decided not to unpack, in case her undertaking didn't work out and she needed to cut her losses and catch the train back to Chicago right away.

She opened the dresser drawers furtively, rummaging for secrets and finding only blankets, pillowcases, and dresser scarves. Lifting the frog bank, she heard a few coins rattle within. When she raised the lid of the music box the maimed ballerina rose and made a half-turn over and over again to the repeated first notes of a skipped tune. She closed it and unscrewed the top of the crown-shaped bottle, and then choked at the stale, clotted smell. Hastening the top back on to stop the image of Delta, dressing for a date with Rudy Johnson, she signed her name with her finger in the mirror's dust and peered at the portions of her face revealed in the curving strip of cleared glass, noticing, as always, her arched nose with its insistent spine, and her focused eyes. Too much, she thought, like everything about me, too much. She stood back from the glass.

Turning, she found that her early efforts at sketching, leaning in the corner, had curled into cylinders as if to conceal their bold and awkward innocence. Although she was curious, she decided to wait until later to look more closely. Two early attempts at faithful landscapes hung on the wall, embarrassing her with their constriction and self-conscious accuracy. She wondered at what point, specifically, she had begun to be able to paint for herself, and repeated the phrase that helped her to accept the flaws and weaknesses of completed work: "process . . . process . . . process . . ." she said, wondering what Delta would think of the labyrinth of overlapping images and colors she was currently trying to find her way through.

Across the top of the chipped cork bulletin board were two time lines of thumbtacked school photos marking the sisters' progress through childhood, which had been carefully placed each year by Dolora, and then Nana, in a thick, brown, string-tied envelope. Delta had arranged them chronologically since her last trip home.

In rows of tiny two-by-threes they moved through braids and Peter Pan collars and missing front teeth, to eye shadow and clinging body shirts. She looked, photo by photo, at the images of Delta, discerning in each one the certain injured aspect in the eyes that had always provoked in Sunday a sense of impotent responsibility, and recognition, too. As she looked from her story to her sister's, Sunday saw a shared wariness, with traces of unsettled grief.

In her sixth- and seventh-grade photos, Delta's face and neck had grown chubby. Shoulders awkward and fixed, eyes evading the camera, she radiated what Sunday remembered was her common complaint: "Where did this body come from? How did I get so huge?" To the further consternation of their mother, who hadn't been able to respond in any way to Delta's misery, her plumpness had resolved itself, later, into full breasts and rounded hips. That fullness had seemed to worry Dolora even more, prompting her to urge concealment, warning her with "Watch yourself," "Don't flaunt," "Don't be cheap." And there she was in the last two photos, in the eleventh grade and twelfth, unsure of her beauty and wearing that meticulous pageboy and reticent half-smile. But then, Sunday thought as she stood and went to the window, "What beautiful woman have I ever known who saw herself that way?"

In her own pictures, Sunday saw a shy and gawky girl whose braids gave way to a pageboy, and then to a loose, curly Afro. She saw a face that was suddenly given the refuge and bane of reading bifocal glasses in the seventh grade. And along with wary grief, she saw hints of determination and daring in her own eyes.

She worked the long-settled window frame against the grooves, unsticking years of dirt and settled paint to make it rise, detecting the cloying odor of the paper mill, and underneath its scorched sweetness, the smells of leaves burned that day and the approach of cold weather.

Leaning out, arms on the window ledge, she wondered, who was this Clement Woods she had just learned about, and what was he doing right then, several counties away? Was he a repatriated country man, or had he stayed put on his home turf, like Delta? Was he watching a late-night rerun on television or making love to his wife? Maybe he was sunk in heavy, work-tired sleep, and maybe he was even thinking about the two daughters of the brother-like man to whom he had somehow become bound. Would she and Delta be able to face finding out who Clement Woods was and what he knew, she questioned, for imagining and confronting were two different things.

And what about Mercury? Had he tried at some point to lose himself in the reel of city life? Where had he gone when he left them, and in what kernels of memory was his experience housed? The downy feel of his girl child's hair or the color of the night sky in winter, seen from the river's edge? A 2 A.M. boyhood hunger that worsened until dawn? Would he ever have been able to forget the smell of the paper mill after it rained?

She hadn't. All she had to do was close her eyes. There were so many past things she had tried to evade, including the slow, walking death brought about by the paper mill and the distant nearness of sisterhood. And here she was, actively trying to remember the things she had sought to forget.

Inhaling the air, the place, she felt as though she had only stepped away on an errand. She knew her hometown and the lives that went on behind her neighbors' backlit window frames, and even though she had left Salt County, she painted it again and again, as if it composed her first language. As if it were alphabet.

She loved the throb and tension of the city, even though people collided and ground up against each other, and interactions with strangers left you raw. After she had been painting, her trips out of the house made her feel porous, and she had to struggle to assume the opaque attitude she needed for basic survival, to conceal her curiosity while she rode the train or walked home through often angry, hopeless terrain. She had to work at not meeting others' eyes, for she was drawn to witness that tender, vital place in people and she painted from there. She thought of herself as a Chicagoan now, but she was also from this river-cleaved paper mill town, and in one way or another, it was always present in her work.

She knew what folks in Salt County were doing and feeling while they wiped their kitchen counters and got ready for bed. How they were looking back over their mornings and afternoons as they turned down the sheets or removed their makeup, or stood before the bathroom mirror rolling their hair on pink sponge and molded plastic, or evaded the relentless sameness of their days with the TV screen. She knew how down the street, Mr. and Mrs. Nowlin's eyes had met from across the room during a commercial, that evening or the night before, passing between them a fleeting understanding of what they had managed to have together and what they had missed. She knew how they folded an extra blanket at the bottom of the bed, sensing the encroaching cold in their joints, and touched bare feet as they gave in to sleep, trying to dream a dream of possibility that was contradicted by the facts of their lives.

Sunday had tried to bring what she knew about the people from

Salt County to the world she had come to inhabit. She had painted the lives she imagined being lived within brick and cinder-block walls. Through rows of windows she remembered them on canvas, people who appeared vaguely underwater and lost at first glance in the anonymous repetition of city living, yet there, always burdened and sometimes joyful, moving their days forward with ordinary tasks and fleeting human exchange.

City folk, she often told Reed, didn't knowingly reveal either the drama or the trivia of their lives in the same ways as small-town people, didn't even speak to you on the street or make eye contact. She entered their realities through arguments that exceeded the thin walls of her apartment or overheard comments in elevators and corner stores. She found out who they were by listening for the ways they spoke to bus drivers and bank tellers, by watching how they walked and dressed, what items they purchased, what they carried on the El. But they didn't mean for you to discover them. They didn't ask you in. Yet city people, she thought, must be touched by the same longings and the same words or chasms where words might have been, as they cooked and ate together, while they made their beds and swept their floors. "People are the same, aren't they," she asked Reed, "aren't people the same deep down?"

As she furtively watched the black people on the bus, she reminded herself that they, too, had migrated to Chicago, in that generation or earlier, and many from areas not that different from Salt County. And before that they had come, by way of the South, from a place with different rhythms and tongues and codes. She was certain part of that survived.

Maybe each person retained a sliver of memory, and it took whole families, neighborhoods, tribes, to make their pieces into wholes. She sat on the decrepit, overburdened bus and thought that maybe the stalwart and exhausted woman across from her, with yellowed eyes and dewlapped neck, maybe she remembered trading secrets over the fence, remembered being a neighbor who had lent a hand. Or the lithe, adolescent boy who stared at nothing through scratched window glass while making his way to his forsaken, run-down school could receive a different, remembered entrance into being an adult. That frowning man in heavy boots and hard hat who stood holding the overhead bar with scarred, leathern hands, perhaps he had kept alive in his heart the smell of wet grass inhaled with his face pressed to a screen door.

Maybe, she thought, one such small thing had come to Mercury Owens at the end. Suppose he had remembered the river's corrugated surface, from the middle of the iron bridge.

While Sunday stood at the window, Delta lay in the double bed that had been their mother's and could swear she felt the river's current churning up refuse from its muddy floor, rocking the order she had been making and remaking with her navy blue tin box since she was twelve.

How long were you supposed to keep a mattress? she wondered as she felt the springs poking her back. This one felt as if it had been around since the beginning of time, and she rose from it aching and stiff each morning, but took no steps toward its replacement. She wondered if it had been there nearly forty years, since her parents had spent their nights together.

She asked herself, as she had many times, how much her father's leaving had revolved around what happened, or didn't, in that bed? And for her mother, had the bed become placid territory after he left, or had her nights been terrible in their blank evenness?

Delta's bed was a vast and lonely place, but it wasn't company in sleeping that she missed the most. She yearned for the erotic, in which she felt completed, alive. She could fully feel herself when touched, when entered, could see her loveliness if beheld. How had Dolora handled losing that after only five short years with Mercury? Had she arranged secret liaisons after her Thursday evenings out, or ached with desire and satisfied herself with her own hands, while picturing lovers above her, their features blurred, their mouths calling her name? Afterward, was she, like Delta, often silent and ashamed?

"Maybe I should move again," she said aloud, and considered continuing the circuit she had made of the upstairs rooms, "maybe Nana's room would give more rest." She had thought and acted on that impulse countless times, but once she got settled into Nana's former bed, she found that she was haunted, still. She had stopped moving her things, and left all the beds made, so that all she had to relocate was her body, and she kept migrating, though the things she fled seemed to follow her. Yeah, but it could be that it's time to try the front room, she speculated, and it's probably warmer, what with winter coming on.

She tried not to think about the trouble in either her mother's life or her own, but it came, along with the other things she was forever banishing. The river, swollen regularly and threatening so often to flood, had carried a locket, had carried Sunday back home. Though she felt the water lift and pull her with the current, she tried to lie still, resisting chaos, and she chose.

She chose the blue bowl, waiting, eyes closed, until she could picture it.

Once she had called it up, it filled with bread dough, and she could see and feel the pungent, sticky mixture before it was taken out for kneading, along with Nana's rich, clove smell. She felt Nana's hands, cabled with veins and missing half a finger, guiding her small ones at folding and pushing and rolling the dough. And then they rubbed it with shortening and placed it, a seamed, flattened sphere, back in the bowl, covering it with cloth. Drawn by the fermenting smell, she focused, through time, on a patch of the blue-striped cloth where the spare weave revealed the glistening, rising dough.

Hearing familiar, low-pitched voices, it was again for Delta an afternoon when she was nine, and the six women came to Nana's as they did each Saturday, to bake. Loaves of wheat bread and rye bread began to expand in bowls, came out of the oven, cooled on racks. Knives tapped against the bottoms of pans to loosen the loaves, and utensils and containers were soaped and rinsed for reusing. It seemed as if they were growing bread, all those hands of different browns, dusted in flour.

Sometimes the women played the radio, but mostly they talked while Delta and Sunday helped to grease pans and listened for bits of grown-up conversation. The Bread Ladies spoke of obligation, of washing and sewing and cooking and preparing the way in and out of the day for their families. They talked of their husbands, children, nieces, and nephews and the things provided them that week. Of the mopping and cooking and serving they did in white folks' homes, and the routines of the offices and factories where some of them found work.

They revealed their joys. Their gardens and the lingering porch swing kisses they had once been given. The mastered verse of a grandchild and the night-blooming cereus that had struck a family speechless.

They discussed politics and gossiped, too, telling who had gone over the line of acceptability in pride or infidelity, and who had failed to do his part.

They laughed as they disclosed recipes and practical ways to tackle all kinds of ordinary challenges. "You know those peelings will help your plants to grow," Opus Green would proclaim, nodding as her hands worked the dough. "It's truth, yes it is, and coffee grounds and eggshells, too. I feed them right back into the soil, and it does seem to do my squash plants good."

"I tried out what you said, Alpha," Laveen Walker might say, "about vinegar in that iron."

"Oh yeah," Patrice answered, "and did you sample the plant medicine I told you about?"

"Mmn hmn, baby, and those things been growing faster than my white hairs."

Delta remembered Nana, so present in her joy at the smallest things, going on about the sweet flesh of her red and yellow peppers and how their red was so red it would stain your fingers and your mouth. She told about the combination of spices she had used in the juice that would float the pale, seed-studded pears she was putting up one year. Secrets for rice pudding and watermelon pickles. What you might do to stretch a meal, or make up for the better cut of meat you could not afford.

Delta and Sunday had received most of their information about the world from Nana's kitchen, even though they had a radio and, later, a TV. That was where they had heard about the danger of violence from "the other group," news of which was sent by networks of friends and family spread out across the states. As the Bread Ladies worked and shook their heads, Delta and Sunday heard about white folks and their troubling ways.

She and Sunday absorbed the little bit they knew, in that gathering place lit by dissipating afternoon light, about Mercury Owens's departure and the things it had wrought. The women expressed their struggle for compassion and their puzzlement. "Life's a messy business," one of them said, her hands tossing flour across the table, "but when's that not been so?" They discussed it indirectly, guardedly, but the girls realized, over time, what they were talking about, and whenever the subject of Mercury came up, Valentine Cross just shook her head and sucked her teeth.

"How's Dolora?" the others would always ask, carefully, and Nana would answer evasively, "Making it. She's making it through."

They liked to pass around a jug of dandelion or currant wine that Nana had brewed, hiding it in coffee cups in case Grandpa returned. Everyone would take some except for Valentine, who never did approve of drink.

At some point, Nana would start the singing. She would begin by clapping and humming, and then a few words blossomed into a hymn or a work song or a shout. The others would join in, one by one, until the place was vibrating with everywhere they had been that week, and there was no stopping between songs. Their voices rolled from one melody into the next.

And Delta liked to wind among the women and make white flour clouds with her clapping hands.

Those women had referred to their Saturday afternoon activity as a task that had to be done. They worked hard to make the bread that would feed their families in the coming week, and the loaves that would go the next day to church, mixing and kneading the dough and lining up the pans as they came out of the oven, putting aside the rising dough to be carried home for baking. But it was their communion time, and they would never have given it up.

As they finished, they washed up and straightened the room, leaving it as it had been when they arrived. They took their aprons off and thanked Nana for her kitchen and their time together, and said goodbye until the next morning at church.

Nana would begin their cherished Prohibition toast before they left. "Well," she would say, picking up her glass, "here's to lying, cheating, stealing, and drinking," and the Bread Ladies would gather round the table, laughing, and lift their mugs of wine, all except for Valentine, who stood with the group even though she refused to drink. The others would pick up the next three lines.

"Lie only to save a friend," one would say, and then another would add, "Cheat death," and they would all respond with "Amen."

"Steal the heart of the one you love," a third would contribute.

And then Nana would finish as they clinked glasses, "And drink only with the best of friends," reaching out to embrace each one of them with her working, praising hands.

It was to those hands, injured so long ago she never even talked about it, that Delta had always turned. Dolora's hands had been there, plaiting and arranging and cleaning, doing for her daughters in a consistent, daily way, even though the person connected to them had seemed ever-distant. But Nana's fingers, warm and receptive, had kept something within their lives vital. They had made a circle of women happen and they had made bread rise.

With the help of the bowl and the Bread Ladies, Delta managed to achieve peace. Smells and images and rhythms had returned, and the feel of Nana's comforting fingers had helped her to drift off into dreaming, where she rediscovered other pieces of the misplaced past that would remain in the world of sleep when she woke.

Down the hall, under the same sky and shelter, Sunday had finally lowered the window and gone to bed, and she, too, was dreaming of what had happened in the kitchen below: of her first easel, set up by Nana and Dolora on spread-out newspapers by the sink after she had returned from school. She remembered standing at that wooden A-shaped easel drawing, making collages from magazine and newspaper cuttings, discovering poster paints.

She still worked in the kitchen, its linoleum layered and spattered with so many colors that the floor was an artwork itself, an accumulated chronicle of her work. Sometimes she got down on her knees and sorted out the blue and green from one summer, chipping it back with her fingernails, and the red abutting orange from another time, recalling the work and the life out of which each color had grown.

She had watched her mother working on her mosaics in her own small, orderly kitchen. Standing just beyond the light from the cracked door, she and Delta had seen Dolora fitting together tiles while they felt their own fascination and jealousy build. Delta's jawline locked and her anger flared; she retreated to her bed, unable to bear how her mother came alive in a way that had nothing to do with them, in a manner that seemed to banish all else. But Sunday had often watched Dolora for hours, undeterred by the painful struggle she witnessed from the other side of the kitchen threshold. She had wanted it in her life, the focus and intensity she saw in her mother's face and posture as she worked on into the night, despite fingers cut by sharp tile edges, oblivious to her blood mixing with the grout to color it pink. Sunday had watched Dolora's mouth relax and open as she made her pictures, evidently whispering some kind of chant, and she was determined to get for herself the thing she saw those nights.

After looking through a telescope in science class, she had begun dreaming of connecting the pinpoints of light to form pictures, and then of making a night sky. It instilled her with awe that the patterns of stars that had magically come clear and close through the tunneled lens were beheld in common everywhere. As a wonder and as a chart, for navigating the way out from home and back.

First she withdrew books on astronomy from the library, and then she sneaked out at night to find which constellations she could discover, amazed that for her, they had just recently been made real. By the bridge one evening she had found them transformed by the mirror of night water, rendered hers by the river, and by the slant of her own vision. Above her, in the bedroom, she had painted sky and water, too.

Sunday had cried and argued about covering the ceiling over in white, but Dolora had been firm, and she had understood, even then, as she watched her mother's hands tremble and mouth go taut with an unyielding explanation, that Dolora knew and feared her unbound need.

As she painted the ceiling over in white, she memorized her sky map so that it would never be wholly lost, and promised herself that one day she would have her own ceiling, palette, and canvas, which she could do with as she pleased.

When Sunday came downstairs the next morning, she found Delta underneath the kitchen sink on her back. Her knees rose up in their taupe panty hose, and her feet had slipped out of their fluffy pink slippers and hovered above the linoleum floor.

"Hey," she said, thinking that Delta looked as if the sink cabinet had caught her in its jaw-like doors, and was swallowing her, chew by chew.

"Oh, there you are," Delta said as she pulled her torso out from under the curving pipe. "I noticed a dripping yesterday and thought I'd tighten the washers under here." As she rinsed her hands and started the washing machine, Sunday laughed at the hammer and pliers that were stuck in the waistband of her ruffled apron.

Although Delta had never finished the education she had begun at the local community college, she had, over the years, taken many courses at the high school and the Y. In recent years she had found that she liked to fix things, and after taking a course on shop and electronics, she had rewired every lamp and appliance in the house, whether it needed it or not. "Nothing electric around here is safe," her friend Dinah had said, for it had become irresistible to snip off plugs and graft them onto different cords.

She was always on the prowl for leaks or malfunctions, for anything that needed mending. On the back porch there was a stack of window screens she had removed for patching, broken picture frames that could be restored, old faucets and handles that needed soldering. Sunday pushed the gingham curtain aside and peered out the window at a collection of disabled can openers, toasters, electric skillets, and clocks. Most of them were missing their plugs. She thought of Nana's basement storage room where she had sent things that no longer functioned, but which she couldn't bear to throw away. "Someone might be able to get that working again," she had always said.

"Appliance purgatory," Sunday said, "you put it out back."

Delta laughed at the name they had given Nana's basement room, through which all broken things passed before leaving the house. Sunday giggled, too, realizing that it was the first real laugh she had heard from Delta since she arrived. But as usual, because Delta's laughter sounded loud and raucous to her own ears, she cut it off, leaving Sunday grinning on her own.

Sunday paused, the sighing and burping of the coffeemaker filling the quiet. "But why didn't you use the coffeemaker yesterday, instead of heating water on the stove?"

"Oh, it's temperamental. It seems to work only first thing in the morning, and then it gets tired. I'm working on fixing another one for the afternoons." Shyly, Delta told about the course she had taken on electrical repair, but she didn't admit that she had taken to combing through yard sales and flea markets for things she might revive.

The washing machine began to vibrate and inch its way from the wall as it reached spin, and Sunday imagined it soon joining the other retired machines on the porch. Submerging her hand in a basket of clothespins, she was lost in remembered images of windblown towels and sheets, and could barely hear Delta's far-off ramblings about repairing the coffeemaker. Sunday said, half to herself, "It'll be too cold, soon, to hang out clothes."

"Yes," Delta answered, puzzled by the change of topic, "I'll be pulling them in, stiff from frost, or going to the Laundromat two blocks down."

"I do miss having line-dried clothes," Sunday said, and together, they returned to that plain, weathered smell. They had run through the flapping sheets and had laughed at the funny little hunched corners where the clothespins had held shorts and trousers to the clothesline. Facing each other, they had stepped forward to fold the sheets after Dolora took them down, and then stacked them in the oval wicker basket of braided twigs.

They heard a knock on the door and felt the edge of autumn's chill as Earlene Hall entered, without waiting for an invitation, holding Delta's latest Avon order in a small white paper bag.

Her eyes widened and she stopped at the kitchen archway when she saw Sunday. Aged beyond her thirty-nine years, and adorned with makeup to compensate, Earlene placed her hand on one of the high, rounded hips that stretched her knitted dress so tight it parted at the seams. "Well, well, look who's back in Salt," she drawled as she strolled in on red spiked heels.

She hadn't expected to find Sunday there, and it sparked something in her. She scrutinized her, moving from wild and wiry hair to loose-draped clothing to low-heeled, chunky boots, feeling the same resentment at Sunday's flaunting of her difference that she had known so many years before.

Delta rose from the table, took the white bag, and turned the conversation to perfume and bubble bath while Earlene chewed the corner of her red-glossed lips, which were outlined carefully with a thin black line. Sunday had seen that cosmetic trick and had always wanted to ask what the idea behind it was, but she didn't want to provoke Earlene and held her tongue. Sunday could tell from a distance that she had some varying design painted on her long, square-cut fingernails, perhaps similar to the palm trees, rhinestones, and gold stars she had seen on women's nails at checkout counters and coffee shops. Once, on the bus, she had seen a woman in sandals with I♥NY painted on the nail of her big toe.

Overcoming her qualms about approaching Earlene, Sunday said,

"Let's see your nails. I can tell they're spectacular from here." Earlene pulled out a chair, sat down, and proudly displayed her fingers, whose nails showed a ripening sunset in ten separate scenes. On her left pinkie finger a ball of fiery orange hovered at the nail's tip, and over the course of fingers it lowered, the surrounding sky shot with reds and then purples, until on the right pinkie it had disappeared halfway behind the cuticle's horizon line. Sunday wondered if it looked like a motion picture when Earlene moved her fingers fast.

"You see, Sunday Owens," said Earlene proudly, as she pulled her hands away, "Chicago's not the only place there's art."

She returned, then, to apprising Delta of the new products from Avon and Mary Kay, while Sunday tried to make herself invisible with silence as she cleaned her eyeglasses with the bottom of her tunic. After slapping a catalog down on the kitchen table, Earlene held forth on the merits of coordinating sachets and after-bath powder with one's cologne. Pausing, she looked Sunday up and down, and inquired, "What's your scent?"

It felt like a challenge. Although she hadn't worn perfume in years, Sunday picked up the catalog. As she flipped through the slick pages, with Delta reaching over her shoulder to turn down the corners of the ones that showed potential treasures, Sunday remembered Earlene's grade-school taunts. From countless moments of exile, one in particular emerged. After choosing an art class museum trip over the spring social, Earlene had come by her locker and said, "So you're too good to come to our little set," and when Sunday had opened her mouth to defend herself, Earlene had cracked her gum, turned, and said, "Un hunh. You think you cute . . . and white, too."

She knew it was meant to be the ultimate insult, yet what were the things that lay within the domain of whites? She had wanted to ask someone why being an artist or liking books belonged to white people. Her family was black. Her neighborhood was black. Her church was black. She hadn't even known any white people, except to nod hello to in school or downtown, so what had made Earlene react to her that way? Many times when she was growing up she had wanted to ask someone, but had been too ashamed that she might be inauthentic in some way she didn't even comprehend.

Sunday flinched at the harshness beneath her temptress drawl as Earlene chatted with Delta about after-bath spray. Sunday removed her glasses, repaired with gray duct tape at the joint, and realized that her own lipstick and blush must need reapplying. She remembered Earlene's look of condolence when, on her last visit, she admitted that she had never had a manicure.

Sunday felt Delta and Earlene receding, and she was farther and farther apart. Their voices, debating eaux de cologne and solid perfumes that came hidden in necklaces and rings, were thin and far away.

Time shifted, and she was again the twelve-year-old who was sprawled on the floor with the new set of colored pens she had saved up to buy, working with the rich marigold yellow and the lapis lazuli blue, loving their soft spread into the texture of the grainy paper, taking care not to press too hard and ruin the fiber tips soaked with radiant color. And there was Earlene, coming through the screen door and calling Delta's name, standing over her, mouth set hard as she nudged the pens that rested by the paper with the pointed toe of her high-heeled shoe, poised to destroy the cherished thing.

Returning to the present, Sunday came to the last page of the catalog and selected some hand soaps she would probably never use. Prepared for her selection to be ridiculed, she stood as soon as she had announced it and excused herself, saying she needed to make a call. Earlene filled out a form, feeling triumphant that she had bent Sunday to her will.

Sunday picked up the phone as if to place a call and pretended to be on the line as she listened to Earlene from a safe distance. She reported the details of an attempted break-in and an incident of disorderly conduct that had happened the night before. And then she went on and on about how she was only on her lunch hour and had to get back to work, how hard her office drove her, how many deliveries she had yet to make.

It aggravated Sunday when people emphasized how oppressed they were at work; because artists so often didn't have anyone to answer to daily, people acted as if they had no responsibilities, as if what they did wasn't work. And sometimes, over breakfast, Reed began to inventory the tasks that awaited him on a given day, getting himself revved up as he described them, and by the time he finished, she was panicked about whether he would get them done and felt as though she had to work her way out of a shrinking box. She had to enter her workday in a different way, starting with a meditative chore, even washing dishes or repotting plants, and she could listen to music or the radio, but she could not begin by thinking about paying bills, setting up appointments, listing what had to get done. Of course, lately, she had barely been able to begin at all.

After Earlene had collected her money from Delta, she clicked through the kitchen, the noise from her tiny heel points ceasing when she reached the living room carpet and turning to thumps as she crossed the plastic runner. She shouted as she banged the screen door that she had started carrying Amway products, too.

Sunday wondered who Earlene was underneath her seductive exterior and her active aggression. Why had Earlene always disliked her, she brooded, feeling the stirrings of the hurt twelve-year-old who resided, still, within. She had invariably been shocked to find out that others felt insecure and alien, too, even the girls in school who had been most popular. Why were the strangers never able to find each other? But then, she thought, look at Reed and me; maybe finding each other was the easy part.

"Well, she hasn't changed much," Sunday said, "though I must say there is more of her. I thought she was gonna put a gun to my head to make me buy something."

"Oh, that's just Earlene," Delta said. "You don't need to look down on her. She's one of the few people I'm still in touch with from school, and she's had a pretty rough time." Delta refused to be a part of Sunday's criticism, especially about Earlene's weight, and at the same time she wasn't sure why she felt the need to defend her, when she knew that she had always been a bully, even toward her.

"Delta, forget it," Sunday answered, "but that wasn't what I meant." She regretted right away her spiteful comment about Earlene's size, recognizing in it her own pitiable attempt at an alliance. But she wanted to ask Delta what black people she knew who hadn't had a rough time. She didn't doubt that Earlene had had one, but she doubted that Delta's indignant response had stemmed from that, and she felt a familiar hollow grow in her stomach and promised herself that she would not let her big sister see her admit to feeling belittled by Earlene Hall. "What was that about the break-in and the disorderly conduct?" she asked.

"She's got a police scanner. I guess it's her way of keeping up on things. That way, she has a kind of inside track on what crimes are being committed. She knows what trouble is happening before anyone else."

Sunday couldn't imagine wanting to be a monitor for trouble, immersed in dramas of disaster and wrongdoing day in and day out. She couldn't bear the nightly TV news, with its salacious account of every permutation of human horror, natural disaster, and accident, and she sometimes found it hard to read the newspaper's chronicle of negative events. But reluctant to say anything that might be interpreted as criticism, she changed the subject to what had happened to other friends and classmates, and then she fell silent.

"It's chilly for late October," Delta said, annoyed with herself for retreating to the cliché topic of the weather, out of not knowing what else to say.

"In Chicago, they'll have Christmas decorations in the stores before long. Seems like they used to wait until Thanksgiving at least to put them up. Now there are all these reminders of holidays past, yet nothing is really the same."

They were quiet, and then Sunday thought of something positive to bring up. "Speaking of Christmas, remember those hard, raspberry-shaped candies we had at Christmastime?" She recalled the way the sour-sweet bumpy tops had felt against the roof of the mouth, scraping it raw if they had too many, and breaking through to the gooey, jam-like centers.

"I loved those things," Delta answered, "and ribbon candy, too. I wonder why we only had them at Christmas."

They talked about the holiday feasts their grandmother had cooked, about wrapping presents and trimming the tree at Nana's house, and how Dolora had given up on real trees and opted for metallic silver, despite Sunday's unruly protest in the aisle of the department store downtown. And the little white, glitter-sprinkled felt skirt for snow that covered the metal legs of the stand, those ceramic reindeer candleholders that marched across the mantel, and the big pink-faced Santa they had on the door in the early years, until Dolora suddenly realized the error of that way and said the door was one place they didn't need a white man, if they could choose otherwise.

"What was Christmas like before I was born?" Sunday asked.

"Well . . . let me see." After a long pause, Delta said, "I don't think

Mercury was so into Christmas, but that's something Opus might know about. I think he seemed to be . . . on the edge of it all. He didn't forbid or ruin it, nothing like that, but he didn't really get swept up in it either. And like you know, Mama was committed to the customs and traditions, like they gave her something to throw herself into. You know how making everything nice and pretty kind of guided her through."

"Do you put up a tree now?"

"Oh yes," Delta answered emphatically, "in the very same way. But I get a real one and decorate it with the family ornaments, the ones we've always used. I try always to go to someone else's for dinner, though. Opus's, or Dinah's . . . she's a friend of mine . . . or a colleague's from work. By dinnertime I can get to feeling pretty low about the lack of company and the lack of presents underneath the tree. Usually, there isn't even any snow, and if there is, it's brown and turned to slush."

"I guess everyone feels bad over the holidays, about whatever way what's going on with them doesn't measure up to the TV and greeting card picture of unity and cheer. Whatever's wrong or missing tends to rise. I feel like I just try to survive Christmas. Celebrating it isn't much in Reed's experience, and we've never had a tree. We do get each other presents, but we try to keep it low-key."

"You could spend Christmas here sometime," Delta said, turning to look for her cigarettes and finding them in her hand.

"Yes. Yes, we could."

Their talk of Christmas brought back Dolora apologizing in advance for the modesty of her presents as she strung lights and hung the ornaments she had made herself out of papier-mâché, ceramics, and painted wood. She refused the money Nana often offered, seeing it as a point of honor to provide her own gifts.

They remembered the strained holiday mornings when they had opened their own gifts before going to Nana's for dinner. Because Dolora said she couldn't bear the sentimentality of Christmas carols, the time leading up to the yearly ritual was quiet. She made breakfast and passed them plates piled high with sausages and French toast, and then they waited for her to declare it was gift-giving time. She worked hard, they knew, to make Christmas pleasant, and she always had more than the one present for which each of them had asked. But they dreaded the time for opening meticulously wrapped and ribboned gifts, for it seemed that Dolora watched the paper tear and slide off with tension that approached alarm.

They tried to meet her apologetic and nervous scrutiny with effusive comments about their gifts, and as soon as they were out of their boxes, Delta and Sunday put them to use. Delta remembered standing before the tree one Christmas dressed in all of her gifts: pajamas, high-heeled shoes, and a winter hat, going on and on about how perfect each thing was. Aware of Dolora's discomfort at having to formulate instant responses to unexpected gifts, her daughters were conscientious about dropping hints that would let her know what she would be getting. "Your hands must be pretty cold this winter," they might say on the days leading up to Christmas, to prepare her for a pair of gloves. She thanked them with quick, dry kisses on the cheek, and began immediately to clean up, taking paper and bows from their hands as soon as they removed them, and vacuuming around the tree as soon as the last gift was opened.

"She was always going. Nonstop," Sunday said, "never, ever resting. Especially her hands."

"Yes, and it was funny how her hands were so big, yet she handled those tiny pieces of things, doing that intricate tile work. I remember when we had those Scrabble games with Nana, how fascinated I was with how fast Mama moved the little letter squares. She would be thinking, not moving a muscle, and then she would lay down a word, quick as a flash. Her hands were always accomplishing something, even embroidery and needlepoint, and I know I thought it looked odd to see them busy with that ladylike kind of thing. And sometimes they were scraped and raw from some job or some project," Delta added, "but to me, they always looked in charge."

Dolora's fingers were making sandwiches and wrapping cookies in sheets of white-veined waxed paper, and then packing all three of their meals in little brown paper lunch bags. Getting their hair braided and her own rolled back and pinned in place, mouth set and barely speaking, except to say she had to fix their "wild and nappy heads" and to inform them of the minutes remaining before departure time. She seldom touched them without a task, without an end in mind, and neither one could remember caresses, forehead kisses, strokes, or pats. Her hands were busy following through, and moving as though they were trying to forget some of the things they had known.

From the moment she arrived to get them from Nana's, where they went after school, she was making dinner and cleaning up and preparing the way for the next day's demands. Present in body, yet somehow perpetually off-limits, Dolora was intent on the tasks of getting them washed and tucked in, announcing firmly how long it was until bedtime, and checking behind their ears for dirt.

On Saturday mornings she was hustling them off to classes at the Y, where they learned to swim and cartwheel and tap dance while she partook of "Ladies' Day Out," working at crocheting and wallpapering and mosaics with the other mothers who tried to provide their daughters with the opportunities they hadn't had, while improving themselves.

Saturday afternoons were for bread-making, and Sundays, for church. Women's perfume and powder smells. Vaseline-polished legs and patent-leather shoes. With Dolora between them, they had shifted on hard wooden pews during the sermons, and then basked in her nearness and lost themselves in the singing that seemed to make the talking worthwhile, giving themselves up to the heartbeat rhythm and the voices, led by Nana's. They could both picture every detail of that red brick house of worship, where over the years they had felt less and less at home.

Often, on Thursdays, Dolora went to the movies with one of her "men friends," and they sometimes went to the same show several times, as the one theater in town only got a new film every month or two. She never had those men, whom they were instructed to call "Mr. Evans," "Mr. Blagden," "Mr. Phipps," over to their house, and saw them only that one night a week, while Nana watched the girls.

On Friday nights, after she was finally free of the week's obligations, she made her mosaics. They had always lived by a schedule, but on Fridays, Dolora was really pushing to have them cleaning up from dinner, squared away with homework, and in their room by eight o'clock. "Let's go, girls; it's seven-thirty, and fast becoming eight." She had thrummed with tension as she glanced at the clock and cleared off the table, hurrying them from the kitchen and upstairs.

Sunday recalled with guilt the times she had flirted with that boundary and dragged on the washing of pots and pans or chosen that time to seek her mother's intimate advice, feeling a certain power at provoking her desperation to get her three or four hours to herself, at making her choose to be mother first.

Once she got them squared away, and there was no one, for that evening, who needed anything from her, she sat down at her gray marble-look Formica table and her large, thick fingers started to speak. She pulled out her box of tiles and materials for building her wooden frames and began. Bits of glass and stone were collected to add to the pieces of tile she mail-ordered, and as she walked to and from work she watched out for bits of metal, rock, or wood that might be of use. They could still picture her hands, busy arranging the tiles into spirals and waves of color.

Alone with her tiles, she had been at ease, but she had bristled at the touch of others, stiffening at sudden demonstrations of affection and pulling away. And neither daughter remembered Dolora disclosing much about her own life. When they asked her to tell them specifics, she got up and busied herself with a chore. But there was one thing she loved to talk about.

Her best memories, she said, were of weekends of discovery at the tiny town library, where she had found books on the Greek gods and ancient Egypt, and the leather-bound encyclopedias that overwhelmed her with their vast collection of amazing information about the world. There had been about a year at fourteen and fifteen when Nana had sent her to the library on Saturdays while she did her cooking and other chores, and Dolora would get lost in that single room of books until it closed at six and she hurried home to set the table and eat.

Of Africa, she had only a sketchy, general sense, and no encouragement to know more. Teachers and librarians steered her to the West, but one place she had discovered, despite them, was Egypt, with its mesmerizing murals and friezes and tombs. Egypt, she felt, was hers, a source she could name, and she found two library books on its ancient glory and sat reading of gods and goddesses, catastrophe and resurrection, life beyond death.

Her interest was thought peculiar by her schoolmates and friends, but one teacher encouraged her excitement, especially about ancient Greece and Rome, and she came home and shared the information she learned. Nana hadn't exactly understood it, finding her own footing in the Bible, but she had listened and tried to ask questions, despite how far away and foreign it all seemed. Dolora talked about the pantheons of deities, and about temples and mummies. She showed Nana how to write certain words with hieroglyphs. And when they worried about the rising of their own muddy river, Dolora reminded them that the Nile flood was caused by Isis's single, yearly tear.

Those library weekends had come to an end when her father had worried that money was thin, and he had decided that she should help out with Saturday work at the drugstore downtown, but she never lost her fascination with ancient heroes and gods, in the symbols and contradictions of their stories and their grasp of ongoing life. For years her interest was buried, kept alive only in the naming of her child and the little stories she made up for her, but after Mercury's departure, it surfaced in the mosaics she put together on the nights she declared to be her own.

Delta and Sunday asked her for stories, but she talked rarely of her own past, and even less of the husband who had fled, or how she had managed to make it across her barren nights. Instead, she told tales of a god dismembered and scattered, gathered and revived. She spoke of pyramids and rulers who were buried with tools for the afterlife. Telling them less with words than with the pictures she composed from tile and stone, helping them pick out the sun god and sheltering Nut, with stars made out of mica flecks. Her mosaics depicted lotuses, Horus's eternal eye, and the papyrus swamps that had been refuge and conception place. She told the story of how she had named Delta out of her love for the ancient site of entombed pharaohs and the recovered head of a god.

Dolora made some of her mosaic tiles herself, out of slabs of clay that she cut into irregular chunks and geometric shapes and ovals. And on Sundays after church, once she had the pieces arranged, she did the grouting and sometimes let them help. They mixed the plaster under her direction and watched as she worked it down between the tiny chips and pieces with her fingertips and covered the whole surface with cloudy grout. And then they waited for the magical apparition of color, as the powder gray screen was wiped away.

In the morning light, while Sunday sifted through clothespins and Delta fidgeted with pliers and wrench, they recalled an adventure of making fish-shaped tiles that would interlock to become a tray for the church auction one year. They had both treasured that single time when she had let them sit at the kitchen table with her and make their own fish out of smooth beige clay. Dolora had taken her daughters with her when she went to fire the pieces at the Y, where the ceramics teacher let her use the kiln. They had treasured those clay fish, made at her side and finished with glazes she had helped them blend.

Sunday admitted that the fish she made had either been lost, misplaced, or broken over the years, but Delta knew that one of hers had survived, for she had found it in the attic, in the rusted, blue metal chalk box she had saved.

So many years later, they could still picture Dolora working and whispering, too quietly for them to make out her language of exhilaration and sorrow. While they watched from the crack in the kitchen door, her large, knobby fingers narrated in fragments of clay and stone. They could both envision her fluid, vibrant gestures, and it made them wonder: What range of things, residing deep in the bone and muscle, did those hands remember and forget?

6

DELTA PUT HER WRENCH and pliers in her toolbox and returned it to the porch. There were so many things that needed fixing and tending, she thought. Her mother had managed to keep the house clean and orderly, but clutter and dust just seemed to overtake Delta, so that she sometimes couldn't make a start. Only two days before she had raked, and yet the ground was covered once again. She wished for their hands, her mother's and her Nana's, and for the smell of baking bread.

Grabbing the rake, she went out front to clear the newly fallen leaves. Five years had passed since Nana's death, Delta thought as she combed at stray leaves, and Dolora had been gone for almost two decades, nearly half her life. When, she wondered, would there be an end to her mourning? When would she be able to leave her grief behind?

She began to make a pile of leaves, thinking as she did so about how strangely bereavement worked, how for the most part the pervasive and disorienting pain of what was lost either faded or blurred. And then suddenly it visited, with a freshness and clarity that were astonishing, years after the fact. Over time it seemed to distill, as it was housed within. "Remember," it demanded as it arrived, and you had no option but to comply.

When Dolora died, Delta had been in her first year at the post office and Sunday was finishing high school. Noticeably worn and pale, Dolora had suffered fatigue and back pain for over a year and had taken more and more sick days from her clerk-typist job, but had never sought medical help. "No doctors for me," she had said, dismissing Nana, "I don't need experimenting on." In the mornings of her sick days she had to drag herself from bed, but once up, she restlessly tackled tasks she had meant to do for years. Only when she collapsed while painting the hall banister did she seek a doctor's help.

Delta had found Dolora unconscious on the landing and rushed her to the hospital, where tests revealed that it was too late for either radiation, chemotherapy, or a surgeon's skill. Although she was discharged a week later, she was soon readmitted, never to leave the hospital alive.

Nana was in constant attendance, but she had told Delta years later that none of it had made any sense to her; present was simply what she knew how to be. Her own parents were dead and she had lost her husband a decade before, and her only other child was a son who never visited and rarely called, who only sent get-well cards as Dolora approached death. He showed up the afternoon of the funeral service, making sure to point out the elaborate floral arrangement he had sent, and left town the very same day. The fact that Nana's daughter was dying before her was barely comprehensible, and though she tried to count Wilborn as a comfort, she had to admit that her family was dwindling to her sisters in bread-making and two teenaged girls.

Cancer at the age of forty was unsettling and bewildering, and no one in town was sure whether to inquire about specifics or to express faith that Dolora would be okay. They said they would pray for her and bring her name to the altar, but they weren't sure that cancer, "of the lower regions," was something to be spoken about any further. Such a stealthy misfortune, suffered by a family that had already seen so much trouble, was hard to accept. She had seemed all right, they thought, if a little thin and peaked, and it made them uncomfortable, made them want to know if disease like that picked and chose, or could come for anyone.

Dolora received their visits and flowers and cards with quiet appreciation, making sure she looked presentable and careful to accept her fate, at least publicly, with refinement and ease, but the worst thing about being sick, she said, was having to endure all the reassuring touching and patting that well-wishers seemed to feel the need to bestow. Delta had held the mirror as her mother applied her lipstick, trying to stay within the edges of her narrow mouth as her hands shook, and had sneaked in a Curl Free perm that they applied in the bathroom, so that Dolora didn't have to look "unsightly" at the end. "Spare me the indignity of an unkempt head," she pleaded.

Dolora tried for composure, but the bitterness and fury she had always kept in check erupted suddenly in tirades directed at the hospital staff. An orderly had a water carafe pitched at him for waking her with his cleaning, and a nurse who had patiently answered her call button throughout the night was chided for both indifference, and for "never leaving me alone." Although she had never before been a complainer, she snapped at the nurses for their inattention, demanding more and faster help for her pain. Nana couldn't help thinking that she had stored up a lifetime of discontentment, and was expressing it while she could. It was how Grandpa would have behaved, she thought, if the suddenness of his death had not deprived him of the chance.

Delta and Sunday had tried desperately to know their mother while they could, but their daily and extensive inquiries as to mood and pain and diet, and their offers to fetch and rearrange things, sent Dolora over the edge. "What can I bring you?" they would ask by phone before coming. "What do you want?" There was nothing she wanted, she responded, nothing, in any case, that they could provide. What she longed to shout, but couldn't, was, "My life. It's my life I want."

So it was "Stop that hovering" that she grumbled as she pulled away from their ministrations and closed her eyes. Wanting to ask and tell her all the things that had never been expressed, Delta and Sunday begged and waited, hopefully, for her secrets and poured out details of their own daily lives. When she said she was too exhausted to talk, they sat with her in silence, moored by the sound, confidential and basic, of her effort to breathe.

In her last days, Dolora had moved in and out of consciousness, raising her head off the pillow to ask what time it was or whether they had completed their homework and their chores. "It's almost eight," she said once, asking them to vacate the kitchen and leave her to her tiles. She woke one evening to their expectant faces and whispered, "I've given all I have. Don't suck me dry."

She was so tired of trying, she told Nana, so tired of following through. At least, she whispered, she could go with the comfort of knowing that although at times she hadn't been sure how she would accomplish it, she had managed to get her girls to adulthood.

As Dolora lost control of her functions and could no longer eat, Delta had been aware of her own panic. "Tell me," she wanted to say, long after Sunday had gone home for the night, "tell me one true, important thing, something you've saved just for me." She spent entire nights curled up in the bedside chair, afraid she would miss the moment of connection she had awaited so long.

She seemed to feel her mother's body folding, cell by cell. Her organs stifled by choking growths, she hung on with sinew and reflex and pride, each breath a triumph. In contrast to the monochrome and order of the room, disinfected and polished and clean, there was the messy life-wish striving against its own end, trying for a poised release when all grace was denied. And Delta was there for the sputum and blood, the jutting bones and stale sweat of a body not abstract at all, but her mother's, and, therefore, in some way, her own.

As Delta swabbed her forehead and held her hand, she had felt and smelled the dying that seemed to vanquish from the center out. She had wanted to know it, and had pressed her face to Dolora's faded skin to take in the stink of morphine and decay. Climbing up next to her, she had seen her pores and moles and wrinkles from up close, had held her mother's shrunken body. She was there for its resistance and surrender, absorbing each extraordinary thing the body which had conceived her told. It seemed to give the only confessions she would ever get.

They had sat around her bed as the end drew near, and just before she died, she disclosed to them her device of selecting and composing a past, a bequest that had as much to do with forgetting as it did with looking back: "Remember only what you choose."

Delta had found herself exuding rage when the nurse pulled up the bedsheet to cover her mother's face. "Wait!" she had urged her, as if there might still be a chance she would still reveal herself with words. She yelled at Nana, "She didn't *have* to go! She could have caught it if only she had cared." When no one else was home, she had hammered one of Dolora's mosaics into tiny pieces with a chisel, and then buried them in the refuse of the Salt County dump.

So quickly Dolora had departed, Delta thought as she raked, in just a little over a month, and it had been nearly impossible to find any outward joy in the year of her death, as Sunday's impending departure weighed on everyone. But in a rare moment of mirth, the August before she left, Sunday had urged Delta to climb with her from their bedroom window onto the roof just before dawn. They had taken a blanket with them and climbed out barefooted, praying Nana wouldn't find them missing from their beds. Up there, stretched out on their backs, aslant with the roof and side by side, they had surveyed the night-into-morning sky. Sunday had pointed out the fading constellations and recited the myths she knew about them, bringing Delta to the point of raucous laughter with her own contemporary version of the tale of Virgo, fighting off the smooth advances of their local Lotharios with her palm branch and her ear of wheat, in order to stay free and self-contained.

The next month she set off for school in Chicago, leaving Delta and Nana with their grief. And for a long time, Delta had resisted releasing a single aspect of her mother's suffering. She had held on to each detail of her living and dying, filling the sudden emptiness by recalling anything, everything, painful and not.

Only recently, she had tried to replace the hurtful and complicated with what was good. Instead of the shrink and disappearance of an unknown and unknowable life, she had decided on rediscovered clay fish and Nana's magic, loving hands. You could do that, she had told herself for years, couldn't you? Dolora had practiced the art of selective forgetting and had passed it down.

Since she had always been out of reach, even her voice, when she had used it, seeming remote, Delta had tried to assemble the mother who was hers, the one she needed and might have known. She had had that person for her first years, so briefly and so long ago that it was mere impression, punctuated with small, discrete images that had tunneled to the present, whole. Those things, a placket of buttons, a lullaby, or the smell of her mother's skin, those things she had worked to keep alive against the consuming force of decay.

And now that Delta wanted her mostly forgotten, Dolora was back.

The dead seemed to stalk her present, she thought, like insatiable ghosts. Those unable to manage showing up in life were always entering, ready to consume what they had left behind, and the worst part was that they didn't come back different, better, unless she recalled them through object or experience, and willed it so. They came back as they were in life: denying, disapproving, remote. There was Dolora, adept and inaccessible, and Grandpa, despotic and proud. There was Nate Hunter, stepping into her light and forcing her into silence with his absolute desire. And her father, returning through his unfinished leaving, again and again and again.

Unaware that she had company, Delta muttered to herself as she gouged the lawn with the sharp tines of the rake, "Absent when you need them and here when you want them gone. Isn't that . . . isn't that just the way life fucking is?"

Sunday stood at the screen door and sipped her coffee. She heard the word "fucking," and theorized that Delta was having a private conversation that just might concern her recently arrived sister. She wondered whether to point out to Delta that she still had on her fuzzy pink slippers, and that they were getting caked with mud and withered grass. No, she thought, the less said about most things around there, the better.

Delta raked furiously, silently, and Sunday kept watching, striving not to make a sound and call attention to herself, until Delta paused and looked up from her raking. "Oh, I didn't see you there." She placed one arm on the rake handle and the other on her hip. "You know what I keep thinking about? I keep thinking about those tickets."

For a moment, Sunday had no idea what she was talking about . . . Tickets? . . . Tickets? . . . and then she pictured the large white shopping bag, its handles torn off and its top rolled down, discovered in the closet corner so many years before. When Nana had asked them to choose a burial outfit for Dolora, they had opened the closet door and released the violet and cold cream and lotion smell that was hers alone.

Opening the door, so many years ago, they had both remembered sneaking into that closet on her Thursday evenings out in order to try on her blouses and slips and nightgowns, and had made believe they were grown-up ladies with her purses and stockings and shoes. Dolora's adult things, with their soft and slippery textures and hooks and eyes, had been mysterious, evoking intoxicating secrets that womanhood would one day provide. Delta had rubbed her face against those clothes, inhaling that near and unattainable scent.

Years later, as they searched for an outfit for her burial, they had gawked at the modest collection of blouses and skirts, aware, in seeing the sum of her personal belongings, that she had worn practically the same things every day. Assembled, her possessions told their own story. Delta's and Sunday's eyes traveled over tan skirt after tan skirt, noting the range from cotton to wool, and then scanned the unbroken, wire-hangered line of pastel blouses, long-sleeved and short. They had turned to face each other, overwhelmed with the uniformity of her clothes.

An even row of low-heeled pumps and flats was arranged beneath the clothes; some needed polishing and others, new heels or soles. In one pair of sandals, dark, indented toe marks were visible, and some were lined with Dr. Scholl's cushions and bunion pads. They were embarrassed to be looking at the condition of her intimate things, from the inside-out. It seemed wrong, a violation, and they both wondered how their own closets and underwear drawers would look to outsiders. Three pocketbooks hung from a thick nail driven into the side wall; their contents were half-open to view.

On the back of the door hung her two nightgowns, five white cotton bras, three girdles, and a slip. A drawstring bag of soiled garments hung with them, along with a dusty sachet, its potency long gone. At first, neither Delta nor Sunday touched the small assemblage of oddly intimate things Dolora had left just inside the closet door.

Delta hadn't even been able to remember seeing her mother undressed, though she sometimes asked for help with the tiny hooks that ran all the way up the back of her long-line bra. The only occasion when Sunday had seen her naked was the time she slipped in the bathtub and broke her collarbone, which ached from then on. They looked silently at the private possessions of the woman who had been so out of reach, self-conscious about their famished curiosity.

"There's stuff back there," Delta had said as she bent over at the waist and peered beneath the row of tan hems. And then they had parted the clothes and reached in.

They had found dusty shoe boxes filled with pay stubs, rubber-banded gas bill receipts, and canceled checks. A manila folder marked "Important Papers," containing birth certificates, old leases, and a high school valentine from Mercury Owens that read "Please be mine."

There were half-filled books of S&H Green Stamps and empty packets of zinnia and marigold seeds with the tops torn away and the care instructions intact. Plastic bags of church programs and decades-old *Ebony* magazines. Napkins and matchbooks from the out-of-town trips she had taken with co-workers. Gloves and hats and hardened cakes of shoe polish. And finally, in the corner, they had found an entire shopping bag of entry receipts for the Publishers Clearinghouse Sweepstakes, and lottery tickets purchased every week over years and years. Pouring the contest receipts and lottery tickets into a mound between them, they were silent and openmouthed at Dolora's private and sustained belief in hope and chance.

"The tickets," Sunday said, coming through the screen door. "Yes. I would have never figured Mama to do such a flighty thing, and there she was, laying her dollar or so down weekly, believing it was possible that she just might be lucky one day."

As the items in that closet came back to her, Sunday decided she wanted to find her mother's things again. Had they kept any of those papers? she wondered. Maybe they would tell her something that would help, something she needed to know.

Deciding that their inventory of her closet had yielded no outfit that was right for burial, Delta had convinced Nana that they should buy something new. While Sunday worked on the funeral program and Nana made arrangements with the church, Delta had taken care of the clothing.

Although Sunday had been horrified at the pale peach, lace-encrusted outfit chosen by Delta, which she was sure Dolora would never have worn, she managed, then and now, to keep her mouth shut about it. Standing silently at the coffin with Delta before the mourners arrived, she recalled that as she had examined Dolora she had thought that her mother's thin-lipped silence was the only thing about her, lying there all trussed up and ornamented, that seemed the least bit real.

It had rained the entire day before the funeral, and all through the church and graveside services, the sky had been bleak, its clouds pent with rain. She and Sunday and Nana had sat in three metal folding chairs whose front legs rested on the AstroTurf that had been placed around the opened ground, and Delta remembered the back legs of their chairs sinking gradually into the soggy grass, so that by the end of the service, they were tilted back and looking up with apprehension at the waterlogged clouds.

"Days like today," she said, pointing to the slate gray sky and kicking at the curling leaves, "always remind me of Mama's funeral. You're sure it will rain, but the sky keeps you waiting and waiting. And there's that same end-of-the-season chill in the air."

"Funny," Sunday said, "how you remember things through weather. I guess it's the backdrop for whatever's going on."

Delta stopped raking and without censoring herself, she let the words spill out. "I think it's weird sometimes how we mark time with deaths. Births and deaths. They're the things that get recorded in a book down at someone's office . . . or in a family Bible."

"Our 'official news,' Nana used to say."

"Yes. But it's the daily in-between stuff that's your life. It's the sandwich-making and hanging out the sheets like we were talking about. The clapping and singing, and the things people said to you or that you remember, the everyday, little things that don't really matter much in the big picture, like the clock that stubbornly stopped working. Like Nana tapping her foot while she hummed and the private feeling of Mama's closet, or the smell of bread."

"Isn't it the small things that lovers do for you that let you know you're special? Aren't those things the deal-breakers, the things that count? I'm thinking of a man who used to bring me boxes of candy, Belgian chocolate and Katy Dids. Sometimes there would be one piece missing, and he'd have left a single word on a little folded-up piece of paper, in the depression where the candy had been."

"Wow," Sunday said, "that's impressive." She thought about how unimaginative she was with Reed. Maybe that was the kind of effort it took to make things work. "What kinds of words did he leave?"

"Oh, things like 'MAGIC' or 'DELICIOUS.'" She blushed, and grabbed her cigarettes. "Or 'HURRY,' if we were going to meet later on. It really made me feel amazing, for such a little gesture."

"Wow," Sunday said again. "Where is he now, this man?"

"Leaving words for someone else, I guess. The problem is, by the end of our time together, *I* felt like leaving words for him, words like 'ASSHOLE' and 'TRIFLING.' I guess that's the way love goes."

"Maybe not. Not always, if you can say yes to it." She hoped Delta would keep on talking.

"No? Well, that's another story anyway, one I don't want to revisit in any case."

Sunday didn't push. "Well, you're right that the details matter. They do in a painting, too. Often they seem inconsequential, but the whole picture turns on them. The whole picture is made up, after all, of individual brush strokes and marks. A photograph is made of tiny dots. Whether something's little or big, I'm not sure you can ever tell."

"Do you know," Delta said, looking directly at her, "I read in some magazine that people need fourteen hugs a day. Now is that a thing that's little or a thing that's big?"

Dolora had been buried in what still functioned as the black cemetery. As Dolora had requested, they had added her name to the double headstone carved for Mercury, whose inscription simply read, "Now at Rest, 1937–1961." Next to his name, it read, "Dolora Owens, Daughter, Wife, and Mother, 1938–1979."

They sat on the porch and discussed what to do about that gravestone, now that the locket and the note had come. After a great deal of talk and no resolution, they decided to go and look at the headstone that had been sunk into the earth with nothing beneath it until Dolora died.

They weren't sure what to do about the body that must be buried in Clare County, either. Should they rescue it from what might be a pauper's grave and bury it next to Dolora's? Should they let him rest where his life had come to a stop? Was it a big or little thing? Resolving the question of the gravestone was hard, but it seemed more manageable than deciding whether to bring his body home.

While neither sister was certain she owed him any further recognition, the inaccuracy of the death date carved upon the stone disturbed them both. They still had no body to bury, but they debated whether to give Dolora her own marker, and whether to correct the date on his. For her part, Delta was concerned that correcting it might notify the people of Salt County that rather than dying, he had merely run.

Sunday called Opus to find out whom to see about changing the stone, and Opus told her that Felix Harris was still the one to contact, but that she would have to go there, since he had no phone. Before she tackled that, Sunday wanted to do some repair work on her bond with Delta. Her comment about necessary hugs had made Sunday feel bad, particularly since Delta was alone and she was not. She knew they were going to need each other, especially through resolving the question of the headstone, and she knew that with Reed a special meal often acted as a demonstration of love.

She wanted to make dinner for Delta, and she wanted it to be a surprise. That kind of special effort she didn't really mind; it was daily cooking she despised. But she knew she had to choose something that was nice and simple, not elaborate, as Delta might see that as an effort to show her up. Maybe, if she could choose the right meal, it would get some goodwill flowing.

She showered and dressed again in her loose tunic and pants, tamed part of her hair back, and put on lipstick. Then she put the buckle and the coaster she had brought home in her bag, feeling foolish as she did it and whispering to herself that she had really lost her grip, but realizing that the objects were becoming amulets.

In light of learning that Mercury had roamed the whole of Salt County, she decided to walk to the supermarket in the white part of town. Although the landscape might well seem like that of a different planet since the time of his taking stock, what with the sprawl of strip malls and car-clogged streets, Sunday wanted to imagine what her father might have felt.

She walked the streets she had known growing up, where there had always been a small, tight-knit community of black folks. Freedmen had settled the area, establishing trades and starting small farms and services and stores. They had provided the whites who lived only blocks away with domestic and unskilled work, and as the century turned, more blacks had come, and some families had flourished. Later it had acquired a few professionals, too, doctors and lawyers, and the pharmacist who worked at Grandpa's store. And when factory and farm work were available, it had been a promising place to settle, especially if you already had people nearby.

The paper mill had been the biggest draw to Salt County, and many had thought that its steady work replaced the need for higher education. And then, when it mechanized and streamlined its operations and its workforce, and the linoleum and tire and lamp factories were no longer profitable there, a lot of formerly contented people had nowhere to turn. Some went looking for work in cities like Detroit and Chicago, and some stuck around and tried to manage.

Salt County had been segregated not by law but by custom and reach. Its divisions were enforced by hostility, condescension, and fear, and as in most cities, including Chicago, the races kept to different worlds. The lines were more or less clear, the services and privileges distinct.

As she crossed out of the part of town where black folks and a handful of Indian, Vietnamese, and Mexican families lived, Sunday found herself among white people who were struggling to get by. She walked by neat, cracker box houses with tiny, hemmed-in gardens that persevered, and sagging, peeling bungalows, whose tired inhabitants had given up the effort to adorn.

Sunday recognized the spirits of these people, some of them resigned to their circumstances, and some resisting by planting and ornamenting whatever it was they had. Many had been drawn, also, by the paper mill, the lamp factory, the tire and linoleum plants. Here, too, folks were jobless, working for subsistence, and "on the county," as her people called the welfare benefits that were fast being snatched away. Struggling with the meager returns their myths and dreams had delivered, fighting to make ends meet. But they could not ally with their darker brethren, for the single advantage they had was being white. And though Sunday wasn't sure they were aware of it, many blacks, to whom they knew themselves to be patently, inherently superior, looked down on them as "PWT." Neither could see beyond the stories they had needed to make, and potential bonds were vanished in the fault line dividing race from race.

Across a fenced-in yard, a woman of fleeting youth glanced tiredly her way. She hung out a mound of spotless sheets, snapping each one open with strong hands before she stretched its length along the line, as her child played in an abandoned, hoodless Chrysler, its entrails exposed and invaded by crabgrass and weeds.

Sunday paused as something in the woman's determined movements, in the proud set of her mouth, made her think of Sheila Flanagan, one of the few white children in her elementary school. Solemn and unaffiliated, spurned by all, Sheila had met her exile with a show of indifference, walking erect and friendless through the school hallways with her jaw fixed in a proud and obdurate line. Sunday wondered what had happened to that girl with the high-water pants and the lush, green eyes, thinking that she could have been the woman before her, pockets full of clothespins, mouth set firmly in answer to her plight, stringing out her wash with anger and pride.

Sunday willed a smile in the direction of the child who tumbled in and out of the abandoned car, but he stared across the yard warily, and ran farther away.

A throng of hardened, blue-eyed, adolescent boys, dressed in the urban hip-hop drag of low-slung, baggy jeans, massive athletic shoes, and name-brand shirts, blared rap music from a tape deck and watched her coldly as she passed. Now there's a contradiction, she thought, walking on. And as she approached, a group of porch-sitting men grew still and followed her progress intently with stares that seemed to come from behind their eyes. The hair on the back of her neck stood up, but she held her breath, nodded, and controlled her stride. What was going on behind those eyes, she wondered, fascination and distrust of the unknown? A defensive offense? Mute and fearful rage? Was it a tangled, recondite desire too historical to name? Maybe, she decided, it was all those things.

As she continued, the houses began to grow bigger and further apart. And then, after blocks of modest and secure, well-tended homes, the streets started to curve and wind. Larger and fancier dwellings were set back from the sidewalks and surrounded by broad, landscaped lawns and flowerbeds. On some blocks, there were matching wrought-iron coach lights out front, and a few properties still had grinning jockeys posted at the corners of their walks.

She found herself getting angrier and angrier, just as she did when she moved north or east in Chicago to the grandeur of the lakeshore or the casual opulence of the Magnificent Mile. She understood the impulse to burn it down or hijack it, to destroy what was inaccessible and splendid. Access, a secret withheld.

Did Delta want those luxuries? she wondered, and thought not. Like everyone she had ever met, Delta liked nice things, but that kind of desire didn't drive her. She stayed, more or less content, in her own part of the world, neither jealous of the way white folks lived nor giving it much thought. Like Nana, she didn't really think white people had anything on her. "Just look at them," Delta would say, with a dismissal that Sunday found unsettling, "they're out of rhythm, and they seem so strange and miserable to me. I'll stay over here in this little house and work my little job," she said, "if you've gotta be like them to get what they have."

But perhaps Mercury had wanted to have what they had, Sunday thought, and maybe that was what he was thinking as he walked the same streets. Extravagant homes and cars, servants and respect. Maybe he had wanted to be what they were, to have what seemed like authority, over his own life and everything else.

In Sunday, crossing over into the territory of "the other group," whether in Chicago or Salt County, provoked something else. She wanted to recognize what drove the order of things, she wanted it to keep on hurting her and burning her up inside. Sunday didn't want to be blind to it, but to see it, understand it, then reject it, choosing something different for herself. Once rejected, she wanted to keep it in mind, to push up against it with her inheritance of suffering and dignity, and of making something, music or mosaics, out of that. She had had her quest for the devotion she had seen in her mother, fitting tiles, from the kitchen door. And she had had painting, something of her own.

Once she got to the market, she wandered the aisles that had once seemed so enormous and replete with new things, and couldn't settle on what to cook. They had rarely shopped in the white part of town when she was growing up, but just before she had left Salt County Nana had found out that the meat and produce were immeasurably better over there. She had put on her best clothes and hat and gloves, and marched in there with her head held high, consciously disregarding the cool reception. The first time Sunday went with her, she thought she had stepped into a different world. Instead of withered apples and dented peaches, there were berries and kiwis and halved melons with succulent red and yellow flesh, exotic cheeses and meats that were free of gristle and fat. Delicacies she had never tasted, like pâté and bottled sauces, mushrooms and capers, and cans of tiny corn. She was so busy taking in the wealth of choices, the clean wide aisles, the music and lights, that she had failed to even notice the chilly stares from other customers.

She and Nana had kept shopping there, and eventually the salespeople grew warmer. Nana said they probably decided, despite her elegant attire, that she was a servant, shopping for someone white. For the short time that Sunday accompanied her, she had enjoyed walking in with the presumption that they were welcome, or at least entitled; she had even enjoyed unsettling and angering the other customers. But Delta hadn't liked going, and said that no merchandise could make the atmosphere worth it. There were only ever a few brown faces, which were tolerated as long as the whole black population didn't overstep its bounds and flood their aisles of plenty. And Nana was careful never to share any information that would make the man behind the meat counter and the checkout clerks jealous or angry. She never told that Sunday had dared to go past high school and study art, but she chatted about the weather and they even notified her of specials and asked, in a general way, how her family was.

It seemed strange to be back there without Nana, and it dumbfounded her that she saw not a single other black face. She ignored the nervous glances produced by her entrance, and sucked her teeth as a woman looked at her uneasily and placed the strap of her handbag over her head so that it securely crossed her chest on Sunday's approach. "I will refuse this," she mumbled, "I will not let this ignorant bitch get my goat." She strolled with apparent leisure, tight as a spring inside, but determined not to turn away or quicken her pace, chanting to herself that such was the territory, such was the territory of black lives. After one circuit of the store, she was tempted to abandon her plan, for the aisles had become a blur and she had made no decisions on what to cook. And it seemed that when she tried her hardest with Delta, she seemed to make her biggest mistakes.

When Sunday returned to the house, she found a note from Delta saying she had gone to get her perm touched up.

Delta had noticed that her hair was a little unruly around the edges, but getting her perm touched up was also an excuse to see Dinah, her one real friend. When she came through the door of Dinah's shop, several pleased and relaxed-looking women were leaving, and she heard Cassandra Wilson putting her signature on Robert Johnson's blues.

"Hey, girl." Dinah snatched the line from the singer's mouth: "You better come on in my kitchen, 'cause it's goin' to be rainin' outdoors."

Delta felt the sudden shyness that usually visited her when she entered the shop, and laughed tentatively. "You have time to touch me up this afternoon, Dinah? My sister's in town."

"You know I've got time for you, sis. Get a cup of coffee and sit on down. You gonna let me cut it different, or you staying with the tried-and-true?"

"Tried-and-true," Delta answered. "Some things have to stay the way they've been." She fixed her coffee and watched Dinah sweep up from her last customer and get ready for her.

Dinah had come to live with her cousin in Salt County after leaving her husband, and they had started up a hair shop and called it A Joyful Process, after the early Funkadelic hit. It had taken Salt County a few months to catch on, but Dinah's enterprise was thriving.

"Beauty is a lasting business," she liked to say, "'cause sisters will be forever spending money on their hair and on looking good. Now if you mix beauty with another staple of black life, which is music, you've got an irresistible combination. They won't be able to keep away from my door."

Dinah declared that she had something for everyone. "We do braids, perms, press and curls, wash and wears, you name it," she told prospective customers. "As you see, I myself have chosen to stay with the 'Fro, while my partner here," she said, nodding at her cousin's straightened, layered bouffant, "has chosen to go another route." She offered manicures, nail wrapping and nail polishing, facials and cosmetic makeovers by appointment with a "Beauty Consultant," and she always had coffee and tea on a table by the door.

On Sunday mornings, she played gospel and spirituals as she did the hair of women and girls who were headed for church. And Monday through Saturday, she had a forenoon discount for "the mature lady," during which she played Ella Fitzgerald, Dinah Washington, Sarah Vaughan. She moved into the afternoon with Coltrane, Monk, Miles, and then picked up the pace with more contemporary R&B and cuts by women rappers. In the evening she returned to jazz and mixed it with the blues. And for the "natural woman," from five to six o'clock, she offered specials on simple washes and cuts. At the top of the hour, Aretha's voice could be heard singing "You make me feel . . . you make me feel . . ." and then Dinah popped in a tape she had mixed of sixties and seventies oldies. She called that time of the day "Nappy Hour."

When the shop first opened, Delta had stopped in after work to find out about prices and services, and stayed throughout the hour, smiling as other customers sang along to War and Rare Earth and the Isleys, Minnie Riperton, and P-Funk and Rufus. "I don't know when I've had that much fun," she told Dinah. "You should be a D.J."

Dinah chuckled and said, "Well, I am. I'm what you call a D.J. Hair Burner, D.J.H.B."

Delta had gotten to know Dinah slowly as she started coming to the shop regularly. At first she had held herself apart, watching the ease and warmth of Dinah and her patrons from a distance, appreciative but unable to join in, and then little by little, she had added a comment or requested a song, until she started showing up not only to get her hair done but to hang out and listen to Dinah's music collection, which was better than any of the radio stations they could get. "You jammin' the box, girl," customers would say, rocking to the music so enthusiastically that Dinah would have to ask them to keep still so she could finish their hair. She and Delta began to go out for a drink or for dinner, and Delta found herself opening up to her more and more. At first they had talked about work and the townspeople, but their talk became more and more personal, and eventually, Delta had been able to work up to telling her about Mercury and his suicide.

It freed Delta up that as a newcomer to Salt County, Dinah had entered their friendship with no preconceived notions of Delta or her family; with Dinah, Delta's life was a story she got to tell. Dinah had leaned across the table and taken Delta's hand when she told about Mercury Owens. "I know it feels like you're the only one who ever grappled with this kind of thing, but many a river has called a person home. In fact," she said, "as Percy Mayfield sings in one of my favorite blues:

> I spoke to the river
> And the river spoke back to me.
> And it said, you look so lonely
> And you look full of misery.
> And if you can't find your baby,
> Come and make your home with me.

"'The River's Invitation,' honey, that's what that song is called. Now I don't mean to excuse or make little of what your daddy did, but he wasn't alone, as Percy lets you know. That call from the water, whether it's from love or some other kind of injury, that call can be mighty strong."

Dinah had a song, or a story about one, for every situation and occasion. She said, "Music is in my blood. My mama didn't name me after Dinah for nothin'. And that's Washington, not Shore."

Delta loved going to the shop, where she heard tales of the outlandish and ordinary things people had told Dinah while she was doing their hair. In A Joyful Process, with its turquoise walls and framed posters of black musicians and singers, she felt enclosed and removed from the world. It was a place of touch and music and familiarity that reminded her of those bread-making afternoons in Nana's kitchen. Sometimes Delta heard herself join in with the trash-talking at the shop, and sometimes she even enjoyed the unmoored sound of her own, robust laugh.

Dinah told stories and joked a lot, but the thing Delta liked best about her was her ease and the way she listened, with apparently true interest. She told Delta that she liked her honesty. "It's no bullshit with you, girl, and when you get comfortable and let loose, you feel like family, like a sister, which I always wanted a bunch of and never had." Dinah didn't seem to measure her against anyone else. And they shared a love of music that kept them listening, and even sometimes dancing, late into the night.

Delta knew that she wouldn't have come through the Nate Hunter conflagration without Dinah's help. She had come over with dinner in foil-topped go-plates and had stayed to make her tea or help straighten up the house, and had brought over her own accounting tasks on the first of the month and sat working while Delta paid her own bills. She had showed up with music for them to listen to or rented movies for them to watch. Like Nana, Dinah was able to offer freely what she had, without feeling diminished by the giving. Whether she extended music, her attention, or her touch, she made people feel that it was she who was privileged to give.

In Delta, Dinah had seen so many women she had known who were uncertain of their own strength and beauty. She knew that Delta was both hurt and capable, and it moved her to see her gradually venture her presence, and then her laughter, and then her past. It was the ease and familiarity of sisterhood that she wanted, and Dinah could see that in spite of fidgeting and reticence, beneath her staid clothes and hairstyle, Delta was a passionate and complicated woman, who was trying to recover from the kinds of misjudgments that she, and most everyone she knew, had made.

Over and over Delta had cried, "Why can't I ever want the right man?" and Dinah had shook her head and said, "I know, I know how it is," and then quoted a song Dinah Washington had recorded in the fifties, "This can't be love because I feel so well . . ."

Throughout the months it took her to recover from her "love vortex," as Dinah called it, she had listened without making Delta feel ashamed, as she went over and over the details until she could see past them. "Did I tell you how he said, 'Give me everything'?" Delta would ask, and Dinah, her only witness, would sit with her and listen for the twenty-seventh time, as if it were the first.

Delta said she wasn't sure how Dinah knew about that kind of responsive patience, but they were "tools of the trade," Dinah stated. "People tell the hairdresser when they have no one else to tell. Feels like receiving confession sometimes, but it's partly what I'm here to provide, I guess." And Delta sometimes worried that she could never return anything that would equal Dinah's listening, but that, Dinah said, was an insult. "I'm here because I care, and it's no more than I'm able to do. I'm here because I've loved and lost," she added, turning to one of her favorite songs for inspiration, "because I know the meaning of the blues."

As Dinah mixed the relaxer for her touch-up, Delta told her that Sunday had finally come home for a visit, after five years.

"What brought her back?" she asked, parting Delta's hair, and she answered, "I'm not sure," without admitting her own role in the process. "It seems to have been a sudden impulse. It hardly ever works, but we're trying hard, anyway, to get along." She hadn't told her yet about Mercury's sudden return from the dead.

"Why don't you bring your sister in?" Dinah offered. "I could do her hair."

"Oh, she wears it all reckless, kinky and long," Delta said, holding her hands out at least twelve inches from the sides of her head. That's what your hair would be like if you didn't perm it, Dinah thought. She had been encouraging her to try a hairstyle other than the tucked-under mushroom she had always worn, but she had gotten nowhere with that campaign. She hadn't necessarily been arguing for long and natural, but for something a little freer that would move the hair off her face.

She thought Delta had hidden her beauty with her armored hairdo and matronly clothes. The first time she had walked into the shop, Dinah had noticed the unusual beauty of her eyes, and when her uncensored smile had appeared in response to the music, her face looked as if it had been opened, lit from within. Now that woman could be stunning, she had thought, and she doesn't even know it.

After Nate, Delta had tried to hide her weight gain with oversized shirtwaists and jumpers she had ordered from catalogs or pulled from the rack and purchased without even trying them on. "I can't face the cruelty of the dressing room mirror," she had argued, "and I have surrendered to elastic waists." Occasionally, when Delta looked in a mirror, she was surprised to see herself in what she and Sunday had once called "middle-aged, wifely dresses." That's what I am now, she thought, without the wifely part.

Delta went on, "I bet my sister hasn't been in a beauty shop since she left Salt County. I bet she even trims her hair herself."

"Well, bring her in for Nappy Hour," Dinah said. "I've never met a person, woman or man, in my life who doesn't like to have their hair washed."

"Mmmmn, I don't know," Delta answered, giving in herself to Dinah's firm and gentle touch.

"Or bring her in for a facial. As I'm always telling you, beauty shops and music together, they work wonders, girl. People get comfortable and relaxed, and before they know what's happened, they're talking and they've let you in."

Delta smiled. It had happened to her. She tried to imagine bringing Sunday there, but she couldn't picture herself being with both of them at the same time. What would they talk about? What would they think of each other? Dinah was the least judgmental person she had ever met, but what if she thought Sunday was withdrawn or stuck-up? She knew that we can rarely give others the same room to criticize family that we allow ourselves. And Sunday might see Dinah's eager choice to be a small-town hairdresser as silly, though Dinah wasn't a bit insecure or apologetic about what she did. She often said, "I make women feel beautiful, and I give them a place to gather, listen, be touched, and talk. What could be more worthwhile than that?" Maybe Sunday would relate to that, and maybe she would like the feeling in the shop. But Delta felt protective of both of them, and she couldn't bear it if they didn't like each other. And then again, what if they liked each other too much? Maybe, next to Sunday, Delta would seem commonplace.

"Well, I'll have to think that over. I'm not sure I would subject you to being around our bickering. We just keep stepping on the same toes we've been stepping on our whole lives. I can't tell you how I miss her and wish for her to come home, thinking of the way we were once, long ago, close, and all the things I'll tell her and what we'll do. Each time I think I'll be able to correct the past, and fix what it is that's been wrong. And then, as soon as she gets here, it's like we can almost see each other, in the distance, but we can't quite reach."

Delta thought of the smashed whiskey glass and the oath she and Sunday had made up when they were kids. Crossing their fore and middle fingers, they had whispered, "Two for one and one for two. You for me and me for you."

"We can't reach each other, and that's not supposed to happen with family, Dinah."

"I don't know, Delta," she responded, applying the relaxer to Delta's scalp. "People may manage and love may win out, most of the time, but who ever said it was easy, or that families get along. Like Sly said, 'It's a family affair. It's a family affair.'"

While Dinah was doing Delta's hair, Sunday was chopping and slicing and grating, and when Delta got home she was ready to start cooking. She had decided on a stir-fry, which was not something fancy or pretentious, not something Delta couldn't or wouldn't make. As she had wandered the supermarket lanes, she had recalled that Delta had loved going to the Rice Bowl with Nana and the Bread Ladies on special occasions.

Delta was both surprised and delighted with Sunday's efforts. And the fact that she had remembered to get Delta's beloved butter pecan ice cream nearly brought tears to her eyes. Sunday did not even resist having on the small, kitchen-counter television, tuned to CNN, while they ate. They commented on news of whatever appalling things people had done to each other that day, and Delta shared the bits of gossip she had gleaned while getting her touch-up.

When Sunday tried to bring up the topic of finding Clement Woods, however, Delta turned to the on-screen cable television guide and watched the brightly colored strips of information scroll across the screen. She was tired, and the prospect of dealing with Sunday's fervent mission to locate a stranger with more upsetting news to deliver was too much for her to bear. "Later. Let's talk about it later," she said, as the TV blinked a succession of fleeting images and broadcast pieces of interrupted speech.

And as Sunday watched her point the remote control at the TV to change channel after channel, she noticed that Delta did not have on the pewter fish earrings she had brought.

While Delta watched her crime shows in the living room, Sunday decided to look for the things they had found, almost eighteen years before, in Dolora's closet. She searched through drawers and boxes upstairs until it occurred to her that she might find what she was looking for in the attic.

She stood in the upstairs hall beneath the rectangular seam where the attic trapdoor met the ceiling, looking up at the place that had represented mystery and fear. As a child she had been afraid it was where ghosts resided, along with all the things her family didn't want to talk about and didn't want to know.

Once, on a day when she was home sick from the fourth grade, she had used a kitchen stool to reach the handle and then climbed the stairs and got trapped. She had pulled up the ladder with her so that her mother wouldn't know she was up there looking around, and the doorway had stuck. At first she had panicked and tried over and over to unlock and release the ladder, sweat breaking out down the back of her shirt, under her arms, along her hairline and lip as she pushed against the jammed latch and pinched her fingers trying to work it free. Eventually, she had accepted the fact that she would be there the rest of the afternoon, until someone came home, and sat on a carton, dreading her mother's disapproval and the disciplining she would face.

More than explosive curses and reproaches, she had feared Dolora's closed, wordless look. She had been warned not to go up to the attic to play, and had already been on punishment once that week for drawing in the margins of a book. While she waited, she was too distressed to investigate the boxes and trunks, and wondered what would happen if no one ever came. The cramped space seemed to get darker and darker and she saw spiders on the rafters and menacing dust balls hiding in the corners of raw, splintered wood. In her pocket she had found a periwinkle blue Crayola crayon, and to pass the time, she had knelt beside the trapdoor and drawn a picture underneath the folded stairs. It would take some looking to find it, but if rescue never came, she thought, and she perished up there, she wanted someone, someday, to see her mark.

When she heard her mother's weighted footsteps dragging in from work, she knocked so hard she scared her half to death. "Good Lord," she heard her mother exclaim, "who the hell is up there in my house?"

"It's me," Sunday had cried. "Mama, come help. It's me."

"It serves you right," her mother had said, despite Sunday's tears, offering no hug or pat or assuagement of her fear, and then grounding her from outdoor playing for a month. She had never gone up there again.

With the faint drone of Delta's television show anchoring her in the present, Sunday stretched on her toes to grasp the panel seam's thicker, hollowed edge, and pulled. The square wrenched free, revealing recessed hinges and accordion stairs.

She climbed, and when her head rose above the attic floor she stopped to take stock, smelling decades of mildew and stagnant air. This isn't purgatory, she thought, training her heavy, industrial flashlight onto trunks and bags and boxes, for the things she saw were not in a limbo of transit; they were at the end of the line. She climbed the rest of the stairs and steadied herself with her palms against the slanted walls. It was so much smaller than she had remembered.

She stepped carefully, as some of the floorboards looked rotted and loose, and sat for a while, resisting the impulse to pull the ladder up after her as she had done that childhood day, and give in to the settled quiet of the past. To seal herself up there with the ghostly spirits and saved possessions, and disappear backward, rather than into the future, as Mercury had done.

Moving the flashlight around the room, she stopped at a corner where a wooden box wrapped in cellophane came into view. She rested the flashlight on the floor, entered the cone of light it cast, and knelt to unwrap the box.

Inside she found Dolora's birth and death certificates, and her marriage license. Staring at the birth certificate, she thought about how her own read "Girl Owens," in place of a name. And the terse, clinical statement of the death certificate, new to her eyes, appeared so dispassionate and mundane, so insufficient to describe a completed life. "Black . . . 120 lbs. . . . carcinoma." She put the document down and picked up the license certain that she had never seen it, either. Focusing on Dolora's signature, she saw it was a self-conscious, clearer version of the one she remembered. She had only been eighteen when they had married, and the date of the license, she observed, was six months before Delta's birthday. Her father's signature matched the handwriting she had been poring over lately, on the back of the riverside photograph, but then they were both from the same youthful time. His five-word note, written at the back end of his life, didn't give her much to go on in terms of changes, but she had noticed, before she ripped it, that his E's had stayed the same. She wondered what besides his rendering of E had been constant in his life.

At birth Dolora had been "colored," at marriage, "Negro," and at death, "Black." That was a story, Sunday thought, in and of itself. Dolora's high school diploma, dated five months after the license, was also in the box, along with a copy of the deed to the house.

There were several Mother's Day cards Sunday had made for Dolora in school and a photo Nana had taken of the three of them, all smiling, on the front porch. Sunday, her front teeth missing, appeared about eight, and Delta a chunky thirteen, while Dolora looked so young they could have been sisters. "I had forgotten that," Sunday said, transfixed by the rare, playful exchange that had been caught by the camera as they sat crowded onto the porch swing, their heads thrown back in laughter. Under the photo was a Mother's Day wish written in pencil on green primer paper, the uneven stick letters made too large to fit the name on the page: "HAPY MOTHER DAY LOVE DE," with the "LTA" on the back.

Beneath those documents Sunday found *Bulfinch's Mythology* and an encyclopedia of Egypt, both inscribed with Dolora Blount's adolescent signature. And there was a dining car napkin from the train that had taken Dolora on her only trip to Chicago and a folded map of the Art Institute collections, with the wing on ancient civilizations circled in pen. Along with those things were a recipe for pumpernickel bread written out on an index card, and an empty dram-sized bottle of Dolora's Emeraude perfume.

What had at first seemed to be a random collection of family papers was turning out to be something else. Realizing that the assortment differed from the things they had found in her closet just after she died, it dawned on Sunday that Nana must have assembled those objects she felt could represent her daughter's life, making a trail of memory that could lead to the person Dolora had been.

Sunday took the items from the box and placed them on the floor in front of her, one by one.

She sniffed a tortoiseshell comb that Dolora had used to French roll her hair, to see if it still smelled of the hair oil she and Nana used to concoct and boil on the stove. Inhaling, she thought she detected the aroma. And then the tourmaline necklace appeared, with the bracelet, made by that early admirer they had heard so much about.

She gasped when she saw two wedding rings on a knotted brown shoelace. Which one, Dolora or Nana, had joined the bands together in that way, and had her mother kept Mercury's ring all those years? On the very lace where he had left it? She picked up the shoelace by its knot and listened to the wedding bands chime against each other.

Dolora had worn hers off and on, and Sunday had never known what provoked her decisions. The gold band would suddenly appear on her finger and stay for a month, or even a year, and then it would just as abruptly vanish. It was never in the jewelry case she and Delta had played with, but she didn't know where Dolora had kept it.

Returning her attention to the box, she wondered when Nana had collected the things it held. She didn't even know if Nana had put them together for herself, or for others, and whether she expected it, wanted it, even, to be found. The box's contents had not been amassed as autobiography, but by Dolora's mother, from her own limited angle of perception and need, and Sunday considered how the assemblage might be different if Dolora had done the choosing.

If Dolora had tried to gather items that would announce the lives of her daughters, what would she have come up with? Sunday wasn't sure her conception of motherhood had included knowing them. Had anyone known her, she asked, in a way that would permit that kind of attempt? She hated to think of how she and Delta might choose to memorialize each other. But maybe Nana had got the spirit, if not the facts, of Dolora's life, and maybe she was declaring that by her collection of the "little things" that make up people's lives. And Reed, Reed, was the person who might be able to do such a thing for her. She would have to ask him what he would include.

Next she found loose buttons and those packets of zinnia and marigold seeds they had uncovered in Dolora's closet. A calendar from the Odells' shop, and a book of matches from a restaurant the next county over that Sunday couldn't place. Two puzzling smooth gray rocks and a faded hair ribbon. Crumbled wildflowers, a clothespin, and a pigeon feather. Sunday laughed when she came across two Scrabble tiles, the letter "Q," which Dolora always said she got stuck with, and a "U" to go with it.

And there was a yellowed napkin bearing Jackie Robinson's autograph that Nana had treasured, and a weathered copy of the *Life* magazine issue on Martin Luther King and the March on Washington.

Nana had included a portrait of Grandpa and herself, taken against a studio backdrop of draped cloth not long before he died. With upright posture and raised heads, they announced their pride and rectitude. Grandpa stood with one hand over the fob-looped vest pocket that held his watch, and the other on a walking stick, and Nana stood beside him with her shoulders squared and hands clasped, gazing into the distance. But Grandpa looked directly at the lens, as if in challenge to the camera's power to reduce his stature and limit him in time and space.

After putting the portrait aside, Sunday removed a steno pad from the clerk job Dolora had worked for fifteen years. An emery board and a bottle of shoe polish, which Nana had no doubt included because Dolora had prided herself on never going to work without "respectable" nails and shoes. Many of the get-well cards she had received at the end were in the box, as well as her plastic name bracelet from the hospital she had left but once alive. At the bottom Sunday found a notice of an Easter presentation from church folded with the program from Dolora's funeral.

There had been strident disagreement over what picture to use on that program, with Delta arguing that the photo showed how tired and unwell Dolora already was, that she would have preferred to be remembered as young and strong. But Nana wouldn't budge. She said there was no disgrace in either aging or sickness, and added, "She was only forty, and that picture shows who she was." Sunday held the program for a long while, thinking that in the picture her mother's mouth was as thin and firmly set as it had been in life.

She felt along the inside of the box and discovered a small, yellowed envelope, caught where the side and bottom joined. The last thing she extracted was something she and Delta had found eighteen years before: the valentine from Mercury. Please Be Mine.

And her fingers found that what had sifted down and settled underneath all the papers and larger objects was a handful of loose mosaic tiles, glazed on one side, and some fragments of china and glass.

As she returned the items to the box and closed it, Sunday realized that in the container itself lay a message. It was a wooden shipping box that had held figs, delivered from Nana's cousin, Boykin, the Christmas after Mercury left. Nobody knew how he had gotten hold of fresh figs, but his gifts were always filled with an aura and a magic. Dolora had loved that box and the fruit that had arrived within it, nestled in straw and chartreuse tissue paper. It was the only time she had tasted figs, and they were unforgettable, she said. She had used the box for her mosaic tools, often telling the story of its unexpected arrival on Christmas Eve.

Sunday sat with the objects from the box all around her. She finally had a way to know Dolora Blount Owens, had a sense of her that was more of a whole. As she placed each item back in the box, she felt both gratitude, and a renewal of her mourning. Finally, she could touch her mother, and still, the revelation hadn't come from her. Nana had spoken for her. As usual, filling in and taking care.

But Nana hadn't been able to add any of Dolora's lottery tickets and sweepstakes receipts, for she and Delta had thrown them away, certain that they would depress their grandmother past reckoning. Now she thought that at least one ticket or receipt, testament to a long-term belief in hope and chance, should have been retained.

She reassembled the fig box so that Delta would have the chance to read its contents as she had. And as she closed it, she wondered about her father's shoes. Just what had Dolora done with them, and were they up there in the attic, underneath or behind something, in a plastic bag or a special case? She would see about that another time.

When Sunday went downstairs to tell Delta about her discovery, she found her engrossed in a show whose plotline was winding up.

"You won't believe what I found, Delta . . ." she announced as she reached the doorway.

"Mmn hmmn," she murmured without looking away from the TV screen.

"I found a treasure . . ."

"Wait, they're just about to solve the crime."

Sunday stood with her mouth open. She felt embarrassed for being so excited and for barreling in, and hurt for being cut off. But Delta didn't feel up to hearing what she had found. Columbo was just closing in on the criminal, and she was focused on the end of her show. When the commercial break started, Delta got up and walked past her into the kitchen. "I found a treasure trove," Sunday murmured as she climbed the stairs, "and I guess I'll keep it to myself."

She decided to take her second cigarette for the day up to the attic. After she had smoked it, she opened and poked at other cases and bags and crates, and then came across a metal, fireproof box, which she recognized as Nana's. She had organized and prepared her papers and possessions, so that no one would have to do it after her death. She had made all of her funeral and gravestone arrangements, and she had cleared out and given away most of her things, keeping Delta and Sunday from having to sift through her possessions, deciding what to keep. In the last year of her life, she had divested herself of everything personal that she didn't wish to survive her, providing that the only things that had to be discarded after death were her clothes and cosmetics. On Sunday's last visit to see her, the Christmas before she died, she had brought out a strongbox and explained to the two of them what necessary documents were included and why and she had gone through the pictures and mementos she was saving with them, leaving little about her own story open to conjecture. She had decided exactly what she wanted them to know and remember, Sunday thought.

Opening the cedar chest, she found tablecloths and napkins, and when she touched them, she could feel something hard underneath. As she unfolded and lifted out the linens, yellowed and forever creased, she uncovered six of her mother's mosaics. After removing them, she lined them up in the order in which they had come out of the chest and she began to read them for common details and changes, before pausing.

How had Dolora intended for them to speak? Sunday wasn't sure who had put them in the chest, or whether they had been saved in that way to make a record.

How would her own life and artwork read if she died at that very moment? she wondered, picturing her kitchen, most of its canvases turned to the wall, the latest ones unfinished and stopping short of blue. If someone were to look at the body of her work, would anyone know her, or see her progress, her missteps and challenges, her aims?

As she stared at the mosaics of different sizes and shapes before her, she thought how people brought what they wanted and could to art, and experienced it through the themes of their own lives. She would never forget the time when, at her first gallery show, she had overheard two men talking. One had declared that her painting of an elderly couple, their faces reflected on their TV and seen, through their patched window screen, to be sharing a simple dinner of beans, was "clearly a trope that theorizes the body . . . complicating the split . . . as a raced and gendered site . . ." Amazed and fascinated by their commentary, she had been unable to move away from the corner where she was eavesdropping, until a woman had approached her to share the fact that she had recently been diagnosed with a malignancy, and to express her appreciation for her tackling, in one of the more abstract paintings, the issue of cancer in women's lives.

At first she had been disturbed when people read something different than what she intended. Of course there were critics who thought they knew better than the artist, who thought the artist wasn't even capable of knowing what she meant to say. She had worked at accepting that people's reactions couldn't be controlled, that whatever she had thought she meant to say, what she had ended up painting had its own truth for whoever was doing the looking. It could be about theorizing the body, and cancer in women, and everything else. Her job was to paint what she painted, and the viewer's was to receive it through her own life.

But here she was interpreting Dolora and everyone else who had left some kind of trace, seeing in them what she wanted and needed to see. She wished she had asked her mother more about what the mosaics meant to her, but Dolora hadn't been big on talking about personal things. Hell, Sunday thought, she wasn't big on talking at all, and she tended to approach her mosaic-making as something that would lose its spell if it were discussed or shared.

Sunday had loved to help with grouting and glazing, but she had never made her own mosaic from start to finish. That was her mother's territory; she didn't venture there. And it wasn't something her teachers would have encouraged, either. Aside from those of ancient Rome, the Byzantine Empire, and a few modern artists, mosaics were hardly considered worthy of attention, and most critics wouldn't even call the things Dolora had created "art," unless they considered her efforts timely political assaults on the order, subversions of "high art" with "low."

At school in Chicago, she had found a line clearly drawn between "arts" and "crafts." But wasn't the art in the spirit, the vision and transformation that were made to happen on any material that could be found or used? She picked up one of Dolora's serving trays and looked at its powerful explosion of color and texture.

Wasn't the art in the imagination and skill, the getting at what mattered, through struggle and devotion? In the union with the material, the speaking through it, the vibrating and resonating that was made to happen, for maker and viewer? Wasn't it in the way you touched the viewer's heart and mind and belly, in the "Yes" of recognition you evoked, and in the making of some kind of form from chaos? Sometimes with beauty and always with power, wasn't it the speaking of something true?

Dolora's mosaics did that, she thought, and she wasn't sure where, in her mother's case, that came from, but she knew it was nothing that could derive, completely, from a classroom or a book.

She had seen scores of competent paintings and drawings that were silent and dead, and she was sorry to say that she had made some herself. And she had seen the cutting-edge products of the urban art world, dexterous and conceptual, clever and contrived. Much of that was loud, but silent. There was so much vacancy and death in the gallery shows she went to in Chicago and New York, that it was seldom she felt the presence of mystery and life, and rarely was the work that spoke to her in its honesty and depth the work that received attention and reward.

She refused the idea that true art could have no practical utility, that, implicitly, the avenues open to dark people, working people, women, were lesser, somehow. They could have crafts, but art belonged to someone else.

Although paint was the thing that had always possessed her, Sunday had worked with other media, and she had incorporated bits of cloth and wood and pottery over the years into her work, refusing to relegate those materials and forms to a domain outside of "art," refusing to forget the traditions out of which she came.

She knew that Dolora had been unconcerned with that kind of division or judgment. She had been celebrated at office and church, and in the neighborhood, and she had often given her mosaics as gifts. She had sometimes visited the library to look at its few art books, and had taken an interest in Sunday's classes and projects, but she probably hadn't even realized there was an "art world" concerned with magazines and gallery openings, and surely would have had no aspirations to belong. Sunday doubted that she even thought of herself as "artist," or struggled with what that meant. Once when Delta had asked her why she made mosaics, she had shrugged and answered, "I like making them. It's what I do."

Sunday was curious about the fact that her mother didn't destroy or discard the ones she thought were unsuccessful. In some, she had lifted out some tiles, possibly, Sunday thought, for reuse in other work, and others had never been grouted, finished, or framed. Sunday had saved many of her less successful paintings, too, and some she had kept working on, or painted over. They weren't gone; they had just become part of something else. Her first piece of canvas, bought with money from her after-school library job, she had worked on over and over again, painting image upon image so that it held, submerged and stratified, every mistake and bit of progress she had made.

Sunday heard her sister climbing the ladder. "Look," she almost shouted as she saw Delta, "I found this collection of mosaics in the cedar chest. I think these are the ones she thought were failures. They're early, I'm pretty sure, 'cause you can tell she didn't quite have the surface even, and they lack a kind of control that the later ones have."

"Well, they look perfectly fine to me." Delta felt defensive, though she wasn't sure why.

"I'm not criticizing them, Delta. I'm not saying they aren't fine. It's just that I can see the difference from the others. The difference and the sameness. I think she was learning with these. I think she was finding her way."

Sunday looked up at Delta standing above her with her arms folded and her face closed. No more talking seemed possible, so she asked Delta to help her bring down the mosaics.

When they had carried down the last one, Sunday grasped the door with both hands and noticed a trace of periwinkle blue at eye level beneath the first stair. It was smudged and faded so that she could barely make it out, but memory returned it to her, freshly sketched. She had drawn a steepled house of worship, as a way to mark her presence with her name.

She said nothing about it as she shoved the ladder back into the ceiling, closing off the attic space again. After she carried the mosaics into her bedroom, she went and got the gold and blue tiled soap dish from the bathroom and the perfume tray that sat in the guest bedroom, and headed for her room.

"Wait . . . but!" Delta said as she cornered her in the hallway. "Where are you taking those things?"

She reassured her that she just wanted to look at them carefully, that she would put them back. The disarray was only temporary, she told her excitedly, and she would return each thing to its place.

She heard Delta in the bathroom, getting ready for bed. The medicine cabinet opened and closed, and Sunday pictured the nail polish, Vicks, and condoms she had discovered there. The tap ran, the toilet flushed, the floorboards creaked beneath Delta's feet. It all seemed a long way off, and then Sunday looked up to find her standing in the doorway. Sitting on the floor and focused so intently on her mother's work, spread out before her, she hadn't realized Delta was standing above her, stilled with both alarm and wonder at Sunday's enormous appetite.

"Isn't it cold and hard down there on the floor? We do have chairs, you know."

Sunday heard the frown in Delta's voice. Glancing up from the pale, defenseless feet that were so like her own, she saw the knuckles of Delta's balled hands pushing out the pockets of her robe. She told herself to stand up and hug her, but her limbs felt heavy. Do it, she said to herself, give her one of those fourteen, but she thought of the earlier exchange by the television, and felt foolish again, and unsure.

The floor creaked as Delta shifted her weight, wishing she could hit a curving arrow button, like on the computer at work, and undo her earlier dismissal of Sunday's news. It was like the night of Nana's funeral, when she had stood outside her door, hand raised and unable to knock. She wanted to have the words to ask what Sunday had found, but it somehow seemed too late for that. She wanted to be able to say the thing that would mend it, the right thing, but as the silent tension grew, she became certain that her presence was unwanted, that Sunday was waiting for her to go.

"Don't worry, I'm leaving," she said, "and you can sit up all night thinking about the precious art that you and Mama shared."

Sunday looked up at her, flushing, and it dawned on her that Delta not only took what she said and did in the least favorable way but seemed to require her own resentment, to nourish it even, for its role in defining herself.

She stared at her sister and then lowered her head as she felt the tears about to come, trying not to notice Delta's exposed ankles and the stray hairs missed in shaving on her ashy calves. What about their oath of sisterhood? She knew she was often at fault, that she tore into things recklessly or disregarded protocol, that she was judgmental and distant, that she guarded what was hers. But Delta's wounded stance was also historical, and Sunday was struck by the fact that they relied on each other to fuel the conflict that was so familiar and reliable.

She got herself to her feet, but when she stepped forward, Delta turned to leave.

"The headstone, think about the headstone," Delta called out as she shuffled down the hall to her room, "we've got to figure out what to do."

7

THE NEXT MORNING Delta and Sunday agreed to meet in town and walk to the cemetery to confront the question of the headstone. They figured that seeing it and the other family markers might guide them to a resolution.

Delta cursed her clumsy hands as she fumbled with her buttons and dropped her scarf and then her cigarettes. She was getting ready to go to the post office to request two personal leave days before meeting Sunday. Although she wasn't sure how long her sister would be staying, she thought it safest to plan ahead only a couple of days at a time. She prided herself on never taking time off and had been working on a perfect attendance record since her unapproved month of absence when she had left town abruptly with Nate Hunter two years before. Her supervisor had overlooked her negligence when she produced a complicated story of sudden family illness, and after all, she had worked at that post office since she was twenty-two and had faltered only that once. Because she often felt that he was waiting for her to screw up again, she never took a vacation or sick day and showed up at work whether she was feeling well or not.

She got as far as the front porch when she realized that she didn't have her umbrella, which she carried whenever the sky showed the slightest irritability; few things irked her as much as being unprepared for rain. She rooted for her keys to unlock the door and found her fold-up umbrella in the closet. After checking her hair and face in the hall mirror, noticing how sturdily middle-aged she seemed, she closed the door and walked down the path that was littered again with leaves.

As Sunday heard the door close and stepped into the shower, she was taken by a wave of missing Reed. Leaning into the steaming water, she lifted her head to feel it on her hair and face. She ached for him in that moment, recalling the way they had showered together at first, before bathing became a merely functional act.

She thought of the way he loved her slowly, immersed and savoring each moment, as they moved deeper in. Closing her eyes, she pictured his full, chiseled lips and his skin, so near the color of hers that when they were naked and entwined, it was hard to tell their limbs apart. She saw his mouth and his unguarded eyes. She saw the slight paunch that made him self-conscious, and the faint scars from adolescent acne on his face, thinking how she had grown to love the very traits that had at first seemed to be flaws.

Even the things that provoked her seemed inextricably him. "I love hard," he had told her, right from the start, and he had not lied. He lived with a commitment she could only manage consistently in her art, and sometimes his need and sensitivity frightened them both, but at least his strategy wasn't to try to shrink his caring. That was her way. While she had always been eager to keep desire bounded, Reed said, "Come for me. Come for me where I live."

Often she wanted to banish him from private territory, but there were so many things, little things, she supposed, that compelled her. The textures of his voice, and the way, if he was running, his hair looked like a comet's tail. The way he read a book sideways, lying down.

She cherished, too, the uncensored delight he showed at the most lovely, simple things, like blowing soap bubbles through a little ringed wand from the edge of their stoop. And also his unguarded admissions of heartache and anguish, which his father had called "effeminate." But it was his capacity for showing up that she most admired, because for her, that seemed to come so hard. As the water rained down on her she imagined him standing before her, reaching out, so apparently able to choose what he wanted. "Wide Heart," she sometimes called him, and he shrugged it off, unsure sometimes if, in a man, that was a weakness or a gift. Unlike Reed, she thought, I get to "Yes" by way of "No."

As she stepped from the bathtub she caught a glimpse of her body in the half-fogged mirror. Despite her temptation to look away from her small, sagging breasts and slackening thighs, she moved the towel and looked at herself. Oh well, she thought, anyone who can't love you past these things isn't worth having. Maybe, to him, this is part of my beauty.

She decided to call him, agitated suddenly about her own recent remoteness, and about not having spoken to him since she left. At that hour he would be at school, between classes, in the English Department office. He might not answer and he might be busy, but she decided to try, since she might not get another time alone in the house.

Hesitating, she dialed part of the number and then hung up, deciding to have one of her daily cigarettes first. In spite of all the things that compelled her and perhaps, even because of them, she couldn't ever seem to reach out for him in a straightforward way. Her path to everything but painting was roundabout.

When she had washed all traces of her cigarette from the ashtray and brushed her teeth, she dialed again, finding herself both anxious and relieved when he answered.

In response to her apology for calling him at work, he said, "I'm glad to hear your voice." The night before, he had picked up the phone to call her a dozen times, but had managed to honor her request that he not press, riding out the withdrawal that had become her shelter once again.

They chatted about his twelfth-grade honors class, her train ride, who had called since she left. When he asked how it was going with Delta, she wasn't sure what to say.

"Like always," she responded. "Some discomfort, some conflict. I guess I'm some work, and she's just as bad."

"Well, there should be common ground then." He laughed.

"Yeah, there should," she said, moving around pens and paper at the phone table, "but we're work in different ways. And nothing either one of us does or says . . . stands alone. Seems like every statement or question we make comes dragging all kinds of stuff from the whole rest of our lives. You can almost hear and feel the crud built up from five . . . and fifteen . . . and twenty-five years ago, pressing down onto the now.

"It's kind of tiring," she added.

"Yeah, I know, I've got my father for a reference point."

In the long stretch of quiet, he felt himself getting tense. "Well . . ." he said, "what else?"

"Reed? Do you think you know me?" She was thinking of the attic, and the wooden fig box she had found, how Dolora hadn't let her daughters near enough for them to be able to put together a collection of the things that had mattered to her. Sunday was haunted by her own retreats from Reed, and she couldn't bear to think that because she panicked at their growing closeness, mistrustful of all that it promised and protective of the life she had fought so hard to claim, that there was no one who would be able to tell her story.

"...Yeah..."

"Yeah?"

"Well, I know the core you, I think. But you're changing all the time. You don't stay one person, none of us does. And as you said, you take some work. You tend to let me in and out."

"I was just wondering," she said, "if you'd say yes. And also, if you'd say the way you know me is through all the little things you've learned. I was just wondering, that's all."

"Little things. What do you mean by that?"

"Oh, I don't know. It would take too long to explain right now."

Oh, don't, he thought, as he felt her pull away. Trying to make his voice sound light and reassuring, he said, "I've got some time."

She was silent, just within reach, and they were hovering on the verge of their familiar pattern, in which he moved toward her abruptly, uneasily, and she pulled away.

"What was it that made you wonder?" he asked.

"I'm not sure." She closed the subject. "Never mind."

He listened to her breathing, thinking how close and far away she seemed, and tried another question. "So, about your father, was it... was it what you expected? Was it what it seemed?"

"Mmn hmn."

"Delta heard from him? Saw him?"

"Heard."

"Heard." He felt her beginning to make a wall.

"Mmn hmn."

He gave her time to go on and when she didn't, he asked, his voice tight, "And what... and what did he say?"

"A man wrote for him, to say he had just died."

"Just died."

"Yes. That's about it."

Reed was silent. Sunday could hear the clock beating and her pulse ticking. He waited, quietly, feeling the wall he knew so well take shape between them, and then he spoke, flinching as the words came out, "Well then, how long do you think you'll be there?"

"How can I know that, Reed?" The wall was up. "I just can't say."

He wanted to cry out for her not to go, to tell her he was trying, trying to be whatever it was she needed, but that he was only human, he had limits and needs, as well. He wanted to have the answers for her. He wanted to know the right thing to say. To make her believe in love without leaving, and undo with his words and his steady loving what had come before, to heal the marks of things gone wrong, things exceeded, things left unsaid.

"Okay." He drew the word out. "Keep me posted, and if there's anything I can do . . . you know . . . if . . . just let me know."

She heard him turning pages and getting ready to get off the phone, but she couldn't seem to stop it and she wasn't even sure why she had raised the wall, because she wanted to be able to tell him all of it. Papers shuffled in the background. The quiet was heavy. She heard a pen tap.

"Before you go . . ." she said, and then stopped.

She wanted to divulge it to someone, and if she didn't tell Reed, whom would she tell? She wanted to blurt out the way the world had careened with the sight of Mercury's handwriting and the message, cryptic and inadequate, with which he had tried to span thirty-six years. Her pulse ticked faster.

She wanted to pour out the love and distress she felt, to let Reed know about the wooden box that had once been filled with enchanted Christmas figs and now held the remnants of her mother's life, about the Bread Ladies and Dolora's hands and the edgy supermarket woman from "the other group." She wanted to tell him about Earlene and her ruined markers, and the way the house had changed and stayed the same. The river's secret history and her father's fedora and pride. About her ceiling stars and the locket and the smell of the paper mill after rain. Mosaic fish tiles and china pieces. Lottery tickets and run-down shoes. About the family photos and the change in Delta's eyes, appliance purgatory and the music box dancer with the broken leg. Her bedroom window, from the outside and from in. Line-dried clothes and the gravestone question. The attic stairs where her small, blue church survived.

All of that, and more, she wanted to tell him, and instead, she managed to say only: "Before you go . . . he did send written word. Or five words, to be exact." Reed waited silently for her to continue. "He did say something to me and Delta. He said, 'I remembered and I paid.'"

Reed had whispered, "Oh, Sunday." He had said it four or five times, at a loss for other language, and she had told him she would call that evening, convincing him, somehow, to hang up.

And he had sat at his desk without even hearing the bell that designated the start of class. He had tried so hard and wanted so much to reach her, but all that wanting and trying had been inadequate. The wall had gone up between them, when they had most needed it to disappear. Outside of fiction, did anyone ever manage to say the right thing? "Oh, Sunday," he said once more.

After she finished dressing and got her bag, Sunday locked the front door and walked down the path, thinking of her father's message, her own muteness, and Reed's two-word offering. How was it that, in times of trouble, when so much needed saying, the people in her life, including her, had so few words?

When she got to the end of the street she stopped to get her bearings, turning in a circle to see where the four streets of the intersection led.

Countless people were idle in the weekday morning. Kids who should have been in school shot baskets off the side of a store, and men and women were still gathered at the bus stop in hopes of picking up day work. A couple at a folding table hawked cheap watches and polyester ties. Just as in her section of Chicago, folks were desperate to make a dollar, any way they could. With crack and crystal meth finding their ways to small towns like Salt County, that crime rate she and Delta had argued about would soon be going up.

She stopped for a moment as she came to the small, red brick church where they had gone every week. Except for weddings and funerals, Sunday hadn't been to church since she moved to Chicago, but even before leaving, she had come to feel uncomfortable and cramped there. As a child, it had been magical, filled with beauty and voice, with hands clapping and holding. Bodies rocking. There was freeness, along with sweat, and even the big women like Valentine Cross had seemed to rise up and float. There was the throbbing organ and the brilliant, colored scenes fitted together, piece by piece, from window glass. People were together, and it wasn't either tight or quiet.

And then she had begun to feel wrong there, unable to fill her expected role. She had wanted to ask about the proclamations on sin and believing, about the rules for righteousness, and even from the Bread Ladies she had sometimes sensed the message that there was something inappropriate about her hunger for elsewhere and her devotion to something that was completely hers. She hadn't felt that there was room for whom she was becoming in that brick building, or in that town.

She walked on into deserted territory, coming to the old, closed-down paper plant and recognizing it as an image that appeared, again and again, in her work. It was abandoned now, exhausted by everything that had gone on inside its walls: the monotonous labor and low wages, the segregation and bitter racial conflict over thankless, necessary jobs. Why had they just left it as it was when they built a new complex of smooth, gray rubber-looking buildings, she questioned, why hadn't they renovated or used it somehow? It just squatted there, decaying, and collected vermin and waste.

The old railroad station of red brick and verdigris lampposts had been abandoned, too, and she had arrived in town at a makeshift Amtrak trailer, blocks from the building where she now stood. She imagined people moving back and forth within the station's dusty central hall, waiting on the wide, wooden benches to depart, and stepping off resting trains. Coming for visits, returning home. There seemed to be shadows and voices inside. "More ghosts," she said, moving on.

Delta emerged from the post office, looked up at the sky, and felt in her bag to make sure she had her umbrella. Everyone had seemed glad to see her, and she had stayed and chatted for a while. It was disorienting not to be working on a late weekday afternoon, and she was at a loss for where to go for the hour she had before meeting Sunday. She stopped by a little store to get two of her few indulgences, fresh bean coffee and chocolate, and began walking without planning where to go.

When she came to the playground, Delta remembered telling Sunday she was her angel as she swung from the bars, and Sunday saying in response that shoulder blades must be the stumps where her wings had been. Sunday had gathered piles of leaves and convinced Delta to jump into them with her, exploding red and yellow clouds and squealing with delight. And nearby was the yard where she had taught Sunday how to skip rope, and the corner lot where she had showed her how to make music from blowing on the mouths of bottles and mold the perfect mud pie. All over town were places where Delta had guided her little sister and witnessed her many firsts. And at a point which neither one could designate, things had changed, and Sunday had no longer seemed to need Delta to take care of her.

They had developed separate social worlds and friends, but even before their lives diverged, Sunday's intensity had daunted both Delta and Dolora. Such focus and ardor were worrisome in a girl so young, and Dolora hadn't known what to do about it, except to counsel temperance, proportion, discipline. Sunday didn't seem to want the knowledge of boyfriends and cosmetics that Delta tried to impart, and instead, spent hours alone in her room, drawing, painting, inhabiting a limitless world of her own creation. She got that consumed and unreachable look which alarmed Delta, and although they had occasional escapades and late-night talks, Sunday's artwork came to occupy the center of her life.

Delta left the playground and strolled by the houses she had passed nearly every day of her life.

"Saw your sister yesterday," she heard a voice call out. Stopping and squinting, she recognized an elderly member of the church sitting half-hidden in the shadows of her porch.

"What's that you say, Miz Martin?"

"Said I saw that sister of yours, but then she was hard to miss, in that purple getup she had on. That must be what they're wearin' up in Chicago, but then, she always did have her special style."

Delta nodded and took silent inventory of her own orthopedic shoes, slacks, and floppy-bowed blouse, with her tan raincoat on top.

"Looks like rain, hunh?" Miz Martin called out.

Delta looked up. "Could be."

"Mmn hmn. Could be. Well, you all enjoy your visit. I had a sister. Sisters should be close."

"Yes, ma'am, they should."

She walked on, glancing now and then at the sky, hoping it would not rain on her touch-up. She knew Sunday didn't have to worry about that, since she wore her hair natural. "Naturally wild," Dolora would have said. Delta had left the house before Sunday, and she wondered about the outfit Miz Martin was talking about. Something dramatic, no doubt.

In so many ways, she had always felt lackluster and unnoticed next to Sunday. How had she ever been outstanding? she asked herself. What had she ever known how to do that couldn't be done by just about anyone else? Processing and sorting mail? Selling stamps?

Growing up, she knew how to be a good girl who minded and took care of things, how to fulfill expectations and respond to what her family and her teachers asked of her, as long as they didn't ask too much. And then in junior high school, she had discovered that she was desirable to men. On her way home from school, they slowed their wide-bodied cars and offered to buy her "a little something special," or pick her up from school. Boys in her own class didn't seem to register her, but the older ones, those on the verge of graduation and jobs at the paper mill, couldn't seem to get close enough.

Love, she had felt, was something at which she could excel, for a time anyway, but then it seemed to fade. As she looked back on it, she guessed her home ec teacher was right when she asked: "Why buy the cow if you can get the milk for free?" Sometimes it struck her as strange that she had known so many men, but was still unmarried at nearly forty-one. On the other hand, she reminded herself, Earlene had had three husbands, and with each one she had gone through an ugly divorce. While no man had stood up in front of people and vowed that he would love her forever, she hadn't been imprisoned, either, by that lie. She was good, at least, at the early stage of love, at the potential part, where adoration thrived.

She had never even found out what else she might be good at. Although she had told herself from early on that she was not an artist, what she did have a talent for was the piano, and her school music teacher had encouraged her and said she had a perfect ear. Her ability to read music and her accurate playing had led her to practice regularly in the church basement, but when she was asked to play the organ with the choir, she could not allow herself to enter the music, or let it enter her. She recalled the choirmaster urging, "Play it like you mean it, honey! Give it up!" but that had not been possible, for she had barely been able to stand the heartache and celebration that were in its sound when others played. She had withdrawn from the choir soon afterward, feeling the disappointment in her limitations too much to bear.

Up in the attic, the night before, she had watched Sunday kneeling down with the mosaics around her, seeing so much more than what she had seen, and thought about what it would be like to have something, anything, other than the Nate Hunters she had known, that could make her feel that awake.

Her little sister, and "Sister" she had been for quite some time, had always overshadowed her, even with her willfulness, her disobedience. "Girl, you've got a talent for trouble," Dolora had told Sunday as she delivered the reproof of the moment and shook her head. Delta remembered when Sunday had painted the ceiling dark blue, knowing enough to lock the door, but seemingly unaware of how upset their mother would be. She hadn't even asked Delta, who shared the room, and then, instead of showing contrition, she had argued, argued, argued against painting it over, only giving up when Dolora shouted and slammed the door.

Delta had always been a good, solid student, but she had never stretched herself. Caught up with cosmetics and crushes, she had seldom studied, and got B's without trying too hard. Since B's seemed good enough for everyone else, they were good enough for her. No teacher had ever taken special interest in her or guided her to certain classes and challenges, and because she was neither a problem student nor an exceptional achiever she had moved smoothly through the minimal demands of school.

"What about college?" Sunday had said one night at dinner, when Delta was completing the eleventh grade. Although she was only a fifth-grader, Sunday had seen a show on television about the United Negro College Fund. Dolora had put her knife and fork down and looked at Delta as if a fog had just lifted, as if she suddenly saw that her daughter had reached that point in life. "Yes," Nana had asked as Dolora nodded, "what about it? What about college?" Delta hadn't known what to say. When she finally went to Nana that evening to ask, "How, where, which ones?" Nana had to admit that she had no idea. "I don't know about these things. Can't you ask your counselors or your teachers the specifics? Or ask your friends?" But Delta didn't have any college-bound friends, and felt herself so foreign from the few students in her class who were headed away for school, that she wouldn't have known how to approach them. And she could never mention it to Earlene and her crew, for they would have accused her of arrogance, nerdiness, disloyalty.

When Nana occasionally said that she and Grandpa had hoped they would both go to college, she had been expressing a general wish that their lives would open out. As far as knowing how to make that happen and helping with the concrete steps, neither she nor Dolora had a clue.

Delta went to see her counselor, who could barely fit her in between the students with disciplinary and truancy problems. She handed her a booklet about the SAT tests and some information on the local community college, and then she scooped up the three brochures that were sitting on her desk, for Northwestern, Spelman, and Illinois State. "Here, take a look at these," she had said as she rushed her through the door, "and see what you think."

With no sense of what it meant to get into or go to those schools, or of the differences between them, Delta locked the bathroom door and looked nervously through the brochures. The idea of the SAT terrified her; it seemed to require certitude, and possession of a language and body of information that were open to only a few. Chicago and Atlanta both seemed planets far away from what she knew, and she strained to see herself arriving with a suitcase, alone, at the gates of the campuses pictured on the glossy pages that unfolded before her, wondering how she would ever be able to afford those schools. In one scenario, she imagined entering the dining hall of staring black girls who all had the right clothes, the right answers, the right charming things to say, while she was mute, hesitant, and wrongly dressed. And in another, hers was the lone black and silent body in a classroom of confident white students from big cities, who answered the professor's questions with casual confidence. She pictured lonely nights without her boyfriend, without a date.

Sitting in his car one night, she had told that boyfriend that she was thinking of college, and he had clasped her hand tightly and asked her why she wanted to go away and leave him when he needed her so. "What's wrong with the community college?" he asked her. "It's only an hour away."

She put the brochures in her dresser drawer, deciding to think about it later, and before she knew it, she had missed the deadline for the SAT. She thought about it on and off during her senior year, but when her counselor asked her, "What's up for you next year?" she shrugged her shoulders and said she guessed she had decided to stay home. She found a job at the five-and-ten, and a few years later, when a position opened up at the post office, she figured she was set for the long term with a steady salary, benefits, and a retirement plan. By then, she and the boyfriend had long since broken up.

She had never been able to envision herself striking out in the world or opposing convention in any public manner. But despite her strait-laced, mild appearance, there was one way in which she had decided not to be a "good girl," and she was partly proud of that distinction. She surmised that Sunday was a virgin at the end of high school, and it always seemed ironic to her that the rule-breaker was an innocent and a prude.

Delta never talked about her sexual life, not even with Dinah, or with Earlene, who told her their business freely and without shame. But if there had been anyone she trusted with her secrets, she could have told a story that would shock. She had slept with several boys in high school, and had later been involved with a married man for years, but then something happened in Salt County that supplied her with a love life for many years.

When the paper plant had expanded, it had brought a steady stream of workers to its regional center for two-week training stints, and Delta knew how to place herself at the local bars where the transient men would find and pursue her. She knew how to be both sexy and girlish, and she made herself just blank enough to fill every man's desire and need. She asked questions about their training workshops and their jobs, meeting their eyes intently, whether she was listening or not. With her skill at making them feel fascinating, and powerful, and central, they gave in to a rapture inflamed by its impermanence.

One of the things she loved best was that she imagined they left Salt County with perfect memories, returning to their tedious routines, their demanding wives, their draining kids with an intact and unspoiled secret that was her. Although she missed each one for a day or two, another soon arrived to take his place.

Nana had never asked her about her Saturday night absences and the Sunday mornings when she didn't rise until early afternoon, but Delta realized she must not have wanted to know, for their mutual evasion of the topic had been conspicuous. Those Sunday morning aftermaths of carnal passion had been the ones on which she hadn't made it to church, which made her feel divided, guilty and unclean.

One brief affair had led to pregnancy, which she had chosen not to see through. Growing up, she had imagined that her mother wished, amid her daily providing, that she could escape, as her husband had done, and she knew there must be times when any parent felt hemmed-in and second-guessed her choice, fantasizing about walking away to regain her life. Sometimes Delta had felt, in her mother's remoteness, the thwarted desire to withdraw, to silence, to flee. And how often, she had wondered, did Dolora wish to leave behind the very body that had trapped her? How many times had she stood by her sleeping children and yearned to follow Mercury to the river, and even into death? Delta had decided never to be faced with those feelings or that choice, and although she had felt a sense of sadness as the time for having children began to pass, she hadn't trusted her ability to do it any better than Dolora had, to do it right. She hadn't been able to see herself managing to want and hold and confide and listen to a child over an entire lifetime, even with a husband. Deciding to do it alone had been inconceivable.

When the paper mill's training center closed, six years earlier, Delta's flow of temporary devotees had dried up. After that, she had had a handful of dates and a few encounters with visitors who passed through town. And then she had met Nate.

After managing to free herself from him, she had stumbled around for months, fulfilling her responsibilities at the post office during the day, and alternating between tears and stunned silence at night. She had made it through that time with Dinah and A Joyful Process, her repository of remembered objects, and her efforts at resurrecting damaged things. When she had discovered those classes in wiring and plumbing and wood shop, she had found satisfaction in correcting small, yet manageable failures. Here was something for which she had a talent, and the best part of her discovery was that there was always something that needed fixing.

Walking toward the place she and Sunday had decided to meet, Delta thought again of being in the attic the night before. One day, a year and a half before the note from Clement Woods arrived, she had remembered a childhood gift, and had climbed the attic stairs to look for it. After searching, she had found the metal chalk box of her girlhood, just where she had put it years before. Aunt Edna had given it to her, filled with smooth, white stems of chalk, for her sixth birthday, and while her mother was busy with baby care, she had spent hours in her room practicing her letters and numbers on the chalkboard Nana had thought to provide.

She wasn't sure what, exactly, had motivated her determined search for the chalk tin, so many years later, except that she had spent the night haunted with the way so many things in her life seemed to have chosen her, and how the few things she had elected had cost so much. Too overcome with the realization of her poverty to sleep, she had remembered the metal box.

At twelve and thirteen she had used it as a place for the small treasures that were hers alone, hiding in its dark interior a silver coin, a special marble, the colored fish she had made by Dolora's side. Sometimes she had put the box outside and let it fill with rainwater so that it became her own, personal lake or trove of water, clear, clean enough to drink. Eventually, as it began to rust and she shifted her focus to boys, she had stopped using it, and had placed it in the attic, where she went looking for it in the night, twenty-five years later.

Kneeling as the splintery raw boards of the attic floor pressed into her bare skin, she had dug it out from beneath a collection of blankets and pillowcases. "I found it," she whispered, working open the lid. The fish, the marble, the coin, were still inside.

She had taken it downstairs and decided to add a few trinkets from her recent past, beginning with an oval of painted corrugated cardboard that Sunday had sent during their five years without visits or telephone calls. And she had inserted the single-word message she had saved from Nate's candy box deliveries, her favorite, "UNFORGETTABLE." The others she had burned.

She kept the metal chalk box next to her bed for several months, opening it most nights before bedtime to remind herself of the small, good things she was collecting and remembering in the life she was making alone.

Soon she was able to picture the box and its contents, and she put it on the shelf of her closet. She could shut her eyes, imagine easing open the dented lid, and visualize each of the articles she had placed within. Each time she needed it, she saw herself opening the box that had come to live in her head, and finding a particular object or adding something new.

Finally, she had not needed to imagine the box itself at all, and could include some things that were too large to fit. Two gifts from Dinah: a cassette tape of Nina Simone singing "Trouble in Mind," and a forty-five of "Change What You Can" by Marvin Gaye. And she had conjured the bowl Nana had used for making bread. No longer constrained by the size of a container, her capacity to call up her treasures was as large as memory and vision. She had found a way to excavate her lost or buried objects and raise them up through all that had happened, a way to give the past a forceful, present life.

The night before, after arguing with Sunday about the mosaics, she had focused on two positive things to add to her cache: clean clothes on the line and raspberry Christmas candies, and she had imagined holding several candies in her hands, and then reeling in the soft, worn line, clothes and springing wooden pins and all, and inhaling their sun-dried smell. When she needed it, she could unreel it again.

Delta had always had an invented, private world, and it was peopled by friends and day trips to nearby places. After Mercury left and the house grew tight and quiet, she and her imaginary friend, Sienna, would go, hand in hand, on forays, hopping freight cars and riding on the tops of trains, their plaits blown back from their faces by the wind, their hands covering their ears from the whistle's sound.

Delta talked to Sienna about the family, about how Dolora was closed up tight and silent, and seemed free and balanced only with her tiles and grout. With Sienna she wondered, aloud, as she walked the ragged edge of the road, whether Mercury Owens had, in fact, died in that brown river that they crossed each day to go into town. When she heard about "amnesia," her and Sienna's hearts leapt at the possible explanation the phenomenon held, and they watched trains approach across the countryside and imagined Mercury coming their way.

Reaching the edge of the area that was once wooded, she remembered how with Sienna she had walked through thick trees, into the graveyard and down by the railroad tracks, places she was afraid to go alone. She wouldn't go there now, she thought as she stood, compelled and frightened by the shrunken patch of densely layered foliage, pondering whether a man could have once been lost or hidden in the dark, tangled unknown.

She and Sienna had ventured into the woods, naming trees and rocks and speaking with them, climbing over fallen, rotting wood, and poking tender mosses with their fingertips. They had found shelter against a cluster of rocks and had sung loudly, with no danger of being heard. Though her own voice had sounded frail and off-key in church and school, she was able to hear herself differently in the woods. With Sienna, she had belted out "This Little Light of Mine" and other songs from church, and pieces of the blues and work songs and spirituals Nana sang as she worked. When they sang in the woods Delta felt she had a soulful power to her voice; she sang "Ain't No Way" and "Respect," pretending she was Aretha, and feeling that she, too, might be a queen.

One day they found that their favorite pine tree, Alice, had been split by lightning, a wedge struck free from tip to bottom, its pale inner wood fired open to the world, and Delta had stood and looked at its majesty, at the burnt bottom and the branches of other trees torn by the crashing of the seared strip. Dropping her book bag, she had backed up slowly, awed by the ruthless strike, and aware that she was looking at the tree's private center, crumbled and soft.

The natural world had its cruel power, she saw. It could split a tree and it could take a man in the swift, ruthless current of a river.

And then, over time, she had found an even stranger thing: Alice's neighbor, barely marked outside by fire and standing whole, was dying from the inside, out.

The sky seemed to be darkening as Delta walked on, and she touched her bag to feel the ribs of her umbrella. The streets looked deserted and unnaturally quiet, and so many homes had become run-down. The steps on one were leaning and she could see garbage accumulated underneath the front porch through latticed wood.

Fall had arrived, she thought, and the isolating freeze of winter was not far behind. Every year, as the leaves fell and things paled and turned inward, she grew resentful and anxious, as though there were any future in fighting against the inevitable, yet temporary death. She hated winter, even though she had never sought a warmer place.

She had left Salt County only once, on her reckless exit from town with Nate Hunter, and even then, she had only gotten one state away. She wondered how she might be able to tell Sunday about that misjudgment, and about the woods, and Alice, and her memory storehouse, too. How could she admit to Sunday that her one really wild choice had taken her to Indiana, of all places. Jesus, she thought, is there anywhere less exotic than Indiana?

How could she reveal that she was even a failure at recklessness? "Oh damn," she said, "I'm about to be late."

When Delta got to the downtown square, breathless from hurrying, Sunday was leaning against a wrought-iron fence, her face turned up to the afternoon sun and her eyes closed. She wore her long, purple wrap and a woven scarf the tender green of newly opened leaves.

"I walked the around way," Sunday said, "by the edge of town, past the retired train station and the old paper bag plant, and I couldn't believe how exhausted those buildings looked. I got as far as the chain-link that closes it in to try to see into the metal-reinforced windows, but I couldn't see much. Then I went by the woods."

Delta looked away; it seemed that Sunday was divining her thoughts, anticipating what she would talk about if she could, but Sunday continued, "I realized how many times lately I've tried to paint those big, spreading trees. When I saw that pair of maples, I recognized something about them, only vaguely at first, but from how I had put them down on my paper and canvas."

Delta's hands closed up in her pockets and she looked at the ground. She felt a tension, felt something else trying to work its way out of Sunday's mouth, and she wasn't sure she wanted to hear it. "We have plenty of time, you know. You don't have to tell me now," she said.

"Well, what I was going to say is that when I saw it, I said to myself, I know that tree from my paintings. It was as if it had been buried in my head, and you know I didn't even know I had remembered it, but it was embedded in some way, and in my painting, its trunk had become a river with branching brooks and streams. A river that's all cut up, severed into pieces."

Delta looked at her and wished she had some idea of what to say. Was she supposed to understand this? What did it mean? She was afraid she might say something stupid, so she asked why she had chosen that particular warehouse to paint, and whether the painting was finished, and what it was called.

When Sunday gave no answer to any of her questions, Delta stood up and said, "Well . . . let's walk."

After a few blocks, Sunday tried to go at things a different way, by talking about her first attempts with papier-mâché, pastel crayons, and poster paints.

Delta remembered how all the activities in art class had felt messy, out of control. Those big tubs of paste and the construction paper scraps were always getting stuck on her shoes and the cuffs of her shirt. She hated the way the paste smelled. And even the time Dolora had let them help with her mosaics, the clay had felt so slick and oozy, the grout so grainy. She had never been able to make order or sense out of things with her hands. Cutting things out with a stencil and making those snowflakes with little cuts in folded paper was the one thing from art class that she could remember liking. She was successful at doing exactly what was expected, just what she was supposed to do.

They walked on, noticing that the smell of fall in the air was so keen, so identifiable, and carried with it all the Septembers and Octobers of their young lives. There was still some sense of autumn being the year's beginning point embedded in both of them.

Children flowed from the huge doorway of the school and headed home with their backpacks and book bags. Delta and Sunday watched a group of boys walk out with hardened, bass-line walks in oversized shirts and designer jeans, projecting both mistrust and ease as they approached adolescence. They looked so much tougher than sixthgraders had when they were growing up, Delta and Sunday thought, as if they were hiding behind their faces. Watching them, Delta and Sunday felt old.

Suddenly they noticed two sisters, roughly five and ten years old, both with hair in two thick plaits, coming through the heavy wooden doors and descending the wide concrete steps, hand in hand.

Delta and Sunday stood still as they watched the girls make their return passage from the world of school. They came down the walkway laughing, book bags hanging from their shoulders. The older, protective one waited while the initiate in side-buckled shoes and white tights stopped to adjust the collar under her rigid, plaid jumper, and Sunday put her hand to her neck as she recalled the chafe of her own hand-me-down dresses, revived with her mother's heavy starch.

Delta noticed the girl's outfit, too, and recalled going to buy new clothes at Sears for the start of school. Most of her things were outgrown by one of the Bread Ladies' nieces and passed down to her, but every season she got to have a few new things. She had turned the racks of dresses suspended on white plastic hangers and stuffed with tissue paper round and round, excited at the prospect of new clothes, but unable to choose. She imagined that kids nowadays would be mortified to be dressed by Sears Roebuck and would plead for certain brands. But when they were growing up in Salt County, there had been no shining, enticing mall one county over; there wasn't such a blatant distance between have and have-not.

Dolora had had no tolerance for her anxiety and tears later, at eleven and twelve, when she faced herself, chubby and developing, in the Sears dressing room, resisting the blousy "fat girl" dresses that her mother insisted she wear. "You'll wear them," Dolora would say, "and you'll be happy you are."

Delta had never understood that kind of statement. Dolora could make her wear it, and she could even make her act satisfied, but how did she think she could actually make her feel happy about it? She would try, but those weren't the types of promises you could make. Besides, nothing had made her happy at that age. She was chunky and friendless and in-between, in every way she could count. She was miserable, just as everyone else was at eleven or twelve, and under the impression that she suffered alone.

Sunday had made fewer of those September department store trips, for she had gotten Delta's hand-me-downs until an after-school job at the library had enabled her to buy a few things of her own. She had been skinny, "all legs," people said, gangly and later flat-chested, but she hadn't agonized openly about her body as Delta had. She had hidden herself in gym class by dressing before the other girls, and prayed secretly for breasts and curves to come. And in high school, she had begun to assemble clothes in her own quirky style. Dolora had been mystified at the platform shoes and patched bell-bottoms, but had soon given up objecting, even to the scarves, the layered tops, and the wild combinations of patterns Sunday had assembled.

Transported into their shared past by the image of the two brown sisters, Sunday thought, I wonder when the next train leaves. She closed her eyes and smelled chalk, and her fingers remembered the surfaces of desks with names and hearts and insults carved into the wood, and the hollows underneath where books and papers were stored. The rough, narrow-folded paper towels of school bathrooms and the wide porcelain pedestal sinks whose drains were always stopping up. She remembered clothbound books that were worn gray and white in the folds, and the pencil box and sketch pad she had carried wherever she went.

Delta had always wanted to ask what Sunday remembered about that day she had taken her to school for the first time, when she had felt so inadequate, so responsible as the lapse that had up until then been only their family's was suddenly public.

"Do you . . ." Delta ventured, afraid of saying the wrong thing, clearing her throat and clutching her umbrella and bag, ". . . do you remember starting school, going that first registration day?"

Sunday looked directly at her and said, "I remember it as though it just happened."

"Yeah?"

"Yeah. It was the day I took my name."

Together, they looked back on that day. Nana had volunteered to take them, so that Dolora wouldn't have to miss work, and she had led the way, with Delta pulling Sunday by the hand into the mustard-bricked school building to register for kindergarten. Stopping to bend and collect the leaves scattered across the sidewalk, she could hear Delta saying, "Sister, there's no time for that," and warning her that she would get her stiff, green corduroy jumper dirty if she didn't watch out.

Delta had been explaining about answering politely and minding, about being a nice, quiet girl who would make them proud, trying to tell it in just the way it had been presented to her. They had followed right behind Nana, crossing into the world of school, where everything was beige and tan and cold.

Nana had told them to wait next to the drinking fountain, letting them know with her firmest look that she expected their best behavior before she turned and marched off to find where they should go. They had stood right in their assigned spot, Delta catching the spreading excitement that the beginning of another year of school evoked. She watched for familiar teachers while Sunday focused on the motion of legs and feet that surrounded her, rapid-fire high heels and authoritative, striding oxfords, the scuffle of playful older children and the small, uneasy steps of other five-year-olds, entering holding grown-ups' hands to begin school.

After Nana returned, she directed them to the office, where they had stood by her side while she handed over Sunday's birth certificate, and a prim white lady began to enter information on her form. The lady had looked at the paper, handed it back to Nana, and pen ready, inquired, "Name?"

The lady's hair had been sprayed into a blond helmet, and her mouth was pulled tight, as if gathered by a drawstring. She looked sternly from Nana to Delta to Sunday as she tapped the end of her ballpoint pen on the edge of the form.

And the moment of expectant silence stretched on and on, interrupted only by the tapping of that pen.

"One moment," Nana had said to the lady, and Delta and Sunday had felt Nana's gloved hands on their backs as she ushered them through the office door, back into the hallway.

Sunday and Delta had sensed from Nana all the cautions they had learned against exposure of their inner, private lives to white folks, instilled through words and distance, mostly by the women they had known. Grandpa had recommended being in close contact with "the other group," so that you could learn how things were done, but he also let it be known that one had to be wary. "You can't tell them family business," they had both heard Nana say, "don't take a thing for granted with them, or ever let them know too much."

"Now people are people," Sunday had heard Nana tell Delta on one bread-making Saturday, cupping her young chin with flour-coated hands, "but you must be careful. Many of them live across a line as plain as that ruined river running through this town." A kitchen full of baking women had nodded their "Amens."

Sunday had rarely interacted with anyone white, and without understanding their foreignness, she respected it as truth. She wasn't sure what those words meant, "Negro" and "white," but she knew, from the thickness of feeling she detected when difference was discussed, that it was huge. When she had asked Nana and Dolora to explain about Negro and white, neither had been able to respond. They had looked at each other, and tried to begin. "We'll talk about it later, and you'll come to understand," Nana had said. After Nana left the room, Sunday heard her whisper, "How do you explain such a thing to a child that age, knowing that you must?" Dolora wondered how, as well, realizing as Nana said it that her parents had never untangled it for her. It had been that little girl who spit in her face and whispered "no 'count nigger" on a downtown street who had begun to teach her how things worked. Somehow, you learned the order; you began to catch on.

For Delta, at ten years old, the world had long since split. She had had white teachers, and there were a handful of white students who mostly kept to themselves at school. There were no white people at their church, where they lived, at their neighborhood hangouts or corner stores. And she saw them, downtown or at the library or the Y, as if from a distance, even when they were right up close. She could sense both aversion and fascination when she got too close in the book-borrowing line, or when she touched the items displayed at Woolworth's or Sears and felt Nana's hand tighten around hers as she said, "Watch how you act, child. The world is not a friendly place." She knew that Nana's posture grew tense and proud when interaction was necessary, when the worlds of white and Negro met.

Once, years before, a girl at the Y had approached her as they stood by the pool in their bathing suits. As she reached out to touch Delta's hair and skin, Delta had stood motionless, curious, afraid. She had been unable to answer the girl's question, "What's your name?" and when the worried-looking mother came and snatched her away, it had been too late to speak.

The world had most definitely divided, and the split had not been even; that much was clear. She could see how those on the other side of the divide had bigger and better houses, bigger and better jobs. She noticed that they seemed to occupy space differently, and many of them carried themselves as if they owned or ran things, in a way that reminded her of Wanda Nelson, the biggest bully in her class. She knew she was supposed to be careful around white people, and now she, and Nana, and her sister, were confronted with the probing and impatient eyes of the school gatekeeper before her.

From the corner where Nana had pulled them, in front of the glass display case, Delta had stared at the pen-tapping white lady, thinking about how she had overheard Dolora say to Nana that it could be a good thing to get to pick your own name. She had held tight to her sister's hand while Nana looked down at her and said, "Choose. It's time for you to choose your name."

Sunday had looked up, unsure of what, exactly, was happening, but aware that something was amiss. She had known that other girls her age had names of their own, and once, when she had asked her mother if she had a name but didn't know it, Dolora had said, "You're 'Sister' to us." Later, when she had questioned how it was that other people came by their own names, and if she would get one, her mother had said, "Just wait. The time will come." She knew, from the way Dolora had stood up from the table, pressed her lips together thin, and frowned, that something wasn't right.

And now she knew, from the helmet-haired lady's reaction, from Nana's posture and Delta's tightening hand, that again, something wasn't right. Maybe she was as different, in some deep-down and undefined way, as she felt. And then again, maybe this was how things worked, with each person facing a time of deciding, and hers had arrived.

Sunday had looked up at Nana's loving and worry-lined face and at the fear in Delta's eyes at her family not having the answer to fill the white lady's box. Delta's hand had begun to feel sticky, clutching hers, and while everybody waited and she watched a blur of shoes hurry by, she thought, This is Monday. This is what Monday is.

She returned to the day before, its singing voices rising in open-ended praise and respect, and its stained-glass light, carrying her in, in to a live place.

"Ready?" Nana asked, rubbing her back as she looked her in the eye. She nodded and they returned to the hair-sprayed white lady and her form.

"Sunday," she declared. "I'm her sister"—she nodded at Delta— "but Sunday Owens is my name."

The helmet lady gaped at her, marveling aloud at the names Negroes had, and entered it on the form.

When Dolora got home, Nana got them seated at the table with supper and went to speak with her in the other room. Delta and Sunday heard whispering, and when they returned, Nana had spoken to Dolora sharply as they sat, and Dolora had looked down at her plate. Finally, she had asked Sunday what had happened, and what the name she had selected meant.

No one spoke of the pen-tapping white lady or the stretched-out blankness while they waited for the name, and there was no mention of the silent caucus they had held. When Dolora asked the reasons for her choice, Delta listened while Sunday explained about the singing and the warm feeling she knew from church.

The name stuck, and though they all slipped for a while and continued to call her "Sister," she corrected them patiently until they got it right.

The thing Delta remembered most clearly from that day was their reflection in the display case at the entrance to the school.

In the glass she had seen them, dark and conspicuous, as she waited for Sunday to come up with a response. There they were, faces brown and lotion-shiny, wiry hair threatening to escape the confines of their plaits. They were inadequate. Sister didn't even have a name. Dolora was always telling her to watch out for her little sister, and there she was, embarrassed, holding her hand as if she, Delta, could protect her from anything at all.

That day, and the silence out of which it had grown, came to mean more and different things to Sunday as she grew older and moved further from the insular world of family and home. But she had revisited her school registration day again and again with paint, and her work held both parts of the story: the way she had been nameless, and the way she had declared her choice. She drew on the whole of it. On that expectant pause and judgment from across the divide, and her sister's hand as Nana urged her to define herself. The smells of school and autumn, and the rough, grainy surface of yellow brick. The memory of stained-glass windows and voices of the worship day.

She painted from that place, that moment, and in each act of creation, she was taking her name.

When the school yard was empty of children, Sunday and Delta began to walk.

"Look, Delta, isn't that the same garage that was there, where we used to go to smoke?" Sunday asked, striving to place herself in the landscape and bring back the person she was in those days. She couldn't say, like people she knew, that life had ever been carefree, that there were "good old days" of purity, not visited by shadows, but she thought there had been times when trouble was more of an abstract presence, not yet built up in discernible layers. Or maybe there had always been the same accumulation of trouble, she thought, and it was one's consciousness of it that grew. She pointed out remembered sights, linking them to specific events.

In response, Delta found herself talking more and more about who in town was doing what. Aware that Sunday was reaching for a bond, she began emitting long threads of looping gossip that might pull her sister toward her and hold her with the everyday power of the home-place.

Sunday tried to concentrate on what Delta was saying . . . *but you know, he really shouldn't have said that to her because she knew he'd bought that watch and paid too much for it* . . . but she faded in and out, in . . . *and then Vonda said to her well you know how he is always showing off like that time he wore those white shoes with his dark suit on Easter Sunday and then didn't even stay to lay out the food at the VFW* . . . and out, in . . . *but then she had the same dress I had on, and look there's Tommy Wilson's car and I bet he brought it home on empty so that she'll be in a rush somewhere and have to* . . . out, and in . . . *but do you think it will rain and ruin that new wax shine* . . . and Sunday was nodding in what she hoped were the right places, but she barely recalled the people Delta was going on about and she couldn't stay with the thread.

She felt a surge of panic that she would never be an artist again, and if that were true, if she knew that she would never, ever, make anything else with her hands, then she might decide not to live after all, inconceivable as she had always thought her father's choice. She concentrated on counteracting her panic with Reed's words to her over recent months: "You haven't stopped being an artist because you can't work right now; artist is what you are."

Painting was how she had lived. But here she was, stuck, able to see, yet not to reach the full spectrum. What else could she do? she asked herself, trying to imagine teaching high school, like Reed, or working in an office, like her mother and sister. She had done her share of cleaning and waitressing jobs over the years, and she could always keep doing her drafting work. But without her painting, what would she care about?

Although she had known, from as far back as she could think, that she wanted to make art, she hadn't thought it was superior to other employment. But it was her work. It was what she did. Grandpa would have surely been confounded by her impractical choice, and unable to think of it as work at all. He would have been unsure what it had to do with either an improved standard of living, or the uplift of the Negro race.

"Nana did every kind of job," she said, interrupting Delta from her litany of local facts, "from reshelving at the library and working at the store to cleaning houses. And those were just some of the things she got paid for. She cooked church dinners and watched children, and who knows what else."

Delta stopped walking while she tried to orient herself at Sunday's sudden change of topic. Had she been listening? Well, they were back to the past, back to Nana, but at least she hardly ever minded talking about her.

"And she was some frugal, too," Sunday went on. "I guess that's where appliance purgatory came from, Nana never throwing anything away. And you know the way she saved her pennies to buy special gifts for us. One of my favorite things was to help her paste in those S&H Green Stamps, and that other kind that said, 'It's Smart to Be Thrifty.' Visions of the things we could redeem them for . . . bicycles and electric kettles and such . . . were going through my head as I wet the sponge and tried to get the stamps angled right between the lines."

"Yes, those stamps," Delta said. "I used to want us to trade them in for the shiny red wagon with the removable wooden sides, and Nana always used them for something practical, that the whole family could use, you know, a card table or a can opener. But once, you know, she let me choose. We didn't have enough for the wagon, and I couldn't decide between the miniature tea set and the paddle with the rubber ball attached."

"Yeah. When I was six or seven I coveted the blackboard and set of colored chalk," Sunday remembered. "I begged Nana to let me start my own book and save up for them. She said, 'Child, you'll be saving till you're twenty-one, and by then you'll be wanting something else.' But she did let me have my own book, and she gave me stamps for doing special little jobs around the house. Eventually, I did get that blackboard and that chalk."

Sunday thought about how Nana had often told her, "You must do what is necessary to get what you need, and try to put some joy into it, while you work."

"She made some serious bread, didn't she?" Delta said, and Sunday's face lit up as she exclaimed, "Matter of fact, all those women did.

Those weekends in Nana's kitchen were something, all those hands in motion, and the talking and laughing. But the singing, that was the best part."

Nana was singing, always singing, whether it was with the Bread Ladies, or in church, or around the house as she did her daily tasks. One day, Sunday recalled, when she was twelve or thirteen and she was looking from the living room window at the steady release of rain from a pewter sky, Nana was raising her voice while they sorted clothes. That piece of something buried and sore that she always heard in Nana's voice prompted Sunday to turn and ask her why her song had to be so sad.

"The basic story's got trouble in it," she had answered, her frown lines appearing. "Once you've seen what you've seen, in other people and in yourself, you can't quite sing without pulling on some of that."

And then Nana had taken Sunday's hands in hers and told her that music, whatever parts joyful and sad, should get you in that tender, live place, where the sensitive flesh is just beyond the shelter of the fingernails.

"In the quick," she had said, "that's where music should come for you. In the place where the blood is, where you freely bleed."

And Sunday had carried Nana's words into her relationship with paint. Telling and retelling what she knew, letting the cobalt and red declare themselves along with the lines of the strong and weighted backs of the bread-making women who sat before her in their pews, their brassieres cutting into their abundant flesh and their working healing feeding hands clapping as their bodies rocked. She painted the backs of all the joycrying black women she had ever known.

While she worked, she listened for those buried generations that had ridden Harris's river north, some passing through and some settling, and she learned about surviving most kinds of hardship, and crafting from that hardship, art.

She had heard Nana's voice and seen her mother's busy hands, felt her grandpa's ravaging, interlocking pride and shame. She had pictured Wilborn raising his income and his stature. She had imagined Delta raising any claim at all.

She had felt Mercury in flashes, sinking with his longing and his fear and guilt, haunting from the boundary line.

And when she stepped back and looked at what she had done, she saw her story, full of joy and trouble, and felt the nearness of blood.

8

.

SEEKING THE QUICK HAD, for Sunday, been a way to self-christening. In painting and in leaving, she had tried to either refuse or redeem what had been unchosen, what had been unknown. And although she had begun to recapture the past, she knew that within the story of silence and choice was the thing she had never asked: What was the reason? Why was I left unnamed? She knew that question was linked to what had drawn her home, and she intended to push Delta, and anyone else she could find, for the answers.

Lost in their own thoughts, she and Delta had fallen silent as they reached the entrance to the cemetery. Through the gate they saw a field of tombstones being taken slowly by lichen and weather. The stones grew from the faded autumn grass, like teeth in different stages of decay, mottled and gray. Recent, unblemished ones rose straight from the ground, while the older, rounded slabs, darkened and eroded, tipped and leaned. Now and then a line of modest tributes was interrupted by a monument to prosperity, ornate with crosses and spreading angel wings.

They were in Our Cemetery, as the black people of Salt County called it. Started on a small piece of fallow, black-owned land, when even in death they were not welcome to occupy the same ground as the white townspeople, its stones were close together, its graves densely packed. Although they had later been deemed eligible to enter all-white Greenlawn Cemetery, most of the black folks of Salt County preferred to keep on being buried with their own. When one black family had decided to buy a plot at Greenlawn, Nana had laughed and said to the Bread Ladies, "I'm talking about getting some *rest.*"

Sunday could remember her going on about exploitation in the hereafter: "Can you imagine rest happening over there at Greenlawn? Why there's nothing more tiring than white folks. They'd have you working to make the way they'd treated you in the former life all right for them. And you'd have to keep such a watch out . . . monitoring them and guarding whatever there would be in the afterlife to guard . . . peace, or room to stretch out, or whatever advantages there might be in death . . . that there'd be no rest to be had. And you *know* they'd have us working; in fact I bet we'd be tending the other graves. No, I'll go right where my people are," she had said, laughing, as she kneaded a hunk of dough, "that'll be good enough for me."

While Delta hung back at the entrance to have a cigarette, Sunday walked in and wandered, veering eventually from the bricked path so that the tips of her shoes pressed into the moist grass. Sunday smelled rain and thick humus, and the clay exposed by digging near a fresh mound of earth. The black-flecked salmon pink of the granite headstone was newly cut, and bending close, she found that it, too, smelled raw and fresh. Sunday had an idea of how hard it was to carve stone, for she had taken sculpture classes in art school and grappled to impose her signs and symbols on a resistant marble mass. The incised message told her that it honored a youngster, barely into manhood, whose brief passage was the only thing recalled. Stepping back, she stared down at the granite, pondering what else might be known if the life could somehow be told. What lover's hand was missing his? she wondered. What small items, key chain and bubblegum and rabbit's foot, had filled his pockets, and what romantic devotions and hopes had collided with what was callous, yet had somehow prevailed?

Each marker declared something of a life lived, and perhaps said even more about those left behind. The granite and limestone retained the facts of naming and dating, selected and chiseled into its grain. Here's what you get in the end, she thought: a designation, two dates, and relationship proclaimed.

The former fig box in the attic had given her a different kind of record of Dolora's life from what she would find at Our Cemetery, had shown an attempt to capture what had been important at different times. As Delta had said, there were the built-up bits of living that happened in between the parentheses of birth and death, some lost to you and some retained. There were the moments for which you were wholly present and the ones that washed over you. There were those that were, somehow, endured. Some of the pieces of your life were preserved through will and desire, and others just couldn't be dismissed.

What had survived in her, below the surface? she wondered. What did her other, early selves recall? Sister remembered the starched jumper and the meter of a tapping pen, schoolhouse brick and a choir of stained-glass voices. And what memories did Girl Owens recall, deep within? The feel of her mother's arms, the taste of her breast? Dolora's mute anger and prayer for Mercury's return?

The fragrance of wet grass or a peerless blue might be remembered. A certain collarbone, the patterns of the stars, or the fleeting sense of being linked. Through telling, those things could persist in the minds of your survivors, or might be fixed through the practice of an art. But here's what the stone remembers, she thought, long after people forget.

She and Delta had been through the gate of Our Cemetery together three times: for Grandpa, Dolora, and then Nana, and now they were back to edit the record they had made. They could do it: Change Mercury's death date . . . separate the names onto different pieces of stone . . . excise "Cherished" or "Wife." They could remove him altogether, for a body had never been buried there at all. They could take off "Father" and "Husband," and leave him unaffiliated, leave him unclaimed.

Short of bringing his body back, Sunday wasn't sure what they should do. In her gut she wanted to claim him, for as low as he had sunk, she didn't want to keep Mercury out there on his own, on the run from his life and from them, and she knew there had to be something else to his existence than his leaving. Maybe she would be able to find out what it was. Wanting, with the curatives of love and time, to make him into Father at the very least, she focused on the fact that he had contacted them in the end. She wanted to read the arrival of the note and locket as an announcement of atonement and regret. That was the story she needed most to make.

Delta, on the other hand, kept returning to the solution of "letting things be." There were things that could be repaired and rehabilitated all around her, toasters and lamp cords and plumbing leaks, and she would rather focus there. Even in the cemetery, she noted trees that needed trimming, and edging that should be done along the path.

As she walked the cemetery grounds she tried to remember something about each of the more recently buried. There was the cobbler, "Mr. Essex" Block, whose leather and shoe-polish scent came to her as she paused to read the "Truest Husband on Earth" his wife had had inscribed. Delta had always been able to smell the labor on his thick, hardened fingers as he had reached out to clasp hers at the threshold of the church. And then a few years ago he had died and the shop had closed, but his wife, who never had the slightest involvement in the business, seemed to maintain his polish and shoe leather scent.

Behind Mr. Essex was a marker reading 1877–1901, whose worn letters honored Sumner Wells. Delta and Sienna had spent a good bit of time before that stone, pondering the quote, "We Shall Know Each Other Better When the Mists Are Cleared Away," and wondering what had taken Sumner at twenty-four, the same age her own father had been. Was it a sudden illness or long-standing disease? A fight with a loved one? An accident? She had liked making up what this unknown town ancestor's life was like, deciding that he had been compelled to Salt County by the remarkable beauty and passionate love of a woman, who had mourned him for the rest of her life and never loved again. Maybe, like her, he had had a weakness for peach preserves, and maybe had carried a silver flask.

Down another row she walked past the sourest woman in their part of town, Rowena Tyler, the only Negro in Salt County who had owned a grand piano, and the only one who hadn't spoken to other colored folks when she passed them on the street. She talked of pedigree, had read extensively on "free colored people," and injected at every opportunity that her ancestors were all "freedmen," who had demonstrated their superiority by either purchasing or being granted their freedom.

Delta remembered the Bread Ladies laughing about Rowena on their Saturday afternoons, when Nana had said that there were no Negroes on U.S. soil who had not descended from slaves. "Unless they made that middle passage by choice, and it was a pleasure cruise, then they were slaves." She would turn to them. "Now don't you forget it, girls"—her hands sending flour into the air as she moved them—"we come, all of us, from the same trouble." Delta wasn't sure that Grandpa agreed with Nana on that score, but she was always too afraid to clarify that point.

Over by a reddening maple, she came to two of the Bread Ladies, Alpha Post and Patrice Hawkins, side by side. In order to get their neighboring plots they must have arranged to be together way in advance, for space had grown dear on those circumscribed grounds.

Neither one had ever married, and people had always wondered whether they were bound by a dangerous and deep-rooted love. Delta wasn't positive, but she bet that Nana knew, and it hadn't ever seemed to make any difference to her. As she bent over to uproot clumps of invading crabgrass and entrenched dandelions with thick, barbed leaves, Delta could almost see the two of them, quietly in tune with each other, their presence conjured so recently through the blue bowl.

Delta realized she could walk the cemetery and nearly see a history of Salt County. Each grave provoked some kind of reminiscence, and she imagined herself buried there, and the people she had known indulging their memories of her. Dinah coming to tell her about some new music she had heard, or a man to whom she had sold stamps for years and years, pausing at her grave to recall the small, but important role she had played in his life.

She saw Sunday touching a marker, pushing her fingers into the grooves that the numbers and letters made, her eyes closed. What is she *doing?* Delta wondered, anxiously; she would probably even try to see what the stone tastes like . . . probably has. Why did she always have to get so up close to a thing, forcing its secrets from it? Delta could see that her sister's shoes were already mud-encrusted and, no doubt, wet, and her clothes would soon be dirty, rubbing up against those slabs.

Sunday noticed Delta watching her before she had a chance to glance away, and moved toward her, so that they approached their family's plots together. They read "Lomax Blount, 1905–1965" on a stone twice the size of those around it, lavishly adorned with angels and trumpet vines, reading, "In Righteousness We Prosper." And next to it was one of the same black granite for "Jetta Blount, 1910–1992." Hers was simple, carved with only a pair of praying hands, and the inscription "Family * Fellowship * Song."

It felt peculiar for Sunday to see her grandparents described by their full names. To her, they had been Grandpa and Nana, and to the rest of Salt County, Mr. Blount and Nana J. Where in them, she mused, had those different selves lived and met? Were they all those selves at once? Sunday wondered, too, if Jetta was short for something, and if so, why Nana had relinquished her full name.

Sunday studied her parents' double marker, carved with a Celtic love knot, labyrinthian, without beginning or end. Sunday figured her mother had selected the joint headstone and had Mercury's epitaph, "Father * Husband, Now at Rest," carved to the left, but that was another thing she would have to ask Opus about. She couldn't remember seeing the stone when she was growing up, but it had clearly stood there, the ground empty beneath it and the right side partly blank. And there was her mother's name, inscribed beside his. Sunday had a hard time understanding why Nana had decided to include the "Wife" part of "Cherished Daughter, Wife, Mother. Taken Too Soon." After all, the wife part hadn't exactly worked out.

She looked at the recessed letters reading "Dolora Blount Owens," remembering Nana telling them that she had promised Grandpa to include their daughter's maiden name. It was intended, Sunday supposed, as some kind of mitigation of the Owens brand.

For nearly twenty years, Sunday thought, her mother had believed Mercury dead and had prepared to someday lie, still alone, beneath their twin memorial. And all the while he was getting up each day to eat and talk and move around, and then settling down to sleep. In what way had they, his wife and children, been dead to him?

"You visit here," she said, looking at the spray of plastic flowers on Nana's grave, and Delta nodded, without revealing that she came twice a month to clip the grass and place flowers, even if they weren't real. A few times she had brought cut bunches of live irises or lilies that would honor her mother's name, but it had vexed her that they faded so fast and died; the plastic ones would last, she had decided, and that had seemed important, too. She didn't tell, either, that she sometimes left other, everyday offerings, for she was afraid Sunday would be judgmental of her bestowal of doorknobs, safety pins, china saucers, and loaves of bread. She wasn't sure why she did it, except that she had read about people in New Orleans and other places paying tribute to their dead in that way. She never left them openly, but concealed them in boxes or bags.

Delta arranged a rectangle of newspaper on the ground and knelt to brush away the leaves and sticks that had collected on Nana's grave. Sunday asked, the strain building in her voice, "What do you think would be best for my stone, Delta? 'Sister' or 'Sunday'?"

Delta watched her take out her glasses and clean them slowly and deliberately on her clothes. "Oh Lord," she said to herself, "there's a storm coming," and she stood up, stepped back a few paces, and planted her feet firmly on the cemetery path, waiting to respond until she had a better idea of where Sunday's questions were headed. Sunday's face had the same look as the last time Delta had called her "Sister."

That time, over ten years before, Sunday had stopped what she was doing and quit speaking in mid-sentence while she cleaned her lenses carefully as her anger, terrible in its constraint, climbed. Finally, she had placed her glasses back on her face and said, " 'Sister' is our relationship. It is what I am to you, Delta, and what I am to other black women, but it's not my identity. It's not who I am. I've got a name of my own, and as long as I had to wait for it, I don't ever mean to let it go." Delta had never again used "Sister" as an appellation, but she was always afraid she would misspeak and provoke that rage.

When she finished with her glasses, Sunday crossed her arms and squeezed her sides, while Delta tried to prepare herself for the coming exchange.

"I do want to know one thing. Were you . . ." Sunday began. She herself was astonished that her question was surfacing at that point. Was it something about the cemetery, she wondered, that pushed it from dormancy, so that it had to be asked? She tried to continue, but wasn't sure how. She didn't mean for Delta to feel culpable, and she knew the question would appear to indict. Delta looked away. Sunday looked away. She got out one more word the next time, "Were you . . . there?"

Delta focused on the green of Sunday's scarf, knowing they weren't finished with the question of Sunday's naming, and that it was going to bring with it things that were even harder to revisit. She was too jangled to find a cigarette, but she wanted to fill the space between them, the space of the full and coming question, with some activity, and she wished she could deflect Sunday's attention with her favorite food or a piece of local news, with something good and constant, like the marvel of rising bread. She prayed that Sunday wouldn't press it, but she figured that was partly what she had come back for, and asking Sunday not to pursue something she wanted was like asking her not to breathe.

"Were you there, Delta," she implored, gripping the top of Nana's headstone, "were you there when I was born?"

Delta stopped and looked at her sister, realizing that it was, after all, a perfect time for a cigarette, that in fact it was the only thing that would save her, having that very occupation for her hands. She rooted for her Kools while Sunday began to speak.

"You know, it's never, ever been talked about," she stated, "but I've always wondered why I wasn't given my own name."

She paused, as if to find language, and then went on, "For a while I wasn't sure how naming worked, and then, when I came to understand that people are named at birth, I couldn't seem to ask. I mean I thought it must have been something about me, or something too, too bad to ever discuss, so I was afraid to know." Delta could see the puzzled child in her face as she talked. "But now I think it's something I should be able to ask about, don't you? I think it's a piece of my life that I've got a right to."

Delta had always been afraid to ask Sunday how the whole naming thing had made her feel. As bound together as they had been early on, sometimes that alliance of two, there were so many wordless gaps between them. She had wanted to find out so many things, but had not known how, so instead, she had always tried to see in it what was good, to focus on the advantage of being free to create who you might be. She also knew that none of that even began to address what her sister felt. The burn in Sunday's eyes told Delta how large the question was.

"What do you remember, Delta?" she ventured. "Were you there when I was born?"

Delta lit a cigarette and tried to think of what it was she did remember of that day. Sunday reached over the top of Nana's headstone for the Kools and lit one, too, while Delta returned to her mother's bedside and told what she had witnessed there.

Delta had been downstairs with Alpha and then Patrice, who had tried to hush the screaming and grunting with closed doors and distract her with stories and games. Delta kept returning, amid paper dolls and Dr. Seuss, to the explanation Dolora had given for her father's absence. He's away, she said to herself, away. And then finally, she had been allowed upstairs. Standing at the bed's footboard, she had gripped its dark, wooden spools with her small hands. Despite the adult reassurances that her mother was fine, she was relieved to see her intact and breathing, and puzzled by the quiet stillness, after the cries she had heard. She saw the two pointed humps of her mother's feet just before her, pushing up the blanket, and the mound of her still swollen stomach. And she saw the fidgeting infant, its face red and puckered, at her breast. Her mother's eyes were closed and the Bread Ladies stood around the bed, encircling Dolora.

As Delta came slowly around to the side of the bed and squeezed between the hips of two of the Bread Ladies, she saw the baby nursing, and was transfixed. Despite closed eyes, her mother's face was wet with tears, and the newborn's head, florid and so delicate, quivered as it sucked.

"Nana," she asked, "what's it doing?"

"Your sister's eating, child," Nana whispered. "That's how babies get their food."

She stared at the baby, locked to Dolora's nipple, its hand a fist.

"Did you feed me like that, Mama?" she had asked, recognizing in a rush of memory the smell of mother's milk, the texture of round white buttons, the faded yellow of a housecoat and anchoring arms.

Dolora had not answered. And then one of the Bread Ladies—was it Opus?—had placed a palm on Delta's shoulder, and Dolora had continued to lie immobile, her eyes closed.

"Did you, Mama, did you?" she pleaded, her voice rising and shrill. The women reached out to touch Delta, one gentle, worn hand smoothing her plaits, one patting her back, another stroking her arm. They all looked at Dolora, waiting for her to open her eyes and speak to the child who was wrenching free of their hold and urgently lifting a knee to climb up to where mother and sister were. "Mama, did you feed me like that, too?"

Nana had answered for Dolora with a soothing, "Come, baby, of course, of course she did," and pulled her from the bed and onto her lap across the room, where she explained that Dolora had had an awful time, and along with the baby, needed rest. Delta saw the three worry lines between Nana's eyebrows. "She'll be back to herself in no time," she told Delta as she settled her against her clove-smelling breast, "in no time at all."

After all of the Bread Ladies but Opus had left, Nana sat rocking her, humming softly. There had been a long time of quiet, when Delta heard only sucking, breathing, and the grind of the chair's rockers against the floor. Opus came in and out of the room, straightening up and putting things on the bedside table.

Dolora handed Opus the baby, and Nana eased Delta from her lap and went to take her. She asked Dolora what name she had picked.

The seat of that chair where Nana had left her was hard, and the edge cut into the backs of Delta's legs. She got up and resumed her place at the foot of the bed, but Nana didn't seem to notice, so consumed was she in getting through to Dolora, who looked at her blankly, unable to form a single syllable.

"There were no words," Delta told Sunday, leaning against Nana's headstone. "What I would say about it now, I think, is that words just failed. And when Mama turned her face away, Nana had said that for the time being, we would call you 'Sister.' "

"That's what I remember of that day," Delta said, "but I wish we had Nana here to ask."

"I can see . . ." Sunday said, "I can see how she was devastated, what with him dying . . . well . . . thinking he had died, anyway, just beforehand. But it's not like you have a baby every day. I mean, wasn't it a major event, wasn't she excited, or a little bit happy about me?"

She had watched her friends prepare for their infants, making rooms or parts of rooms for them, gathering clothes and toys and supplies and reading up on birth and development and baby care, knitting things. She saw them shifting their lives and homes around. Yielding. Making a place. And the care that was taken with choosing a name made for an entry, was part of one's passage into the world.

"She must not have been ready for me. I bet I wasn't planned or even wanted. For me, she had not made a way."

Delta didn't know what to say to that. "Planned? Who do you think was planned?"

Sunday pictured the marriage license and birth certificate for Delta that she had found in the attic, dated six months apart.

"Does it sound to you like she was able to make any kind of way for me, either?" Delta asked. "After he left, she had nothing but silence, as I said before."

"Okay. Well, what I was driving at was that I can see how, right after I was born, on the heels of Mercury's leaving, that Mama was too floored to cope. So she fell into some kind of silent depression and was devastated, daunted by the needs of an infant and a five-year-old, the whole nine yards. But what about later? What about then?"

"Later?"

"Yes, later, for five more years. What happened? Did they forget about me?"

As Sunday wandered in and out of the plots, Delta thought back to the time just after her sister's birth. Nana had stepped in to provide the attention Dolora didn't have to give, but Delta had wanted to climb into the arms that Sunday occupied. And whenever she sought her out, too often with a cry or a whine, Dolora responded with irritation, and focused on the task at hand. "I've got my hands full, Delta," she would say. "It's time.to wash up for dinner, while I put your sister down."

Looking back, Delta imagined that her mother must have felt like lying in bed forever, with her eyes shut. She must have wanted to get rocked and fed and changed herself. Nana, the Bread Ladies, and Aunt Edna had helped, and then, eventually, Dolora must have started to feel ashamed of how depleted she felt. Grandpa had probably criticized her, asking when she was planning to get out of bed, get back to normal, or some such thing. And so she rose and faced what needed doing. She cooked, and straightened up, and fed her baby. She washed her and diapered her and put her down. And then she got herself and Delta ready for the morning, and then for bed. Her daughters needed everything from her, and it must have been all she could do to provide food and keep them clean and dry and safe.

Probably, Delta thought, looking at her headstone, there was no part of her which was able to yield. She must have felt as if she were drowning, rising repeatedly in the tumult of the current to get her breath, and when she measured herself against her own mother, she must have felt guilty and poor. Trying to block out the emotions that crept up on her when she let her thoughts go, Dolora threw herself into a roster of daily demands, adopting a strict schedule, where rules became important as never before.

She could not move over her sorrow to make space even for the new child, let alone give her gratuitous kisses and hugs, for there was a hollow at her center, and if she shifted the precarious balance of silenced rage, disappointment, and doubt the slightest bit, everything might spin into the vacuum of that hole.

As Delta thought about her attempts to be near her mother, she was again witnessing something that had changed her world. She closed her eyes and looked down, but it was still there, inside of her, not with the memories that were savored and preserved, but demanding its very own place. Why remember it? she asked herself. What she saw had made her childhood world careen.

She tried to block it out, but she found herself, again, at the doorway of Dolora's bedroom. Having shed her muddy shoes from playing in the yard, she rushes up the stairs, eager to see and maybe get to hold her month-old Sister, whose tiny perfection and growing repertoire of facial expressions can fascinate her for hours. She can kiss and stroke her again and again, and while she is holding her, she is the baby's world. As she climbs the stairs, the crying she heard from the front door grows louder.

She can see it all again, from her child's height. As she crosses the raised, wooden threshold to Dolora's room, her mother stands at the window, looking through a lifted slat of the blinds, her back to the baby, who floats on a puffy comforter in the middle of the bed. Delta keeps quiet, savoring the image of her mother, unnoticed, before she has a chance to retreat.

Delta looks up from mother to baby to mother, who stands gazing through the parted blinds, apparently oblivious to the baby's squalling. And then she drops the blinds suddenly and lets them fall back into place, clenching her hands and shaking them at the child.

Holding her breath, Delta steps backward over the threshold, into the shadow, without making a sound.

And her mother crosses the room in one fluid split-second step to reach the baby, whose crying has risen, risen, risen in pitch. But instead of lifting her from the bed, she clamps her hands, one atop the other, on Sister's mouth.

Delta stands in still terror as she sees the baby sink into the comforter with her mother pressing the small bud of a mouth, fury and vexation showing in the bulging vein on her temple and her clenched teeth. The cry becomes a mewl and the tiny arms flail, as if Sister struggles to fly free of her inherited grief.

As Delta is about to call out or step forward, her mother gasps, removes her hands, and lifts her child to her breast, while Delta withdraws into the hall closet without ever being seen, and pulls the door closed, completing the darkness she feels inside her chest. She waits there for at least an hour, encased in the smells of mothballs and wool, shivering despite the closed-in heat, until she can safely slip downstairs and begin trying to forget what she has seen.

But where, she had never stopped questioning, where did Dolora put that small act that was so huge? Sometimes Delta had found her mother looking at her with odd concentration, and wondered if she had seen her in that doorway for an instant, for a flash. And then again, without knowing for certain if she had been witnessed, maybe she was able to make believe, even to herself, that she had never done it at all.

Over the years, Delta, too, had tried to find a place for that image of her mother, behind and underneath the other painful pieces of the past that she had decided she could not use. She had tried to keep it buried, but it returned, often after an absence of years, and it always made her stomach fume.

Feeling that searing in her middle, Delta looked over at Sunday, who was peering at the ground between the family graves, and reached back into her repository for a different memory.

Instead of the blue bowl, she chose the placket of faded flowers and its button trail. She also imagined something just remembered two days before: a Mary Jane candy, sticky and molasses-sweet. She freed it from its red and yellow wrapper, tasting its treacle as she chewed, and then released it from the present just before it was swallowed, so that she would be able to conjure it once more.

Why tell it? she asked herself, after letting go of the buttons and the candy and finding herself back at the cemetery. Why even recall it, if you didn't have to. She hadn't been able to stop remembering, but silence was something she could choose.

"So what do you think we should do about Mercury," Delta asked, "now that you've seen the headstones again?"

"I don't know. We don't have to decide yet, but we could go to the stonecutter's shop that Opus told me about, and find out what our options are."

"Let's go, then," Delta answered, happy to get in motion and leave the vision of her mother's stifling hand behind.

9

THE STONECUTTER'S SHOP was on the edge of town, among the defunct factories and warehouses where Sunday had walked earlier that day. In that industrial and commercial graveyard, only the paper mill and the Rock of Ages monument shop survived. Pieces of stone filled the yard next to the shop, and although some surfaces had been polished and cut with names and images, many were rough. Still others were carved, yet unfinished, bearing only parts of illustrations or names.

Because Nana had made arrangements for her own marker well in advance of her death, Delta had never visited Felix Harris's shop. At Nana's request, Opus had taken care of her mortuary and burial matters, leaving the sisters to focus on the service, whose components she had discussed with them, and provide comfort to each other. With Dolora's death, eighteen years before, Sunday had gone with Nana to handle adding her name to Mercury's marker, while Delta had seen to choosing burial clothes. This time, they were there to see about undoing what had been done.

They entered the shop, smelling damp stone dust and feeling grit beneath their shoes. The cowbell on the door sounded as they pulled the handle, and the whine of the lathe ceased. Sunday prepared herself for Felix Harris's attention, which would place the two of them within their family history of death and shame. She remembered Nana's weary recounting of her previous visit to the shop: "Imagine getting to know people in this way. The whole of Salt County passes through that man's life."

Appearing in the doorway to the back room, Felix Harris wiped dust from his hairless face with a handkerchief. "Soon's I get washed up I'll be back," he said, speaking so quietly that they had to strain to make out his words.

To Sunday, nothing in the shop seemed to have aged, not even Felix Harris, but then he had been "born old," Nana had said. Although he had the height and wiry strength for lifting and working stone, his spine and shoulders had acceded, early on, to gravity. His expression, in which each facial feature seemed to participate, said how troubled and disappointing people could be. As rumor had it, Nana said, his wife had left him on their honeymoon, but no one ever remembered hearing it from him.

Despite the fact that he was a witness and a record keeper of sorts, the people of Salt County didn't have to worry that he would pry into their private business, for he learned what he knew with a minimum of personal questions. He had beheld the more righteous aspects of human nature, for in some people, loss seemed to refine away what was irrelevant and petty and bring them to him in moments that were clean. But he had also seen his share of indulgent bereavement, dramatized and fraudulent. Felix had observed base quarrels over assets and net worth, family discord that was historic and unending, and he had heard the consolation of mythmaking, and tales of middling lives. Although he had never got the chance to tell anyone about his inspirations and his disillusionments, Felix Harris had kept his own kind of chronicle, and he thought he had been given unique access to people's lives.

"It's him," Delta said after Felix had appeared and disappeared. She pulled at Sunday's sleeve. "Harris, the scuba diver, from the river yesterday."

Sunday said, "Harris. Felix Harris," as she brushed dust from the stone bench along the wall and sat down. While Delta stood beside her they both tried to integrate the story of Harris the diver and historian with the shop where they stood.

When he returned, Sunday stood up and looked into a face that was freighted with knowing.

"How can I help?" he asked, drying his hands on a towel, recognizing them from the day before at the river.

Sunday tried to speak directly, as she imagined Opus Green would. "We haven't yet decided what action to take, but we might want some changes to a headstone that you made. We have three questions," she said, raising a finger to account for each one. "What does the most simple, basic stone cost? As far as the message is concerned, do you charge by the letter? And . . ."—she paused to clear her throat—"can the message on a stone you did over thirty-six years ago be . . . edited?"

His eyes grew wide and he tossed the towel aside as she went on, "That is . . . can part of it be removed or changed?"

He stared at the sisters in turn, looking as if he wanted to moan. Sunday felt terrible that she had added another disappointment to the burden that he carried, for their question could only be provoked by human error. He seemed to shake his head as he went behind the counter and dug out his price chart, and looking away toward the workroom, as if he were more comfortable with inanimate company, he said, softly, "I've added, but I've never cleared away."

They didn't know what to say next, and then he answered, "I couldn't make nothing where something has been without it showing, but I might be able to put an image in its place."

The sisters nodded, and focused on the printed sheet and Mr. Harris withdrew to his workroom, pausing at the doorway to whisper, "Let me know."

"Wait," Sunday wanted to shout. "Wait, and tell me who you are." While he was talking, she had noticed that his thick coveralls had a dime and something else pinned to the front pocket, but she hadn't been able to discern what the second thing was, and she wanted to know if it was one of the charms he had worn when he was working the river. As he vanished into the back room, she had a picture of him slipping into the water's surface in his wet suit.

She had so many questions for the peculiar and mysterious Felix Harris. She wanted to know what the river and the stone carving had to do with each other. Would he return to his diving in the spring, or was he done? And where he had put the things that he had found?

"Wow, is he strange. He's even stranger than I realized during the river thing, and I didn't know he was the gravestone man. I wonder what his story is, with the diving and the carving and all. I just wonder."

"I wonder, too," Sunday agreed. "I met him when I came with Nana, after Mama died, and she sure did say he seemed burdened by all the death he had seen. I know he's got some serious stories to tell."

She had already wanted to meet Harris the river diver, and now she knew she wanted to talk to Felix Harris, the gravestone man. "Delta, didn't they ever say he was the stonecutter in the articles you read?"

"I didn't read any articles. I just saw him on TV, and they never made that connection. Maybe they thought everyone knew him, or maybe he has that kind of job, like mine, where you serve people and they go on and on about their needs, without ever really seeing you."

"Yeah, could be." They were quiet, while Delta continued to look through her bag. "I wonder if he *has* anybody," she said, "or if he's alone."

"Yeah. I wonder if that story Nana told me about his wife leaving him on his honeymoon is true."

"On his honeymoon?" Delta gasped. "That's just plain low-down."

As they were leaving, they noticed a fenced-in yard at the back piled up with rusted scrap metal, machinery, and crates of smaller objects. "Look," Delta exclaimed, "I bet those are the things he brought up. Look at all that stuff."

They stood with their fingers through the chain-link, staring at the recaptured things, none of which looked much like treasure. "Just think," Delta said, "all that stuff was dropped or thrown or lost to flooding by somebody. And it wasn't just forgotten, or people wouldn't have been out there watching to see what he would bring up. Some of it was missed. You know, Earlene came to watch the diving for a few days. She said she was looking to get back something she had lost."

"Her heart? It's been at the bottom of the river all these years?"

Delta shook her head, as if Sunday's resentment of Earlene was merely pathetic. "She said that twenty years before, she had dropped the All-State trophy she won in freshman high school track in there. And I guess she wanted it back."

"Really? I wonder why she dropped it there."

"I don't know. She didn't say. But I wonder if it might be here. I wonder if it's worth her taking a look."

Sunday folded the price sheet he had given them and put it in her bag. "Anyway, I'm glad we took some kind of action. At least we can start thinking about what to do about the markers."

"Well . . . and I just don't know, Sunday . . ." When she had finally located both her cigarettes and lighter, she pulled her sister close to shield the flame from the wind. "I don't know if it's right. Don't you think it's kind of like exhuming a casket or disturbing the dead to change a gravestone?"

"That's just the point, Delta. He wasn't dead."

The best thing about cutting stone was that it allowed him to move past his own trouble. When Felix communed with the rock, he forgot the solitude that came down on him sometimes, blade-edge-sharp. He forgot all that the years had taken from him, the promise of youth and lost loved ones, and the abandoned and alien feminine possessions, corset and lipstick stub, brush with its few trapped hairs, that he had only had two days to get used to before he was alone, once more. Unmindful of the dust that covered him, he dipped from the water barrel to reveal the grain and flecks in the stone and to cool his chisel and gouge. He had invested in expensive power tools that got the job done faster and more perfectly, but he found that they took some of the satisfaction and joy out of the effort, so he used them for certain things, but still did part of his work by hand.

He liked marble best, but no one could afford it much. There was granite of different colors, and limestone. Each material had its own responses and he knew how to deal with them all. He understood stone, and when he was working slow and steady on a monument, he felt all right with the world.

As long as people were dying he had work, for the white population had their headstones cut and installed by him, too. Though they weren't keen on being buried next to colored folks, they didn't mind having one do their memorial work. The stone he was cutting was for a white man, a "cracker," most of his people would say. A Marine and farmer and husband and father and son, unknown to him personally, perhaps the kind of man who wouldn't have ever spoken or even nodded at him if they had passed downtown. But they were connected now, past everything on the level of skin.

"So . . ." the dead man's wife had said, bending and unbending the strap of her pocketbook while she had told him what she wanted, "he's gone now, and somehow we'll get on." He had nodded and let a hush settle over the shop so that she would have room to tell him about the man she was mourning, and what he had meant to her. Felix knew it was relief from the prospect of an ongoing acquaintance that enabled her to speak, and he figured that hearing her out was part of his job. After she told her story, she asked for images of a heart and corn stalk, and said that the Marine Corps should appear somewhere.

He preferred it when they left the rendering to him, just telling him the elements they needed and giving him the liberty to carve them as he wished. He was working on the swell of the heart and its intersection with a stalk of corn, but he couldn't focus. It was no good because he was thinking too much, so he stopped and put his chisels down.

He remembered Sunday, the one who did the talking, from a good many years before. Her hair had been different, but that emphatic quality in her was unforgettable. The other one had a kind of fierceness, too, but it was turned inward, he thought. Without a doubt they were sisters, for their common fire and the set of their mouths were unmistakable, and his years of watching families interact had told him that their relations were charged and difficult. He had known something was wrong between them the day before, when he saw them sitting so stiff and far apart.

And they were kin, he realized, to the woman everyone had called Nana J. Although he knew people said her husband, Mr. Blount, had been money-hungry and unforgiving, nobody ever had anything bad to say about her. He recalled making that marker for the family of those girls, nearly forty years before. There was some kind of hard story, harder than usual, of a lovely young woman left alone, and something . . . a tragic accident? No, he didn't know the circumstances, but remembered that it had been a suicide.

Now what had brought those women to him, he puzzled, and what did they want to change? It couldn't be a happy story, but then, happy wasn't his domain.

He washed his hands and shed his coveralls, transferring the dime his granny had given him to ward off haints nearly fifty years before, to his shirt, climbing the stairs to the flat above his shop. Nope, he thought, he wasn't interested in the happy stories, as the used-book and -furniture seller was fond of pointing out, although he never minded having Felix relieve him of all kinds of dusty and unwanted volumes. The shelves with which he had lined his room, made of planks and pieces of stone, were filled with dictionaries, encyclopedias and atlases, reference books on plants and birds and stars. But most of all, he had devoted himself to collecting novels and stories.

"Thirty-six years ago," he muttered as he went to the fireproof strongbox for his thick, cloth-covered notebooks. He searched among them, putting aside the one listing items recovered from the river, and pulling out the one marked "1950–1969." Starting with 1957 and flipping forward, he ran his index finger down the pages until he found what he was looking for under 1961.

Felix carried the notebook back to his easy chair and began to read, curious suddenly to see what that whole year had meant for him. By that time, he had been in Salt County carving tombstones for a decade, and that year there was a flood, his general, end-of-the-year notes told him, one of many he had weathered, and racial unrest involving brick-throwing downtown. He read through his description and drawing of each marker he had carved.

He had made notations about his impressions of those who had come to order stones, about appearance, deceased's occupation, cause of death. There were sketches of angels and flowers, crosses and hearts, praying hands, and he had added reflections on the people who came in and the things they had told him about their lost loved ones. He wasn't sure why he made his chronicle, for he had no descendants to whom he intended to pass it down. He just knew that something drove him to do it, to make a story of what he had seen.

Finally, he came to the entry for Mercury Owens, and when he saw his sketch of the headstone, a little piece of the past returned to him.

"That's it," he mumbled, as the details of the story came back to him, "that's it."

He decided to quit carving for the afternoon; his back was tired from the hauling he had been doing down at the river. Maybe he would go back downstairs later, but for a while, he would try to lose himself in a novel. When he finished a book, he wrote a paragraph on its inside cover, jotting down the things he had liked and disliked, and what it had made him think about in his own life.

Felix borrowed from the library, but he also combed the Goodwill bins and the used-book shop's shelves for discarded and discounted books. He tried never to pay more than a dollar, and he didn't mind the creases and underlines and cracked spines, which showed that people had been there before him.

The new chain bookstore he had visited once felt to him like another planet, and he didn't like the slick, cheap feel of brand-new paperbacks. Peering through the window of a fluorescent-lighted store at the mall in the next county, he had shaken his head and thought how cold it seemed. "It's like a clinic in there," he said to himself. "That kind of thing could turn you off the printed page altogether."

Though he knew they were less valuable to tradesmen, he liked the smell and feel of his old books. They took him back to warm and safe afternoons at the tiny, local library that had been made from a clapboard house, where his mother had taken him when he was eight, introducing herself and her son to the librarians so that they would watch over him with special care while she went to her second job. Barely able to read herself, she had known enough to make it possible for him, and there he had found that he was not alone.

He had dropped out of the eleventh grade, in a hurry to grow up and start earning money in his uncle's stonemason shop, and had, over the next few years, ceased to read. And then, after he found himself abandoned, following a two-day honeymoon cruise from Detroit to Cleveland, he had turned to books. After a string of sleepless days and nights in a rented room, fingering the few traces he had been left of his vanished bride, he had remembered reading. Taking her few discarded possessions, he had hit the road, bent on finding his way back to the afternoon feeling that his mother had provided.

Wandering the narrow aisles of another small-town library and flipping through drawers of faded catalog cards, he had looked for a place to begin. After reading description after description, he had settled on two authors who seemed to be writing lives he knew something about, and he had begun with Zola, going down, down into the narrow miner's shaft. And then he had been led by Balzac down winding city streets, and into the life of a fellow stonemason by Hardy. With continuing hunger, he had read everything he could get his hands on, without much plan. Sometimes he moved through the shelves in order, or went alphabetically through the catalog until snagged by something else. He fed an interest in geography and history, but always returned to fiction, and if he liked a novel, he read everything by that writer he could find.

Felix would have to admit that he had spent many a lonely hour in his sixty-odd years. But in depending on the characters he met through reading, he felt that he had chosen well. His stone-carving had provided him one safe way to see people on the inside, his recent river excavations had told him more, and the rest had been given by books.

After warming a can of soup, he settled into his easy chair and reached for his latest novel. Occupied with working his way through Dostoyevsky, he was in the middle of *The Brothers Karamazov*. It had sent him many times to his dictionary and reference books, and he had the damnedest time trying to pronounce the names in his head, but he loved the Russians, with their thick, complicated plots and their tackling of trouble and grief. Sometimes he had to put the book down and shake his head at how piercing it was. That Fyodor surely did know people, Felix said to himself, he surely did.

He tried, but he couldn't quite depart from his life to enter the world of the book. When the author had taken him almost to a bridge in St. Petersburg, he found himself back at the water and the river of Salt County.

The next morning he would see what he could make of the gravestone he had dredged up. It was thick with muck and algae, but maybe he would be able to make out some of the words or the dates. And he needed to do some cleaning and cataloging of his more recent finds. As he planned his tasks, it dawned on him that he not only recognized the one sister from years ago, and the two of them from the day before. The prim and guarded one had come, day after day, to watch him dive, and he wondered what it was of hers that she was thinking he might find.

His mind kept returning to Dolora Blount Owens and that 1961 flood. Over the years, he had worried a great deal about the flooding, from which there was now and then a reprieve, but never full deliverance.

Although it rested on a bit of a hill, Our Cemetery was on lower ground than Greenlawn, and it had always been susceptible to the rising water. He wanted to believe that his people had finally found untrammeled peace in death, but he dreamt at times of sunken and dislocated headstones and caskets that floated off and were never seen again. And sometimes he dreamt that he was back in that giving, taking river, surveying all of its sunken treasure and waste. There he would be, swimming through its obstacle course of lost objects, unable to surface from the watery dark.

"Please," he said, thinking of the gravestone he had uncovered, "not that dream tonight." He hoped the river he knew so well would keep within its banks and not wreak havoc on the living and the dead. Sighing, he opened his book, determined to return to a St. Petersburg past, investing his faith in Fyodor to take him somewhere that was different, yet known.

10

When they got home from Felix Harris's shop, Sunday declared that it was time to visit Opus again. Reluctant to join her, Delta talked about getting started on dinner and began to list other pressing responsibilities, but instead of giving up, Sunday urged her. "Come on, Delta," she said, "I need you with me. Don't you see?" She remembered Opus's stern gaze at the news that they had been estranged for five full years, and told her that her presence would mean more than she could know.

When she called, Opus told her to come on over, and asked how she felt about inviting Laveen Walker, the other surviving member of the Bread Ladies. Sunday thought it was a good idea, for although Opus had been Nana's closest friend, all of those women had been instrumental in raising them, and Laveen might be able to help, too.

"We're here," Sunday said proudly when Opus unlocked the door, leaning on her cane and patting the fine net on her hair. As Delta stooped to hug her, Opus smiled over her shoulder at Sunday, acknowledging her effort to repair their rift.

Laveen arrived, as always, in a color-coordinated outfit, her skirt, blouse, jacket, purse, hat, shoes, and jewelry all a color she called "garnet." Sunday remembered her signature custom: When she found a pattern she liked, she sewed seven identical garments, out of different fabrics, in the colors that she had decided, early on, suited her. She rotated them, according to season, for several years, and when she was tired of them, she started over with seven of something new.

She entered the room with the spry, bowlegged walk Sunday remembered, handing out souvenirs she had brought back from her latest trip and looking even livelier than the last time Sunday had seen her, at Nana's funeral. "Miz Walker, I swear you have somehow found the secret of aging backward. I think you get younger as the years wear on."

Laveen rolled her laugh around in her mouth, as if to taste it before letting it go. "You know the right thing to say, Sunday Owens, and it makes me wonder, when you compliment me like that, if you've brought me here to steal the little bit of my fortune."

Opus laughed at their long-standing joke. Ten years before, Laveen had taken the money her husband, DeLoach, had left her from his funeral home business, and had invested it well. Against the advice of many of her friends, she was spending that money to travel everywhere she had ever dreamt, and to give her friends and family special little gifts. Nobody would ever have to steal from Laveen, for she offered whatever she had, saying, "Money is for spending and sharing, and as my mama used to say, love is the one thing you can multiply by dividing."

Sunday looked at the garnet ensemble and remembered that the Bread Ladies had relished teasing her about her eccentric approach to clothes, and she had said they were just jealous of her "sartorial splendor." She had loved coordinated clothes and linguistic precision, and her job as school librarian had put her "in propinquity," she used to say, "to words."

"Why say in a few simple words what can be said in twenty-five you've got to look up?" Opus had often asked. Although Laveen's intoxication with language sometimes tried the Bread Ladies' patience, they understood that rather than putting on airs, she was enjoying herself, and they had loved seeing such delight and facility with language in someone who had gone back for her GED and pursued library science while she had a full-time job. And they got a kick out of her description of herself as a "wordologist," and her fervor to develop something she said "white folks don't think we've got a clue about." Each time they baked bread, she would have a new word, "peregrination," "tumescent," "aqueous," which she would try to "throw on them" throughout the afternoon. As Sunday listened to her, she thought about Mercury's attachment to "quandary," imagining that Laveen would like that word as well.

"Do you still do crosswords?" Sunday asked, as Laveen was pouring the tea Opus had brought out.

"Oh my, yes. Now that I'm retired, I do them every single day. And the more arduous, the better. There was a time I did the Sunday *Times* puzzle in pencil, but no longer. Now I do it in indelible pen, even if it takes me several days."

Opus shook her head and told Laveen she ought to "stop her bragging," and continuing the banter they had been keeping up for decades, Laveen responded, "Just jealous. Just jealous of my extraordinary linguistic prowess."

All four of them laughed, and then the chatter turned to Salt County news. *Did you come on the train? You know they're redoing the station.* Sunday half listened, moving back into the past, tethered by the last two Bread Ladies, and then forward to the now. *They're going to restore it to its former elegance.* Back and forth she moved. *And did you see the wrought-iron clock down at the bridge? And the new courthouse steps?* She wondered how they would transition into what had brought her and Delta there.

When Opus had dialed Laveen earlier on her heavy, black rotary phone, she had told her about Mercury Owens's sudden reappearance, and Laveen had forgone elaborate language and exclaimed, "Stop your lying, girl. Say it isn't so."

"It's no lie, honey," Opus had reassured her, "it's truth," and then filled her in on the details Sunday had shared. Laveen had interrupted several times with "Are you *certain?*" demonstrating her typical resistance to accepting bad news. "Laveen, listen. What I'm telling you is fact. I know this is hard to digest, but please do try. Maybe there's something good in it, for the girls, I mean. Now do you want to come on over and help them work it through?"

She had paused, overcome with feeling for the Owens girls. "Yes, of course I do. But it's just too much. I didn't really think that story could get any worse. And I don't mind telling you that I just can't help imagining what Valentine would say."

And there they sat, quietly sipping tea, each unwilling to be the first to speak about why they were gathered. Delta's eyes were cautious and evasive as she fidgeted with the buttons on her cuffs and stole glances at the purse that held her cigarettes. Laveen's garnet form was perched stiffly on her narrow chair and she focused intently on stirring her tea, looking as though she wished life were a crossword, where things fit sensibly together and there are right answers to fill up all the interlocking blanks.

"So . . ." Sunday said, figuring it was on her to get the talking started.

Three pairs of eyes met hers. Three pairs of eyebrows lifted in wary curiosity.

She decided to plunge in. "I guess Opus told you about why I'm back home, Miz Walker. About," she said, nodding at Delta, "our father reappearing. By mail, that is. Well, it has raised a lot of questions for us," she said, "questions about long ago, and we're trying to make some kind of sense of what happened. The fact is, I've always had a lot of questions. More questions than answers, I sometimes think."

She stopped and took a sip of tea. "Well . . . one of the things we've been talking about is the way I was not named."

Delta noticed Sunday's reliance on the word "well," and didn't feel so bad about her own inadequacy.

Laveen put down her cup and cleared her throat. "I'm confounded," she said, looking around at the others, and when no one spoke, her anxiety grew and she asked, "Not named?" as though her question was reluctant, but necessary.

Sunday smiled nervously. "I guess you weren't aware, Miz Walker, but . . . my mother never gave me a name."

Laveen looked as though she couldn't fathom what accounted for such a thing. After all, she was a believer in words. She looked from face to face in bewilderment. "I *have* read," she said, "how some tribal peoples avoided naming to confound the deities, or how, in times of famine, they gave their infants disagreeable assignations that would discourage the deities from taking them. Dolora must have had a good reason. Was her logic something along those lines?"

When she got no answer, she went on, "We called you Sister like your family did, but I just thought it was a nickname. It never occurred to me that you didn't have an appellation of your own. And then, when they started calling you Sunday, I thought it had been yours all along." She couldn't help but ask, leaning forward, "Are you positive? Are you absolutely sure?"

Sunday and Delta stared at her with no idea how to respond, and Opus shot her an impatient look over the top of her glasses and rescued them from silence. "Really, Laveen. What is it that you're doubting, after all?"

Sunday directed her next question to Opus. "Delta says that you were there when I was born, and just after, when Nana tried to get Mama to pick a name. And I was wondering," she said, hearing her voice quaver, "do you remember what went on?"

"Yes," Opus answered, "I was there when you were born. We all were, in fact. Nana J. made it clear to me that I was not to repeat her words, but she talked to me over the years about it." She hesitated. "I guess all those who would ask for her silence are gone. I don't mind saying I've had some misgivings about you all dredging up these old, painful matters, but I guess it has a place in what you're needing to do. It's all related to your daddy, and in any case, I'm aware that there are things, sometimes hard things, that people need to know. But I do want to say that whatever heartache and complicated feelings there were for your mama, the day you came into the world was a blessed day. For all of us. We were all there."

"Standing around the bed," Delta volunteered.

Laveen nodded, recalling Dolora's silent tears. "That's right. And you, Delta, you got very worked up because you wanted to get on the bed with your mama, like the baby was. You were feeling excluded, and Nana J. tried to comfort you."

Delta blushed as Opus spoke. "And then the others left, and it was just me and Nana J., with Delta on her lap while Dolora was nursing you, Sunday, and I recall that Nana J. got up and went over to your mama, who was silent as could be. She asked her what name she had decided on, so that the midwife could register what she had picked.

"And . . . Dolora didn't say a single word, but the tears kept running down her face. Nana J. kept talking, to fill in the quiet, it seemed. And then she looked at me anxiously, frowning, and back to her. 'Maybe you need a day or so to figure out what strong, lovely name is just right for this precious girl,' she said. 'Isn't that right, sugar,' she cooed, taking you from your mama, 'a name that's special and just yours, that you can live up to.'

"When Dolora still didn't say a word, she said, 'A child's got to have a name, Dolora. It wouldn't be right not to give her one.' Nana J. said she thought about how Lomax had chosen Wilborn, and how she had picked Dolora after seeing it somewhere and thinking it was musical and unique. And after a long stretch of waiting and looking at each other across the bed, Nana J. had said, 'You just take some time to think on it, and till then, we'll call her "Sister." That will do for now.'

187

"Nana J. sent Delta down to the kitchen to tell the midwife she could go, and then we collected up the diaper cloths and got your mama comfortable. 'You get some sleep now,' Nana J. said, stroking her hair, and when we reached the doorway, Dolora finally spoke.

"What she said was something I could never forget. She turned to us, her head against the pillow on its side, and said, 'Leave the naming to her. There'll be little enough in life that she can choose.'"

"Say it isn't so," was the first thing out of Laveen's mouth.

Opus pursed her lips and shook her head, fascinated that, in moments of amazement, Laveen relinquished her extensive vocabulary and blurted out her comments plain.

Delta was stunned by the last part of Opus's story, by the statement from Dolora after she had left. She sat back in her chair, realizing that even if she had heard it, it wouldn't have made much sense to her at the time. After so many years, it closed a gap in her understanding, for the story she had made about the strength in choosing had been right; her mother had intended something positive, after all.

Astounded and speechless, Sunday stared at Opus, who, meeting her look, declared, "It's truth."

They all got up to refresh their tea and Delta excused herself to the patio for a smoke while Sunday went to the windowless bathroom and stood in the dark. She leaned against the sink and hugged herself. There had been love for her in it, she thought, and a gift, however mishandled, had been intended, after all.

When they reconvened in the living room, Sunday was the first to speak. "The thing is this, Miz Green. I was never named, but I was never told, either, during the next five years or ever after, that letting me choose was what Mama had in mind."

At that, Laveen looked even more stricken. She jumped up and went to the kitchen. "Don't you have anything to nibble on in here?" she called out. "I'll bring this banana bread out."

"I swear, Sunday," Opus said, "I had no idea she and Nana J. never told you her reason, and I can't imagine why not." Laveen returned with enough sliced bread for twenty people and Opus passed the plate while she collected her thoughts.

"I remember, after leaving your mama in her bed and closing the door, that I pulled Nana J. by her sleeve into the next room and argued. 'A girl's first name is extra important,' I said, 'because she'll likely marry and give up her last. Her first name is one of the few things of her own she has to carry through her life.' And Nana J. reassured me not to worry. It would all work out, she said. 'She'll name this baby yet.' You see, regardless of Dolora's parting statement, Nana J. clearly thought that she would change her mind.

"It always seemed to me that Dolora, and even Mercury, must have picked, or at least thought about, some names. That's what people do when babies are on the way. And then, with his . . . his death, she must have let them go. And maybe once she had failed to speak, it was harder and harder for both your mama and Nana J. to face it and to fix it. Once they had given in to silence, it must have been tough to renounce. And maybe, as time wore on and Sunday became old enough to receive their explanation, they couldn't seem to extract that tiny bit of providence, without meeting the problem, whole."

"Does that seem like Nana J. to you?" Laveen asked.

"No, it doesn't. That kind of lapse doesn't fit with my idea of her, because she had such strength and drive. But you know, I've been thinking lately of the way people have these pockets of inconsistent things in them. My Wilson was like that, in these funny ways. I guess there was a part of Nana J., seldom seen, that could fold in the face of trouble."

Opus gazed into the distance. "Once, at church, she suddenly gave up the fight we women were waging for more decision-making." She stopped talking again and thought back. "Time and again, she let both son and husband interrogate her and order her around. She was strong, but just like most of us, she was deferential at home, making sure to have dinner on the table by six o'clock . . . fixing Lomax's plate." Opus knew that both she and Nana J. had sometimes been passive in the face of disaster or doubt. She declared, "I'm sure that Nana J., knowing how wrong it was for you to go unnamed, pressed Dolora for weeks that turned into months, each time thinking she would take care of it, each time saying, 'Well, tomorrow, then.'

"We've all wanted and needed to believe certain things. Here's the point: People aren't absolute, and this is truth."

She had been astonished every now and then, by Wilson's abrupt lapses in functioning, like the time she found he had been putting letters from the IRS in a drawer for a year. Sometimes he just hadn't been able to cope, and whenever it happened it was shocking, good as he was in general at meeting things head-on. And her own mother was divided, prone to enormous kindness, but sometimes selfish and small. And just look at the two of you, she thought, glancing at Delta and Sunday, you've undermined your love with holding back.

"As for your mama," she continued, "she might have doubted the rightness of her decision, later on, but for quite a while, I figure it was like this: On the outside, she went on taking care of things, deciding what needed ironing and what needed doing at work, while inside, something in her just closed up, like a fist.

"I ask you," she said, looking around, "who has any of us ever loved that's not divided? Who have you known that's just one thing?"

Sunday's eyes were huge as she listened to Opus. Divided? She knew it described her. Look what had happened with Delta. Look at the push and pull with Reed. She sighed, overwhelmed at the truths told and silences broken in the space of two days. At least her mother had had a reason, whether or not it made sense to Sunday, and at least she was putting together an account of things that would help her to understand and forgive.

Laveen weighed in with her opinion. "I don't think your mother was in her proper frame of consciousness. I don't think she was really herself."

"Maybe not," Opus said. "She had been so taken with Mercury, at such a young age, and I don't think she could fix her mind around the fact that he had gone and left her, for the grave, or so she thought. Nana J. once told me she believed that unfinished task of naming might just force Dolora to pull herself together. Nana J. talked about it a lot for a couple of years, and then she stopped bringing it up. But maybe it just got more and more difficult to do, and at some point, she just surrendered, as all of us sometimes do."

"I'm sure Nana J. put forth her most strenuous effort," Laveen said passionately.

Opus went on, "And then I think she decided on a way to think about it that was easier. That it was Dolora's to handle, that it would all somehow work out. One thing's for sure, no one could argue with you, Sunday, unusual as the name you picked turned out to be. Nana J. and Dolora both felt proud of a five-year-old with that kind of ingenuity, and I think they both felt relieved, along with guilty, that the issue had finally been resolved. I think they suspected you would eventually change it to something more standard, but for the time being, you would be Sunday if you wished." She reached for her cup. "I guess they did the best they could, but my, my, people do mess up."

Delta felt the image of Dolora's muting hands edging into her consciousness. My, my, people do, she thought.

Sunday was nodding. "And what about Grandpa?" Sunday asked. "What did he think?"

Laveen folded her arms and sucked her teeth with utter eloquence. None of the Bread Ladies had been fond of him, but she had a bottomless well of rancor where he was concerned. It was as if she had focused her entire ability to see the human potential for wrong onto Lomax Blount.

Opus looked at her and thought, Oh Lord, here we go, aware that the mention of Lomax Blount's name worked like an ON switch for Laveen. She quickly continued, "Nana J. told me much later that she had managed to keep the situation from Mr. Blount, and he was so preoccupied with the store and the Masons that he didn't know until you were almost two that Sister was the only name you had. 'You mean to tell me the child's not been named?' he yelled, demanding that Nana J. take the situation in hand and choose. He didn't understand women, he said, and tried to force several names on them, insisting that he could decide if they were incompetent to do so. 'How hard *is* it, J.?' he hollered. 'Just pick something. Pick Sarah. Pick Mildred. Better yet, pick Linda, it's a perfectly good name. It doesn't have to be fancy or mysterious, and it means pretty, which is a good enough thing for a girl to try to be. Just take care of it, for God's sake, woman. Just follow through.'

"I guess he didn't live long enough to be truly disgusted by their failure to do so."

Laveen placed her cup and saucer on the table and said with satisfaction, "Expired of a massive heart attack, though he'd scarcely been sick a day in his life. Collapsed right over the cash register, arms embracing his most beloved thing."

Sunday and Delta knew Grandpa had died at the store, but they had never heard that detail. They looked to Opus for confirmation and she shook her head regretfully, and said, "I'm afraid it's truth."

A lull in the talking gave Delta the chance to ask a question that had always interested her. "That's another question: How did they get together, then, Nana and Grandpa? How did they meet?"

"Well, I know all about that," Laveen volunteered, "I was there. Opus and the others came later, but Nana J., of course we called her Jetta in those days, she and I went all the way back to the paper mill."

Sunday interrupted her to ask why Nana had changed her name from Johnetta, to Jetta, to Nana J.

"Well," Laveen answered, "she had been named after her father, and she said her name meant 'little girl version of John.' She decided she didn't want to be a little version of anything, least of all her father, who was prone to penury and had a frigid temperament. So instead of doing away with the name altogether, she made it into something she was comfortable with, and later, when Delta came along and she became Nana to you all, she let the rest go and adopted Nana J."

So, Sunday thought, she had shaped her bequest to fit her life.

"When she met your grandfather," Laveen continued, "Nana J. had already been wedded once. The first husband had expired in a farm accident of some nature, and she had come to Salt County seeking employment at the paper mill. She worked tirelessly to support herself, prior and subsequent to her unfortunate marriage to Lomax Blount, until his investments began to pay off, and she continued to toil tirelessly and thanklessly for him at the store.

"But you see, he was from the northern part of Illinois, and Nana J. was from Mississippi, which he considered backward and uncouth, its brutal history of enslavement and debasement something tantamount to shameful, something to be escaped. He was of the opinion that marriage to him would elevate Nana J., endow her with class. Of course, he failed to understand that class does not derive from affluence, place of origin, or noble birth. Class derives from how one treats people.

"In any case, they had encountered one another at the paper mill. He walked, or rather strutted arrogantly by, like he was the center of attention, and she didn't even notice him, didn't even look up. And more and more he tried to get her attention, but she didn't seem to know he existed, and that was probably what fed his determination to have her most of all. To him, it was partly a triumph of will.

"She wasn't so sure about Lomax Blount at first. Moreover, she was supporting herself and liked not answering to anyone for the first time in her life. He was stiff and formal, what your generation calls 'square' and ours called 'gentlemanly,' and he was always humorless. But he was ambitious and serious about the future, and he customarily spoke about how he was going to have security and lasting, 'quality things,' and one of them would be a gold pocket watch, which he coveted through the window of a store down on the main street. She finally consented to accompany him to get a cold drink one afternoon, mostly to dispose of him, I'm sure, and he continued talking about what he would have and remained in steady pursuit of her, without receiving even the most chaste of kisses at the evening's end. I must say, Lomax Blount had tenacity, and I guess it served him well.

"I was working alongside her, and I'll never forget that day when she got her finger caught in one of those machines. She didn't even cry out, though, but bore her misfortune with the reserved strength for which she came to be known. When she lost half of that finger, he appeared to be of the opinion that her prospects for marriage had diminished, and that he would have a better chance. And he was also impressed by her fortitude. 'That woman could go the distance,' he said aloud, to no one in particular, on the factory floor.

"Me, however, he treated like refuse, or worse, as though I were invisible. I was too poor and backward, from the country, and far too dark. He viewed me as a 'common' or 'no 'count nigger,' to use two of his favorite terms."

"Wait a minute," Delta said, "he wasn't exactly light."

"Correct. But when did that kind of logic restrain the colored man? In any case, Lomax Blount was indefatigable," Laveen said, and noting the perplexity on the faces of the others, she again abandoned her customary diction and declared matter-of-factly, "I think he wore her down. He was hardworking, ambitious, driven, and he was not the type to be either physically violent or unfaithful. And I believe, as well, that in addition, she badly desired the experience of motherhood. Once she married him and he started making money, he began to institute a program not unlike a monarchy."

Sunday found her anger rising on behalf of her grandmother. "I would have put my foot up his ass, that's for sure. Reed knows he better not come talking about where's my dinner, or be quiet, or bring me my robe. I wouldn't have it, that's all, and men have to be trained to understand that."

Opus broke in with, "Honey, women of our generation catered to men. We both did it." She nodded at Laveen. "I acted like every word out of my Wilson's mouth was brilliant, and asked questions about mundane matters I could have given less than a damn about. I built him up, and shrunk myself sometimes, so that he would feel special and safe. My mother showed me, by example, how to keep my man. It was what we learned. Nana J. liked being taken care of, and maybe she liked being the wife of a prosperous man."

"Yes," Laveen said, "I guess she did, but that seemed like such a minor part of who she was. And did she get the benefits she thought she would? In my opinion, nothing could have been worth the price of waking up next to Lomax Blount."

Delta and Sunday listened, wide-eyed, struck by the depth of her contempt, and Opus added, "When he died, she was only fifty-five. We encouraged her to find another husband or companion, but she said the thing she wanted least was to be tied down to another man. She made a point to say that Mr. Blount had been decent to her, but she wasn't ever waiting on or answering to anyone again. Two husbands were plenty, she said, for one lifetime."

"So what did he think of our . . . father? Did he ever give him a chance?"

"No, he didn't, Delta," Laveen answered, "but that had less to do than you might think with your father. Anyone to whom Lomax Blount took a dislike could forget ever receiving his respect."

"Then what was it about him, about our father, that is?"

Opus thought for a moment, and then spoke. "Mercury was good-looking in the easy-smiling way that made Mr. Blount suspicious. You know, he had those delicate features that made him 'damn near pretty,' Lomax said. He had the loose way of a charmer, too, and he talked real big. Also, Mr. Blount thought he had no manners, that he was 'low class.'

"He did things like keep his hat on in the house, and he put his foot up on the coffee table once. Sometimes he chewed on a toothpick or a stick of gum while he talked his big talk, and Dolora always defended him, which seemed to make your grandpa even madder. 'If that boy worked as hard as he dreams,' your grandpa would say, 'he might have the chance of becoming something one of these days.'"

Delta and Sunday both thought of how they had just learned that Grandpa had been a dreamer, too, trying to impress Nana with his intentions of being a big man and wearing a pocket watch. If he hated that in Mercury, did he hate it in himself?

Sunday asked, "But didn't he work at the plant? That was always what we heard."

"Yes, indeed, he worked hard at those paper bags," Opus answered. "Hated every minute of it, too, as anyone with a smidgen of sense would."

Laveen spoke out angrily again. "And then he had to come home to confront familial contempt. Now Lomax could have assisted him, don't you think? He could have helped him get ahead."

"Yes," Opus added, "but no one had done that for him, Mr. Blount argued, and he wanted Mercury to make his way, just as he had. Of course he certainly didn't apply that standard to Wilborn, and that was a boy with no respect at all."

Opus shook her head. "I've never really understood his blind spot with Mercury. Even at the memorial service, his posture and his callous expression seemed to say, 'I could have predicted this. I told you so.'"

"Once," Laveen said, "Nana told me it was partly the way Mercury talked. Mr. Blount was embarrassed by the slips he himself had sometimes made early on. I remember when he misused a word and a co-worker corrected him, and his face looked as though it might combust. He was embarrassed that he had dropped out after one year of college. And he didn't like the ease with which Mercury spoke, or the 'fancy words' he used. 'He's a dandy. A braggart,' he said. 'There's something deep down trifling about that boy.'

"But I don't think he really liked anyone very much. You know, he didn't approve of us meeting to make our bread," Laveen said, smiling, as if the idea of his discomfort pleased her. "Too much feminine power concentrated into one place."

Opus shared her recollections. "When we first got started, in nineteen fifty-four or fifty-five, Nana J. had the idea that the church could earn money and feed its struggling members by making bread. She invited us over without asking him, and he had a fit about it, telling her she should get permission for such a thing. Now that, she wasn't having. 'Isn't this my home?' she demanded. 'You've got the Masons and this is my fellowship.' He was offended by the comparison of a bunch of cackling, cooking women to his formal brotherhood of gentlemen, who had earned their community's respect. But that was one time she didn't back down, and he let the permission thing drop, seeing how it had failed to fly. But he called us The Ravens, and fussed that we were always 'caw, caw, cawing.' He always made a show of putting his coat on and leaving the house as we arrived.

"But well, he did tithe, and he was generous enough to help fund the church renovations, and build the Masons' lodge, things like that," Opus pointed out, feeling the need to redeem him in some way.

"Nonsense. He didn't have a benevolent corpuscle in his body. Any contributions he made were for recognition and social prominence. He gave the church money to get his name on a pew, and he didn't even attend services unless Nana J. made him."

Delta and Sunday squirmed. They hoped the conversation would move on quickly from the topic of church, for both of them were waiting to be asked when they had last been to a service, and neither one wanted to reveal how long it had been.

"Laveen, that's extreme. You don't know what motivated his good works, and you're talking about their grandpa, after all."

"Well, I thought you believed in honesty. Isn't that what you're always saying, 'It's truth. It's truth.' These girls are here for the unadulterated picture, are you not?"

In response to the challenge, they nodded, hard as it was getting to accept more bad news.

"All I'm saying," Opus added, "is that what you're telling is your truth."

Laveen rolled her eyes, happy to go on with her tale. She told how after Mercury died, Grandpa had refused to give or even loan Dolora any money toward buying a house. He felt she should earn it, and learn to make better judgments and choices. "But you insisted that she marry him," Nana J. had said, arguing that it would help to give Dolora and her children a start of their own. "And you can afford it, with the earnings from the store this year and the rent those apartments are bringing in," she had said, breaking his house rule of never speaking about their assets.

When he still refused, Nana had gotten a job answering the phone at the funeral home that Laveen's husband owned, and although he preferred her not to work, he wouldn't budge on his refusal to help Dolora buy that house. Together, Nana J. and Dolora had saved for a down payment, and when he died, four years after Sunday was born, Nana J. gave Dolora the rest.

"That was the only financial help Dolora would ever take from Nana," Opus told the others, "and she paid every bit of it back. Through that effort to stand on her own, she was trying to prove her strength to her father, and she was redeeming her faulty judgment about Mercury, too."

Laveen's face was flushed as she shook her head and muttered, "You know that was a gotdamn shame."

Delta and Sunday marveled at the depth of her animosity toward Grandpa. It had to involve more than what had been said. What had he done, they wondered, to inspire a wrath that would survive his death by thirty-two years?

Sunday had barely known him, but even for Delta, he had been less a man than a figure. Stern, exacting, all-powerful. Delta wondered whether he had let go with his Mason brothers, whether there was anywhere he was just an average man. With Nana he must have been, she thought. But Delta had been afraid of his starched clothes and his scrutiny, and the forced way he talked to her made her sometimes feel like Bertha, her favorite doll. He had often volunteered compliments about her poise and grace, and said he knew she would make him proud. But he had required that "I love you" from her and others; he had been able to compel the answer he wanted, without accountability for what produced it.

"So tell me," Sunday asked, steeling herself for the answer, "what was the 'no 'count nigger' thing?" She hadn't been able to get that phrase out of her head since Laveen had first uttered it.

Laveen sucked her teeth. "He thought of himself as committed to his race, but he used phrases like that without apparent shame. It had bothered Nana J. and she never stopped letting him know it, and sometimes I thought he said it just to get her goat."

Opus admitted that one time she and Wilson had gone to dinner at their house and she had been surprised to find that Mr. Blount had a flair for drama and timing, for she had rarely seen him jocular. They had all laughed at his "nigger" jokes. Willie Jones, Attorney-at-Law, signing his name with an "XX, XXX." Things you could leave in a "nigger" neighborhood without fear of them being stolen: books, the employment Want Ads, toothbrushes. Later, when they got home, Opus and Wilson had trouble falling asleep, unsettled as they were by the undertone of self-hatred in the jokes, and by their own laughing complicity.

Both Sunday and Delta looked at the floor. Maybe that's what the Masons did, sat around and talked about "no 'count niggers," and "nigger" women, no doubt, except that maybe they were so low they didn't merit mentioning. There was another part of their inheritance, then. Would the bad news ever end?

They knew it wasn't unusual for Grandpa's generation to have had shame and contempt built into the idea of "uplifting" themselves. Some people were better than others, house and field, light and dark. But their family had been laborers on both sides. People of their own generation who talked that way were ridiculed, openly vilified, as embarrassments of the race. Except that aboveboard self-hatred seemed to be making a comeback, and it was no mystery why blacks who talked that talk seemed to thrive.

Opus couldn't deny that Mr. Blount had been like that, but she tried to find a way to think about it that was not so harsh. "Laveen," she said, "in some of it, I have to believe he didn't really mean any harm. It was the times, don't you think? People talked that way. I remember my father saying he would like to get as far away as possible from black people. 'I hate niggers *and* white people,' he would say. 'Only folks I like are the four of us in this room.'"

"Go on. You can't be serious. That doesn't mean it meant and did no harm."

"But don't we have to laugh at ourselves?"

"Who do you believe he was laughing at?"

"Well . . ."

"Was he laughing at all?"

Opus thought for a moment. "He was set in his ways, Laveen."

"Lomax Blount was that way at thirty-one."

"Yes, but by then he had already had a trying life."

"Unlike the 'no 'counts' he despised?"

They paused, as if they suddenly heard the rising pitch of their voices and saw themselves through Delta and Sunday, whose heads were turning back and forth to follow the exchange.

"There's an excellent word for this," Laveen said. "I had it in a crossword yesterday. 'Contrapuntal,' that's what this conversation is."

That took some of the momentum out of their arguing.

"But seriously," Opus said in a calmer voice, "I know Mr. Blount was in some measure all the things you've said he was. But let's give his granddaughters something else to remember about him, too. I know you must have your reasons, but you've only ever been able to see one thing in him. There was his dignity and his achievements, too. He made his way from nothing with his will and his brain, and that was no small feat for a black man. My father was of that ilk, disrespected and reduced, and trying with hard work to distinguish himself, to make himself fully human to others by proving that colored folks could do the same as white. And I loved that proud and serious aspect of my papa, even if it had made him unyielding and harsh. He was a stand-up kind of man, and Wilson had that dignified and proper way, too.

"It couldn't have been easy to grow up then as a black man, seen and treated as subhuman . . . 'Move over, boy . . . don't look at my woman or you'll be swinging from that tree downtown . . . tote this and lift this . . . come through the back door . . . stay in your place.'

"Gardening for white men and taking their sweaty, funky clothes to the laundry, when you only had one shirt of your own. Toting and lifting at the sawmill and then the paper plant, where you got no respect as a man. And seeing light-skinned colored getting the chances in life," she argued, as if she felt guilty about her own, fair complexion, "that would make anyone mad, wouldn't it?"

Delta jumped in, surprising everyone, including herself. "Didn't my father grow up black and hungry, too? And toting at the plant? And who were these 'niggers' Grandpa looked down on? They must have looked just like him."

"And for that matter," Sunday added, "Nana worked at the plant. I'm tired of the black man blues. Men might have been two-thirds human, but women didn't count at all. It's not that I don't feel for them, in this world where male is supreme, but what about the sisters? Women didn't even get the vote till 1920, and sisters weren't exactly sitting home doing their nails and hauling in the respect. Why do you think Nana tolerated it," Sunday asked, after pausing to collect herself, "when she was so . . . so not that way?"

Laveen had a ready answer for that. "She had a truly capacious heart. She was adept at forgiveness, and at making up for what was wrong in him." Shaking her finger, she added, "I think her singing functioned like an antidote to his poisonous ways."

"Well, I think," said Opus, "that she hated that quality in him, and she never gave up arguing about things like the 'nigger' jokes. And I guess what she got from him was bigger than what she didn't get. All relations weigh out like that. And you must remember that in our generation, people stuck out their marriages and made the best of them."

"Nevertheless, our children don't choose us. And the ones who had to suffer from his rejection of Mercury were his daughter, her husband, and their girls. Treatment like that can wound people," Laveen said, tears collecting in her eyes, "and I should know."

They all looked away, to keep her from embarrassment, and then, when she had got her feelings in check, Opus asked gently, "Is there something you'd like to tell us, Laveen?"

She cleared her throat and dabbed at her eyes. "I'm cognizant of the fact that I'm speaking of your maternal grandfather and I mean no disrespect to the two of you, who are so . . ."

"No one will hear it as that," Opus said. "Now why don't you just cut to the chase."

Laveen straightened her shoulders, as if slightly hurt by Opus's direction. "Well, my quarrel with Lomax Blount is quite historical, though I didn't find out just how nefarious he was until much, much later.

"He had finally got Nana J. to marry him and was rising in stature here in Salt County, as he acquired property and joined the church. And after he got himself that gold pocket watch he had been coveting through the jeweler's window, he used to stroll along our part of town in the early evening, and he would stop and take it out to check the hour, every block or so it seemed to me, as though he had such important things to do that he had to keep a close patrol on the passage of time. So he had Nana J. and he was on the social climb, joining the Masons and the church. And I had moved on from the plant to working for a caterer, but still, I had no one, no husband or even beau. I never did have a plethora of suitors, for I was poor, from down South, skinny, and jet-black. People used to say, 'But you have sharp features,' as if that were a compensation for my color, as if that were the highest compliment. 'You are so lovely,' my very own grandma told me, 'if you just weren't so very dark.'

"As it turned out, Lomax Blount had a distant cousin from the more uppity branch of his family who relocated to town to initiate a funeral home enterprise. And shock of all shocks, this cousin was sweet on me. We started courting, and we really fell in love. Finally, finally, I had found someone who loved me for myself, who didn't follow observations on skin tone with 'but,' and he proposed marriage.

"However, Lomax Blount didn't think I was acceptable for his cousin, and he undertook a campaign to abort the betrothal. He went to his cousin and told him I was 'no 'count nigger trash.' 'You can do better,' he said, and he told him that he had detected a lassitude . . . my word, of course, not his, for his vocabulary, as I have noted, was quite limited . . . he had detected a lassitude in me at the paper plant. He said I came from 'common' people and would make an unsuitable mother and wife.

"DeLoach disregarded him, and married me despite his objections. But Lomax Blount refused to attend the wedding or to 'give his blessing,' as he called it, as though that were a prerequisite." Laveen was sitting on the edge of her seat, her garnet-clad arms moving and her neck rolling with indignation as she spoke. Her tears had stopped.

"DeLoach Walker married me nevertheless," she said, shaking her finger, and we were together for thirty rewarding years. But no thanks to Lomax Blount, who tried to take away my one blessed thing."

She sniffed as she pulled out a handkerchief, monogrammed in garnet thread. She felt foolish for letting her hurt show. "I know it seems like an inconsequential matter, a little thing, after all, and practically antideluvian, it occurred so long ago. I never knew about it until just before DeLoach died, ten years ago this December. Otherwise, I would have never set foot in his house, despite my love for Nana J. I knew he was mean-spirited, but I didn't even know how I had been disparaged, as you see.

"I can tell you this, though. I loved my husband for protecting me, but I have been angry at him, too. Because I never got the opportunity to confront Lomax Blount for the lowly injustice he did to me."

Delta and Sunday were stunned. My God, they both thought, she had held her story like a kernel of rage that had burned and burned beneath the surface. They wondered if Nana had had any idea

Grandpa had done such a thing, for she had seemed so intuitive. Did he have her imprisoned, too, by his prejudices? Had she spent her life with him trying to measure up and follow through?

"Did you tell Nana," Delta asked, "after Mr. Walker died?"

"I was on the verge more than once, but I chose not to. Until this moment, I decided to carry it alone. I knew it would hurt her and make her feel guilty, and I wasn't sure what it would achieve."

Laveen and Opus stood, and Opus went to her, placing one palm at her back and one on the nape of her neck. So that was it, they all thought, and all that time she had kept it to herself. The sisters sat carefully on their dainty chairs, wishing they were capable of embraces that were neither greetings nor good-byes. Sunday thought about Delta's advice on fourteen hugs per day, and wondered if it was the first prolonged and loving touch that either one of the elderly women had felt in years.

"I'm so sorry," Sunday said quietly, and Delta said, "Me, too. I'm sorry for him. Sorry and ashamed."

A "little thing," Laveen Walker had called their grandfather's act. But it was another confounding piece of information, something both little and big.

"There's something else I wanted to raise with you," Sunday said, once they had settled back into their chairs, relieved to have a reason to shift the subject from Grandpa. "We went to Our Cemetery this morning, and I wondered, did Nana choose the inscription for Mama's gravestone, the 'Cherished Daughter, Wife, Mother'?"

"Yeeeees," Opus drew the word out as she thought, "I'm sure she must have. Nana J. had her own arrangements all planned out with Felix Harris, and she asked me to carry out those plans. But as for Dolora, she said she couldn't get her to talk about any practical matters, like finances, or her burial, or what she wanted for her service. Dolora said she was finished with being responsible and making decisions any bigger than what she wanted to eat. So I'm sure Nana J. tried to do what she thought your mother would want."

Sunday nodded. "And to go even further back, Mama picked the stone and the message for our . . . for Mercury, I would guess?"

Laveen and Opus shrugged. "I don't really know, but I guess so,"

Opus answered, "for who else could it have been, other than Edna, and I don't think she would have made that kind of decision on her own. What I do remember is that there was no stone made for quite a while. For at least a year or two."

Delta asked, "Where was Aunt Edna during that time, right after Mercury disappeared?"

"Aunt Edna," Laveen said. "I haven't thought about her in epochs. She seemed like such an amiable woman."

"Gentle. Humble," Opus said.

"Whatever happened to her, Opus?"

"Well, she tried to be there right after Mercury died . . . or that is, left. And she helped us with arranging the service for him, and did a lot of washing and cooking for Dolora and whatnot. Her face always had such a pained, embarrassed look, but she watched you girls and brought you presents, trying to make up for her nephew, I think."

"Like the chalk box. She gave me a dark blue metal box with gold writing that was filled with smooth, white chalk. I just loved it, and I found it recently in the attic."

"You see, Delta, that's what I mean," Opus said. "Edna was a nice woman. Quiet and a little defeated-seeming, but she had cause to be. I think she was oppressed by the burden of raising that boy on her own, and the Blounts weren't too welcoming. Everyone felt uncomfortable, even angry, though they mostly kept that under wraps. Edna hadn't done anything wrong, but like I said, I think she felt responsible. I think she took on Mercury's shame."

Laveen was distracted, still recovering from her revelation. She tried so hard to keep things to herself, but it only ever worked for so long. As a girl, her mother had told her that the whole world showed on her face and she had tried hard to cure that, but here she had gone and bled all over everything. And the Owens girls were the ones with the problem, not her. She just hated how disappointing people were, and she never wanted to believe the bad things she heard or read. Lately, she had been unable to read the daily newspaper's accounts of individual, human wrongdoing, of organized, collective systems of depravity, and to maintain her faith in the basic decency of people. But these girls would have a hard time believing in people's goodness, with their family history of wrong. She almost wished she could take her story back.

"So," Opus continued, "it got to be too much for Edna, carrying her own as well as someone else's crimes, and she found a job doing something or other in St. Louis and moved away."

"For a long time we got birthday and Christmas cards from her," Delta said, "but they never had a return address, just a St. Louis postmark, as a matter of fact. And then they stopped coming, but she did send flowers when Mama died, though I don't know where they came from, and I don't know how she found out. I haven't had a card or note in years."

"I wonder if she's alive, and whether she, or any of her people, could be found. I wonder if she should be told about him being alive."

"Oh goodness, Sunday. I don't think that's news she would welcome," Laveen exclaimed. "That would make her feel even worse."

"Well, she might have a right or a need to know. It might be the proper thing to tell her, whether it's welcome or not," Opus said. "And I don't recall knowing about any other kin of hers."

"How do you think I might find her," Sunday asked, "if I wanted to, that is?"

"I have a very old address in St. Louis," Opus said, as she went to get it and write it out.

Delta glared at Sunday. As usual, she seemed to think it was her decision alone to make. Sunday could feel Delta's resentment and decided to let it drop. She would bring it up with her later, once they got home.

Laveen was watching Delta and Sunday closely. She wanted to give them something good. "You know, there was more to your father than you think. I knew him in secondary school, and I could see a colossal inquisitiveness in him. He used to come to the library and read books about geography and history. He liked things about kings and queens, and great adventurers and conquerors.

"What stuck out in my mind was how solitary he was. He looked vulnerable, like a boy who was trying to pass for a man. I never saw him with other students, and he just sat for hours, until the library closed, looking at maps and encyclopedias, even reading the thick, unabridged dictionary sometimes. On many occasions he fell asleep in a corner, and I would have to wake him and send him home. He was a dreamy young man, and the library appeared to be a kind of refuge."

Returning with Edna's address, Opus contributed what she knew. "As I told Sunday the other day, he had a wanting in him. I remember Nana J. telling how once, when he was falling farther and farther behind in Scrabble, he stood up and turned the board right over, sending the tiles flying all over the kitchen. Afterward, he called himself cleaning it up, but she said she was finding letters for the whole next week. An 'E' under the toaster or a 'W' in the sugar bowl."

"Yes," Laveen said. "According to his teachers, Mercury was often reprimanded in school. You know, for disrupting the class, telling outlandish tales, and not submitting his homework in a timely fashion. He was a bright young man, but if there was any criticism at all of his work or his behavior, he became antagonistic, convinced that he had failed completely, and either withdrew or did a sloppy job."

Opus added what she remembered. "But Dolora seemed to believe in the person he put himself out to be. She loved the bigness of his thinking. She loved his reach. Dolora had been so sheltered, and her father was so stern and into discipline. I'm not sure what she had in mind for after high school; maybe she was just drifting along, following the rules and hoping she would get married to the proper gentleman, or work at her father's store. And here comes this smooth-talking, big-thinking boy-man who was absolutely gone on her. In Dolora, he had finally found a disciple. It's truth. And if someone didn't believe in him, he seemed to set out to fulfill their low expectations. I guess it was that way with Mr. Blount."

"Amen to that," Laveen chimed in. "Now I'm not saying what Mercury Owens did was justifiable, or that he is any exemplar of rectitude, but Lomax Blount must have made his life a living Hades, that's what I think. He made it clear to him that he thought he was no 'count, and so that's what he became."

"Everyone's been made by their pasts," Opus said, "and there are reasons for everything we do. Neither one of them was the finest specimen of black manhood, I guess we could all say. Now I see what you've been holding all these years, but I'm not sure we have to bend over backward defending Mercury Owens in order to reject Mr. Blount."

As they listened, Sunday and Delta were both fleshing out the figure who lived in their imaginations, trying to envision a person who did and felt the things they had heard described. They were developing the character they had known from fragmentary details and photographs.

When they fell silent, Sunday leaned forward, her eyes intent, and asked, "What else can you tell us about him? What else?"

My word, there's a hunger in that girl, Opus thought. "I don't know much more, child," she said, beginning to collect the cups and plates. "At least not for today, anyhow. He knew next to nothing about the in-between things in life. He knew how to make babies . . . and to soak up things in books . . . and how to dream big dreams." She paused at the doorway to the kitchen. "And as we unfortunately must admit, he knew how to run."

11

THE NEXT DAY, Laveen phoned to tell both Delta and Sunday, in turn, how worried she was that she had revealed such unpleasant information about their grandfather, and that she hoped something positive would come of it. Delta and Sunday reassured her that she had nothing to apologize about because they wanted their full family history, ugliness and all. When Opus called to say she was thinking about them and hoped the conversation hadn't been more than they could take, both sisters told her that they were fine. In fact, they both felt troubled and stuck.

Few of the disclosures had been pleasant, but the man who had once been merely Grandpa to them was becoming Lomax Blount. He intruded on their waking thoughts and their dreams; they had new reasons to be ashamed. And neither one of them could figure out where his crimes left them. In what way was his behavior theirs, they wondered, and did they have the obligation to atone?

It was Sunday's third day in Salt County, and that was all the time she had allotted for her visit. Part of her wanted to say, "That's it, I'm out of here. That's all the time I've got." But another part of her knew that she was just beginning to have a sense of her family story, and of the possibility of reaching Delta. She was on to something, however uncomfortable, and if she fled, she could forget discovering more. Leave or stay? She fought with herself about what to do, and then decided to try to give herself a little more time before bailing out.

Trying to lose themselves in household tasks, Delta made a roster of things that needed to be done on a little, spiral notebook she kept tucked in the waistband of her pants. Like meter maids Sunday had seen, she pulled the notebook out and flipped it open, as if she were issuing tickets for infractions of a serious, but common kind, fascinating Sunday with the way her gestures had the directness that her speech so often lacked. Sunday hoped the roster of projects would mean the chance to clear away some of the dilapidated and cast-off objects that filled the house, and maybe she would consider removing the heavy drapes and worn pieces of carpet downstairs, discarding piled-up magazines and mail order catalogs, or clothes that hadn't been taken from the closet for over a decade. Maybe she could convince her to air out and lighten up the house. For three days they worked away at the list, with Delta drawing a thick black line through each completed job.

Delta supervised as they cleaned the furnace and changed its filters. She showed Sunday how to spackle ceiling cracks and even out the walls. Hoping they were going to paint over the white scars that had begun to spiderweb across the ceilings and walls, Sunday volunteered to do that work. "I'll tell you when we're ready for that," Delta said; "we'll do that, if we do it, last." She surrendered to Delta's plan and her managerial tone, helping to take down and repair window screens, replace seals on commodes, and recaulk the bathtub.

When they took up the runners to clean the carpet, Sunday seized the opportunity to argue for discarding both the plastic strips and the rug, but Delta countered that there was nothing wrong with them that a little elbow grease wouldn't fix, and took offense at Sunday's penchant for looking down on her old belongings and small-town ways. "Do you think I'm made of money?" she asked, prompting Sunday to withdraw her suggestion as quickly as she could. As a matter of fact, Sunday figured, she must have a great deal saved up, since the house had long ago been paid for and little in it had changed. She clearly didn't spend much on clothes, and what local outlets for entertainment could claim her nest egg? What *did* she spend her money on? Sunday asked herself, wondering if her sister had inherited her mother's penchant for playing the lottery, or Grandpa's tendency to hoard.

During breaks in Delta's program of household jobs, Sunday returned to the mosaics she had assembled in her room. After propping them up along the baseboards of two adjoining walls and trying to put them in chronological order, she asked Delta for help, and they found that some story of related events surfaced for each piece they tried to place. "That one," Delta said, "she made for Alpha Post's retirement, and Patrice returned it to Nana when she died. So let's see, that must have been done in nineteen seventy-five or seventy-six. Remember that retirement party, Sunday? All the champagne?" Delta pointed to a tray. "That one has the floods of nineteen seventy in it. See the water carrying that tree and covering the house?"

Sunday did see it, and she noted that each mosaic contained water, rising or abating, with human figures and emblems of daily life in its thrall. Sometimes there was green sprouting, new, from its rain or flow. In one, a single corner of the composition was claimed by a wave, while in another, the tiny, dark figures that she had always seen as swimmers within the band of blue and mica chips seemed suddenly to sprawl and cartwheel at the mercy of the water that had the power to both endow and take.

Sunday sat before the mosaics of different size and type: coasters and jewelry box lids; trivets, trays, and paperweight cubes; tabletops; wall hangings and a clock; pieces of the half-done countertop she had begun just before she died. Knowing that she would never be able to remove herself, as daughter, and approach the mosaics as a fellow artist or critic looking with detachment for technique and theme, Sunday tried to bring her full self to her reading of the pieces. She immersed herself in all that she had been finding out and remembering, and closed her eyes to imagine her mother working on them, bit by bit, in the sacred-seeming full moon of artificial kitchen light.

She strained to put herself in Dolora's place, drawing on her own experience with clay and wood and paint, and tried to feel her mother going to the quick. Here was her story, told not by Nana in retrospect, but narrated by her own hand. Sunday knew that the images Dolora had selected and constructed, tile by tile, moved her. She responded to them "in the belly," which Reed argued was the truest place. "The head alone's not enough for art," he said, giving examples of his favorite books that engaged him both "above and below the neck. The head might betray us, in the end, and the best thing about your painting is that it gets the belly involved."

Sunday could see ambiguity in each one. Figures shifted, rain taking the shape of either teardrops or fish, and long, sinuous blades of grass interwove with snakes. In some pieces, she found the fluctuation existed in the shapes of the individual tiles, and in others, the composition or context made it known. Looking at the collection of mosaics as a time line, she saw increasing control and abstraction, and in the later ones, Dolora had begun to use the grout for more than joining the tiles, as part of the design. Some of them had more pebbles, pieces of glass and metal, or irregular found objects worked in with the tiles, but Sunday didn't know what to make of that. She couldn't find a pattern to it, but maybe there had been periods of scarcer money, when she had made do with the materials she had. Maybe she had needed to break free of known constraints. Maybe they had been statements about what could be of use.

Up in the attic, amid her search for weatherproofing materials, Delta came across something else to add to Sunday's treasury. She found three life-sized masks wrapped in plastic, dry-cleaning bags. Sunday couldn't remember seeing Dolora work on those masks, and she had no idea where to place them in the chronicle they had arranged. They stood apart from the other work, and were striking in their marriage of authority and peace. She put them at the end of the time line of work.

Reminded of the brass and bone and beads of wooden, African masks, and of entombed, Egyptian death faces, Sunday began to wonder what, or who, had inspired Dolora's efforts. Were they ceremonial in some sense, or merely exercises? Did they represent specific lives? Dolora's faces, composed of tiny chips of brown and reddish clay, both glazed and raw, studded with ceramics and glass, were images of endless repose. Maybe they expressed Dolora's hope for the release of death, for the serenity of afterlife.

After a day of moving back and forth between decoding Dolora's compositions and the house improvements that sometimes freed her from thought and left her exhausted by evening, Sunday would rest her forearms on the windowsill and watch the neighbors' lights come on, imagining the routine lives unfolding within each home. Were Mr. and Mrs. Nowlin fumbling for a way to share with each other their doubts and fears, or making one another pay for the ways they had settled for what was safe and known? Was Exie Claybourne sitting down, ruefully, to a solitary meal? And was there a couple, somewhere, who were moving past their fear to embrace the rolling current of mystery and deep desire? Saying, "Come for me, where I pulse and bleed?"

She often pictured Reed moving around their apartment, reclining on their paint-marked couch with a book, making coffee, raising the window shades. She saw him twisting his locks while he was deep in thought, running his bathwater, stepping out of his shoes to get in bed. And there he was, entering the kitchen studio filled with canvases that had been turned to the wall. Did he move among them to wash dishes and cook?

She yearned for him to call, and when he did, she felt both solace and the urge to escape his attention, worried that he would go right to the heart of her trouble, as his ability to ask and answer the intimate question seemed to underscore everything of which she found herself afraid and incapable. For a long time, she had asked him to step away, and then panicked as she watched him respect that stated wish, fearful, in the midst of her evasion, that she was stretching his patience to its snapping point. Just how long could she count on him to trust and wait? Sunday hoped that he would see in her gesture of phoning that she was fighting the safety of her cherished distance.

She was relieved when she called him and got the message machine, to which she could speak freely of the ways she loved and missed his touch, his voice. But when he answered, she found herself able only to make surface chatter, enumerating her and Delta's refurbishing accomplishments and recounting the day's events. She didn't say how she was trying to decipher her mother's mosaics, or seek his help in where to focus next. And she didn't tell him how Grandpa was emerging as a more and more distressing character, although this he would have understood, knowing firsthand about begrudging, chiding family.

After one botched conversation, she found Delta standing in the doorway, holding her black marker and her list. "Venetian blinds and windows," she announced. "That's next on the list."

"I bet Windex would help with these."

"Who needs Windex. I make my own cleaner with ammonia and water."

"Go 'head, girl," Sunday said, impressed with her enterprising spirit. Looking at the window, bare of its slatted, metal covering and holding the bucket and cloth while Delta rubbed at the glass, the smell of ammonia wafting up, she said, "You know, I've never liked venetian blinds." Delta rolled her eyes as Sunday continued. "We could leave them down or even throw them out, rather than taking the trouble to clean them. Can you imagine how much brighter the house would be without them?"

Delta scowled at her from the stepladder. "Then people could see in."

"Well, raise them in the daytime then, so some sky can get in."

"Oh, please. What's wrong with the blinds, anyway? We've always had venetian blinds, and these are relatively new. I put them in ten years ago. Remember those big, wide ones Nana had, and how she and Mama used to try to keep track of us playing outside by pulling them down in the middle, and you could see that they sagged where she had parted the slats to get a better view?"

Delta scrubbed at the window, refusing the image of Dolora peering through her bedroom blinds and then turning to silence her sister's infant wail.

"If you had to pull them apart," Sunday added, wondering why Delta was suddenly scrubbing so furiously, "why have them? Don't you just prefer the sky whole?"

Delta stared at her. The sky whole, she thought. What the hell did that mean? The sky, as far as she knew it, had always been interrupted by smokestacks and rooftops. Filtered through smudged, rattling windows or the tiny waffle-holes of screens. Even outside, it was split by telephone poles and power lines, if you could see it underneath the smog. Sunday was so romantic. What did either one of them know of that a person could have whole?

"I see, Sunday," she said, climbing the ladder at the front window, "but blinds suit me fine, and I accept the sky as it comes to me. They just need washing, that's all. Now come over here with that bucket and mop so I can hand the next one down."

Sunday did as she had been instructed, deciding to try to keep her musings to herself, imagining the window clean and uncovered, picturing undisturbed expanses of night and morning sky whole as she worked. She helped to eliminate items from Delta's list of tasks while she tried to figure out what remaining concrete actions she could take to extend her search. Mercury was starting to come into view, but where could she look next? What more could she unearth about him, Dolora, and Nana, even Grandpa? And what else might lead her to Girl Owens and Sister?

She had discovered the family Bible at the back of a closet, but she could hardly bear her disappointment when she found that all of the places at the back for recording dates and milestones were left blank. She had almost exhausted her sources of information about the person

Mercury Owens had been before he left, and Clement Woods was her only way to learn about the man he had become afterward. She was trying to work up to the effort of confronting him, and finding out all the things he might know, but it was easier to track down the small bits of the farther past than to go headlong into the more recent unknown.

She decided to write Aunt Edna at the address Opus had found, on the slim chance that her letter would be forwarded and somehow reach her. She and Delta had argued about contacting Edna, with Delta maintaining that the news of Mercury's reappearance could add nothing positive to an old woman's life. They had reached a standoff, and then Sunday had agreed that she would only ask for family information, and would not tell Edna that Mercury had been alive.

After drafting and redrafting her simple note, she came up with a message that apologized for the years of silence and asked for Edna's memories of the kind of child and young man her father had been. In explanation of her sudden curiosity, she said she had become interested in local and family history. She told her that Nana had died five years before, and that only she and Delta remained.

In the middle of scrubbing baseboards, Sunday mentioned that she had written to Edna and was ready to mail the note. She decided to interpret Delta's silence as assent, and before she knew it, her sister was whipping out her notebook and marker, instructing her to rinse out the sponges and rejoin her on the second-floor landing.

Sunday couldn't recall her sister ever having been so bossy, and she consciously worked at tolerance. When they argued, Sunday coached herself in acquiescence, reminding herself again and again that it didn't matter if she let Delta have her way about such things. But she marveled at Delta's frenzy to fix what could be righted with immediate results, watching her work until she was insensible, unwilling to rest before a job was done, even if it took until 2 A.M. When she did stop, her eyes darted around for some other little thing to take care of before she turned in, and on her way from bathroom to bedroom she might suddenly stop and go get a cloth to make a brief onslaught against the dust that had collected in a corner, or a sponge and spray bottle to clean the switchplates in the upstairs rooms.

Sunday had to admit to herself that she was obsessing on her own list, which comprised a different sort of task. She didn't even pretend to try napping, and she lay awake at night, going over what she had discovered and what action to take next. "Documentation," she said one night, sitting up in bed to think it through. "I have to find out what documentation there is."

She wasn't sure what information she thought would be recorded, or even what she was looking for, but she remembered that in high school everyone was searching county records and doing family trees with a post-*Roots* fever. She had never wanted to dig for the specific facts about her family, preferring to see her life as something she could create, free of the choices and misdeeds that had come before. But such information might just be important, she supposed, warming to the idea of the certain and objective truth that records could provide.

The next day, Delta's executive approach to raking pushed her past tolerance. When Delta told her she was holding the trash bag into which they were stuffing leaves "all wrong," Sunday dropped it where she stood. "Do it yourself, then," she said quietly as she walked away and kicked the rake, heading for the county recorder's office downtown.

She approached the information desk without having thought through what she wanted to ask, and when she glanced up, she found herself looking at Earlene Hall's smirk.

Earlene stood with her ten-part fingernail sunset spread out across the sign-in clipboard. "Well, if it isn't Sunday Owens. What, I wonder, can I help you with?"

In an instant, Sunday was on the floor again with her new marking pens, and there was the point of Earlene's shoe, just beside her face. Sunday nodded her assent when Earlene asked to try the markers out, and then looked on in panic and anger as Earlene mashed them hard into the paper, blots of yellow and blue spreading like wounds into its weave. Earlene's interest waned when one of the pens' tips flattened and broke off. "These things don't last," she said, tossing the pen aside as she stood up, "they must be cheap."

Amid both past and present, Sunday stammered as she tried to get her balance. "I, I'm not quite sure. Let's see." She cleared her throat and prepared herself for an abrasion of some kind from Earlene. "I guess I'm here to do some kind of family trace treeing . . . tree tracing, some kind of . . ."

"Genealogy."

"Yes. Genealogy, that's it."

Earlene stared at her inquisitively, awaiting further disclosure, and until Sunday heard herself say, in a conspiratorial whisper, "Delta doesn't know I'm here."

"Follow me," Earlene said after a scrutinizing pause, rounding the counter and sauntering across the room on high-heeled pumps that matched her purple sweater dress. Sunday followed her, feeling vaguely disloyal to Delta, but relieved that Earlene had not decided to oppress her for either uncertainty or mere presence in her domain. She didn't know if it was her need of Earlene's help that had pacified her or the potential bond of something treasonous.

Earlene led her to a worktable, where she brought Sunday the books she needed to begin. She was explaining imperiously how to use them when she stopped and demanded, "Why are you here then, Sunday Owens? What has brought you back?"

"Why does she *always* call me by my full name," Sunday asked herself. It must feel like leverage of some kind, she thought, and considered Laveen referring to Grandpa as "Lomax Blount." She could sense Earlene homing in on the possibility that her return to Salt County had been motivated by difficulty, and she recalled what Delta had said about her monitoring potential distress and violation on her police scanner. She hadn't worked out what to say about why she was home, but she knew she couldn't tell about Mercury's return from the dead.

"I'm not sure what I'm looking for . . . whatever I can find. I just want to see what there might be about my family, however far back they go. Birth dates, death dates, marriages and such. Property ownership . . ."

"Yeah, I'll bet," Earlene said.

Sunday looked around her, like an airplane passenger locating the nearest door as turbulence sets in. It must be Grandpa again, she thought, for Sunday knew that in addition to the store, he had owned some rental property. She lowered her head and played with the worn creases in the record books, flooded by the things she had learned from Laveen and Opus only a few days before. She wanted to disclaim Grandpa and his crimes of greed and condescension, to blurt out that she wasn't like that and hadn't even known he was, but she was afraid that her denial would sound false and make her ire increase. She wondered if Earlene Hall had suffered personally in some way. Certainly she was too young to have really known Grandpa, but maybe, somehow, he had something to do with her scorn.

Sunday swallowed as she glanced at Earlene's resentful pout, unsure if she should give her a chance to release whatever it was she had been dragging around all these years. She thought of Laveen's long-standing wound.

"My grandpa . . ."

"Missster Lomax Blount."

"Yes," she said, making room inside for more bad news about him as she glanced at the door. The office felt small and the air thick, but she decided to meet Earlene's challenge and try to let her settle her score. "He died when I was little, but I'm finding out more and more about the price of his prosperity. Was there something, Earlene . . . that he did to you and yours?"

Earlene was surprised by the admission and the question, and she examined her nails before she spoke, debating whether she could give up the thing that had been passed down and entrusted to her to keep the family's indignation fueled. She wanted to tell it, finally, but if she did, it might lose its force.

"He was the landlord," Earlene finally said, drawing the last word out contemptuously, "and he put my folks out of their shitty little run-down apartment, where they had to fix whatever broke themselves because they'd grow old waiting for him to do it. When my uncle died in an accident at the lamp factory, your grandfather evicted my aunt and put her stuff out on the street. 'Just business,' he told her, 'nothing personal at all.' I heard that story many a time growing up. It was like Lomax Blount had never died, but just lived on and on through that story."

"I'm sorry for him," Sunday answered, removing her taped-up glasses to clean them with her scarf. She looked around at the walls of record books and then at Earlene. "It isn't much, but it's all I've got, my being sorry . . . and ashamed. You know he couldn't stand my father, or anything that came from him, which probably would include me and Delta, if Grandpa had lived that long."

Earlene watched Sunday intently, noticing how defenseless her face seemed as she worked her lenses clean. Sunday glanced at her and put the glasses back on, wishing she could do something more to make up for the past. And perhaps it was the dishonor of her inheritance that made her offer her own misfortune as amends.

"It's my father that's brought me back," she said, almost relieved to state it plainly. "Turns out he's been alive."

Earlene searched Sunday's face to see if she was deceiving her. "Damn, that's heavy-duty. I know a lot about trouble, and that's rough." Sitting back in her seat, she said, "You know, I've got a scanner, and whatever illegal wrongdoing is going on in Salt County falls on my ears. I know the code numbers for offenses so that I've got an inside track. I think it's a good idea to have the whole picture of what folks are up to, don't you? To keep in the forefront of your mind just what people are capable of. But this business about your father is another kind of thing. I wonder," she mused, "if there's somewhere in the penal code where this might fit. 'Fraud and Misrepresentation,' or 'Child Endangerment.' Maybe 'Neglect and Abuse.'"

Is she enjoying this, Sunday wondered, or what? She seemed to be savoring the information with a kind of abstract detachment that made Sunday want to scream. "Look," she said, hitting the table with her palm, "let's get things out in the open, for once. I don't know why I just told you what's been going on. It probably wasn't for any reason that was good, but this is my life and my sister's that we're talking about, and not some disembodied perpetrator's or victim's whose story is coming over your scanner. I know you've never approved of me, Earlene, but it's been more than that. You didn't just dislike me and ignore me; you messed with me, every chance you got. And where does that fit in your wrongdoing code?"

Looking as if she had been slapped, Earlene's face registered both shock and respect. "Well, okay, Sunday Owens. I've never heard you speak your mind, and I guess I deserved that."

Earlene focused on her nails, and Sunday decided to put something else on the line. "Do you have any idea what it felt like to be an outcast? For you, socializing was effortless. You were . . . popular and sexy. You were at the center of every group. So what was it that you had against me, in addition to my grandpa's crimes? Do you have the guts to tell me, all these years later? Can you say what it was?"

Raising her glance from her fingers to Sunday's face, Earlene spoke. "Your grandfather wasn't the only thing. I knew you all got a raw deal with your father's checking out and all, and to us, it was a standard for messing up.

"But that got you some kind of recognition, too. After all, lots of folks got useless relatives who are too trifling to support them or who only every now and then come through. But here you were, handling it all

217

with the kind of poise you get in charm school, walking a certain way, shoulders even, carrying your head high, all on your own. You never seemed to need anybody. When you didn't get invited or you were picked last, you just sat alone, looking content." Her eyes narrowed and she leaned toward Sunday. "You held yourself apart. Above it. Above all of us, and that really used to burn me. You made not fitting in an advantage, and you always seemed headed somewhere else, with your weird clothes and your sketch pad underneath your arm. I never could get to you, and when I tried, I always came out feeling small.

"Now me, I had track and field in junior high school, and I was fast. I had the body and the boys, and I could make other girls jealous, except for you. And where did all that get me, in the end? I used to think, she may not have a pot to piss in, but she thinks she has."

Earlene was thinking of how she had flung her high school trophy in girls' track and field off the bridge downtown, after no one from her family had shown up at the meet. As she launched it into the air, she had cursed the mother she could never please, the father who was too tired to pay attention, the siblings who were too distracted by their lovers and kids. Nothing's worth a damn, she had thought at the time, taking the only revenge she knew how to enact, by letting go of her one good thing.

"People don't always make sense from the outside, do they, Sunday Owens? I've done some crazy things in my life. You know, once I threw away something that mattered to me a lot, and I never could get it back."

Sunday's head jerked up. She wanted to ask Earlene if she was talking about the trophy Delta told her she had given to the river, but she decided not to imperil the careful balance they had somehow established. She could hardly believe that she and Earlene Hall were actually sitting down together, having a conversation, and a confessional one, at that. A crack seemed to have opened, straight down through the layers of enmity and insecurity that had formed over the years.

But she had forced the crack herself, hadn't she? As far back as she remembered, she had been volunteering whatever it was she had to appease the Earlenes in her life. Her colored markers, her sister-rift, her pain, whatever good or bad she had to give had been extended, and she was doing it still. She had felt like a hostage, and she wondered whether Earlene had any concept of her distress. Did she have any idea of her pain and discomfort at the inventory of her uppity "attitude," her skinny legs, her "different" clothes, as she walked by the lockers of Earlene and her crowd. At choosing a seat in the cafeteria, where Earlene was surrounded by mocking devotees. Did Earlene have any inkling that she had often tried to find a way to paint or help some teacher or administrator through lunchtime, in order to avoid the moment of nonchalantly entering the room, teeming with adolescent uncertainty and desperation, and merge, seeking a way to belong.

They seemed to be sharing a moment distilled of impurity, released of freight. But was any interaction unburdened by the past? Even if the moment really was clean, Sunday knew it was temporary, for no one could manage that kind of meeting for long. You took those moments when they happened, if you could, but often they led to more ruined markers, or something even worse.

Sunday folded her arms and looked for the EXIT sign, closing off the connection before it was polluted, and the question of what had been forfeited to the river hung, unbroached, in the inert office air.

But "that's another story," Earlene said, carefully opening one of the large, clothbound books so as not to harm her fingernails. "Now let me help you get started here."

Sunday's search of the county records yielded little information. The only thing she learned was the exact property Grandpa had owned. In addition to the store, he had some rental apartments, a coin-op Laundromat, and a parking lot. Those apartment buildings, as Earlene had been delighted to inform her, had been run-down and poorly maintained when he owned them, despite their steadily rising rents, and Nana had sold all the property in the few years after he died.

As she tried to sort out what she should do next, she found herself asking why she was there, back in her narrow bed and her star-printed room, cleaning and repairing, probing futilely into the past. She pictured Felix Harris diving the river to no avail, submersed and then resurfacing, empty-handed, until he gave up and returned to the pursuit of burial and stonecutting in which he had been trained. Neither the record search nor the Bible had paid off, and Aunt Edna was probably dead or long ago moved to someplace else. She wanted conclusive answers. She wanted for her and her sister to stop their foolish conflicts and understand each other, for things to be smooth and clear with Reed. She wanted to be able to face Clement Woods and accept whatever it was he had to tell. She wanted to know what to do about the tombstone, about the color blue, about anything at all.

Enough, already, she said to herself, my three days passed, and I stayed three more; now let's get on with all of this. After all, she reasoned, Mercury didn't elect the role of father, so why am I bent on pursuing him?

The house, haunted and flood-stained, would never seem fresh and new, no matter how much cleaning and mending they did, and she and Delta would never really get along. This is not my present, she insisted, this is lost and old and riddled with questions. My life is in Chicago, she thought, my life is now.

When she called Reed and got her own voice on their answering machine repeatedly one day, she pictured an empty apartment, the walls and floors painted over white. Maybe he had finally gotten fed up with her and left, discarding her possessions, her finished and uncompleted work. Or maybe he had simply walked away. What if her painting and her lover had both disappeared, and she was nobody but one of the Owens girls when she returned.

She told Delta she needed to return to Chicago to take care of work-related things, since she had only intended to visit for a few days. Deep down, she knew she wasn't finished with Salt County, but she couldn't bear to stay and face all that was unresolved. She would check in with Reed, arrange some freelance work to bring in some money, and get more clothes. Privately, she admitted that she wasn't sure if and when she would ever come back, but she had decided to tell Delta that she was just taking a break. Once she had finished filling her bag, she sat on the edge of the bed. "That was easy," she said, "since I never really unpacked." But before she left there was one thing she wanted to do.

After pulling down the attic stairs, she climbed them, aware of her crayon drawing as she ascended, and got the wooden box where Nana had placed Dolora's things. She took it down and replaced the stairs in their ceiling recess, tracing the ceiling seam with her fingertips.

She found Delta in her room putting on her lipstick and knocked lightly. "Don't trouble yourself to drive me to the station; I'd rather walk. But I did want to give you this before I left. I found it the other day and tried to tell you, and I don't know what you'll think of it, but there's a story in it, and it belongs to you, too. Nana put it together, I guess partly for us, and I didn't want to keep it to myself." After putting the box on a chair in the corner, she said, "I'll probably be back in no time."

Just as Sunday was leaving, Earlene arrived. She had made a special trip to bring over the hand soaps Sunday had ordered. Sunday repeated her reasons for leaving and wrestled her bag onto the foldout wheels.

"What's up with her? Something wrong in Chicago?" Earlene asked. "She's hightailing it out of here like she saw a ghost."

Delta didn't even try to respond. They stood at the screen door, too bereaved to speak, and watched Sunday disappear down the street, bumping her bag along the sidewalk cracks and seams. Earlene pressed her nails against the screen's mesh and reported the information she had gathered the night before from the police scanner: one assault and battery, one incident of trespassing, and two domestic disputes.

After Earlene left, the house felt eerily quiet. Delta walked around with her list, noting the jobs that had been completed. She tried to resume her project of fixing all the objects in appliance purgatory, but she had lost her momentum. Abandoning a disassembled can opener on the kitchen table, she decided to lie down and rest.

From the bed she could see the box Sunday had put in the corner of the room. She recognized it as the Christmas fig box from Boykin, but she wasn't sure she wanted to know what was inside. She turned on the radio, but every station seemed to be playing a love song, and she didn't know whether to cry or smash the dial. "No," she said aloud, "I will not break it. If I do, I'll just have another thing to repair."

She turned off the music, grabbed her pillow, afghan, and Kleenex box, and decided to try a different bed. Down the hall, in what had been Nana's room, she settled herself on the twin, four-poster bed, closed her eyes, and began to fantasize about the comfort of a stranger's body, exhausted and grazing hers after an afternoon of abandon and heat.

She pictured the stranger's familiar bony knees, and his smooth, dark chest, and then, inhaling his pepper-citrus smell, her eyes snapped open and she realized abruptly that her blessed stranger had transformed into Nate Hunter. "Damn that man," she said, "he shows up uninvited every-fucking-where." Closing her eyes again, she willed the image of her blue bread bowl, and this time, as she invoked it, an array of other bowls and serving platters appeared. The blue bowl was filled with steaming greens and was being borne by pairs of brown hands around a table, and there was a casserole of macaroni and cheese, and a bowl of sweet potatoes going round, a loaf of Nana's honey whole wheat bread and a dish of gravy, too. Plates were circulating as they were heaped with pieces of turkey that Nana had carved, and Delta could smell the succulent aromas of the meal.

"Thanksgiving," she said. Growing up, she and Sunday and Dolora had helped themselves from the stove each night, and there had been little joy in eating, just seven meals rotated over the weeks. Obligation food, designed to fill the stomach, cover the food groups, and come together without too much fuss. But at Nana's, and on holidays, there was pleasure in food and company, and they had served themselves from common bowls that were passed from hand to hand.

She had asked her mother again and again if they could eat "family style . . . you know, with the bowls at the table," and Dolora had said it made more work that way.

Delta imagined the bowls circulating and then released them. Her hunger was so aroused from the memory that she went downstairs to figure out dinner, but she couldn't cope with the idea of making anything from scratch, so she pulled a frozen dinner from the freezer. It would have to do.

She tried to watch one of her crime shows, but she couldn't follow the plot for thinking of the wooden box up in the bedroom. She turned off the TV and went up to find out what it held. Lifting the lid, remembering the story of the bounty of figs that her mother had loved to tell, she began to go through the contents, item by item, stopping to remember every small thing she could about each object.

Delta had always wanted to know her mother, and here had been the revelation, through someone else. It was a way to have something of Dolora, through odd bits and pieces. It was something to hold in her hands, something concrete, like her chalk box had been at first, but it also left her groping, with a sense of discovery only begun. When she came to the last thing in the box, she could hardly believe there wasn't more.

Maybe Mercury had left some things behind that would help to tell about him. If they found Clement Woods, he might be able to fill all kinds of voids, but the opposite could happen, too. It might open up a longing for her father that had an even slimmer chance of ever being satisfied than her yearning for Dolora. And who knew what things might come rushing forth if they really did find out who he was? How would they be able to control, as her mother had advised them, what to remember and forget?

After going back through the contents of the fig box and debating whether they should try to find Mercury, Delta wanted the warmth and conviviality of the shop, but was afraid she would not be able to be light and playful, to join in. When Dinah answered the phone, "A Joyful Process," Delta heard Queen Latifah in the background and almost hung up. She felt near tears and unsure she could be in a truth-telling, plain-speaking frame of mind.

"Hello?" Dinah asked twice before Delta answered, "It's me, Delta. Just wondered what your customer backup was like."

Dinah could hear pain in Delta's voice. "Come on over, girl. I've been wanting to know how you are."

"Well . . ." Delta hesitated, and then said, "Okay. I'll be there during Nappy Hour, and if I could put in a request, some Earth, Wind & Fire would do me good."

She arrived with cartons of shrimp fried rice and egg rolls from the Rice Bowl, relieved to find the shop almost empty. After she finished a wash and curl, Dinah put on the music Delta had requested, and they took advantage of a lull in business to talk. They sat in the swivel chairs while Delta told about what had been going on, starting with the news that Sunday had gone back to Chicago.

"Gone? Already? I guess it's like that old blues from the thirties: 'Goin' to Chicago, sorry that I can't take you.'"

"Except that she's not sorry, Dinah, not about that anyway. She practically ran back, and all of a sudden, too."

"So it's more like 'St. Louis Blues,' then: 'Feelin' tomorrow like I feel today, I'll pack my trunk and make my getaway.'"

"Yeah. It's more like that. More like a getaway. And I can't say I blame her, given the way the family story's been shaping up."

"The family story? What story is that?"

Delta told her that Sunday had been interested in digging up family history, and that they had uncovered things in the attic from their mother's life. She surprised herself by talking freely about Dolora and the present-absent mother she had been. "I can't say I ever knew her in life. That's because she didn't . . . want to be known. After my father . . . left, she held me at arm's length always, as if she just couldn't move over her hurt and her order and determination to make a place for me. Now Nana, she was different. She lived right up close to everything."

Dinah listened raptly as Delta talked about Nana's singing and affection, and the Bread Ladies. Pasting S&H Green Stamps at her side and helping with the garden, composting leftover peelings and pulp, eggshells and coffee grounds and such. Rubbing Nana's arthritic joints with liniment and getting back rubs in return.

"The only way Mama had for saying 'I love you' was providing for us. Coming through with food and shelter and clothes. Paying the bills and arranging swimming lessons at the Y and church on Sundays. I'm not knocking it; she was steady and she always fulfilled her parental duties. That was something, that taking care; it was more than some people get. But there was never any way to know her in it.

"Maybe it happened gradually, with each disappointment, but there was a coldness in her, and I feel terrible saying this, but I used to wonder if that was why my father left, because she was so out of reach, and sometimes I felt so angry at her for driving him away. I longed for her so, and I always came up feeling poor.

"She must have been bitter at what she'd been dealt, and you could kind of see that underneath her rigid ways and her withholding. She made us finish every morsel on our plates, and she washed dishes in boiling water, with the perfection of an alien. And there were rules, all kinds of rules. For bathing and straightening up and permission to go somewhere, being home by the time the streetlights came on, watching TV. At six o'clock sharp we served our plates from the stove and either ate around the table in silence, or in later years, took our food to TV trays in the living room, and ate while we watched the evening news. So anyhow, I'm only just now getting some sense of who she was, apart from a mother, that is.

"And then there's Grandpa." Delta was happy that Dinah had no past that was grounded in Salt County; she wouldn't be able to give any firsthand information on Lomax Blount. Delta told what they had learned, confessing, also, his treatment of Laveen. "It seems like he should pay, Dinah, for a thing like that."

224

"Yes, I guess it does. But listen to this." She was relieved that she had the perfect verse for that revelation, and shared two lines from a favorite spiritual: "'Rich man dies, he lived so well. When he died, he found a home in hell.'"

Delta nodded and said, "Amen. Tell it, girl," and then resumed her story. "So my sister's been hooked on all of this, like a kind of mystery she's determined to figure out. She was getting more and more information, and then she up and went back home. Who knows what answers we'll get if we keep digging, but they may not be neat or pretty ones."

As she talked, Delta realized that she, too, was hooked. Although she doubted the wisdom of their digging up old problems, she wasn't sure she could stop. Of course, she wasn't sure when or if Sunday would be back, but maybe she would keep looking on her own. "Anyway, we know who done it, we just don't know what exactly they done, or why."

Dinah was puzzled about why the sisters were on a mission to get information. "But why did you start this digging?" she asked. "What caused this nostalgia trip?"

At that, Delta made her final disclosure, and Dinah had no song, blues or otherwise, in response to the news that Mercury Owens had been alive. Rarely was she stumped in that way, but she promised she would think of one, and when she did, she would let Delta know what it was.

12

As the train doors closed, Sunday saw the white bag that held her Avon soaps peeking from the pocket of her suitcase. A glance back at the house when she neared the end of their block had revealed the image of Earlene and Delta, watching her from the screen door as she fled for Chicago.

Every time she had left Salt County, Sunday had closed her eyes and chanted in a whisper as the train separated from the station and pulled away on its tracks: "I can have this. I am allowed to go." She did it again, even though she suspected that payment would always be exacted for being the one who got away.

After Earlene had gone, Sunday thought, Delta will resume her rehabilitation of can openers and electric skillets, following through with her schedule of tasks, cursing her for her sudden exit, no doubt. Meanwhile, Reed was in Chicago, sitting, perhaps, on the edge of his desk, gesturing with his hands as he praised his favorite passages from "Sonny's Blues." Either that, or maybe, she thought, as fear overtook reason like a consumptive disease, maybe he was at that moment leaving their barren, whitewashed apartment behind, closing the door to abdicate his faith in helping lift the very cup of trembling.

And she was in between, bent on leaving behind Salt County one more time, returning to her unfinished canvases and her unclaimed love.

Grounding herself in the present, she saw the graffitied names and alliances go by, and then the paper mill, disgorging its afternoon shift, and the strip malls that were overtaking the land. Aside from the trees, thinned of leaves in just a week, and the sky, which was taking on a thin, autumn-into-winter light, the view was the same. It must be she who was different, she thought as she looked through the rectangle of glass. The colors appeared slightly altered, and everything she passed appeared to weigh more. And she was aware of water, water underneath it all.

Sunday noticed how the new boxy offices and shopping plazas seemed to press into the land, and the persistent windmill, too, looked as if it might just surrender and slump. And there it was again, looking positively pocket-sized, the Smallest Church in the Whole Midwest.

It had always seemed a strange distinction, a funny way to think about things. And she doubted it, she really doubted its assertion, for she had seen storefronts and alcoves that had served as churches. She had seen smaller. In fact, she had seen people call up churches in their heads, but maybe that was not smaller, but bigger. There she was, back at Delta's question of what was little and what was big.

The fieldstone wall slipped past and she sat back in her seat and closed her eyes. She hadn't even called to let Reed know she was coming, she had merely packed her bag and left.

She was going back to him, but why, she asked herself, did she always seem to stop just this side of really showing up? She couldn't help wondering if she would be able to choose him if she didn't want him so much. She had had less trouble committing to lovers with obvious limitations. With one or two she had felt sexual chemistry, but no real pull of intellect. Another had been physically striking and sophisticated, but had left her feeling more solitary than when she was alone. With some, she had enjoyed conversation and movie dates, but had felt no danger of truly being touched. Until Reed, love had been containable, and she was still in charge. But he came for her in the belly, demanding that she bring her total self.

If she didn't restrict it, her desire for Reed might bleed into everything else, sending everything topsy-turvy, wrenching control. There was no telling what could be lost when you lived that way, and the only kind of home she knew how to make was one where things were clearly separated, and her art, over which she had full ownership, received her passion.

Sometimes she had wildly drawn whatever lines she could in order to make painting inviolate territory. It had to do with borders, she thought, and borders were tricky when you were trying to create.

After her work space was emptied of competing demands and distractions and her materials were all prepared, after she was situated and ready to begin, she often had to move past terror at the starting place of blank canvas or paper, at the midway place of what was started, but still only a raw and nascent grope. But when she made that passage in, she lost herself and felt the thrumming of her blood. To focus her way in, she had to let her protective borders down, shifting consciousness, pulling image and sense from her belly and her head. Tapping into the place where the skin was thin and the pulse near the surface, she made herself permeable. Perception was heightened. The ordinary was sacred and large.

She had to paint to be able to live, and in order to paint, she needed vision, including other-sight. As she traveled inward, things imagined and concrete began to flux. Fiber, cloth, and pigment were transformed, as she gave form to the seeing, as she found her tongue. But when she broke from painting and washed her brushes, she hadn't brought her borders back up, and she found herself out in the world like that, seeing and seen. Yearning to draw in everything around her, she would raise the window and lean out, wishing she could put whole cities in her mouth and feel what plant seeds felt as they broke open, pushing green. She wanted to place her fingertips on contentment and grief, to know the will of ocean currents and glaciers. To ride a constellation and understand, from the inside-out, the friction of tectonic plates.

Undressed and alone when she was working with paint, she found it painful out on the margin, and she yearned for a witness, for the communion of language and skin. And at those times of shifting frontiers, she had often made reckless judgments, allowing people in and entering their lives without passage being earned. She made professions with immediate regret, took actions she knew to be unfounded in other times. She found that "Yes" was so much easier to say with recklessness.

Her work brought her into the common, live place, but it made her separate, too, and she wanted to be able to say, this is where I've been, let me show you where I live. She was out there, skinless, on the margin line, and she needed help getting back.

She thought how once, she had seen the inside of a baseball. Walking by the apartment building across the street, she had heard a group of prepubescent boys call her over to see something "cool," and found that they had cut through the ball's red, bird-track stitches and peeled back the scuffed, leather skin to expose a densely layered mass of winding thread. The sight of tangled, speckled gray, both ordered and haphazard, was unforgettable. She felt like that baseball inside.

Everybody had an inside mess, she figured, but most lives allowed for containing and hiding it. While her paintings weren't reproductions or records of her insides, they had within them, available for deciphering and translation, the pieces of her life, her inside mess. She knew no one made art without revelation, without putting something crucial on the line. If you meant to avoid self-exposure, then that intention got revealed.

Often, when people looked at her paintings and were touched, they felt that she was speaking directly to them. They thought they had a relationship with her, Sunday, through her work and what it might mean to them, and that it entitled them to something more of her. They had walked into her head, her heart, her past, and it seemed to them that she had invited them in, given them access to her life through what she had pulled out of herself and offered up.

In her painting she chose the quick, despite its costs. How could she bear to choose it in the rest of life?

But she also knew that she was willing to mistrust Reed; he was a man, and anything else would be naive. Early on, they had argued about things that seemed minor to him, like unwashed dishes or speaking with authority in public for both of them. He didn't mean for that to be about privilege, and asserting that his actions were "old habits," he denied any consciousness that he acted out of advantage or dominance. "If it were a matter of race," she argued, "you would find it clear."

She wanted to say "Yes" to him, but she was fighting to keep what she thought was hers. Sometimes she held Reed responsible for everywhere else she had been, and was comfortable construing his actions in terms of both of their pasts. "You're always ready to give me a citation," he complained.

Pieces of the conversation with Opus and Laveen returned to her. "Women of our generation catered to men," Opus had said. She and Nana and Laveen had all done it, conspiring to keep the secret that their men were no better, no more savvy or ingenious or able, than them. And the deference, the endless pleasing, for most women, was coupled with anger. Sunday didn't intend to defer, and she wasn't altogether certain that wasn't what "Yes" meant.

Often she responded to Reed's appeals for her to let him in by accusing him of wanting her "endlessly available," like the other women he had known. When she felt him pulling at her, pulling, pulling at her with his expectation and need, she couldn't help but retreat. He wanted to discuss their buried feelings, their intentions, their status, and it had to be right then, right when there was discord or distance between them. When he wanted to inspect and analyze the ins and outs of their interactions tirelessly, she turned to her painting, knowing that he understood it as the terrain where he dared not trespass.

She gave painting her devotion, and sometimes he had asked her why they had to work against each other, arguing that love and passion were not, after all, finite resources. As she was nearing forty, Reed had begun to raise the question of having children, but it was a conversation she was never ready to have. She wanted a child in some general, shapeless way, but where would the time and energy for mothering come from, she wondered, and what of herself would she have to give up to accomplish it? "Later," she told him, "let's talk about it later. I just can't think about that yet."

She and Delta had been remembering their mother's feeding, plaiting, cleaning, and arranging hands, recalling how she did for others before, during, and after her office job, with neither ardor nor daily choice, her own calling compressed to Friday evenings after eight. Sunday knew the small, routine tasks that moved life forward were what living and loving were mostly made of, but she wasn't sure how to have passion within the even and mundane. She knew how to be responsible to her art; at that, she could work in steady devotion, in order to be actor not object, in order to reach the quick.

Sunday imagined her own face and Delta's as they looked from the doorway at Dolora trying to have something for herself. If she had seen them watching, their eyes would have seemed like sieve-holes in the dark, through which her passion might drain. And she had persisted, breaking up pieces of stone and tile and striving to arrange them carefully into some kind of sense, so that the river, which had marked her as it stole her husband, wouldn't seize her, too. Trying, with every bit of will she had, to turn the water from taker to giver, to let it baptize.

She meant to have more than a little something for herself, and no one handed over anything, of that much she was sure. She loved Reed and she didn't want to lose him, but she had to admit that she felt safer reserving the option to leave, and safer not being anyone's mother or wife.

As Reed made his way home on the El, he thought back over the class that had just let out. He was invigorated during lectures and discussions, but as soon as he crossed the threshold of the classroom, he felt so drained that he sometimes wondered how he would make it home. He would have stood on his head if he'd had to, in order to make his students see why "They passed nations through their mouths" was an amazing line, and why it was about them. But his public high school students, especially the males, were resistant to liking stories and poetry. Despite their desperation for nourishment, they had accepted the view that literature belonged not to them, not to colored folks and tough guys, but to someone else. Yet he thought he had detected light behind their eyes when he got them talking about how they kept their people's stories alive.

When he leaned his head back against the wall of the train car, he noticed the ceiling graffiti in stylized red and black. As the train stopped and started, and with it the metal rumble and scrape, he went behind the noise and let his thoughts ramble, wondering whether Sunday had left a message while he was at school. Though he had missed her calls the day before, he had tried to honor his commitment not to crowd her, hoping his instincts had been right. Sometimes, when he backed off as she asked, she said she was afraid he didn't care.

Since her departure for Salt County, he had thought back over their relationship, groping for a sense of the big picture, the pattern, the whole. They had been together a year and a half, and she still wouldn't talk about the future. Was he foolish to think she was moving toward him?

They had gotten past the early tensions of their relationship, where there was always conflict about sharing the cooking and cleaning, and she was vigilant about him not pushing his points unfairly, even in conversation, or getting his way about things that seemed minor to him. She was watchful of the "underlying sexism" in the language he used, of presumptions of dominance or acquiescence. "You walk into a room and start talking," she told him, "as if it were all about you. You feel a permission to express your anger or expectations that women just don't feel. It's about respect, Reed, respect that is shown in the smallest things." She was always "on the muscle," in his view, and it got hard to take sometimes, the vigilance about even his choice of words, the tireless effort to understand. "Reed, I know it's good to be the king," she would state after hearing him out, "but those dishes need washing and it's your turn."

In his parents' marriage, the rules had been clear. His mother had not only cooked his father's meals, but had brought him his plate. She had asked his permission to spend money, deferred to him in conversation, and tolerated his moods without a word, suffering in silence if she was cold because he preferred air-conditioning, never asking him to pull into a rest station so that she could use the bathroom because he disliked "stopping unnecessarily" on the road. And she had tolerated his abuse, too, as he laughed at her opinions and pinched her waist to suggest that she was "putting on weight." One Christmas he had given her a dress two sizes too small and told her to "get into it."

It had often hurt him as a child to see his mother treated that way, and also to see that she had decided it was easier for her to maintain a known and superficial calm, to keep the peace. "I like doing for your father," she told him. "It fulfills me, you see." Once, when his father had exploded with an ultimatum about not asking him how his day had gone until he had had a drink, she had begged Reed not to intercede on her behalf, arguing that he would make things harder for her in the end. She said she felt she was lucky, because at least he didn't raise his hand.

Reed knew he was a far cry from his father, and he had few friends who belittled their wives, or ordered them around. Sunday told him he would be surprised if he scratched the surface, what base ideas his male friends might express. The things they struggled with weren't the obvious issues, having to do with workplace politics or legal rights, and this puzzled him, for he had been known to argue a feminist position as fervently as Sunday. But he felt so lost sometimes.

He had always believed that women liked strong, self-confident men, but sometimes, when he thought he was showing those things, Sunday saw something else. What *do* women want? he wondered. She advocated throwing out the order they had both grown up with, but then she clung to a narrow idea of what strong was. He suspected that she found it partially disturbing that he was sensitive and deeply moved. It was confusing, the in-between country in which he found himself, where the old code didn't work, and he didn't quite have a new system to replace it. Sometimes he didn't even know why she got suddenly irate.

"Don't be upset, my little squirrel," he had said early on, and furious, she had answered, "I'm not your little anything, and especially not an animal, and since when is your anger cute?" He recalled his confusion when she had cursed a man on the street who had lowered his eyes to her breasts and said to him, "You sure got a fine one, my brother." Perplexed, Reed had argued that he meant well, he meant it as a compliment, and had found himself struggling to see why, for her, it was the opposite. Or her dismissive ire toward a man who had said, in passing, "Smile, baby, you too pretty to frown." "Fuck you," she had replied, "I'm frowning now, and neither my face nor my mood has a thing to do with you."

"But you're so angry," Reed had said to her, incredulous. "I've never known a woman like you," and she had responded, "I'm gonna let you in on a secret, Reed. All women are angry, but most of us have learned to be polite."

Vestigial, like the appendix, which had once been of service and was now useless or lethal, the old ways were embedded, and only sometimes recognizable as dangerous and outmoded. Things had changed between men and women, and he was working hard to catch up.

He still dreaded the outrage he had come increasingly to share, as well as the disgusted look she sometimes gave him when she heard a chauvinist comment on TV and left the room, muttering, "Men." But there was a way he understood it. When they saw a white man cut in line in front of an old black woman he hadn't even seen, exuding his entitlement as he walked ahead, Reed and Sunday turned to each other and said, "White people." It must be like that. Black folks carried untold rage at violence and inequity, past and present, as they moved through the world, and the knowledge and understanding of how such things worked was like a vital sense, akin to hearing or sight. They read all-white rooms as they entered, presuming enmity as a strategy for survival, careful to determine what possibilities the landscape held. And he knew how self-proclaimed liberals could be the worst, in their certitude of completed consciousness, in their attraction to a comfortable level of guilt and recompense.

For women, he imagined, it must be that way. They had to be wary and watchful, aware of the danger darkness brought, screening out hostility and the daily come-ons they didn't think were compliments. They must feel the weight of history, and the hints of power and ownership, in every interaction they had. And yet, the role of potential enemy was a difficult one. He wanted to say, as he had heard white boys in college whine, "But *I* haven't done anything. I didn't own slaves or join the Klan." Sometimes he did complain. "I'm not those other men you've known, and I live in constant fear of getting a ticket." "Good," she had responded, "that should make you a safe driver, at least." And he had countered, "But I'm not even sure of the rules of the road."

The one thing he had never said, but often thought, was: "I didn't leave you; it wasn't me who ran before you were born." Did she understand how hard he had worked and how much he wanted to be with her? he wondered. Did she know how her moving in and out of reach could ruin even the deepest love? He knew that she was trying, too, and that her mistrust had to do with things much deeper than the gender war. Yielding was what she could not seem to do, and as he had grown more able to show his tenderness and hurt, she had retreated, with painting often the reason she gave.

At times he did wish she were less complicated, less devout. The one and only time he had called her "high maintenance," in their first month together, she had shot back acidly, "Why is it that the male imagination always defaults to an automotive metaphor? I'm a person, so don't compare me to a fucking car! And if your ingenuity isn't any bigger, and you can't help but go there, then tell me why you'd rather have a Pinto than a Benz."

There were still plenty of women who would accept whatever he wanted, and for his first few months with Sunday, he had hedged his bets by continuing to see a few of them. His oldest childhood friend from down the block had told him, "Look, man, Sunday's phat, but there's lots of fine women out there. Take Tanya, for example: She's happy just to be my girl."

As he often did when troubled by their impasses, he remembered a night when he was getting ready to go home after a weekend at her apartment. More and more of his clothes had seemed to be making their way to her place, and he had decided to take some of them home and lighten up things between them a bit, when he had come to the door of her kitchen studio, and watched her working with paint. Look at her, he thought with astonishment, she's right at the axis of her life. A warrior she had seemed to him, feet planted apart firmly, wholly focused, brush in hand. And when she looked up and their eyes met, recognition had passed both ways. He had felt her potential to live and love without measure, and her eyes had told him that it would destroy that very thing he was witnessing to yield on who she was.

They had drawn out that wordless exchange, and he had returned to the bedroom and unpacked.

He knew love could be ocean-deep. It had the rhythms of the moon-pulled tide, and the turbulence and strength of currents that could shift and tumble. If he and Sunday could manage to surrender, he believed they could keep from drowning.

When he opened the door, Reed found Sunday in the kitchen, sitting on the floor in front of an array of canvases.

Engrossed in touching the surfaces of her uncompleted work, she didn't hear him enter. Where, in what she was looking at and feeling, she wondered, were her former selves speaking? Had Sister taken part in the work she saw? Was she straining to come through?

In art school she had had a teacher who had warned her not to let life interfere with work, and she had often felt herself a bungler for failing to keep those lines distinct. But she had never been able to master that approach, and who, she wondered, could afford to live that way? Only someone who was taken care of, who didn't have to face trouble . . . or earn a living . . . or make dinner . . . or be black. Even if that were the goal, how would anyone ever accomplish it? If you had it like that, wasn't that reflected in the work you made?

And what did people mean when they said that? she wondered. Were they saying, "Be disciplined"? Were they saying, "Don't give up your work"? She thought of her mother, making Friday evenings non-negotiable so that she could do the one thing she insisted on for herself. She understood about choices, but didn't you paint from your life?

Could you have the life without the work, the work without the life, or were they inextricable, parts of a whole?

Focusing on the paintings, she saw, in her fumbling toward that uterine ocean of blue, a story line. What unlocking was she after in her return to Salt County? If Reed was right that she was always in some way rendering that homeplace—its buildings, its people, its terrain, and its river—then she had never managed to transplant herself. And where did all her fragmentary reimaginings of that homeplace and that story leave her? How could she find a place to live, and work, between home and home?

Reed stood in the doorway and watched her, guilty that his silent observation was a trespass and afraid to interrupt. Quietly, she surfaced and turned her head.

When she came across the room into his arms, he pulled her hair free of its elastic and they walked to the bedroom, talking in the way they were able, with body for voice. But it wasn't the furious, death-defying love they sometimes made. It wasn't like the time, in their first week together, wrestling free of garments, when she said he was an electrical storm. They had christened every surface, horizontal and vertical, letting it be doorways, tables, floors.

This time, this time it was reverent. Tender and attentive to every hollow, each fold and bone, they moved slowly, lest the filament between them break. She caught her breath as he entered and they held each other with their eyes, bringing all that they had and were to their crossing, and if words had been possible, she would have sworn that she could see the man, the boy, the old person in him all at once. Attuned to every tremor, every sweat bead, every inhale and exhale, they moved just a little, just enough, and their tension swelled, with his hands on her breathing, the tips of her fingers on his neck to catch the pulse. With her mouth just above his, lips almost meeting, they were sharing air.

In the ease of the warm, moist afterward, they lay pressed together, drifting into sleep, which required greater trust, Sunday said, than sex. When she felt him stir, she wanted to speak and pull him closer, and instead, relaxed her hold. Accept this shallow water, she told herself, as their mouths were returned to them, and their limbs, which had for a short time been inseparable, became their own. To keep her body from crying out against his cleaving, Sunday stood and accomplished the separation herself.

She returned in a T-shirt with a cigarette and sat on the edge of the bed.

"So tell me more," Reed said, turning toward her. "He was alive. What else?"

Sunday didn't know where to begin. The more she wanted and needed to explain, she thought, the less she was able, for comfortable with images, she found that words were sometimes the hard part, except for "No." She couldn't start with the failure of language that had left her without a name. She couldn't start with her first day at school. How could she ease into her story, building from something light to the crucial information, in a way that made sense? How could she take him there with her, bit by bit?

She took several drags on her cigarette and decided to focus on what she had learned about Mercury. After explaining about the package from Clement Woods, she summarized the information she had learned about her father from Delta, Opus, and Laveen. After that, she outlined her fruitless trip to the records office, her discovery of the family Bible, and the letter she had sent to Aunt Edna. She explained the dilemma of the gravestone and recounted the visit to Felix Harris's shop.

But she really wanted to tell about her christening, about choosing, choosing a name. She opened her mouth and only smoke came out.

Maybe she could talk about her time in the attic. Stretching out beside him, she began with the accordion staircase and the rediscovery of her little blue church. She described finding the fig box and the memorabilia of Dolora's life. "You said you know me . . . somewhat, anyway," she said, "so what would you put in that kind of box if you made one for me?"

"Are these those little things you were talking about?"

"Well, yeah."

"Let's see, a paintbrush. I would start with that."

"A paintbrush, that fits. That and what else?"

He took a drag from her cigarette. "Maybe a lock of your hair, because it seems so you. Untamed and quirky."

"That's not what my mother called it. She said hair that was the least bit nappy needed to be confined."

"Will our people ever stop being hair-obsessed? What do you think she'd have to say about mine? Maybe she would approve when it's tied back. But you know, if I put a lock of hair to represent you, I'd have to put one of those rubber bands, too," he said, touching her wrist, "because you go in and out having hair that's free." Sunday nodded, thinking how Opus would say, "It's truth."

"And okay . . . I'd put in a coffee bean, since you love your morning elixir so much. And I know"—he smiled—"maybe I'd include an emblem from a fancy car. A Benz. Remember the thing you said that time about being a Benz and not a Pinto?" She punched him playfully, and asked, "What else?" resuming her position on the edge of the bed, unaccustomed to the role of pressing for intimate dialogue. She wanted to ask what single photo of her he might decide to keep.

"I'm not sure."

She watched him silently, and when he could not continue, she was desolate. Sunday was sure Reed knew her better than anyone ever had, and still he couldn't really say who she was in the way she had asked. His silence came down between them, and suddenly she imagined Delta, on the other side of her bedroom door. She had kept herself separate, and that was what it cost.

"It's not an easy question," he offered, and she had to admit that she valued Reed's honesty, difficult as it was to bear. If he didn't like or understand something in her painting, he usually said so. "This is interesting, but I don't feel it," he might say, or "I don't understand what you are after here."

She waited quietly while he thought, realizing that she would have little trouble assembling a box for him. She would put in poems and stories . . . his favorite bracelet . . . classroom chalk . . .

He finally spoke. "You know those pairs of shells you can sometimes find on the beach, where the two parts are still joined?" He hinged his hands together. "Maybe I'd put in a halfway open one of those."

When she closed her eyes again she felt awash in shifting blues, as if she was trying to live in one of her finished canvases. And she had the dawning sense that there might be renewal in that wellhead, in that color that kept calling her back.

Reed coaxed her to lie down while he massaged her scalp, and when he asked whether she was making any progress with Delta, she told him about the possibility of a bond she could feel, amid the ongoing discord. She revealed about their childhood oath, showing him the gesture that had made it concrete.

"Did she like the earrings?"

"Well, she wore them, for a day. But I knew as soon as she put them on that they were wrong. They were what I would have picked for me."

He watched her as she talked, noting the concentration in the muscles of her face. As always, her eyes burned, but there was uncertainty in them, too, and he caught its flare.

Placing his hand just below her waist and drawing on faith, he said, "I know I'm in there, in your belly, and you're in mine. Go back. I'll be over here in Chicago, loving you, and I'll give some more thought to what I would put in a fig box for you."

She stayed several days, and then he woke one morning to find her repacking her suitcase. He watched her from the bed as she looked around the room, as if memorizing both it and him, in the tumble of sheets. Sitting on the bed, she ran her fingertips along his naked, rosary spine. "What would you think of us putting up a night sky on the ceiling?" she asked. "Could we do that, do you think?"

"I've got to stop doing this," Sunday said to herself as the train began to move. "Life's becoming a blurry Amtrak ride, and I'm not sure if I'm coming or going."

She fell asleep to the rocking of the train and woke as her landmarks came into view. Buildings and fields. Windmill and loud graffiti. Like the river, back and forward, her life seemed to flow both ways.

Impatient and afraid, she leaned forward as if to make the train go faster. How was it that she was wary of knowing and at the same time anxious to discover everything right away? She wanted Reed to keep his distance, yet to know and be able to say who she was. She wished she could allow herself to want him fully, and to run when she needed to. And she yearned to be close to Delta, without either conflict or mess. Her desire was filled with contradiction, that much she knew.

Sunday wanted her family and friends to forfeit their stories, now that she knew she needed them. She wished they could present themselves like the dioramas she had seen at museums, in three-dimensional unfolding, viewed through a private opening. But finding and accepting these stories, in whatever dimensions were available, was a process, entailing risk and doubt.

At some point she had learned, in painting, that she had to work at not getting ahead of herself in her yearning for a piece to cohere. It took discipline, and belief, to embrace the discomfort of her initial brush strokes and marks, and to release her uncertainty that they would come to anything. If they did begin to amount to something, she had to fight knowing what that would be. The task was to begin and be able to live with it, and then to take only the next step and the next, trusting discovery as she went along. As she reworked and painted over, reconsidering and rearranging, she had to practically chant a belief in the way of things, to tell herself that nothing, nothing started whole.

Returning to her sister and all of the questions they had begun to answer, she felt her stomach knotting at the need to explain and redress her last act of leaving. Despite the safety of extremes, she knew that reaching Delta would take patience and a gentle care that didn't overwhelm. Love entailed both mystery and trust.

As she looked from the window to see that she was crossing Salt County's brown river, she thought of Felix Harris, persistently diving to raise its sunken secrets, one by one. Not everything could be yanked immediately into the light and forced to give up its truth. And whatever you found beneath the river's rippling surface, its rhythm and its double flow had to be respected, or the thing you gave the water was your life.

13

SUNDAY WENT DIRECTLY from the train to the Salt County Post Office, before she could change her mind. She pulled her luggage cart up the front steps, across the lobby, and over to the counter where Delta was standing.

Noting her difficult entrance as she struggled to fit her cart and suitcase through the narrow doorway, Delta had a chance to empty her face of surprise and expectation as she organized folders of commemorative stamps. People like the flowers and birds best, she thought, putting those on top.

"I'm back. And I'm sorry," Sunday said quietly.

Delta paused from her task. "And what is it, exactly, that you're sorry about?"

"Running. Leaving you in house repair purgatory. Evading the family ghosts. In fact, I'd like to submit a blanket sorry," she said, stretching her arms wide, "for my lifetime of crimes. You think that kind of bargain is ever accepted, an apology that's wide enough to cover the entire past?"

Delta smiled slightly, in spite of herself, at the dramatic gesture, wondering if there was something about her uniform and the counter behind which she stood that motivated people to express themselves in terms of transactions.

"Guess not," Sunday said, beginning to smile, too. "Then what I'm sorry for is the way I left." She placed her hands on the counter and leaned forward. "What do you think about going to Clare County and finding Clement Woods?"

Delta took a step back. Although she had suspected that Sunday was headed toward the idea of tracking down Mercury's envoy, the suggestion still took her aback. She realized that she was holding a sheet of stamps, and the stamps were getting sticky from the sweat on her fingertips. "Well . . ." she said, letting go of the stamps, "since I get off work in twenty minutes, why don't we talk about it then. Basically, I'm not so very entirely sure that finding him is what we really ought to go ahead and . . . do."

Wow, Sunday thought, that was a lot of qualifiers for one sentence. "Okay. I'll go to the house and when you get there, we'll figure it out. But maybe, just in case, you should look him up in your postal book for Clare County."

Delta watched Sunday inch her cart through the door and down the steps and turn toward home. So much for patience and gentleness, Sunday thought, upset with herself, even though her impulsive declarations and proposition seemed to have gone okay. Damn, Delta thought, shaking her head with both bewilderment and affection, she blew in here like a tropical storm, and I could resist, but what's the point? I got up this morning thinking I knew just what this day would bring, and before I know it, I'm on the road to Clare County.

Delta entered the house carrying a letter. She handed it to Sunday, merely saying, "I should have known you'd go ahead and write her, whatever I thought of the idea. Anyway, the address Opus gave you must have been good. You've got a response."

Sunday was tempted to take the letter upstairs and pore over it privately, but knowing the explosion that might cause, she opened it at the table and read it, passing it on to Delta when she was done.

Dear Sunday Owens,

What a shock to get a note from you after all these years. I never thought you would of wanted to hear from me, of all people. I kept up with you all through Alva—down at the county office—and that's how I learned that they come to call you Sunday, and not just Sister. When I would send you and Delta those cards over the years, I was never sure if hearing from me made the hurtfulness your father caused either better or worse.

I want you to know I never did blame your granddaddy or anybody else for not wanting me around. I know I was your reminder of how things went bad.

Since you asked, I'm not so bad for the shape I'm in—old woman with sugar, who can't see too good. My neighbor from cross the hall is writing this for me. I never was too fond of either letters or figures—and now I don't even see. She's old as I am, so I guess we're the blind leading the blind.

You got me to thinking back to so many things. Ask your sister if she reclects the chalk and little blackboard she just had to have, and how she tried to take charge and be a little mother with you. Now I wasn't there to see you grow into a girl and then a woman, but I remember what a watchful type baby you were.

I tried to think on what I would say about the kind of boy and young man my nephew was. As a little thing he was very attach to me, but then when his mother left, he was only four. When I would go to work—in the laundry at that time—and keep him with a lady down the street, his eyes would get all worried and he would bounce up and down I would try to hold him and resure him that I was coming back. But after while—he started to pull away and say GO. I WANT YOU TO GO.

I'm not for certain what kind of memory he had of his mother—my sister Annie—but when I explained later on that she hadn't no choice but to leave him with me he got real mad and said he didn't understand how a mother could give her child away. It was like he just wouldn't hear my explanation that she couldn't feed him, and she was afraid he would catch the consumption—now they call it TB—if she kept him. He never got to make it up with her since she died so fast. And he never did want to talk of her. All he had to say on it was—she walked out and she left me behind.

Mercury always wanted things I could not afford to give him. A microscope and a set of cyclopedias are things I remember. He would cut out pictures from magazines of the things he was gon to get and he had stacks of those pages tied together with shoelaces or pasted on the cardboards from shirts I brung home from the laundry.

That boy always did want everything or nothing at all. If he wanted a quarta pound of hard candy and I said he could get a few pieces his eyes fired up hot hot and he said he'd do without. And unless he could win a game he would not play.

Early on in school he made good marks and he was the curious sort. But he started getting in trouble for not minding his teachers or for drifting off into some dream place where he mostly lived. One time I got a note to come in and see somebody, and they told me when he got called on, he wasn't paying tention, and the other kids laughed when he didn't know the answer, let alone the question she asked. He broke his ruler in half and called that teacher stupid right in front of the class. I didn't know what to do about him, but I put him on punishment by making him stay home for a month. I guess that was pretty much like putting Brer Rabbit in the briar patch, since the thing he liked the best was to be holed up in his room alone.

Then we moved to Salt County—I spec that was when he was in the seventh grade. And he still didn't have no friends. I would ask him didn't he have nobody he wanted to have over for a Coca-Cola or go out with but he just shook his head. He didn't seem to know how to make friends cept by bragging or stretching the truth.

He sure was crazy bout your mama though and she was a beauty with all that pretty hair and I never will forget the way she took what happened to her with her grace. They was always together at first and she seemed to just hang on every word he said. I know things changed after news of your sister coming without there being no intention— and he just kinda folded up. Got more and more withdrawn.

But the thing I want you to know is he was a good boy too. And I did love him—spite his faults. He was mine I guess and a mother will still love her child, no matter what he done.

I did promise Annie I would raise him the very best I could. I spec I didn't do too good after all, but it weren't for no lack of love or trying either.

I wish I could say to you that I know why he did what he did— leaving you to get on without a father—but I really can't. That's the question I go to sleep with still. And I never do get an answer—either then or when I wake.

I sure am proud of you and your sister. You all both—and your mama—made something of yourself from what I heard. And I know none of that credit is mine or my Mercury's.

For what it's worth I'm still your Aunt Edna. Some things never finish off.

Both sisters wondered what it must have felt like to be Edna, driven by her nephew's incomprehensible act to leave behind the little bit of family she had known. But she had remembered them, and felt a lasting, long-distance pride. She didn't blame Grandpa and had struggled to see the good in Mercury, despite being mystified and ashamed of his choice. They were moved by the report of Mercury's motherless pain, and by Edna's chagrin and enduring love, and her letter helped them, along with the things told by Opus and Laveen, to picture their father in his youth.

"Now that we have this letter, things are coming together," Sunday said. "Don't you think it's time we went to see Clement Woods?"

"Well . . ." Delta stalled, "another way of looking at it is to say that we have some answers and we could be satisfied . . . content with what we know."

They sat at the kitchen table and hashed it out, with Sunday making a case for them being able to finally put Mercury's life and death to rest, if only they could get his story from Clement Woods. Delta maintained that they were taking a risk, since what Clement could tell them might be even more disturbing than the little they already knew. "We don't have much to work with," she argued, "but as it stands, we can still . . . I don't know . . . decide to believe something at least partway good . . . about who he was and why he left. Even though it's hard having questions, there's sort of a . . . kind of a . . . comfort in it." What Delta ultimately responded to was the suggestion that making the trip together might help them with their own bond.

"I can't say I'm for it, but I'll go if you want me to," she said.

Sunday considered that, and then folded her arms and said, "No. It can't be that way. You've got to decide you'll go, but not just for me. Not because I've pushed it, if you're really against it."

Sunday thought of the stuck places in her own life. She thought of all the missed moments to do and say what was called for, and the memory returned to her of hearing Delta just outside her door on the night of Nana's funeral. The wounding words, spilled whiskey and broken glass, and her standing on the inside of that door and doing nothing but waiting, silent, as she listened to her sister's breathing, and then heard her walk away.

"You know, Delta," she said quietly, "not choosing is a kind of choosing, too."

Delta fought the impulse to smooth her eyebrows or reach for her Kools as Sunday unfolded her arms and leaned toward her, tapping her finger on the table's edge. "You can't just go along, as if you didn't pick it. You've got to be in this on your own."

With the number she had found in the postal book for Woods, C., Photographer, Delta placed the call, hollering for Sunday to pick up the other phone when it began to ring.

Sunday asked, "Is this the Clement Woods who knew Mercury Owens?" and when he said, "Yes, ma'am, it is," she said, "Well, it's his daughters calling. We got your note."

She could hear his breathing, but he didn't speak. "My sister and I would like to know if we could come and speak to you," she said, and still he did not respond.

"Hello?" Sunday practically cried, showing her distress that just as they were confronting their final source of information, it was slipping away.

When he cleared his throat she knew he was still there, and then he spoke. "Figured you might call. Guess that's why I left off my return address, so's you'd be positive that's what you wanted. I thought if you had to work a little to find me, that would make you sure."

He told them they could come and they made a plan to visit the next day, figuring that if they left early, they would get there by afternoon.

Delta rose at 6 A.M. and began to get ready for their trip. She dressed for tasteful practicality in a navy turtleneck, gray wool slacks, and her crepe-soled walking shoes. And although they were more noticeable than she preferred, she wore the silver fish earrings Sunday had given her, hoping that at least they would declare that she was on board, and that maybe they would act as good luck charms.

She fried chicken and made deviled eggs, filling Christmas fruitcake tins that she had carefully lined with waxed paper. Sunday remembered those tins, with their rusted reindeer and manger scenes, but she couldn't recall when she had last seen waxed paper. She rarely ate eggs, much less deviled ones, and never fried her chicken or even ate it with the skin. Delta's efforts made her think of the Bread Ladies' trip to her graduation, when, mistrustful of the train food and the promise of its safe and polite delivery into their black hands, they had cooked and brought their own fried chicken and pound cake, as well as linen napkins, thermoses, and cutlery, so that they could eat in style.

The only real out-of-town car trip Delta had ever made was when she and Nate Hunter had quit Salt County, and that time, they had left without either provisions or plans. This time, she filled a cooler with black cherry Kool-Aid so they wouldn't have to stop if they got thirsty. She didn't know if they would even stay the night, but she packed a small suitcase with toiletries and another turtleneck and pair of slacks, in case they got delayed or stuck, and several changes of underwear. It was always good, she felt, to have extra underwear.

She backed the 1978 LeMans she had inherited from Patrice and Alpha out of the garage to wash and Armor All it for the trip. She drove the car to go shopping, on her rare trips to church, and to dinner at the Red Lobster or the Rice Bowl with Dinah or co-workers. And sometimes, in the middle of a sleepless night, she took the car out on the highway and drove. She never went more than twenty miles from Salt County, but she liked to put the windows down and push the speedometer to ninety for just a little while, when there were no other cars on the road.

Nervous about leaving, she checked the refreshments, the directions, and the suitcase, and then honked, and waited for Sunday to join her. "If we're going, let's step to it, before I change my mind and unpack." As she climbed into the car, Sunday noticed the pewter fish earrings, and she knew Delta had worn them as a gesture of solidarity.

They pulled away and wove through the neighborhood toward the river, and then the car hummed and vibrated as the tires took the grating of the bridge.

"It'll be good to get away from here," Delta commented, "but I guess you know all about that."

Focusing on the spokes of the bridge that were flashing by in the side mirror, Sunday let the comment pass. "Two for one and one for two," she said quietly, and Delta looked at her own face in the rearview mirror and finished it: "You for me and me for you."

Before they had reached the county limits, Delta had opened the chicken and pulled out a drumstick. She was steering with one hand and feeding herself with the other.

"Chicken at ten A.M.?" Sunday said, chuckling.

Delta put down the chicken leg and snapped back, "Why don't you look at that road map instead of worrying about what I'm doing?"

Sunday unfolded the state map and pretended to read it, but its roads and rivers looked like that tangled skein of the peeled baseball she had just, days before, been thinking of. Her face burned and she regretted the comment, which she was pretty sure she had meant as a good-hearted tease. How quickly things could turn. She thought of that line Reed liked to quote from a play he often taught: "Things have a way of turning out so badly."

Delta saw that Sunday was leaning tensely toward the door and staring fixedly at the outstretched map. She's retreating, she thought, and reached out to pull her back into conversation. "I didn't mean to bark at you. I'm sorry. It's just that Earlene's not the only one of us there's more of. I myself have surrendered to elastic waistbands. That should give you a sense of where I am."

"I shouldn't have said what I said either. Maybe we can start over."

"Maybe so. Then, let's see . . ." She wanted to chat pleasantly, but she also felt bad that she hadn't asked about the thing that was most important to her sister. Her avoidance of the topic of Sunday's painting was probably becoming conspicuous, but she was never sure what she might be stirring up in asking hard questions, or what ignorance or misinterpretation she might reveal. Sometimes it was safer to keep quiet, or at least to keep things light.

"You know, I've been thinking, it's been a long time since I've seen your artwork."

"It's been a long time since you've seen me."

"Yes. Yes, it has."

"And I haven't seen you in at least as long." How much time had passed, she wondered, since they had really seen each other? She couldn't even think how long it had been.

Delta's eyes filled with tears. "You know what I was thinking of yesterday, after you left? I was walking around looking at all the things we had done to the house. And I remembered when you painted the ceiling, and Mama made you cover it over."

Sunday laughed. "Yeah, I've been thinking of that. It's not something I could ever forget. Even the ceiling hasn't completely forgotten. But you know, since that time, I've always been captivated by stars."

"Me, too, that is in terms of astrology. It's kind of a hobby of mine. And you, you've kept painting them, the stars?"

"Yeah, like in the watercolors in the dining room, the ones of the night."

"You mean the hand-type things?"

"Mmn hmmn."

"So . . . they *are* hands?"

"I guess they are. That's what I had in mind in any case."

"And so . . . the little white things are stars? Stars in the night?"

"Sure."

Delta grinned. She had sometimes wondered if they might be salt or snow, or whether she was supposed to think about what they were at all. She cranked up her nerve. "You know . . . this may be a stupid question, but there's something I've always wanted to know about that painting . . . or drawing."

Sunday faced her, turning sideways in the car seat. "What?"

"I've always wanted to know whether those hands are collecting, or tossing out those stars."

"That's a good question. It's for you to decide. I don't really know."

She didn't know? What did she mean by that? Delta wondered, focusing on the curves of the road. If she didn't know, who did?

"And why, in the dining room pictures, is the night all apart, in . . . in sections?"

Sunday looked at her, thinking of the figures and bodies she had painted most recently, but she didn't answer.

"Do you always paint things broken?"

"Broken?" Sunday was surprised. It was not the word she would have used, and in fact, she had never quite thought of it that way. When she had depicted things with overlapping and superimposed edges, she had thought of them as having separate components or pieces.

"Well, I don't know," Delta said. "To me, they're broken. But I guess it's all a matter of . . . perspective." Her questions and comments were flowing, for she finally had the chance to ask about things that had seemed mysterious and closed off. Even in other times, when they had talked as girls, or by phone from Chicago to Salt County, they had hardly ever discussed what Sunday thought she was doing in painting, or what the images and colors and her ways of putting them down meant to her. Delta was too intimidated to venture there. She didn't even know what questions were appropriate, or what artists felt about talking to someone ignorant, like her. That time she had gone to the art museum in Peoria on a school trip, she had felt that she had failed, somehow, to know the right things to think and say about the paintings in their heavy gold frames, to really understand the excitement and meaning they held. She had tried to either keep her comments and questions as general as possible, or to focus on some concrete aspect, like a color or a texture, and say, "I like that."

"So what I'm wondering is this: In what you paint, are things coming apart, or coming together?"

Sunday was quiet for a full minute. "Neither. Either. Both. They just are that way, I guess."

"I see," Delta said.

I guess you do, Sunday thought. Unsettled, exposed, she tried to absorb her sister's comments, as well as the role-reversal that had somehow taken place; she couldn't think when Delta had asked her, really asked her, about her work. For her part, Delta was feeling exhilarated from asserting herself, but she sensed Sunday's disorientation and in order to sustain the conversation, she pursued a less loaded line of questioning.

"I remember a time you would get up in the night and sketch out something that was bothering you. I guess you couldn't sleep until you got it out, so I'd wake up and there you were, hunkered down in bed with your pad and charcoal pencil or pastel crayons. You wouldn't even notice I was up. You were that into whatever you were doing, like Mama with her tiles, and sometimes there would be charcoal smudges on the bedding and the pillow, which would make her crazy when she found out."

Sunday's face glowed and she rested the map on her knees. "I guess I've always been that way," she said, "though the painting has been . . . slow . . . lately. But there's nothing like it when you find your way in." She started talking about how it was when things opened up. "You know how you can be tongue-tied, or unable to find the right word?"

Delta nodded. She knew all about it.

"But then when things come together, it's like you've found language, and it flows from you, like water from an unstopped tap. You get lost in time and space, I guess. Once, at a moment like that, I had the chance to see myself through Reed's eyes." As she talked animatedly about losing herself in painting, the air snapped with electricity and Delta was relieved and at the same time, uneasy, that she had found the right question to ask. Sunday, sitting right beside her, had become a foreigner, and it was the thing she had seen in Dolora, from the kitchen doorway as she went deep within. And she recalled Nana lifting her head to sing, and noticing the distended artery in her neck. Frightened, Delta had been unable to avoid picturing her blood, pounding through that channel, and she felt that same way as she listened to Sunday. Both afraid and envious.

"So there I was," Sunday said, her voice rising, "paint on my face and neck and arms, and Reed came through the door and looked at me, and I had no idea that I was covered with it, and I was so completely absorbed that I couldn't say anything out loud. We just stood and watched each other from across the room, neither one of us moving, and I felt like some untamed, nocturnal animal caught by the side of the road in the headlights of his eyes. Until he looked at me, I hadn't seen myself at all, you know, because I was just in it. In the groove. I was so deep in it I was up under it."

Delta remembered the time Sunday had been so caught up in working on a watercolor, standing at her easel in the basement, that she hadn't even noticed flooding water seeping into the house until her feet were soaked.

"Do you know what I mean?" Sunday asked. "Have you felt that way?" Their eyes met in the rearview mirror.

I know about that in one way, Delta thought. The intoxication of a naked stranger. The freedom to meet unencumbered only because it would be mercifully brief, and would have no chance to go awry. "Well . . . I'm afraid the only thing I could ever throw my whole self into, the only thing I ever felt that way about, was love."

Sunday knew as Delta spoke that the scorch she had seen in her eyes had to do with a man.

Since she was fourteen, Delta's boyfriends had ruled her life, but even when she had had an admirer like Delmar Watson, who had pursued her with pedestrian sincerity throughout the eleventh grade, she had yearned for something bolder, something riskier.

"Who? Delmar?" Delta had said, when Sunday had suggested him as a date. "He wears a tie to school. He carries his little pencils in an organizer and sits in the front row, where he raises his hand straight up and answers the teacher's questions in a monotone." About the heart-shaped card he gave her, she said, "He's sweet. And predictable. He's not for me. I," she had said, "I am looking for something else." And Delmar, disqualified by his sincere and reliable devotion, didn't even know he couldn't be seen.

Delta thought she had found that something in Rudy Johnson. Sunday pictured the room she had shared with Delta, and its closet, trailing a winding phone cord. She had heard muffled sobbing from behind the closet door, and then Delta had emerged, phone in hand, to say that again, Rudy had decided he wasn't sure he "could be tied down." For two years, he had been unable to resolve the question of whether or not he wanted Delta, and he had had her riding a roller coaster, with troughs as overwhelming and pronounced as its crests. After each upheaval, he would return and win her over with his intense and mer-curial passion, and before long, she had retreated again to the dark and confidential safety of the closet to urge and agonize, convinced with each episode that she was losing her only chance at love.

Sunday had always wondered if Delta would have been able to rec-ognize a "Yes" that didn't arrive coupled with a "Maybe" or a "No." She had wanted to be wanted, however intermittently, in a desperate way, and the breakups with Rudy pitched the reunions higher, for it was intoxicating each time they shifted from off to on. The something else for which she was looking in a man was the aptitude for making the extraordinary out of what was commonplace.

When Sunday had first moved to Chicago, Delta had asked for her reassurance in their fortnightly phone calls that she would find "the one." For a decade she had had a string of steady interests, each con-suming her for a time. And then, for a stretch of years, she had men-tioned no single person, but had said that she was "playing the field." But by the time of Nana's funeral, Delta had stopped talking about men at all. She had seemed tired, and resigned to the evenness of life alone.

Sunday had tried to avoid that very intensity and imbalance that Delta had seemed to crave, resisting, still, with Reed, the letting go. She thought of how, in the chronology of school photos she had stud-ied the night she first arrived, each picture of Delta confessed a reti-cence. In the earliest—second grade—one, her eyes seemed wary and older than her softly rounded face, and later, she looked afraid. Sunday recalled how mistrustful Delta had been of the voluptuous body which had somehow grown, seemingly of its own will. In most of the photos she avoided the camera, glancing to the side or down, her mouth undecided about whether to smile, or even stumble into speech. But when she had left the house on Rudy Johnson's arm, Sunday thought, riding the high of his fluctuating ardor, she had exuded confidence with a full, radiant smile.

For a while, Delta had refused to undress in front of Sunday, and had complained anxiously that her body was turning on her. "Wait," she had said to Sunday in the darkness, "just wait till it happens to you." Later, she must have decided to flaunt what had been a source of nightly worry.

Delta's suddenly curvaceous body and giggling shyness had combined to demand male attention. Neighborhood men watched her pass with tightly wound restraint, and on things intimate, their mother had offered no specific guidance, repeating Grandpa's admonitions on "following through," "being a lady," and "seemly conduct," and never speaking overtly of sex. Rather than talk to her daughters plainly and confront her own acquaintance with the ruin that unleashed desire could bring, she had tried to communicate strength through silence, while praying for them to come through puberty unscathed.

Gangly and bespectacled, Sunday had not had to resist the pursuits of worldly men and eager boys. She had not had the all-consuming bond of a best friend, or been part of a group. Delta traveled with a pack of girls led by Earlene Hall, who had hung out at the train station or the playground, watching boys play basketball. They rode around in Earlene's borrowed Camaro, listening to the eight-track and drinking Yago Sangria or Boonesfarm Strawberry Wine, trading information on clothes and hit singles and eligible boys, and never, ever confessing their doubts and fears.

Sunday hadn't even had that, and until she left Salt County, she had never had a boyfriend or a date. Nana had persuaded her to ask a fellow drawing student to the prom, arguing that she shouldn't miss such an important event, but their attachment had never transcended drawing and school. When she reached Chicago, she had never been kissed. That had probably been good, she thought, for if she had had a lover, she might not have escaped her hometown.

But she had felt herself a refugee, yearning for the ties that also threatened peace.

Delta was right. Love and lovemaking promised the feeling of affiliation, and she guessed that was what she had been seeking in the casual and brief sexual encounters of her twenties. She fantasized that with that kind of experience, she would become more herself, become healed, but those couplings had left her feeling even more deeply estranged.

Years before, at thirteen or fourteen, she had planted a patch of daylilies out front, unaware that their life span was declared in their name. She had been ecstatic when she saw their rockets of flesh splitting into stars, moist and pollen-heavy, and then heartbroken when their deep orange and mauve shriveled in the space of a day, closing when appreciation had barely ripened, as if beauty so lush and incandescent had to pass quickly, had to almost hurt. If they were not painful in their banality, Sunday's one-night encounters had reminded her of those daylilies.

Remembering Delta's soft sobbing from the closet door, she considered the hurt in her eyes. What was the nature of this burn? What had happened this time? Maybe Nate Hunter had been the desperate lover, the "one" she had kept praying for, and maybe he had appeared after she had given up. ". . . if you had met that Nate fellow she took off with . . ." Opus had said. Sunday wanted to know what had happened, but she was afraid of the anger she might provoke if she pried.

Delta gripped the steering wheel and watched the broken lines delineating her highway lane. She had seen Sunday's penetrating look and in the quiet that followed, she knew she was putting pieces together from the past and the present to imagine what was going on. She wanted to tell her sister about Nate Hunter, for Dinah was the only one who knew that everything in her life had shifted, and she wanted her sister to know, too, how at first it had been glorious, that crazy plunge, that inebriated loss of boundary lines. And then she had found herself out at the margin of her life with a man who had become a danger. She had found her way back with the help of Dinah, her blue metal chalk box, and the endless, imagined objects it had come to hold.

Sunday noticed they were picking up speed. Driving with other people always distressed her, a subway-riding girl. She only drove Reed's clunker to get art supplies, and really trusted her feet better than machines governed by someone else. She realized she was pressing her own foot against the floor, and although she didn't want to aggravate Delta, she said, "Hey there, aren't you going a little fast?"

Delta hadn't even realized she was creeping up past eighty. Easing her foot off the pedal, she leaned back and gripped the steering wheel with both hands. She wanted to tell her sister how when Nate Hunter had entered her life, insatiable, asking all the questions she had waited to hear, everything had given way. She didn't have all the words she needed to begin there. All she managed to say was "It came like fire." And once Delta started talking, her story came rushing out.

When she had looked up to find him standing at her postal counter, seven feet tall, burnt-almond brown and absolutely bald, it had been impossible to look away from the hunger in his gaping eyes.

He had returned the next day and the next, waiting in line each time to buy a single, thirty-two-cent stamp. "Do you have anything black?" he had asked, and when she said, "Not right now," he said, "Then what have you got that doesn't have a person or a flag?" She had showed him flowers and trains, hearts and angels, and told him about the self-adhesive books. "I like to lick 'em myself," he had said, smiling secretively as he examined them, "and I'll take that one, the one with the train." While he waited he flexed the muscle in his jaw and rocked from foot to foot, his body taut with longing held in check.

At four fifty-nine on Friday of that week, he had appeared again at her counter emitting a pepper-citrus smell, and requested one stamp. "This time, a flower," and then asked if he could know anything about her, anything at all that she was willing to tell. She gave her name.

He reappeared on Monday and every day that week, each time asking for one commemorative thirty-two-cent stamp and a single piece of information. She gave him her age, her height, and then her address. On Friday he asked for the heart stamp and his question was what time he should come.

Despite her answer, he had showed up early and helped himself to a seat on the couch. After passing her a box of Belgian chocolates, he had said, "Tell me all about you, Delta Owens. Tell me everything." When she paused to remove the lid and offer the candy, first, to him, he had lifted his impossibly long fingers to catch the shiny, quilted paper that lined the box as it floated up, and then plucked a candy from its pleated nest. Consuming it whole with closed-eyed rapture, he had licked melted chocolate from his fingers, lips, and teeth, and she had started, transfixed by pleasure that was oversized.

"But where did he come from? What brought him to Salt County?"

"I still don't know, and I didn't ask. I just welcomed him into my life, from that time with the candy on the couch. His passion for chocolate seemed like a good sign. To have that kind of wanting was . . . impressive, I guess." But something about his lust had been vaguely disturbing, she had to admit, on looking back at it, and she wasn't sure if she had smothered her discomfort, or transformed it, with romance and ingenuity, into something virtuous.

Sunday nodded as she heard the story take shape.

"He said I was his fantasy," Delta went on, "and instead of that scaring me, it made me kind of . . . drunk. He called five times a day, and it felt absolutely wonderful, even as it irritated and hemmed me in. He wanted complete loyalty, and if I didn't get off the other line and call him back right away, he questioned my love. I was careful not to doubt him in any way, intent on showing him that I was capable of rock-solid devotion. I was sure he was misplaced in his job at the gas company, convinced that he had talent that was either unawakened or overlooked."

On weekends they stayed up all night, making love, watching vintage movies, playing cards. They had barbecue and champagne for breakfast, and then slept till dusk. They sneaked into the community center pool and skinny-dipped, or climbed to the roof to see the moon.

Messages arrived in chocolate box depressions. HURRY. DELICIOUS. NOW.

She tried to make Sunday understand, explaining, "He hardly ever did anything halfway, and when he did, he gave the impression that it took unbelievable control. There was just so . . . so *much* of him. He was seven feet of dark brown fineness, with an appetite to match."

"Were there other signs of . . . trouble?" Sunday asked, and Delta considered the question.

"Signs? More and more there were. When it was good, the air was hot and electric, and it made all the empty places in my life feel okay, but I think there was a hint of something else, some partway-hidden edge. When we argued, it was this huge dramatic thing, with him storming out, only to come back later, of course, and his moods were apt to change suddenly, without me knowing why.

"You know I'm no stranger to drama, Sunday. I'm sure you remember Rudy Johnson, and all the other boneheads I told you about. But Nate might yell, or even worse, he might refuse to speak to me for days. I never knew what would happen, and I reminded myself of people who come to live with terrorists in their midst. You might be doing the most everyday thing, like going to the market or brushing your teeth, and a bomb goes off. I keep trying to figure out how I could have heard what I needed to hear, because it took way too long for me to accept that Nate Hunter's flair for pleasure and imagination was matched by a talent for hurt."

Delta knew that one thing she had either disregarded or declined to fully hear was a comment Nate had made on his first visit to her house. In between Belgian chocolates, he had told her that the courtship, the falling, was the very best part of love, for it was in that choreographed plummet that he got to use his ingenuity; it was then that love was fresh, and open, and pure. Nate Hunter relished the license to express himself, and he was blessed not only with imagination but with the fact that his feelings came to him easily.

It was as if Delta had added a few words to her mother's verbal bequest: she had worked at restrictive memory, and at selective hearing, too.

A "Gas, Food, Lodging" sign appeared and she moved into the right lane.

"I know one thing," she said as she approached the exit. "I've read about people being drawn to trouble. The edge of a tall building can make some people want to jump, or something really dangerous, like a raging ocean storm or a burning forest, can have a pull to it. And I know, now, how that kind of thing can happen. I know how that kind of thing can be true."

Sunday didn't like hearing that feeling put into words. "So . . . it was . . . like a storm or a height?" she asked, half-afraid of the response.

"It was fire, Sunday, a forest fire."

It came, the thing Delta had yearned for all her life, as those who live with drought pray, recklessly, for wild rain, suspecting it will tear through things, knowing it will come with thunder and lightning, rocking things to their roots and maybe striking.

Striking a still thing that is there, ready, rising from the ground. A church spire, or something sleeping, even, something alive like Alice, her favorite tree. Searing to its center with fast, white fire that flares orange and yellow once it hits. Claiming what is in its path.

Delta was that still thing. She was a lightning rod.

Recalling the sweeping burn, she felt she had been colored like a tube of Sunday's cadmium red paint, from the inside out. She was lit from within, once again, as she remembered what she was trying to tell.

Fire had caught to the tinder of her life and spread, eating past the dry wood to the still-supple center and reaching her sunken roots, dumb in the darkness and slow with the weight of resignation and memory.

Fire came and took her, and she found herself leaning toward the heat.

"So here's what I've come up with," she said, pulling into the gas station parking lot and bringing the LeMans to a stop. "I think it was the idea of love that we were into. The idea of unchecked love." She turned off the car and looked at her sister. "So you asked if I've ever felt the way you do when you are painting, deep in the groove, like you said."

"Yeah. Nana called it 'the quick,' that place where you're most alive and plugged in. Where the blood flows."

"Okay, well, my answer is that love is where I've tried to find the quick."

For six months, she and Nate had been consumed with their splendid invention, sharing the tale of how they met and got together with anyone who would listen, refining it with observations and pauses and jokes. "We're soul mates," they announced to each other, narrating their tale as they lived it, "brought together by the U.S. Postal Service and chocolate . . . We're perfect for each other . . . We're forever, you and me." They were lost in the story they were building, unable or at least unwilling to distinguish between desire and love.

On the day when he said, "Let's leave this place," she had barely paused to get her coat. Locking the door to her house and driving off in his silver Electra 225, she told herself that his impulsiveness showed a clarity that was both courageous and virile. Thinking that finally she had found "the one," that something else she craved, she had wished she could tell Sunday the news.

"That's when I sent you the card with the sunset that was blank inside. I hoped you would catch my meaning, that something bigger than words was happening, and understand."

Sunday hated to admit that she hadn't. "I knew you were trying to say something, but I didn't know what. It was so different from the other cards you sent, but I thought it was something about a trip to the beach, with the sunset and all."

"Don't you ever wonder," Delta said, "how it is that people are ever understood?"

"Especially when they try to relate with codes and symbols and silences," Sunday replied, "like we have always done."

"Yeah. Well . . . I've got to admit that I often didn't know what to make of the things you sent. They were unusual, beautiful, but I wasn't even sure which was top and bottom."

Sunday laughed and Delta continued, "But I saw you in them, and I was glad when they came. I knew you were saying something about what lasts.

"Anyhow, Nate. After several weeks in roadside motels, watching the daytime stories and waiting for him to reappear with food, with leads on work, with a plan, I realized that my revelations had inspired no similar disclosures about his past. 'What do I know about him?' I asked one long afternoon when he was gone for hours, supposedly trying to drum up some work. He was employed by the gas company. He has been renting a room from a retired schoolteacher. He loves sweets and movies and looking at the moon. I knew next to nothing about Nate Hunter's life.

"I felt like I had glimpses of these key things that allowed me to know him in a way you hardly ever get to understand most people. But then, when we were out there, away from Salt County and our lives, in some kind of suspension, I started to feel like I couldn't zero in on him. He was stretched out, all long and beautiful, with those bony knees and elbows and his polished, hairless head and chest, taking up all this space, but I looked at him and he seemed to be a huge blur. And I would wake up and try to focus in on something about him or what we were doing, but everything around me and everything inside was a jumble."

She admitted to Sunday what she had come to understand. When he told her she was his fantasy, he hadn't lied. But what did he know about moving love from fantasy to real? Before they went to bed at night he asked her to recite their story. "Tell me," he commanded, and she obliged: ". . . postage stamps and chocolate . . . soul mates . . . forever you and me." Nate loved his idea of Delta, loved "all the ways you feed me," he said. But when she expressed her own desire and need, he realized that he didn't "get to be himself" around her. She cramped him, she taxed him. She was demanding, sensitive, hard-to-please. The expectations, all of the expectations, were more than a man could bear. If her presence, or some reverberation of a conflict, invaded his newspaper reading or his morning push-up routine, if her expectations or hurt interfered with his determination to speak and act in the way he saw fit, she had disturbed his pleasure, and for that she was to blame.

"The aspects of my body he had once praised," she said, gesturing at her breasts, "he began to criticize. He took issue with my hairstyle, my clothes, my everyday, common underwear. 'What about those lace things,' he asked me, 'with the string in the back?' He started interrupting me, teasing me about little sore points, like my waistline and my way of saying 'I'm not sure.' And sometimes, when I was talking, he would turn his back. I felt so confused, Sunday. Confused about even the order of events, or how we had gotten there from the rooftop, about how I had all of a sudden failed to please."

And yet . . . and yet, she told Sunday, she had felt so alive in the unpredictable, careening blur of Nate, gasping as she competed with the wildfire for air.

It was a relief to get her story out, but the last part was harder, still, to tell, and she hadn't even shared it with Dinah. As she got out to clean the windshield, Sunday watched her clenched face through the glass and noted her deliberate strokes. Delta got back in the car and blurted it out. "Sometimes . . . not always . . . he liked to . . . well . . . blemish me, too."

"Blemish you?" Sunday ventured, again afraid of the answer. "What . . . do you mean?"

Delta rolled down the window. "I'm sorry, I know I shouldn't with you cooped up in the car, but I'm gonna need a cigarette."

Sunday nodded and reached out to get one for herself. When they were both exhaling deeply, Delta continued, "It started with him going at it kind of hard. She looked at Sunday. "You know, sex, and I'd be sore sometimes. And then there were hickeys, and those things I thought were kind of turn-ons. They were urgent, you know, even the little bit of hurt or soreness was a reminder of our passion from the night before. And then . . . well . . . he bruised my neck."

Sunday's lifted eyebrows asked her question for her.

"With his hands. And then, one night, he bit me . . . on my breast."

Sunday swallowed and tried to breathe. She wanted to vent her outrage and curse Nate Hunter, to vow that she would find him and make him pay, but she wasn't sure if showing how appalled she was would make Delta feel monstrous and even more ashamed. She crushed out her cigarette and moved over to place her arm around Delta's shoulder.

"I let him do it, Sunday, and that's what I can't figure out."

"Yes," she answered, trying to think of what to say. "But every one of us draws the line somewhere different than we think we would. What matters is that you're not in it, you're not there anymore."

Delta let Sunday hold her, reversing the roles they had known in childhood, and then finished what she had to say.

"You know, later, just before I left him . . ." Sunday breathed a sigh of relief that she had done the leaving, and not the other way around. ". . . I decided that one thing about his face was clear. His eyes were like mouths. I swore I could almost see, deep within them, a kind of smooth and fleshy pink, edged with the sharp white ridges of teeth."

Horrified by the image, but impressed with Delta's imagination, Sunday clutched her sister's shoulder with one hand, and tightened her hold on the map with the other.

"He liked to watch me while I slept; that was when I was in my 'full beauty' he said. And when I asked him, more and more, what our plan was, where we were going and how we would support ourselves, he started telling me he 'needed quiet,' cutting me off in the middle of a word with some piece of information about the weather or some statistic on unemployment he had seen on the news. I would ask him things and he would refuse to answer, saying, 'I'll tell you what you need to know,' or . . . or, 'You've asked me that before.'"

With the comfort of Sunday's arm around her, she recounted how the day she left him in a mildewed motel room with pressboard furniture and paint-by-numbers art was the day he went too far. In a round of afternoon lovemaking, she had surrendered to the opening, to the heat, and adrift in their mounting pleasure, Nate above her, around her, Nate within her, time stilled and the world was, for a short while, peopled only by the two of them. The bed beneath them had become a raft, its surrounding sheets rippled water, and lost in his exorbitant kisses, his fingers, his thrusts, she had surrendered to the deep, brown expanse of him, until he brought it to a halt. In the midst of loving, pushing deeper, he had covered her mouth with his hand.

Delta glanced at Sunday, pausing for a moment before telling how the passage of time resumed, returning her to the tawdry room in an instant, taking in all at once the creeping ceiling stains and mass-produced, framed landscapes, the cobwebs and torn lamp shades and chipped, fake-wood furniture. The bed was just a bed. The sheets were sheets, and not too fresh. Paralyzed in the sudden and airless reality of the moment, she had looked up into his mouth-eyes, and bitten into his hand as hard as she could.

Freeing herself from his body as he pulled away and screamed, she had scrambled to collect her things, warning him with a restraint that was glacial never to contact her again. "He knew I meant it," she told Sunday. "He didn't reach for me, or say a word.

"I caught a glimpse of myself in the dresser mirror," she told, "blood on my mouth like a picture of an Asian goddess I once saw in a book. And then I slammed the door and crossed the street to get a taxi to the nearest town. And I wondered, while I waited for the taxi, if Nate Hunter knew how infectious a human bite can be.

"We were both shocked when I bit him, and it was terrible. But staying would have meant my silence, and in this family, there had been far too much of that."

After locating the tissue box on the floor behind her seat, Delta carefully removed and folded eight tissues. Half of them she put in her pocket and half she gave to her sister. "You never know about these bathrooms," she said, "it's best to be prepared." Sunday watched her enter the gas station, approach the Plexiglas-enclosed counter, and reach out for a key that dangled from an Illinois license plate. When she disappeared behind the metal door, Sunday put the map in the glove compartment and got out of the car, shaking her head at the things people went through, fighting back tears for Delta as she waited her turn in the bathroom.

Once they were back on the road, Sunday began talking. With everything Delta had told her, she could surely find a way to disclose her own problems. "You know, Delta, it may seem to you like everything in my life is right, up there in Chicago pursuing my grand calling and having found my man. But I've been having a struggle of my own, and though I don't mean to compare it to what you've been through, I haven't been able to talk about it either."

She tried to explain why she had left so abruptly for Chicago, fearing that Reed would lose his patience, and she would suddenly lose the best chance she had ever had to be known. And then she said, "Lately . . . I haven't really been working. The fact is, Delta, that for the first time in my life, I haven't been able to paint. I haven't been making anything at all."

Delta was surprised at the alarm she felt, and she consciously controlled the impulse to speed. "But are you sure? Oh God, I sound like Laveen Walker. What I mean is, are you sure it's not just below the surface, about to break through? Have you kept trying?"

"Trying? Of course I've been trying." She noticed that her voice was shrill.

"I'm sorry, I didn't mean to say you wouldn't . . . either be trying or know. But what happens? I mean, do you stand there holding a brush and nothing . . . nothing comes?"

"It's not quite like that, though for a while, after I got your note, it was. Now, some things come, but only up to a point. It seems I can work with some colors, but not with blue."

"Blue?"

"When I try to use any kind of blue, or when I add colors that begin to approach it, I get stuck. It's the damnedest thing. After not being able to do anything at all, not even the drafting and paste-up money work I've always done, I was waiting and waiting for some shift, some small rupture to break things open so that I could see or speak differently, and in fact, I'm not sure if it's a matter of sight, or speech, or both. But things would just not open, not even a crevice. And then I had a burst of being able, where things just poured out of me onto the paper and canvas. And then . . . I couldn't work with blue. I'm locked away from it. Painting, but not with the full palette. I feel like I've regressed or something, like a child with a limited vocabulary. Like a stroke patient who's lost certain parts of speech, or at least access to them."

"But don't artists have phases when they only use certain colors or techniques. Like somebody or other's blue period, right?"

"Yes. It would be okay if a certain color or method called me. I would go for that. But this is different. I want blue, and I might even say it's calling me, but I can't reach it."

"Well . . . don't you think it will pass?" Delta asked tensely. "Don't you think it will just take time?"

"On its own? I hope so, Delta. But I decided it wasn't going to happen without coming home."

"Oh, I see," she said, concentrating on the road. So that's it, that's why she's back. She wasn't sure whether to be hurt that Sunday hadn't come just for her, or comforted to know that home and the people connected with it could play such a powerful role in her sister's life.

Sunday saw Delta's face tighten up and realized what she had said, and the way it had been misunderstood. "What I mean," she added, choosing her words carefully, "is that Salt County, which is home, my people, and you, are all necessary to who I am. And the painting comes from there. I'm beginning to understand that I need all of it. Everything and everyone I am and have been."

Sunday circled back to her reasons for returning to Chicago. "In the same way, when I left the other day I felt like I had to get back to Chicago. I was afraid I couldn't be both places. If I was here, I would lose there, and vice versa. But things were just how I had left them. My work was still there, unfinished. It hadn't disappeared or magically completed itself. And Reed was still there, along with the bounty there is between us, and the hard stuff, too."

"Well, no one can run, can they? We're carrying the whole mess around, whether we want to or not, underneath the daily stuff."

They both thought of the anger and injury that Laveen had been holding. They both thought of the range of things they had tried to deny or forget.

"You know," Delta said, "here I go about fire again, but bear with me. I've heard that coal mines deep down in the mountains can ignite. Well, those mine fires don't just die out. They can keep going for ten, or even twenty years. Even when you can't see the fire any longer, they say that sometimes, you can see smoke coming off the mountains, from the fire burning down below."

They decided to leave the highway and make the rest of the trip to Clare County on small, country roads, Delta at the wheel and Sunday plotting their course with the map. Again and again they met the meandering river, tapered to a fordable stream or coming into view, wide and churning once more, flaunting its power to give and take. Which parts of the land, they wondered, had been marked by flooding, along with Salt County? Sunday found it thrilling that they were still in contact with the water of their growing up, "our river," she called it, and when Delta asked her which they were tracking, father or river, she laughed and answered, "Both."

They could feel the intractable silence of winter arriving. Through the car windows, they saw the leaching of light, as fields, and trees, and even painted barns relinquished their color. Pulling their coats closer and their collars high, they turned in and toward each other, and Delta brought up something she knew Sunday must have also thought about. "Don't you think it's funny that he died so near to home? Could he have been this close all along, and us pining for him, imagining him just a ways west, along some little branch of our river? In the same farm and factory land?"

Before Sunday could comment, she went on, "Well, I've also wondered about this. He . . . Mercury . . . ended up so near where he began, as if his life had almost made a circle. And having made that almost-circle, I wonder what flashed before his eyes when he died. If what we get is a chance to relive or come to terms with our lives in that just-before time, what do you think he was thinking about the beginning and the end points of his?"

Sunday considered the question. "Maybe he thought of himself as having two lives. The first one ended when he left us, and that's where the second one began. So maybe what you'd have to ask is, at the end, what was he thinking about the two beginnings he had? And then another question is, where would he mark the transition point? When he stepped out of his shoes? When he knotted in the ring? At the moment he made his decision to leave, or when he crossed the county line?"

"Well, I wonder. Maybe Mr. Woods will be able to tell us those kinds of things."

"And maybe he'll know how Mercury looked back on it all, on whatever it was he did right after he left, and in the later years. God, it's hard to believe he's been breathing, eating, and sleeping all this time. For all we know, we've got siblings; Clement Woods called him 'brother,' after all. And I've been wondering what was going through his head as he made his plans to leave. How long did he have the urge to do it, and did he wait until nightfall to slip away?

"He must have moved fast," Sunday said, "to get away without being seen, hiding along the way. I'm curious, too, about what he said to people about who he was, to keep word from getting back, unless he went really far, and only came this way recently, just before he died. Do you think he might have been planning on coming the whole way, but fell sick? Do you think he meant to reach Salt County before he died?"

"Who knows. I'm sure there must have been lots of lies. Lies or evasions and silence. I mean, how did he explain his situation, at first? How did he ever explain it to himself?"

They were quiet for a stretch of road. "He must have been in a quandary," Sunday finally said.

Their giggles started low and welled up through their bodies until they were laughing hysterically, from the belly, and had to pull over onto the shoulder of the road.

"Oh hell, did I leave the tissues back at the gas station?" Delta groaned, searching unsuccessfully in the backseat. "I can't seem to find them. Now I'm in one. Quandary, that is."

Their laughing and weeping took them in waves, and they gave up on containing any of it. Gradually, they grew quiet.

"Whew," Delta said, wiping her face with her sleeve, "I don't know when I've laughed like that. I think I even snorted a few times. That felt mighty good."

"You did snort, and I enjoyed hearing it as much as you did making it."

They rolled down the windows and let the last of the tears dry, feeling the car tremble as an occasional car sped past. A chuckle erupted now and then, until Delta sighed and started the car. "I guess we'd better get going, if we want to reach there when we said we would. And maybe, if it's okay with you, Miss Sunday Owens, we could have some chicken and deviled eggs."

14

WHEN THEY REACHED the three-room brick bungalow with the address Clement Woods had given them, Delta kept on driving.

"Hey, where are you going? That's the house."

"I know. I know it is," she said as she turned the corner. "I'm not sure what happened, but I just couldn't stop. I'll go around the block." Having done that, she eased to stop out front and made a case for having a cigarette before they rang the bell. "He might be one of these health fascists, for all you know, and I won't get to smoke until we leave. I'd better get one in while I can."

They got out and looked at each other over the roof of the car, making the crossed-finger sign that cemented their oath.

Clement had watched the dated and immaculate LeMans roll past and then reappear, from the blue velour La-Z-Boy recliner by his front window. He watched them sit inside the car for a full five minutes, one smoking and the other squinting through the window at the house. What would they be like, he wondered, and what would they expect of him? They were undefined characters in a tale he had heard, where even the teller had had little to go on. When he saw them emerge from the car, he hurried to the bathroom before answering the door.

In the mirror he saw a shaved, slackening face and a trimmed mustache. He saw a man who was nervous, wary of what was to come. Quickly, he patted on some aftershave, straightened his collar, and shoved in his teeth.

Delta followed Sunday up the walkway and hung back while she knocked. They both waited, hands in their pockets, until the door cracked open and Clement Woods's face appeared, backlit by a living room lamp. They considered one another from inside and outside, the partially opened door between them.

The sisters hesitated before the tall, heavy-set man in jeans and polished boots. Although on the phone he had said he expected to hear from them and told them they could come, his face resembled a shuttered housefront. Was it the eyes themselves, Sunday reflected, that made a screen, or the heavy eyebrows, which met to guard the bottom of his face? Maybe it was the stilted mouth, inured to disappointment of some kind, she thought, seldom known to celebrate. When he spoke, she saw that a set of ill-fitting dentures was partly to blame for the unyielding appearance of his face.

"Come in," he said, looking away and stepping back to let them pass. "You made good time."

They introduced themselves and Sunday focused on the furniture and ornaments for what they might tell her about this man. Anxious that he not take offense at her scrutiny, Delta reached out to touch her arm, but Sunday pulled away and approached a series of photographs on the wall. "These are striking," she said, reaching in her pocket for her glasses. "Who took them?"

"I did," he said, his voice filled with apprehensive pride.

"Oh yes," she said, remembering his telephone listing, embarrassed that she had lost sight of the fact that he had his own story, this man, apart from what he might know about Mercury Owens.

"My line's photography. I've got a shop down the street. Mostly, I do portraits, since that's what pays. But in my spare time, I try to take some of my own."

He stood back, both pleased and uncomfortable with Sunday's attention to his work, and while she studied the mounted photographs, he took the opportunity to study her. What, he wondered, did you call that cape-looking thing she was wearing? He looked at her deep red hennaed hair, the many rings in her ear, and then glanced awkwardly at Delta, who stood rigid by the door. She was dressed all prim and homey, he thought, except for those earrings. Her hair was disciplined and her clothes were sensible, but there was something else about her, something different underneath.

When Delta turned to him, a long-established comfort with the ways of men spread through her, stirring, also, the abandon that slept beneath her tamed exterior. He was so close that she could identify the

Lifebuoy soap on him, and ironing, she could smell that, too, along with a hint of spray starch. She noted that he had ironed the creases in his jeans.

"Let's see," he said. "Why don't you have a seat and I'll get some refreshments."

As he rattled around in the kitchen, they scanned the room for indexes of the man who just might have answers about their father. Delta concluded from the simple furnishings and scant decoration that Clement Woods had no steady woman in his life. The recliner's velour and caved-in bottom told her that it was his seat of choice, and across from it sat a television on a block of wood. In a pair of aged metal milk crates, a lamp, and a set of stereo components, Delta recognized the essentials of an even, solitary male life. She couldn't help thinking that Nate Hunter's furnished studio apartment had been just the opposite; while he had owned no furniture, he had collected dozens of small trinkets, antique bells and enameled boxes, candles and chunks of quartz, signs of a man in tune with pleasure, who was on the move.

Sunday stretched from the corner of the brown tweed couch and tried to peer into the other room, whose door was ajar. Unable to make out anything beyond the edge of a bed and a worktable that was covered with camera equipment, contact sheets, and a light box, she considered a trip to the bathroom to check out his medicine cabinet, and deciding to wait until later, she returned her attention to the living room.

Although the other walls were bare, one displayed the black-and-white photographs that had drawn her as she entered. Clement had shot furnaces and car engines, boiler rooms and clockworks and coiled pipes, the pilings and wires exposed by splits in plaster walls, and the mechanisms of a telephone. In the mysterious and intricate innards of his subjects, he had found and captured an ordinary poetry.

He appeared in the doorway, holding an unopened jar of instant coffee in one hand and a box of Lipton tea in the other. Glancing at him from the couch, Delta decided that he was between fifty and fifty-five, he had never been married, and he was the loner type. She could sense his unease and his longing, and she knew she could reach him if she tried. Sunday opened her mouth to ask if he had any herbal tea, but checked herself and chose coffee. Delta said, "Coffee for me, Mr. Woods," and he went back to the kitchen to make it. When he returned with cups he had bought that morning at K Mart, and the jam-filled coffee cake he had settled on after puzzling over and over about the right thing to serve, he couldn't help but apologize: "Nothing fancy. I guess I lead a bachelor's life." Unzipping the cardboard strip to open the windowed box that held the coffee cake, he added, "Barely domesticated, you might say."

"It looks great," they both responded, then Delta asked, "And have you ever been married, Mr. Woods?" impressing Sunday with the way she went straight for the information that was always her greatest concern.

"Never," he declared, and then steering the conversation away from himself, Clement said, "Like I mentioned on the phone, I figured, sooner or later, you'd call. Thought maybe you'd even come. But now that you-all are here, seems mighty strange, since we're really strangers. I know the two of you in connection to what your father told. You're almost like a story, come to life."

They nodded in unison and he offered coffee cake.

"And how was it that you came to know him?" Sunday asked.

"Came through the door of my shop one day."

Although he tried not to, he glanced away. Telling the tale he had pieced together was going to be harder than he had imagined, but he could also see how needy the two women before him were. One was gripping her mug with both hands, and the other was fidgeting with her eyebrows and clenching her jaw.

"Came in my shop, and the thing that impressed me about him was that he seemed so definite, so . . . sharpened, as if everything in him was all built up and right at the top of him, getting ready to burst out of his lanky body. Didn't have to do or say anything; he was just that way, full of energy, even standing still. I remember thinking he looked like an exclamation point. Well, I'm a man who lives quiet, and keeps to myself, so I wasn't sure what to make of this man when he showed up."

"And how long ago *was* that," Sunday asked, "that he came in your shop? Did he make his home in Clare County for a while?"

"Three years ago he came to town, but I don't imagine he ever made his home anywhere."

Delta's anger flared at the sympathy she heard in Clement Woods's voice. "You do know the truth about his desertion," she said, emphasizing the middle syllable of the last word, "I gather from the note you sent?"

He took a moment before answering. "I know about it, though it took a good while for that to come out. He was close to the end by the time he told that part."

"Yeah," Delta practically hissed, "I bet he was. At least you . . . a stranger, I might add . . . were told the truth of what happened, if it was the truth."

Clement frowned, and his eyebrows became a protective, wavy line. He shifted his dentures around with tongue and jaw, as if trying to reconcile Delta's fury with her restrained exterior. "Doubtful. Doubtful, I'd have to say. Truth's never the same for two people, do you think? As for the waiting, I figure he wanted to tell me right away. Matter of fact, looking back, he always did seem to be on the verge of speaking it. I don't think he had told anyone until he told me, but you might say he led with that fact."

They sat quietly, digesting his speculation. Delta smoothed her eyebrows, one and then the other, and let loose a rush of questions. "Well, did he have a family? Other children? Did he get an education? Travel? Join the circus? Learn a trade? What was he doing, Mr. Clement Woods, all the years he was dead to us?"

Clement's eyes widened as the questions surged out. He backed up his chair slightly and held out his hands with the palms turned up. "Miss Owens," he said, "I'm afraid you're getting ahead of things, all those questions at once. This isn't easy for me, either, but I'll tell you what all I know. Let's begin at the beginning, if that's all right with you."

Both sisters nodded.

"Okay . . . so he came to my shop window. Walked in, asking if I knew of a place to stay and a place to pick up some work. Now as I told you, I wasn't sure what to make of him, but I was needing a little bit of help at the shop. There was a long-traveling look in his eyes, and I must be honest, he had the mark of a smooth talker, too. His smile was easy, and if he wanted them to, the words just flowed." He looked at them steadily. "I could lie, like they do in those speeches folks make at funerals, but that's not why you're here."

Both sisters shook their heads.

"You see, he did come into my shop partly to try to hustle me for some light work, or a handout, or a place to hang his hat . . ."

"He had a hat, then?" Delta sat forward, excited by the image of his gray feather-trimmed fedora.

"I, uh, meant that as a manner of speaking, but in fact, he did. Always wore a hat, and had it on when he first showed up."

Delta smiled with satisfaction, comforted by the continuity of one remembered fact.

"So, as I was saying, he chose me, partly by accident, to get a foothold and ask for help, and probably, at that point, he was just moving through Clare County, gathering no moss. But I saw him at the window before he came in, staring at the portraits I had up. When I look back on it, I think he chose me, too, because he had the idea that as someone who takes pictures, I could fix things . . . feelings, people, events . . . in time. Maybe he had the idea that he might want, somehow, to fix himself like that."

Sunday thought about how the camera had captured Delta in the parade of school photographs.

"So he took out this gold locket . . . the one he had me send to you, and showed me the photograph it held. It was faded and tiny, but I'm used to looking at small things. 'Detail-orientated' is what they call it, so I hear. Well, I asked him who the lady in the locket was, and all he said was, 'Someone who was lovely. Someone I used to know.' Thing is, I think he might have said that about himself if he'd been in the other half of that locket, 'longside her. Got the impression he might well have said, if I had pointed to his own face, 'Someone I used to know.'"

"Did he say where he had come from?"

"I'll get there," he told Sunday, "but we may need something stronger than tea. Can I get you a drink or a beer? I got Black Jack and Michelob."

"Black Jack," they said in unison, and Sunday added, "On the rocks."

He raised his single eyebrow in surprise and respect, and Sunday thought of how Opus had pulled out her Hennessy when the story had got rough. Delta added, "Just a little bit for me, since I'll be driving home."

When Clement came back, he started to apologize for the Welch's jelly glasses, but changed his mind. "What the hell," he said, "the whiskey's good." After several introductory phrases that went nowhere, he was able to pick up the thread he had dropped: "He came in for the reasons I said, but there was something else that happened. There was some kind of tie, and I suspect we both felt it, even that very first day."

At that, the sisters concentrated on Clement Woods. They had come to Clare County to discover Mercury, but they found themselves wondering what it was about this man that had enabled their father to see himself.

"I'm not what you call an open man. Never one to go on about feelings, or to go on at all. And I suspect your father could tell we were both closed off from the world, and carrying around something that weighed a lot. It's not that we had all that in the forefronts of our minds, though, or that we got to telling, really telling about ourselves for a good, long while. But what I'm aiming to say is that I think he recognized something . . . down below the surface, something buried in me."

Clement told how he had offered Mercury some work cleaning up his shop and arranging the studio for portraits, and had put him in touch with a woman in town who rented rooms. And when he had shown a facility for working in the darkroom, Clement had expanded his duties. Mercury had been eager to help and to prove himself, offering to do extra tasks and asking about how the camera worked, and they had taken to walking together and tinkering on the engine of Clement's flatbed truck on weekends. Before long, Clement had come to depend on him at the shop, and Mercury had moved in to share his house.

"Seemed like he could fix most things. Machines especially. Fixed a broken camera for me, and knew all about vehicles. Said he had built himself an engine once, from scratch. Said he worked better in the open, with fewer rules and regulations, and less supervision. So I gave him things to do and let him alone. He always got them done, though he spent his share of time dreaming and relaxing, too. Said he believed in breaks and naps. Found him stretched out and asleep one time, under the truck. Said couldn't nobody bother him there."

Delta wanted to go back to what he had said earlier. "So you knew he had something, as you say, 'buried,' too, but you didn't know what it was?"

"That's right."

"And you weren't moved to ask, Mr. Woods? Didn't you want to know what kind of man you had working and living with you? I mean what if he had done something violent? What if he had committed a homicide or some other violation of the law?"

Clement lifted his whiskey glass to his mouth, steadying it with both hands. "You might say I don't ask questions of other men," he said, "that I wouldn't want to answer myself."

To Sunday's relief, Delta backed off. Her preoccupation with the drama of criminal activity was out of hand, Sunday thought. She and Earlene were probably doing surveillance on their neighbors for evidence of buried bodies, racketeering, money laundering.

"Now, I'm not an educated man," Clement went on. "High school's as far as I went, and even in taking pictures, I'm what you call self-taught. But I do know something about people, 'cause even though not many folks come through my home, they come to my studio for sittings, and I study them and try to make that camera catch something of what's inside. And what I can say is this: I knew he had a hurtful past.

"Oftentimes your father would mutter to himself about 'wanting' and 'desire.' Or he'd just say one of those words and shake his head. I've been thinking about this a lot lately, and it was like he was looking back at his life through a little window, like the one in a camera, that would open for a fraction of a second, now and then. That window was just about the size and shape of wanting, and I'm not sure if I can explain it, but you might say he was looking at himself through that lens, through that very idea."

Delta and Sunday both knew about wanting, and they knew how tangled it was. "And where did his wanting take him," Sunday asked, "over all these years?"

"When he first left, he went west, he said, one town at a time. Got himself to Kansas City first, before stopping, and then pushed on, town by town, through Kansas, then Colorado and Utah, moving away little by little, until finally, he got to California, and there was nowhere else to go. In those on-the-way places he did cleanup and drove a delivery truck. Took him two years to get to California, and he stayed close to ten, picking fruit and laying cement, and driving trucks. And then he learned to be a mechanic and worked at a garage. When he first come into the shop, I asked him where he was from, and he said, 'Everywhere. Nowhere,' and gave his name as Percival Jones."

"Who?" both sisters asked.

Clement remembered they wouldn't know about that part. "You see, I didn't know him as Mercury Owens till later, though that's who he ended up being for me. Told me he'd changed his name. Told me how, but didn't tell me why.

"Turns out that on his way to Kansas City, he stumbled upon the black section of a graveyard and ended up sleeping there one night. The next morning, he woke up and started getting caught up in the names. Said he knew it was a black folks' cemetery 'cause some of the stones made mention of slavery. It was at that point that he stood in front of a marker that read . . . wait, let me get it right . . . Oh yes, it said, 'Percival Jones. Born a Slave. Died a Man. 1843 to 1929.' He stood there wondering about the life of that man, looking at his name, and he decided to take it for his own."

Clement saw the startled anger in both sisters and held out his hands. "I'm not defending him, mind you, and I can see what you think of what he did. No doubt it was dishonest, but he said since the man was dead, he couldn't see how it would hurt him. And after all, he told me, people named their children after folks to honor them, and maybe taking that man's name was even a compliment. In any case, somewhere, on his way to the West Coast, he found a way to get himself ID that had his new name."

Sunday asked Clement to stop and repeat what he had said, and both sisters thought of their recent visit to the cemetery. Delta recalled all the people she had envisioned and known, Mr. Essex Block . . . Sumner Wells . . . Rowena Tyler, who were being remembered. There was no end to Mercury Owens's criminality, she thought, for he wasn't merely a deserter or the "deadbeat dad" of the century, he was a thief. Sunday was overcome, as well, with the knowledge that her father had claimed a name for himself, as she and Nana J. had done. But it was different, she thought, that place in her stomach burning, it was clearly different. While her effort had been a widening act, his had meant a narrowing, for by dropping his name, Mercury Owens had tried to erase all links with his family and his past. He had left behind his own, and he hadn't stopped at that. He had taken someone else's life.

"So according to him, Mr. Woods," Delta asked, "he just stole another man's name and wanted himself across the country for thirty-six years?"

Clement poured himself some more whiskey. "To hear him tell it, yes, he did. Wanting kept him going, but it was never satisfied, 'cause you see, he moved too much for that. Said he drove and walked, hid in the backs of trucks and rode the rails. Hitched rides and when he had the money, he traveled by bus, or train, or even, a few times, plane. And did all kinds of odd jobs, hiring himself out as a laborer, on construction. Custodial work. Did whatever needed doing, I guess. Then, like I was saying, he learned more and more about mechanics and fixing cars.

"Got as far away as Mexico, which was too bright and sunny for his liking, and Alaska, where he went to work on the pipeline, hauling and digging, deep in the earth. Loved Alaska, he used to say, where in the winter, there was the shield of night all day. 'Fugitive's what I was,' he said, more comfortable in darkness than in the daylight. Though no one was chasing him, he was always running. Always on the move. Said he didn't know what was constant in his life, besides regret."

"His E's. He made his E's the same."

"What?" Delta asked.

"In the note he sent and on the back of that picture by the river, he wrote the letter E in the same, exact way. That's something that was constant."

Delta rolled her eyes. "Okay, Sunday. At least we have that. Go on, Mr. Woods."

"Wait. I want to ask did he know whether folks back home considered him dead?"

"For a while he didn't know, he just kept going. But then, the next time he was back this way, he went to a library and searched through newspapers to find a notice that said he was missing and presumed drowned. Said it was a mighty strange thing to read about your own demise. That's the word he used, 'demise.' So he kept moving, and had a rule to never stay anywhere longer than a year. Day three hundred sixty-four he started packing his sack, and the next day he was gone. And he saw almost the whole country. Put his feet on the soil of all but three states, Hawaii, Rhode Island, and Vermont."

"What an achievement," Delta said, rolling her eyes again. "Did he ever come back this way before the last time?"

"Said he would go a long way, and then, like he couldn't help it, he would return to Illinois. He left, and came back again, time after time, getting close to Salt County, but never going the whole way there."

Delta thought of the way Grandpa would have viewed Mercury's departures and near-returns. She could imagine his commentary: "That boy never could follow through."

"But he stayed put here for those three years?" Sunday asked.

"Not quite. Left after he'd been here six months, but was back in a couple of weeks. Said he had gone to Indiana to see a man about some money. When he got back he said, 'All my life I've been leaving, and making my way back to the place I tried to escape. I've got to admit that I've been haunted by that river out there. It always seemed to pull me back.'"

"'The River's Invitation,'" Delta thought. There was that song again.

"Said his mama named him Mercury, and whether she knew it or not, it was the name of a Roman god, who stood for, along with other things, travel. And, boy, did he. Traveled his entire life. Also said though he took Percival Jones and was ever mindful of him, he never stopped thinking of himself as Mercury. Said it was 'bout the only thing he had from his mama, when all was told."

The room was suddenly too quiet and too hot. Sunday removed her glasses and folded them into their case, and then she stood up, urging Clement to stay seated, and said she was going to the kitchen for ice, leaving him and Delta to figure out how to talk to each other while she took a break. As she forced the ice cubes from a tray and filled a bowl, she felt the heavy silence in the other room. She had noticed the tension between them before she left, and was intrigued to see that her sister hadn't lost her access to the male heart. Toward Delta, Clement was awkward and vaguely adolescent, which was strange in a man of his age. Sunday figured that chemistry with men was something basic, and Delta had always had an elemental understanding of the moorings between men and women.

When she returned, Clement resumed his story: "Now he never could have spelled out what all he had been doing all those years, but I got the feeling that in the end, he didn't think it amounted to much. After all, when you spend all your time leaving, you never really do get anywhere.

"So I can't begin to fill in those years for you. Hell, we didn't even really get to any deep talking till the end. Men are that way together. We talk real good about basketball and women. We tell jokes and shoot the shit, pardon my expression, about happenings. But it's hard to go deeper down, you know?

"He did say the best things were done out-of-doors. Picking fruit and vegetables, digging and working construction, tinkering with engines in an auto yard, driving the open road. Whatever made him feel less closed-in, that was what he liked the best. The one thing he promised himself he wouldn't do was work at a bag plant or any other factory, if he could help it, was what he said. And even though the stuff he did for me was mostly inside work, the more he got interested in picture-taking, the more it seemed the same way. It was a going out, he said, even if you did it by going in. Another thing, too. Mercury talked a lot . . ."

Delta interrupted to ask something she had often wondered: "Did he ever marry? Were there children, other than us?"

"Said he decided never to let anything get that far. Now I'm not saying he didn't have women, and I wouldn't be surprised to know that he lived off the generosity of more than a few, 'cause he had that sweet charm and he wasn't bad-looking, I mean if a man can judge that about another man." Sunday noticed how intent Clement Woods was to let them know that his relationship with Mercury Owens was purely one of brotherhood. "Like I said he hadn't wanted any ties, and as soon as he felt them growing, he was on his way."

"So he didn't have another family," Delta said. "Did he . . . did he know anything about us at all?"

"Said he read the county newspaper, whenever he could get his hands on it, whenever he had circled back close. And that's how he found an article that said your mama had died, and told him that you, Sunday, were a girl, and what you had been named."

Sunday and Delta looked away. Neither one was going to touch that, and Sunday swore to herself that she would not offer her suffering in exchange for whatever Clement Woods was going to tell.

"As I started to say, your father kept on moving, and he talked a lot about how he spent many a night sleeping under the stars."

So, Sunday thought, on some evenings she and Mercury Percival Jones Owens just might have been looking up at the same night sky, squinting to recognize constellations among the jumbled pinpoints of light.

Clement poured Jack Daniel's as he talked. "So he went a lot of places, back and forth, back and forth, and then he found his way to this little piece of Illinois with the same river, or a branch of the one he had known. Then, a year ago, he started feeling poorly. Turned out he had a bad heart. Had one attack that laid him low. He never recovered from that one, and just got worse. It was during that time that he seemed determined to get something, his story I guess, fixed."

Hoping he had left something even more concrete, Sunday asked, "And did you ever take a picture of him, Mr. Woods? Did he ever, as you say, fix himself that way?"

He shook his head. "Talked about it. Brought it up more than once. But I think he couldn't do it. Couldn't decide to set himself down in time and space, since he'd been in motion all his life. And his vanity wouldn't let him decide to be remembered at that very point, when he was old and worn-out and sick."

"And did he take any pictures, from behind the camera, I mean?"

"One roll of film he took, after learning all about the technical aspects, you know, light settings, developing, and whatnot. But he was dissatisfied with how it came out. It was all landscapes, and he didn't feel he got the spirit of it down, or got the light or the composition right. 'All unremarkable,' he said, 'not a single one outstanding in the bunch.' I tried to tell him that a photographer takes many, many shots to get one good one, and after all, it was his first try. But he couldn't seem to stand that he didn't make something beautiful the first time out."

"I see you've told us some about how he was trying to outrun what he had done," Sunday said, finding her glasses and putting them back on, "and what I want to know is this: Was he successful? Did staying in motion give him just some kind of shapeless sense of loss, or regret, while he outran the particulars? Did he avoid everything specific except our mother, who'd been 'fixed' in time in that locket, at age sixteen?" She was talking fast, using her hands for emphasis. "In his note he said, 'I remembered,' but if that's true, what was it that he never forgot? I guess what I'm trying to find out is, in just what way did he feel regret?"

Clement nodded. "Early on, before I knew what was deep in him, he talked about that time just before sleep, when you are what you are. Said when he spent six months in prison for petty larceny, he felt the same thing." Delta shook her head and muttered, "Mmmn," as if to say she just knew it, she knew he'd had encounters with the law.

"It was a process of taking away, and 'How are you going to survive this?' was the question you asked yourself. You had your wits, your body strength, your imagination, and everything you had done. All your acts. None of the outside things counted for much, because everyone in there had done wrong, and you couldn't get rid of yours. Matter of fact, your wrong was the very reason for your presence in that place, and your fancy house, or your diamond-studded watch and car, the fine lady on your arm or the split of champagne you always ordered . . . even your reputation or your college degree didn't matter very much, once you were stripped down to the same clothes everyone else had on, owning nothing and closed up in a little cell for home. What made you who you were was on the inside, was in the choices you had made.

"Point is, your father said he felt that same way every time he stretched himself out for sleep," Clement added. "That was when he paid the cost of wrongdoing, like a nightly tax. He was owner of nothing, stripped down to the nitty-gritty, to his flesh and his deeds."

Delta and Sunday both knew what Mercury had meant, how in that time just before sleep, you were divested of all trappings, unable to rely on those things that protect you in the waking world. Delta tamed her nighttime chaos with conjured objects, with moving from bed to bed in the hope that she would lose herself. And Sunday knew well how the things people fought and tried to dodge could surface as they were waiting for sleep. But she wasn't sure that every life included a space for answering up.

She had always wondered about the ways people found to accept and think about the things they had done, and Nana had said she thought folks came up with all kinds of stories to understand and justify their deeds, and that, just as surely, some people didn't think about things much at all. Sunday had wanted to know for certain that people had to reckon for what they did, at least with discomfort or guilt. "But, Nana," she had lamented, "in some kind of way, people should have to pay," and Nana had said that there was payment, there was. "It would be easier and fairer if God sent obvious punishments that fit our crimes, or if we had proof of inside suffering and coming to terms. You want a justice you can see." And then she had asked Sunday if she didn't think there was a kind of payment in merely living a life that was mean or small.

Sunday had accepted Nana's wisdom. For some, there would be no conscious reckoning. But if it did happen, she thought it occurred on that borderline between waking and oblivion. In that span of time, still and silent except for your own bloodbeat, you were faced with the person you were.

"One evening," Clement said quietly, "when we were talking about those nights, he said, 'Clement Woods, I've told you my recent life, about what brought me here and what I was into before I came, but I haven't told you the early part. What's a story without the beginning?' he asked.

"I got us some drinks and tobacco, and we settled in. 'Most of my life . . .' he said and then stopped, rolled a cigarette, and started again. He looked me in the eye and said, 'Most of my life has been about desire.'"

Clement returned to his last days with Mercury and did his best to tell his daughters the things he had learned. He used other-sight to take them to Mercury's bedside so that they could hear what had been revealed.

As the sisters had been told, Mercury had read avidly of foreign lands as a child. He had traced the outlines of other countries from library books, putting in the rivers and mountains and roads as he imagined the tastes and scents of tamarind and curry and peanut stew, the feel of desert sand on his bare feet, of thin mountain air and ocean spray. And he drew maps of fictional places, with volcanic craters and languages only he could understand, aching for the day when he would break free, vowing that he would leave Salt County and see the world, as soon as he was old enough. After school he built models of trains and rafts and boats to carry him away and into life, plotting his route across the Gobi Desert and down the Amazon. And when his aunt Edna forced him to go to bed, he lay and felt the wanting expand and contract within him until he could finally fall asleep.

At night he dreamt of the mother he had almost forgotten by day. There she was, calling his name, her body shaken by its consumptive coughs. There was her softness and her pain, and the gut-aching hunger that had consumed their nights. And when he cried out and wakened, there was the aunt who had taken over. Edna, with her chapped hands and thankless work. Edna, who did her very best.

Friendless as they moved from place to place and left alone while

Edna worked long hours at her dry-cleaning and laundry jobs, he made up solitary games with cards and words, and drew on paper, cardboard, magazines, the backs of scavenged envelopes. He built playthings from discarded springs and bolts and chunks of wood, and sat at the tracks down by the bridge, getting so close to the trains that were leaving and arriving that he could see the sparks and smell the hot metal of the tracks, could close his eyes and feel the wind the trains made against his face while rushing by. Each one he envisioned bound for some place with its own mysterious landscape and customs, waiting to be explored.

Mercury wandered around Salt County, absorbed in dreaming his constricted world into something else, trying, trying to leave his mundane reality behind. Each puddle he stepped over became a continent or region of the globe. "Now Saudi Arabia," he said aloud as he hopped them, "now Antarctica."

And then, crossing into the white part of town where Aunt Edna worked, he thought he would die of yearning. He watched her leave the dry cleaners, bent-over tired and hands raw from wringing steaming sheets and feeding them into rollers in oppressive heat. And in the bowed walk of steady, determined Edna, he saw a defeat, an acceptance, that made him want to ball up his fist and punch and punch and punch at everything in his path. She made her way slowly home, and he turned the other way, to find what else there might be to try to choose.

After-school deliveries of groceries and prescriptions took him into the homes of prosperous white people, and on those visits, he was amazed to see the ways that other people lived. He tuned out the deprecating questions and looks in order to find out what they had in "the other group," discovering that he, too, wanted a wide green lawn, neatly edged with impatiens, and a bubble-shaped car that gleamed with chrome and a spotless shine. He wanted a maid who would make him dinner and use the back door. He wanted tall windows with a view.

As he roamed through town he wished for countless things, but most of all he burned to climb up casually next to a bank president, place intact soles on the iron footrests to order a shoeshine, and give a handsome tip.

Mercury wanted to know what success felt like, and could imagine its texture and taste, and as he gazed across the line at the lives of the fortunate, he decided that maybe he could get those things for himself. He could have a home like that to return to while he traveled the world. And one day, after he had seen everything that lay out there, he could fill that house with a family that was his.

When he first saw Dolora in world history class, he noticed her attentive face and quiet, determined note-taking. "That girl's patient and accepting, she's not a dreamer," he thought, but when she raised her hand and spoke, he saw something else. When she talked about ancient times she was radiant, and he felt a sense of longing in her, coupled with a sense of exile, and although Mercury didn't quite understand the source of her excitement, he wanted to be a part of it, to cause the transformation of a shy, old-fashioned girl like her.

He dreamt of pulling those tortoiseshell pins from her twisted-up mass of hair and watching it come down in his hands as she gently scolded him. He wanted to make her laugh and see her face light up as he came her way. As he started walking her home from school and taking her out for a movie or a stroll, he was overwhelmed by his prosperity, for she believed him; she believed in him. As he talked about his plans to see the world, he was certain that she looked at him with admiration for the arrogance, the magnitude of his plans.

His hunger for her grew, and they began to spend every weekend together, even if she had to lie to get out of the house and meet him at the riverbank. He delighted in convincing her to break her household rules and defy the order of her world, but soon her reverent company was not enough, and he clutched her urgently at the door of her parents' home, pressing his hardness against her, whispering his longing, as Dolora felt a beating aliveness, his hands and his whispers awakening her to her own wanting. His "You will if you love me" became a challenge she wanted to be adequate and adult enough to meet, and she was part of his huge desire to have, to know skin against skin. She acquiesced, her appetite increased by fear, and they met again and again in the back of a borrowed car, until she found herself desperate at two missed periods, just short of finishing school. And it seemed to him that at the moment when she told him she was pregnant, she became the enemy of his desire.

Mercury had tried to convince her to travel to Chicago with him and find someone who would "fix her up," but she had refused, terrified by the stories she had heard of infections and bleeding. He would never forget the cold, condemning eyes of Mr. Lomax Blount as they sat together on the couch before him, confessing the news of their mistake and the life that was growing out of it. At the same time that Mr. Blount expected him to "do right by her" and marry his daughter, he seemed to have written him off. But Dolora knew how to stay and face her family; she knew how to follow through.

While he had felt some warmth and understanding from Mrs. Blount, Mr. Blount never gave him a chance, treating him, instead, like a sorry loser with whom his daughter was now burdened. And the question of love had seemed to be irrelevant; duty was what they discussed. They should make the best of things by marrying.

"We never even talked about love," Mercury thought, "love never even came up." He wasn't sure what he would have said, or what he even felt or knew about it, but he would have liked for it to have been raised. He would have liked for her father to have asked him, "Do you love her, boy? Do you care for my daughter at all?"

Her father's eyes were with him, had become her eyes, and as the years wore on in their sameness, they made him desperate to escape. He was sure that she watched him closely from the moment he came through the door, as if she knew he might try to flee. He was pinned, like an insect, by the wings. She no longer believed in him, of that he was sure, and he could feel her scrutinizing gaze, even when he was away from her, at work. But the eyes of the girl in the gold locket she had showed him on the evening of their first kiss were not the imprisoning, disappointed ones he now knew; they remained innocent and open with belief.

At daybreak he would go to the jewelry box and lift out the locket by the chain while she slept, looking in the eyes of the Dolora he had first met, seeking the freedom to imagine things as different than they were.

At first they had lived with her family, until he could save enough money to rent them a flat. And during that year, under the oppressive scrutiny of her father, he had thought he would burst with the desire, the need to be free of them and their orderly house. He had thought that everything would be okay if they could only get out on their own, but once they had managed to get their own place, all he could see were its deficiencies. It was cramped and dim and ordinary, and that came to seem too much to bear.

As he walked home he wound his way through town, extending his route as long as he could without provoking a comment or question from her. He peered into the puny windows of people's makeshift houses and saw them setting the table or talking to each other about their days, and often he stood and watched for passing touches of easy harmony, for signs of trust. They seemed to have love and belief, those other people, but maybe that was just from the outside-in. Maybe, like him, they had had no choice.

At night he built and razed his columns of solitaire, and then sat at a silent dinner table, Delta eating quietly between him and his distant wife. He went to bed earlier and earlier, and in his dreams he found himself underwater, held down and tangled in objects from his life, paper bags and children's toys and maps, trying to swim free. He heard other people's voices chanting all the things he wished he could say, and woke breathless, his lungs about to burst. There was no serenity in sleep, and he couldn't even tell his wife about the nightmares that pulled him under.

Sometimes it appeared to Mercury that his wife and daughter were united against him. He had never really been able to identify with Delta, whose name Dolora had chosen without him, asking for his assent as a mere formality. He had watched her pregnancy with detached fascination, astounded as Dolora's body changed, utterly apart from will. And once the baby was born, he was overwhelmed by the crying and the mess of diapers and food and soiled clothes. Dolora had been consumed, barely noticing him and never having time for his plans and dreams. In a rare moment of spinning out a plan to cross the ocean in a schooner, she had fallen asleep.

When Delta was just born he had felt afraid he would hurt her or disrupt things, for she was so small and soft, jerking about in such disquieting ways, her head falling back if you didn't hold it. He just didn't understand what was so fascinating about a baby, and he couldn't fathom the endless gazing and cooing in which Dolora was absorbed. At a loss for how to interact with her, he returned her to Dolora's arms as quickly as he could, and she did the feeding and the changing while he looked on.

His child seemed like some different species, unsettling him with the concealing grasses of her eyes and the way she was quiet, without ever being still. He couldn't see that she looked like him either, at least not in any recognizable way. And what did one say to and do with girls, anyhow? You couldn't throw a football with them or teach them to do boy things. You couldn't talk about baseball or women, or what it meant to be a man, or take them for their first bourbon when they came of age. He had to admit to himself that he was disappointed when she was not a boy, although he knew it wasn't her fault that she was female, and she was still his. Maybe when she began to talk and do things, he had thought, he would be able to connect.

By the time she was walking and talking, she was guarded around him, approaching her mother, rather than him, with questions and observations. He was convinced that he remained outside of their laughter and their affection, and when he did attempt to talk to her, he felt ridiculous, as though he tried too hard. Speaking to her in simple language, with a deliberate, louder voice, he tried for a bond, but she stared at him from behind the striated browns of her eyes, as if he were the child. And the things he brought home to her, in efforts to redeem his heavy, separate heart, seemed to fall flat. He would hand her the little trifle he had brought, a plastic coin purse, or a hair ribbon, or a piece of hopscotch chalk, and most of the time, she would politely thank him and ask permission, formally, cautiously, to go to her room.

Now, with another baby coming, he would never manage to get away. He would never have his life. He had tried to keep another from arriving by seldom making love with Dolora, but she was still beautiful to him, and he, after all, was only a man. So the thing he had dreaded for years had happened, and he envisioned three expectant faces surrounding him, like links in a chain.

"I am a young man," the words throbbed in him as he pulled paper bags off the rack, one after another and another and another, and slid them into the folding machine, "and I haven't done anything yet." He had barely come to manhood when Delta was born, and he had married Dolora, managed to finish high school, and stayed. She was only the second girl he had ever slept with, and although he would be able to enjoy another, and another, he would never achieve a different life. He would have no choice but to return each night to his house and his wife and his children, limited to stolen evenings that were broken before dawn.

He would never ride those trains whose heat he had felt, those planes and ocean liners he had read about. He would never see the world.

It seemed that all the things that were closed off to him lined up in the presence of his wife and daughter, their very existence announcing what was finished for him. He would never see past the paper mill that emptied into the ocher river, and his whole world would be that tight fist of a town, that house, those people and their narrow paths to the corner store and to their unremitting jobs. Their common little church with stained-glass windows no bigger than themselves. He would never climb up next to the bank president for that shoeshine, or have a broad, jewel-green lawn, and servants who called him "Mr. Owens" or "Sir."

The tan fibers of paper bags clung to his skin as he made his way home through the seared sugary smell that entombed the town. He never seemed to rid himself of the odor of the factory, though he showered as soon as he got home. Maybe it was in his skin and pores, or maybe it was part of the town. His life felt so compressed as he approached his house and his nights of silence with Dolora and Delta, that he felt it would fit into one of the brown paper lunch bags he turned out hour upon hour, day after day.

In Salt County, the rim of which he had never had the chance to see over, he would, after all, be small and inferior, a "nigger," as the foreman at the plant often said, straight to his face. "Trifling," and "no 'count" as Dolora's father described those he had written off. Those words and that life, which was not a life for a man, not for a man, pushed in on him, swallowing his imagination of himself. And yet leaving, what kind of man's choice was that? He couldn't put it together, and with no way to even voice his fear and inability, the condemning words circled round inside him, in a ring of enslaving fire, and like a scorpion, he prepared to self-destruct.

When Clement took a break from telling Mercury's story, Delta and Sunday felt a mixture of tension and relief. They were putting together what Clement had told with the pieces of information they had collected elsewhere, and Mercury Owens was coming to life as more than a father, as a child and a man.

They silently digested what they had learned, while Clement heated up the barbecued ribs and greens he had bought in anticipation of their visit. Eager to chat for a while about lighter things, they talked about how you never could get enough of certain foods, laughing as they named their favorites. Delta said she couldn't understand the concept of *enough* barbecue, and Sunday said she had to agree, for she was a vegetarian who still ate ribs. After eating, Delta and Sunday settled back on the couch and Clement continued his tale.

"Just before the end, your father asked me to go to the closet and take out his nation sack, and then to find a box inside. In the box, folded up in a piece of soft flannel, was the locket. He held it for a while, and opened it to look at the photograph within, and he recited your grandma's address, assuring me that if I sent it there it would find its way to you, whether you still lived in the house or not. I promised to send it along.

"The next thing he asked for was pen and paper, and I propped him up against a bunch of pillows while he wrote you those five words. He said them aloud for me, as he folded the sheet."

Sunday and Delta pictured the yellow paper, and wasted hands folding it smaller and smaller.

"As I lowered him back down to the bed, he explained how he wanted them sent together, the locket and the note, with whatever words of my own I saw fit.

"You know, I never did hold a man's hand before, except to shake it. But I'm telling you, I ended up holding both his hands for hours, and rubbing them, too." He looked down, embarrassed, as if unsure such acts of tenderness among men were truly okay. "I was soothing him, you know, to make the going easier, and he was getting weaker and weaker. I asked him if there was anything I could get for him, anything I could do. And he looked up at me with the most pressing eyes I've ever seen and said, 'You can listen.'"

"He said, 'I've said a good bit about myself, and it's more than I've ever told anyone. You see, I've been dodging this kind of thing, dodging myself, since I was at least twenty-four. I guess you're querying why you,' he said. He loved that word, query, and I had to ask him what it meant. 'You want to know why I decided on you to tell? Well, that I can't really explain, but something familiar about you made me decide to stay on here in Clare County. And now I seem to have stopped moving, and my time's run out. This is my last chance to own the bad I've done.'"

Clement told Delta and Sunday, "Everyone's got some bad in them, but I've known people who were mostly bad, and people with terrible things to hide. Matter of fact, I've seen a good many lowlifes and predators, and most of it I couldn't explain or approve. What's more, I've seen a lot of men fail to do right by their children, but I've never heard a story quite like his. As I tell you, I'm not judging him. Not defending him and not condemning him. Just telling you what I learned.

"He was lying there, the night he died, and little things kept coming back to him, like the slick and shiny surface of a deck of cards he had used for solitaire."

Delta glanced at Sunday, and without words, she returned to the conversation they had had earlier that day about pieces of life flashing before you at the brink, death throwing into relief the life you've led.

"He remembered the eyes of his father-in-law, and what he had seen and wanted on the other side of those windows where he used to look. Through one window he saw a boy with an electric train that ran through tunnels and along mountains. And in another, he saw a picture of contentment, made up of a family gathered at the fireplace with mugs of cocoa or something in their hands. There were all kinds of split seconds he had lived. He said he was 'reseeing' things. The cards, and what was it . . . oh yes, your mother's unpinned hair and the way her eyes squinched up and almost disappeared when she was really happy and smiled big."

Delta and Sunday realized that neither one of them had seen that often enough to remember it.

Clement pointed at Delta as he recalled something she might remember, too. "He said he could see and feel and taste those Mary Janes he used to bring home to you. He still loved them and he described your little face all sticky and your teeth sunk into them, his one surprise that had been a success. He wondered if you still liked them, too."

Delta nodded as her eyes filled with tears. He had not only taken the locket; he had kept something of her.

"About you," he said, nodding to Sunday, "he had a whole running fantasy. Said he used to picture the whole family sitting down each night at the dinner table, you all reporting how well you were doing in school and then talking about the fancy careers and houses he hoped you had. He didn't know if you were a boy or girl until you were practically grown, so he said he would picture it both ways."

They were rapt, absorbing each detail he was giving, and Clement knew he was closing a gap. But as he talked, he got carried away, embellishing what he had learned. When he heard himself say that Mercury dreamed about them, he realized he had ventured far afield of the facts. It was intoxicating, this making up, and he had moved into telling his own dreams of what life would have been with children of his own. Disconcerted, unsure if his impulse to fill things out was wrong, he stopped himself and returned to the specific things Mercury had said.

"Anyhow, about his aunt, he remembered her laundry smell and her hands. And when he was five she had taken him to a Ferris wheel that was in town for the weekend, and held his shoulder gently as they had stood in line, and as the Ferris wheel took them into the air, crested and made its circuit to take them down, they had both let go of the bar and raised their hands. Said, too, that he could picture the gray rectangular shirtboards she had carried home for him."

And Clement told another thing that Mercury said had come back to him over the years. When he was six or seven, a neighbor boy had shared with him a jar of soap bubbles, and they had sat on the back stoop. The boy had offered Mercury the jar, and he remembered dipping the ring into the pink liquid and blowing carefully, slowly, into the wet circle and watching with wonder as incandescent, fragile globes grew from his patient breath. That was perfection, Mercury had said.

Clement stared into his whiskey glass and then went on: "'It's funny what small things rise, in the end,' your father said. 'They seem to float up, like air bubbles that you desperately need, through water, and when they reach the top, all shiny, they seem to open out, 3-D and multicolored, whole, into the present.'

"Your father was trying to breathe and coughing instead, and I took his hand and asked, 'What is it, man? Why don't you go on and get it said.'

"'It's not that I've been loathsome through and through,' he said when he stopped coughing, and he mentioned that he liked that word, loathsome, and that it was amazing how many enjoyable words were coming to him at the end. 'On the other hand,' he went on, 'I haven't been awful good.' His eyes drifted away. He was thinking back over who it was he *had* been, I guess, and I could relate to that.

"'Ain't no one I know's lived a perfect life,' I said. 'Everybody messes up, man. Only difference is, some folks own their mess-ups, and some don't.'

"'Well, here I am in this fix,' he said. 'I'm not dying alone, and that's good. But I've only got this one person, who has known me for three years, to hear me out. I am grateful, don't mistake me. I guess if most of us get the death that goes with the life, then I'm a lucky man.'

"He had a fit of trying to get his breath, and his eyes were terrified. 'Man, I loved to make those maps as a kid, and I found my way these many years, across this country, with one in my pocket. I sure wish I had one for this part.'

"I took his hand, and he said, 'There was a thing I did, some thirty-five years ago, that was worse, much worse, than most of the stories I've heard. It marked a line between things, and you could date everything by it. There was life before it, and then after, everything was changed.'

"'I'm listening,' I said.

"'I couldn't undo it, it seemed, once it had been done, but I'm not gonna lie. It's bad.'

"I told him, 'Speak.'

"He said, 'You know that wife and two daughters who I had you to send the locket and note? Well, what I did was run out on them. I tried to leave them all behind.

"'One girl was five and the other not quite born. And I knew that my wife's father . . . well, not just him, probably everybody, expected something like that out of me. They knew I'd disappoint, and that has haunted me to no end, how I fulfilled their expectations, after all. I'm gonna tell you how I ran out, because that's what I did, but what I want you to understand, Clement Woods, is that wherever I went, all the things I was dodging went with me, too. I never, even for a second, forgot.'"

He hadn't planned any of it, the day he left. Walking after work to defer the homegoing, he stabbed the ground with a long, staff-like tree branch, moving toward the river, which had risen from the season's rains and seemed to ease his ache with its wild rushing. He stood at the edge as dusk came and pulled out the locket he had taken to slipping into his pocket in the morning, so that he could go to the rest room at the plant, raise the window, and look at Dolora's young and trusting face. He put it back in his pocket and kept his fingers wound in the chain. His desire had moved into new territory, and he wondered, day in and day out, why he shouldn't make his crossing complete.

Mercury pictured himself falling and then taken by the water, turning over and over in the current and desperate as he coughed and gasped, his chest a hot bursting, choosing not to reach for any solid thing that might float near him. In a flash he could picture them grieving him, his aunt and his wife, and his girl who was an alien mystery, could see them moving down the narrow church aisle, weeping in black, could see them standing at his grave. Among the torrent of things he felt was the means to choose a different ending to his life, and his power, in doing so, to make them understand and hurt.

He had thought that maybe, maybe, Dolora and their children would be better off without his appallingly small presence. They could make a fresh start without him. He wasn't any good at being a father, anyway. There would be an end to his pain and entrapment. There would be release. He knew he wasn't far enough above the water to die from the fall, but he was a weak swimmer, and he would surrender to the strength of the current, about which people were always warning the reckless. He would surrender until he was breathing water and had finally found escape. He removed his shoes and knotted in his wedding band.

Perched on the edge of the riverbank, he moved toward dying, his heart beating wildly and tears streaming down his face as he made his choice. Stepping into the air, clutching the locket, he forgot about the hat that rose from his head in the wind and followed him to the water below. He glanced at the hat and then saw nothing but the roiling yellow-brown water, and then he entered its murk and was pulled under, tumbling and gasping, panicked as he was taken, flailing to find which way the surface was. It was dark and he felt the water rushing as the pressure built within his chest, within his head, dark and dark and darker, and he was helpless in its thrall. Blind and unable to help himself from seeking air, he sensed light and broke past water, only to be pulled beneath the surface again. And as he fought the seething current, a severed tree limb rolled into view. He bumped against it and tumbled with the current, choking and gasping and flailing his arms and legs.

He bumped and grazed the log again, and then Mercury found himself reaching, reaching for that tree limb, choosing life.

After he got his arms around it, he managed to stay afloat, struggling to snag the half-soaked fedora that the water had returned to him. He took the river south and west and lay concealed amid the brush and trees at its edge until dusk had passed. With feet and hands he felt his way among the weeds and rocks and tree roots at the edge of the river, joined by the darting of fish and the sunken debris that rocked with the rhythm of its flow.

He climbed from the water, dripping and bruised and shaking with cold, amazed that he was still alive. And opening the locket to let the photograph dry, he resolved to leave all else behind.

Instead of dying, he would disappear, and let the shoes and the ring be his voice.

Finished with the telling, Clement sat back in his chair. "That's his story," he said, "that's what he told."

Delta and Sunday tried to show him that they accepted what he had revealed, but their minds were spinning. Now they had the puzzle piece that told them he had entered that river meaning to die. And all that desire, for a home and a car and a shoeshine, to what had it come? He had wanted ownership and comfort, but his life of constant motion had denied him those very things. And respect? Had he gotten that?

The sisters threw themselves into cleaning up from the food and drink Clement had served. They washed and dried the dishes and straightened the counters, and when they were finished, Sunday took advantage of the familiarity and honesty of kitchen space. "I was wondering about something you said, Mr. Woods . . . I mean Clement. You said there was a bond between the two of you, and I wanted to know about your half of that. What was the buried thing our father sensed in you?"

Sunday watched him measure what it would cost to tell as he ground his dentures together, his face shifting back and forth between shuttered and exposed, and she was struck with what a memorable face it was. It had relaxed and come into its own over the course of their visit. She thought she would like to paint a face such as his, with its combination of hard and unprotected, and she studied each aspect of it as he talked, trying to fix it in memory.

"Done my own piece of wrong," he said, and they nodded and stacked the plates, saving him from embarrassment and giving him, also, a way to go on. He took the plates and set them down. And then, moving toward the living room, he announced that they were welcome to stay the night and drive back in the morning, if they wished. They could use the foldout couch and he would sleep on a pallet, so that one of them could have his bed.

They looked at each other and decided, without speaking, that they needed to return to their own shelter for the night, no matter what time they reached home. Sunday followed him to the living room and thanked him, but said they needed to get back, and he tried to show his understanding by nodding his head, but he hadn't been able to close off the grief in his eyes.

Delta joined them and she and Sunday sat down, knowing it was not yet time to go. Their conversation was unfinished, and they couldn't leave Clement Woods with Mercury's account and his death still reverberating, and with no way to get his own story finished.

Walking over to his wall of photographs, he peered at the edges and adjusted them with his fingertips. Then he sat down and worked his mouth from side to side, trying to get the full cooperation of his false teeth before he began.

"Tell you what," he said, "my half goes like this. Growing up, I had a little brother, a brother by blood. I was the oldest, and it was my job to watch over the younger one. Made breakfast for him, packed his lunch, walked him to school. Taught him how to wash his hands in the bathroom, how to add and subtract, how to dribble and pitch. He was a good enough kid. Good enough. And he came to me if he was in a jam. If he was having it rough at school or getting jumped on by the local boys. Mama trusted me to do it, and she had plenty to tend to on her own. So I did as I was taught. But I thought that once he had made eighteen, my job was over, and I stopped watching."

Again, his face was open, and his eyes fresh with hurt.

"That job's never over. Not then, and not now, twenty years after he died.

"My mother never could tell me she forgave me, and I cannot forgive myself, and I didn't mean for what happened to happen. You might say I just stopped paying attention."

Clement Woods's eyes grew inaccessible. That was as much of that tale as he could manage; it had been hard enough to say what he had said.

"After your father confessed that last part, about the river, I told him the whole thing about my brother and me. I'm not even sure he really heard or understood me, in and out of sleeping and waking as he was, and I will say I've thought about it some, what my reason was for grabbing the chance to say my piece.

"I don't think it was to undo his weight, or to trade my bad for his." He watched the two women who had moved from strangers to intimates in so short a time for their reactions. "I think . . . I think we respected one another with what we told. Seems weird to me sometimes that this stranger came into my shop and stayed. He seemed to mark me so far down inside. 'What was it?' I've asked myself, that the two of us could come together like we did, neither one of us righteous or open men. But one of the things that made us brothers was our common shame.

"I know your father was a student of human nature, among other things like engines and fancy words, and I guess, as soon as he walked into my shop and we got to talking, he could tell there was something shut off in me. And maybe it was kindness made him stick around, too. Might have wanted to do something for someone before his life was done. But in the end, maybe the most important thing was speaking and hearing about the wrong done, and then seeing one another as more than that. You might say both of us got to witness, and to tell."

Delta wished she could think of something to say. She wanted to comfort this solitary man who lived out on the edge of human contact. She knew him, she was certain, for she lived there, too. She had carried the burden and blessing of sisterhood, and she wasn't even sure of the ways she had succeeded and failed.

"Yes," Sunday said for both of them, amazed, once again, at the things people endured and the ways they struggled to make places for those things. This man with the contradictory face hadn't even been able to fully disclose what he had done, at least to them, and yet she sensed its enormity, its lasting presence, and felt for him. She knew, also, that Mercury's story had become Clement's. Maybe through the card he had sent to accompany Mercury's note, he had also asked forgiveness for himself.

*　　　*　　　*

As they gathered their things to go, Clement left the room and then reappeared in the doorway. "Thought you would want to know where he's buried." He handed them a small map he had drawn on the back of an invoice from his shop. "It's a plot in the cemetery at the edge of town. Don't know if I was doing right not to send his body home, but I just followed through on what he asked. The marker has his names, is all. I'll take you there if you want, or you can use this little map to find it on your way out of town.

"And he did leave this," he said, holding out a canvas, drawstring bag. "I figure he'd want you to have it, what he called his nation sack."

"What's in it?" Delta asked, reaching for the bag.

"Haven't been through it. Didn't seem my place. But it's the bag he had when he got here, and I think it has his few possessions, the everyday things of his life."

"The little things," Delta said.

He walked them to their car and told them anytime they came that way they had a place to stay. Sunday thought she detected a bashful smile exchanged between Clement and Delta, and planned to tease her sister that she hadn't lost her touch.

"So," Sunday ventured, "you said when we got here that we were like a story made real. Are we what you expected? Are we who you thought we would be?"

"I'm not sure what all I expected, but you know your father had a lifelong fantasy going about who you might be, and I guess I took those imaginings and added my own touches. What is most clear to me, though, is the bond between the two of you. Your . . . styles . . . are altogether different," he said, gesturing at their hair and clothes, "but there's something . . . something there between you that's the same. I guess it's that sister thing that I can see."

They looked at the sidewalk, suddenly shy.

"The other thing I'll say is this. Wasn't oftentimes a whole lot to be lighthearted about. But sometimes me and your father sat up jawboning about crazy things that had happened, things that didn't make no sense. Guess there's always something to laugh or smile about, else you'll die. Thing is, if Mercury Owens smiled, his face changed altogether. Seemed like he smiled with his whole self."

Delta and Sunday weren't sure if their father's laughing, smiling face was the picture they wanted to leave with. Delta opened her door and got in the car, but Sunday didn't turn away. She wanted to ask him for a parting piece of information that would be easier to bear. They didn't begrudge him a bit of levity, a bit of happiness, but they weren't sure they wanted to drive into the night with the image of him smiling, while they had considered him dead.

Clement could feel their discomfort. "Anyhow," he said, "I figured there would be some way you would favor him. I was looking at the two of you before, when we were talking about the barbecue, and I saw that if you let them go, your smiles were total, just like his."

15

BEFORE THEY LEFT CLARE COUNTY, Delta and Sunday stopped at the cemetery and found the plot where Mercury was buried, using Clement's hand-drawn map. Standing before the stone that read "Mercury (Percival Jones) Owens," they felt grateful that his grave, and his birth and death, had been marked.

They decided to let both body and headstone stay in Clare County, where Clement Woods had paid his own respects. After all, they reasoned, the body wasn't what was important; it was the story that had counted most. But as they looked at the stone, they realized that although it accurately reflected what had happened by including both men's names, something about it still felt wrong. Did Mercury have a right to that other man's name and the past it carried? What if someone took Nana's name, they wondered, and made it hers? Did a person own the facts of his own life?

Despite their discomfort, they weren't sure what it would mean for them not to include the name he had taken, as their father had lived in some way as Percival Jones for the balance of his life. And yet, despite his outward efforts, he had never been able to stop being Mercury Owens, no matter how hard he tried.

Delta and Sunday couldn't help thinking that their father had chosen the name of someone who had accomplished what he lost in deciding to run. "Died a Man," the marker of Percival Jones had read. Maybe, in passing on his story and contacting them, he had tried to do the same. And maybe, in addition to a name, Percival Jones and Mercury Owens had shared an ancestry that could be honored at Our Cemetery.

After each one said her own good-bye, they headed home, digesting what Clement had told. They were connected to their father by Clement's story, and they were linked to him by their full smiles.

The open, deserted road felt good to Delta, bits of information and images returning to her as she drove along. She saw a child making maps and loving words, a child who played alone. She saw a man impassioned, and on the run. And then there he was, no longer a boy and unable to live up to the man's life he had somehow selected for himself. She couldn't stop thinking of him wearing that gray fedora, or of the fact that he had both remembered and told about the Mary Janes.

Delta wanted to turn off the headlights, floor the gas, and open the night with the speeding car. She yearned to put the whirl of testimony aside for a moment and merely move, possessing a present free of her parents, one itinerant, the other constant but just beyond reach. Free of sister love. Free even of the blue bowl, the button road, the box that had once held chalk.

Sunday thought about her father, longing, as she had, to transcend Salt County. She imagined him beneath a limitless, star-pocked sky, dreaming endlessly, unavoidably, of the lost source. She thought of Percival Jones's incarnations, recalling what Clement had said of Mercury's departure marking the shift of their father's entire world. In the end, two strangers, one known strictly from a gravestone and the other only at the end of his life, had helped Mercury Owens through.

As the car tunneled through the darkness, making the past present, the present past, both of them pictured their father closing in slowly on home, and then turning to take flight once more.

After an hour they stopped for coffee and Delta took a smoking break. Leaning against the car door, she breathed out into the crisp night and wondered how she could ever give up the comfort of cigarettes; they eased her into and out of herself and provided occupation, pleasure, and prop. Sunday sat inside the car, blinking in the gas station glare that had yanked her into the present. Closing her eyes, she wished she could worry Reed's spine with her fingertips or smell his neck, and imagined herself with the words and faith to tell him everything. After getting back in the car, Delta pressed her hair down from its middle part, looking in the side mirror. "Okay, then, we're ready to roll." When they pulled back on the road, Delta turned on the radio and tuned it to a 1970s soul station, thinking of Dinah's "Nappy Hour."

When they pulled into the driveway and turned off the motor, they were overwhelmed by the sudden silence and the pervasive sweet burn of the paper mill. They decided the empty food containers and extra clothes could stay in the car until morning, but they took in Mercury's sack. When they entered the house, they found an Avon bag tucked between the screen and inner doors. Earlene had scrawled a note on the bag, saying that whenever Sunday decided to return, she might enjoy relaxing with some bubble bath. They put the nation sack on the dining room table to save for later, and Sunday took Earlene's peace offering upstairs. Although they knew they wouldn't sleep, they said good night and went to bed.

Sunday looked up at the hints of sky and stars she had made and painted over. Delta looked around at the walls she had sought, only once, to leave behind.

Underneath the same roof that had been a nighttime vantage point, a spot for secrets, adventures, and oaths, the same roof that had served as refuge from rising flood-waters, both sisters tried to imagine the confinement and aching desire of Mercury Owens, through their own acquaintance with those things. They pictured him in constant motion, but never managing to outrun his life, and they imagined what it had cost him, not only to abandon them but to create and re-create a story about it that had allowed him to live with himself.

Sunday envisioned the ceiling clear and open, as the canvas it had been for her in youth. Delta closed her eyes and pictured the blue bowl, bringing it into the present in the cradle of Nana's nine and a half fingers.

Sunday and Delta worked at receiving the news that had been offered about their family and the people of Salt County who had touched their lives. About each other and themselves. None of their local drama's players, living or dead, was free of complication or fault. And knowing some of the ways in which he had paid, they tried to accept the truth that Mercury had chosen to leave them, and decided to track him no further. Now that they had him, in some small measure, they would let him go.

Sunday had read that the ancient Egyptians had assessed a person's life by whether his heart weighed more than a feather. Mercury's heart had been heavy beyond calculation, and the course of his life had surely been shaped by that weight. Sunday surmised that Dolora had known about that ancient outlook, and wondered if a sense of Mercury's pain, in the time between planning and managing to die, had caused her to select his epitaph. For her and Delta, it had become an irony: Now at Rest.

Facing death for the second time, he had had a witness, and the sisters believed that in learning his confession, and connecting it with the other pieces that had been recalled and discovered, they had heard him speak. Although in his life of endless travel he had achieved neither escape nor peace, maybe, for his daughters, he could rest.

They braved a late October rainstorm to go to Felix Harris's shop. After they entered the pungent, damp stone air of the anteroom, he emerged from the back wiping his hands, looking for all the world as if he was marked by every failure of the human race. He had been worrying about those Russian brothers. Ruthless intellect . . . confession and passionate guilt . . . brutality and the faithful quest to be a brother's keeper, after all. Felix was relieved to be called by the doorbell for a respite from the beleaguered family that lived in the pages of his book and in his head.

Felix had also been thinking of the Owens sisters since they had entered his shop a week and a half before. He could tell immediately, on seeing them again, that they were changed, although he wasn't certain how. Looking them over, he found himself coveting the jointed pewter fishes that swung, incongruously, beneath Delta's neat pageboy; they would make good fetishes for his overalls.

"We've thought about our father's gravestone," Sunday proclaimed, digging in her bag for her glasses. "But you know, Mr. Harris, before we go into that, I wondered if I could ask you something else." She was afraid if she didn't come out and inquire, she would never know what conclusions he had reached about the river's history.

Delta clenched her teeth and pleaded silently with Sunday not to push the strange and grief-laden man so hard. She was just astounded sometimes by the way Sunday stalked the things she wanted. But he didn't seem offended, just awkward and shy, and Sunday pressed on. "My sister told me about your river diving, and in fact, we saw you out there. And I was just interested to know . . . what it meant to you. Did you learn what you thought you would?"

Felix shrugged and looked at his feet. "I just wanted to see what secrets it might give up. What it could tell me of these people and this place."

He had spoken so softly that they had stepped closer in order to hear. Sunday looked at him directly, willing him to go on.

"I . . . I guess the things that were underwater tell a kind of tale. Some were really old and some were newer. Some were common and some were rare. It was the range. Things rejected in anger and love. Hidden signs of wrong.

"There were lots of familiar, everyday bits of life, and there were lost items, precious things that must have slipped by chance from people's hands as they crossed the bridge. And traces of lost lives, from accidents, misjudged currents, even hatred, I suppose.

"Some of the things that were down there were considered garbage, thrown in to defile the river, or in disregard. And some, I figured, had been carried off in floods.

"All of it said something to me, and I could picture the circumstances . . . the life that had brought it there to rest. And you know, sometimes, I imagine, the very things people had once forsaken might have haunted them, and they either wanted them back, or to see what had become of them. Somehow, even though they were down there, under all that brown water and mud, they had lived on in memory. What people thought and hoped . . . and maybe even dreaded I would find . . . and what they came to claim . . . that has told a tale, too.

"It's all been in there," he said, looking from sister to sister. "I even threw a few things in that river myself," he said, thinking of the abandoned lipstick stub and brush of his vanished wife.

"So," Sunday asked, breaking the quiet, "is it a great river?"

He looked her in the eye, deciding if her intent was ridicule.

"Yes," he answered. "In its own way. It brought people from bondage . . . it delivered goods . . . the current's often powerful, and deceptive. It's connected to bigger, to other things. And it's got a life. That is to say it tells a small, but basic, tale."

After answering, Felix looked at Delta. He wanted to ask her something, but questions were not his way. He looked away and conquered his shyness, "Didn't you come to the river regular? Around midday or so, this past July?"

She touched her eyebrows with her fingertips. "Yes. I was interested in your effort. And, you know, I've wondered what happened to the stuff you found."

"People have claimed some of it. Some of it I've got out back. And the things the county decides are garbage get taken to the dump." He hesitated and then spoke again. "What brought you down there? What were you looking for me to bring up?"

Sunday watched her sister, curious to know what she would say.

"I really don't know, Mr. Harris. I wasn't looking for anything I could ever get back."

"No," he said, "I don't suspect so."

"I do know someone, though, who was looking for something she lost. Could she come and look out back?"

He nodded. "Certainly. Certainly she could."

Sunday leaned on the counter. "Can I ask you something else, Mr. Harris?" He jammed his hands into his overalls and lowered his head slightly. He had done more talking in the last half hour than he had in years.

"Why do you wear them?" She pointed at the pocket where his safety-pinned dime and other trinkets trembled.

Felix Harris studied her cautiously, and Sunday thought she saw that he had decided she was some kind of kin.

"My grandmother gave me the dime," he answered. She had to bend close to hear him, his voice was so quiet. "She said it would keep me safe. I didn't and don't question the truth of that, I just wear it and always have. It's a kind of amulet, you call it. A prayer for luck or peace."

She nodded with respect.

"The others are trifles I've picked up along the way. Found things mostly, little things with no meaning to anyone but me. I just keep them. They name where I've been, and they're part of the same prayer."

He rocked from foot to foot, shoving his hands beneath the bib of the overalls and bringing them to rest on his stomach. Although he felt himself in uncertain territory, there was something in their candor, their story, their curiosity, that encouraged him to speak.

"You know . . . I'm a historian of sorts, and I keep records of a kind on the work I do. I went back to my book after you came the last time. And I'm not accustomed to asking questions of the people who come to me, but this time, if you wouldn't be offended, since you asked me several things, might I ask you something, too?"

Sunday's heart lurched and she looked at Delta to make sure it was all right if she spoke for her. "Certainly. Ask away."

"What happened came back to me when I looked at my records. So how is it that you are redoing the headstone, when he died so long ago?"

Delta and Sunday each willed the other to explain. "For us," said Sunday, "he seems to have come back to life, and we want to commemorate that."

Felix murmured, "Un hunh. I've heard a lot of strange things in my lifetime, and my grandmother believed without question that people could come back to life. She would warn me that restless spirits sometimes roamed the earth. I wasn't sure if she was talking fact or not, but who am I to say it isn't true? Un hunh," he repeated, "just let me know what you need."

"We will, but before we do, will you tell us what you've got in your records, about the stone you made?"

"Well . . . there was a sketch of the design and the inscription she ordered." He hesitated, uncomfortable with their focused attention and sorting through what had surfaced as he consulted his record book for what to tell. She had been so young and lovely, Felix had remembered, but she had been brittle and strained, too, and she had seemed distant, never looking directly at him the whole time she was there.

"She came in to order the stone," he said, "but she wouldn't sit. And she explained how she wanted the center of the stone to have a love knot she showed me from a library book, and I remember it was hell to carve. And she wanted the marker to be double-wide, with a blank place for her own information to be added, 'when the time comes,' she said. She had no idea what her own epitaph would be, but she knew just what she wanted to say in memory of him."

Felix paused again, recalling that when she said the name to be carved on the stone, he had realized that her husband was that suicide he had heard about from someone who had visited the shop. Even though he hadn't known Dolora or Mercury, he had been disturbed by the news of a black man giving up on his wife and kids. And when he had found out, from the inscription she ordered, that it had been two years since her husband had died, Felix had not known what to think.

When she told him that she had just ordered a plot, he realized that the body must have only recently been found.

"She wrote down the number of the plot for me and asked me to install it on my own."

"Yes . . . ?" Sunday sensed his hesitation and urged him on.

He looked at the two of them, wondering if he should tell the most memorable detail.

"There was . . . one other thing," he ventured. "It wasn't in my notes, but when I looked in my record book, a particular sight came to me, entire."

They stared at him expectantly, and he wanted to tell them, in case it mattered, in case it would somehow help. "I got to Our Cemetery at nightfall, to put up the stone, and she was the only one around . . ."

"She?"

"Your mother, Dolora Owens." He took a deep breath. "She was on her knees, with a garden trowel, digging a hole."

"What was she burying? Could you tell?"

"She had two pair with her, one that was run-down, for work, and the other that was Sunday-best. Shoes. She was burying shoes."

Felix Harris came out from behind the counter. Unable to bear their stunned silence, or the responsibility for having caused it, he offered to make them coffee or something else to drink.

When he got back with two glasses of iced tea, Sunday steered the conversation back to their decision about the headstone. She told him that instead of replacing the one he had carved before, they would leave it standing, and add two more. On their mother's they asked Felix to carve a pair of tile-fitting hands and the words, "Dolora Blount Owens, 1938–1979." Their father's stone was to read, "Mercury Owens (Beholden to Percival Jones), 1938–1997," and under that would be the words, "Never Forgotten. Never Forgot."

When deciding what to do, they had acknowledged that since Dolora had ordered the joint stone, it didn't seem right to remove what she had done. They wanted to honor her truth, while respecting the others they had been given.

"Let's face it," Sunday had said to Delta. "Each and every one of us makes the story she needs."

*   *   *

305

After Delta got the recipe for honey whole wheat bread from Opus, she and Sunday gathered bowls and pans and measuring cups, and cleared the kitchen countertops. They planned to bake one loaf each for Opus, Laveen, Felix Harris, and Earlene. And they would send two by overnight mail, one to Aunt Edna and one to Clement Woods. They put on a tape of blues ballads that Dinah had made, and Delta took the blue bread bowl from the cabinet where she kept it safely wrapped in towels.

"This bowl's been big in my life lately," Delta whispered as she held it in her arms.

Sunday stopped opening packages of flour and turned to face her, noticing the tremor in her voice. "I remember it, too," she said.

She held the bowl tighter, adding, "It's more than that," and Sunday waited for her to speak.

Delta took stock of the familiar things in her kitchen, the toaster cover and the half-moon handles and the canisters she knew so well. She said, "Okay," and began to tell about her practice of closing her eyes and remembering things into being, beginning, always, with the blue bowl. She told how she made her ordinary objects real in ceremonies of recollecting until she could see and smell and touch the things invoked.

Sunday nodded, looking neither surprised nor disapproving, and said that she was doing something similar in painting: picturing symbols and images or bringing them up from some stored place inside, and then making them concrete again, on canvas or paper or linen, rather than keeping them in her head.

She asked what kinds of things Delta pictured, and Delta told about the blue chalk box with which she had begun, and about the clay fishes and the housecoat buttons, the records from Dinah, and Mary Janes. And she told how when the bread bowl filled her hands, it brought whole pieces of the past along with it.

Together, they remembered their times with the Bread Ladies, each one filling in her own details, and as they kneaded and turned and oiled their loaves, they felt themselves returned to those afternoons. Singing along with the music, they thought back to the Bread Ladies, to the meditation and ceremony of their efforts, to the flow and order of their task. As they worked the bread dough, simultaneously in the present and the past, Delta and Sunday realized that what went on in Nana's kitchen on Saturdays was as much church as the things that happened on the Sabbath, under the roof of their little house of worship.

Their bonds to churchgoing had weakened long before. Although Sunday and Reed talked about missing the kinship and the rhythms they remembered from their childhoods and wondered about finding a church where they could fit, they never managed to go. Delta went on Christmas and Easter, but it seemed to deepen her grief for Nana, and she couldn't help but feel disconnected and slightly foreign, judged, even though her sexual life was her own secret.

As Delta mixed flour and yeast in the blue bread bowl, responding to the trouble and joy in the music, she thought about the conjuring she had just revealed. Maybe that imagining was her own way of going in to the live place, and of healing. Her own language of remembering and praise. She thought of the bread-making and the things Sunday and her mother had done with their hands as devotional, and she wondered if her conjuring, also, might be a kind of prayer.

They got home from delivering their bread as dusk was falling, and Sunday looked up at the roof.

"Let's go up," she said, touching Delta's arm.

"Up?" Delta asked, and Sunday responded, "To the roof. Nate Hunter's not the only one who can get you up there, is he? Come with me, like you did that other time."

They were laughing so hard as they climbed through the bedroom window that Sunday almost fell, but they got up and out there and settled back against the slant. As they looked at the night sky, Sunday pointed out one of her favorite constellations, Pisces, and told Delta how that gathering of stars stood for the return to the great ocean from which life first evolved, where all boundaries are dissolved.

They could see the stars, and they could see the river, gleaming from the moon and the smattering of downtown, man-made light.

"Look," Sunday said, sitting up, "the water. Seems like it's always within sight. Someday I want to travel it, by boat or inner tube or raft. Any kind of vessel will do. Maybe Felix Harris will ferry me, familiar as he is with river navigation. And I want to see where it meets up with something bigger, with the lake and the sea, even if it disappears beneath the earth before it surfaces again."

Delta looked at her quizzically. As close as they were feeling at that moment, she could never quite anticipate the caliber of her sister's passion. Sunday was really out there on her own sometimes.

"Delta, do you think a person could be the child of the ocean, having really known only river and lake, having grown up landlocked like we did? I've only seen it a few times, but I think maybe the ocean's deep in memory, beyond even what we've known in our lives.

"I bet you didn't know this, but there's water under most of Illinois. And I like the idea that there's water connecting things, even underground."

They were quiet, and Sunday lay back against the roof, barely able to contain her longing. She wanted so much, painting and Reed and family and so much else, that her body seemed at times unable to contain it all. Stretching out her arms as she had done in youthful yearning, she wanted the blue of the night sky and the ocean, of a beginning place that was vast and eternal. Of somewhere that could mend.

A few days later, Delta and Sunday loosened the drawstring neck of Mercury's nation sack. Knowing it would be their last communication from their father, they had saved it for as long as they could. They took turns removing Mercury's possessions, one by one.

There were jeans and khakis, T-shirts, sweatshirts, and a pullover sweater. One expensive dress shirt, still in its package, and a pair of woolen slacks. Delta smelled the clothes, curious to see if they would strike her as familiar, but they had the faint and unrecognizable aroma of the aftershave they found in his toiletry pouch. Sunday went through the pouch, thinking how it was a variation on her practice of reading people's medicine cabinets; maybe she had been preparing for just that moment. The possessions told her that he was clean-shaven and that he had dyspepsia, sensitive gums, and hemorrhoids. Wow, she thought, this kind of thing will demystify even the most cryptic man.

Underneath the clothes, they found a well-worn dictionary, with many words underlined and comments in the margins. And they found a rubber-banded shoe box holding smaller things. Delta pulled out a film container filled with orange seeds. They didn't know what to make of them, but they had clearly been special to him; perhaps he had once grown an orange tree, Delta conjectured, and the seeds had come from its fruit.

"Maybe so," Sunday said, removing a fistful of Mary Janes and handing them to Delta, whose eyes filled with tears.

"Well, he traveled light, didn't he?" Delta said when they reached the bottom of the bag.

"I'll say. For you, he had the candy you had shared, but for me, he was stuck with imagining. I might have been a painful, vacant space, or I might have been anything he wanted or needed me to be."

They stood at the table with their father's belongings, impressed with how peculiar it felt to be touching the personal possessions of a man they hadn't known. When Delta started returning the objects to the sack, Sunday said, "Let's add to it. Let's put in other things."

They spent hours talking about their contributions, and how the addition of each thing changed the assemblage. First they put in Edna's letter, of which they had made photocopies for themselves, and then Delta got the packing envelope from Clement and emptied it. She put Clement's sympathy card and the repaired and folded note from Mercury back in, but kept the locket out. They had decided, instead, to include something of the woman their mother had become, and to reclaim the innocent and hopeful one who had been lost to them. For that, Sunday volunteered the mosaic coaster she had brought from Chicago in her pocket, and Delta pressed the locket into her hand and said, "You take this, then. You had even less of her than me."

"What else should be included?" Sunday asked, and they sat and thought for a while. Delta went out to the car and got two maps, the one of the roads that had taken them to Clement, and the one he had made to direct them to the cemetery plot.

They added a shirtboard in honor of Aunt Edna, who had mostly done her very best. And in the name of the common and all-too-human desire for something fine, they added the silver belt buckle, mono-grammed with the initials of his given name.

"Put something in there of you," Delta urged Sunday, "to go with the Mary Janes," and she selected a pocket-sized *Field Guide to the Stars and Planets* to represent the night skies they had unknowingly shared.

In memory of the inescapable past that had helped to form him, they added a brown paper lunch bag with a half-moon notched away, which had been made by the local plant.

"We need something for the river," Sunday said, "that's what's missing," and Delta recited the lyrics to "The River's Invitation" for her, with particular emphasis on the last line: "Come and make your home with me."

Sunday suggested that they get a copy of the song and put it in the bag, and then she noticed the pewter fish tails swinging beneath the neat roll of Delta's hair. She had worn them every day since they had gone to see Clement.

Sunday touched her sister's jawline gently. "Delta, I know those earrings really aren't you. They're bigger and way more theatrical than you like."

Delta laughed. "Well . . . I might not have picked them. They're more what you would wear. But you see I've had them on, and I like it that you gave them to me."

"Nana said I always gave the gift I would have chosen for myself. Remember that time I bought you charcoal pencils for your birthday? Well, I wouldn't mind if you sacrificed them to the nation sack. To signify the river, if there is, indeed, life down in that murk, as Felix Harris reports."

Delta examined Sunday's face to make sure she would not be hurt, and then took them off. It was a relief when showing your love didn't mean trying to be someone you weren't. "I'll give one fish to each of them. One to his sack, and one to Mama's wooden fig box."

"Good. I like that. And since we're adding to her box, let's make an exchange. Let's take a few of his orange seeds and include them with her things."

They seemed to be finished. Sitting on either side of the table, the bulging sack between them, they gave it a final meditation.

"I know," Sunday said, jumping up to get paper and her fountain pen. Let's make Nate Hunter count for something, and give Mercury Percival Jones Owens some words he would like." In elegant blue calligraphy, Sunday wrote out the words they selected, and Delta folded up each one and placed it in a sealed envelope. Delta decided on TRIBUTARY, inspired by Felix's dive. Sunday picked ULTRAMARINE, her favorite shade of blue. And together they chose QUANDARY.

They found a place for Mercury's sack in the attic, and decided to improve in one more way on the fig box Nana had put together for Dolora. After going down to the corner store to buy a lottery ticket, they tuned in to the local TV news, waiting to see what the winning number would be. They laughed together with delight as the numbers were announced, even though they hadn't won, and put the ticket in the box.

Knowing that she would soon leave for Chicago, Sunday began to straighten up and restore her room to the state it had been in when she arrived. And then she rolled up her awkward sketches and watercolors, which she had earlier relinquished to Salt County, and slid them into cardboard mailing tubes to take with her on the train. After finding a box in the basement, she bought tissue paper and bubble wrap for Dolora's mosaics, which still lined the bottom of the wall, and as she started wrapping them, she found that their wooden backs were marked with faint pencil signatures.

"Delta," she called from the landing, "come up here and see what I found.

"There's another way to tell how they relate," she said. "Her signature changes over time." When they arranged them by those gradual variations, from a bold and upright "Dolora Blount Owens" to a series of slanting, wavy lines, they could see that their memory of the order had been mostly right. The masks, it seemed, had been the last things she made, and each of them decided to keep one.

Through her signed mosaics, Dolora had demonstrated the belief of her beloved ancient Egypt that the dead live on and on.

With each gesture made and each thing settled, Delta knew that Sunday moved a step closer to leaving. She ached when she contemplated again occupying her house alone, moving from bed to bed and resisting her ghosts. She tried to forestall the separation by thinking of things she and Sunday could do together. They went out to dinner at the Rice Bowl and to the movies. They played cards and shopped for food and drove to a nearby mall where Sunday convinced her to buy a formfitting, turquoise dress.

One evening, while doing dishes, Sunday told her sister she would return to Chicago the following day. She explained that she had to get back and make some money, and she had to face her life and work. Her promise to return when the gravestones were installed made neither one of them feel better. Too disconsolate to talk, they played tonk and watched a rented movie.

Her mind only partly on the game, Delta tried to figure out whether to take her last opportunity before she left to tell Sunday about Dolora's silencing hands.

When Delta thought of Clement saying that their father had been visibly burdened both by his choice to run and by all the consequences of that act, she thought, also, of the many things his desertion had set in motion, about which he had never even known. Mercury hadn't been aware of those reverberations; he hadn't known about the silences and silencing his choice had brought about.

While she waited her turn at tonk, Delta looked across the table at Sunday. Her eyes were tired and distant. Her hands had never been so free of paint. As Sunday studied the fan of cards held by her left hand, the fingers of her right traced absentminded circles on the tabletop. Delta wanted to get up and take her on her lap, as she had once done, or sit her on the floor between her knees to oil and plait her hair. She tried to step outside of her own grief about Sunday's leaving, to think about the challenges awaiting her in Chicago, and in that moment, Delta decided that there was territory between total silence and unbounded speech, that not everything need be disclosed.

There was still something she could do to watch over her. She would choose to carry what she had witnessed on her own.

The next morning, Delta opened the screen door and stuck her head out to address Sunday, who was having her coffee as she rocked in the porch swing, wearing pajamas, house shoes, and Delta's coat.

"Get dressed, girl. I'm taking you somewhere."

Sunday opened her mouth to object, but Delta held up a hand. "No ifs, ands, or buts. There'll be coffee where we're going, so get ready."

When they got to the door of A Joyful Process, Sunday stopped and asked, "This is where we're going? You brought me to the beauty shop?"

"That's right. Remember now, for many years after Mama entrusted it to me, I used to do your hair, and I thought as your big sister, I'd take charge of that one more time. Don't worry, I'm not pushing you to change it or get it processed, I'm just giving you a treat."

Sunday decided to surrender her attitude and accept Delta's gift. After all, what woman didn't like to have her hair washed? They entered the shop just as Otis Redding's "I've Got Dreams to Remember" was playing on the box.

"Dinah, meet Sunday. Sunday, Dinah. That's after Washington, not Shore."

Sunday understood that she was being introduced to her sister's truest friend.

"It's a pleasure," Sunday said, stepping forward. "I've heard about you, but I didn't know you did hair."

"I sure do. It's my belief that beauty is a lasting business. And it's a pleasure to meet you, too, Sunday Owens, an artist from up Chicago way."

Sunday climbed into the chair and turned to Delta. "Thank you, Sister," she said.

She was grateful for the luxury she seldom allowed herself, for she cut her own hair, and she couldn't remember when she had relaxed and had someone else do it. As Dinah worked the water and the soap through her hair, Sunday leaned back and closed her eyes. She heard the familiarity and care between Dinah and her sister as they caught up on ordinary news, and the murmurs of other women who had a moment to themselves. She took in the aching voice of Otis Redding in the background, and the sound of water as it poured on her scalp.

She was too lost in the music and the water to hear Dinah confess that she was still trying to come up with a song that would express what she had told her the week before about Mercury Owens's bogus suicide. "I may have to make one up, Delta, and this could be the beginning of a songwriting career. For the life of me, I just can't think of a song that will do your daddy justice."

"Just wait, girl. There's a lot more to tell."

Delta drove Sunday to the train station and they stood on the platform as night began to fall. Delta wanted to hear her say again that she would come back before too long, and Sunday wanted to encourage Delta to visit and meet Reed, and to reassure her that she would find a man who was different from Nate Hunter. But when she ran those statements through her head, they sounded idiotic and falsely blithe.

As they waited for the train, Sunday tried what she had learned from Delta about conjuring. She pictured the frown lines on Nana's face as she taught her about the quick, where music and art could reach her, and along with that face came the praising church choirs that had inspired her name. Attached to that was a kitchen filled with black women, creating sustenance and song.

The night before, when approaching sleep, she had closed her eyes and tried to let her imagination go, and she could just about see the river, connected to an ocean. Looking down from above, she could almost smell and taste its salty water, and could almost picture the whole of it.

When the train pulled up, they hugged for a long time and then Sunday boarded . . .

She settled into her seat, reaching out to touch the cardboard tubes that contained her drawings and the suitcase at her feet, which held the mask. Although she had relinquished the belt buckle and the coaster to the nation sack, she had the riverside photo of her parents in the inside pocket of her coat. As the train jerked and slid from the station, she saw Delta wave, and then sit on a bench, and then fade from sight.

Although she had set out to find their father, she had begun to recover the rest of her clan, as well. Dolora, Grandpa and Nana, even the Bread Ladies, living and dead, had been revealed. Their efforts had even pulled in Earlene Hall. She had found a way that could lead her to Girl Owens and Sister. To artist, lover, and kin. It was almost too dark to see, but Sunday could still make out the sights that marked the distance from home to home.

Delta sat on the platform bench long after the train had gone. She lit a cigarette, fighting back the barren feeling in her chest that had swelled every time Sunday had ever left. She would go home and attend to a loose floorboard she had noticed the day before, and then, in a couple of days, she would return to the post office. Her sister was gone again, and she would have to fit together her own truths about the exploration they had made.

She hadn't meant to undertake a search, but had only wanted Sunday to come home and live the return of Mercury Owens with her. And she had been pulled along by her sister's quest until they were a team.

They had made some crossings and named some things. With acts of invention and remembrance, Delta and Sunday had made a different story. They had prayed. Together, the Owens sisters had chosen things that were little and big.

They had found out how the time for naming had been lost and come again, and discovered enough about Mercury Owens and his weighted heart to let him rest.

He had spent a lifetime on the run, transporting, despite himself, all those things he had sought to leave behind. Along with his single memento, were the judging eyes of Lomax Blount, his abandoned wedding ring, and all the windows through which he had stood and looked. There was his desire, and his solitude and shame, and a hollow where a family might have been. His past was with him, sometimes buried, but never gone, and he had been marked by all of it, not least, the river that had moved both ways.

And like Mercury, Delta and Sunday Owens were learning that in life there may be leaving, but there is no leaving behind.

Trying to Pray

This time, I have left my body behind me, crying
In its dark thorns.
Still,
There are good things in this world.
It is dusk.
It is the good darkness
Of women's hands that touch loaves.
The spirit of a tree begins to move.
I touch leaves.
I close my eyes, and think of water.

JAMES WRIGHT

ACKNOWLEDGMENTS

I would like to thank the Corporation of Yaddo, The MacDowell Colony, and *Callaloo,* in which part of this book appeared.

I would also like to thank Dorothy Anne Hicks Lee and George Victor Lee, Charles Rowell, Robin Lewis, Ellen Miller, Martha Hoefer, Magda Lynn Seymour, Deborah Atkinson, Renée Raymond, Evelynn Hammonds, Alexandra Shields, Claude Summers, Carla R. Dupree, Faith Hampton Childs, and Gillian Blake.

And in memory of Lee Goerner.

WATERMARKED

DISCUSSION POINTS

1. How does Helen Lee set up tension and familiarity between Delta and Sunday? Pick a few examples of how the author uses body language, description, and interior monologue to provide the reader with a deeper understanding of the characters' discomfort with one another. As a jumping off point, review Sunday and Delta's discussion of their mother's mosaics in Chapter 6. How do they interact with each other? Are they really talking about art?

2. What is the role of the Bread Ladies for Dolora, Delta, and Sunday? Do you agree with Miz Opus Green when she says of Sunday's difficult relationship with Delta, "All families have these problems; they can't stand each other and they care, both"? Examine some experiences you've seen or had in your own family, how this notion manifests itself, and how you've been able to move past the difficulty to build more understanding and trusting familial relationships.

3. Discuss why Sunday is fixated on "staying only three days" in Salt County. Why do you think she reminds herself of this over and over again?

4. In general, what purpose does it serve for people to hold on to a story and use labels to retell a few facts again and again? In *Watermarked,* in Salt County, why would Sunday, "always be a story others needed and told?" See Chapter 3 and discuss how Sunday realizes that "she doubted Dolora had ever been free of the label of 'abandoned wife, raising children of her own.'" In your own life, do you label others yet find yourself resistant when others label you? Why? What happens, in Chapter 11, when Earlene and Sunday rehash the old experiences and feelings between them and really talk about their feelings for one another (see the paragraph that begins, "Earlene searched Sunday's face to see if she was deceiving her")?

5. What did you think when Mercury returned the locket and when you read his note, "I remembered and I paid," in Chapter 2? Compare how the sisters react early on to the news of their father's having been alive all these years with their reaction later, after they hear Clement Woods's story. What do you make of Clement's explanation

of why the locket—containing Dolora's hopeful, youthful picture—meant so much to Mercury? What is the significance of Mercury leaving his work shoes with his wedding band tied to one lace? Why does this cause the sisters so much pain?

6. Explore some of the significance of the river that runs throughout the story. What is stonecutter-and-river-diver Felix Harris's role in *Watermarked*? Even though he's shy and reclusive, how do his avocations have any relationship to Mercury's transient life? What is the significance of the hanging "charms" on his overalls? How do they remind you of Mercury's returned locket? Why can't Harris give up his dredging project? What is he looking for? Examine Felix's explanation of the things he finds in the water in Chapter 15. How does this tie Felix to Sunday, Delta, and Dolora? Why does Delta watch Felix dive, day after day?

7. Consider how art is woven throughout the story and extends from Dolora to Sunday. Examine Sunday's musings on her mother's mosaics in Chapter 6: "How people brought what they wanted and could to art, and experienced it through themes in their own lives." How has art affected and impacted the book's characters? What about in your life?

8. Why does Delta say to Sunday, "Do you always paint things broken?" Discuss how Sunday views her work not as broken but as overlapping and superimposed and separate components. Is this like her mother's mosaics? Could the sisters have had this conversation before their journey to find the truth about their father? Why?

9. Explore how Sunday uses her mother's mosaics and "was interpreting Dolora and everyone else who had left some kind of trace, seeing in them what she wanted and needed to see." How does the author show that Dolora's mosaics reveal anger and pride and everything in between?

10. How does Sunday use art in her life? What does Sunday mean when she admits that "in her painting, she chose 'the quick' (that place where you're most alive and plugged in), despite its costs. How could she bear to choose it in the rest of her life?" What causes Sunday to get stuck, rendering her unable to paint?

11. Consider that Sunday is relieved when she gets Reed's answering machine instead of Reed in person; why do you think she holds back from Reed? Do you agree with Sunday when she tells Reed, "All women are angry, but most of us have learned to be polite"?

12. Why does Delta focus on the blue bowl and other cherished objects from her youth to calm herself? Why is Sunday unable to use blue? What does Sunday do when she learns about this "recall" technique from her sister, and how does this affect her relationship with Reed? How does it affect her art?

13. Discuss the difficult scene in Chapter 8, when Delta sees her mother covering Sunday's mouth with her hand. What did you think when you read this? How does this affect Delta's relationship with her sister? Consider Delta's dilemma about whether to tell Sunday what she had witnessed and her decision to carry it alone. Are all truths for telling? What are the implications of this question for your life?

14. In Chapter 13, share your reaction to the sisters' discussion that begins, " 'Don't you ever wonder,' Delta said, 'how it is that people are ever understood?' " Discuss the shift between Sunday and Delta's relationship from tension to understanding. What breaks the ice and why, and how does Helen Lee create this sensory shift for the reader?

15. Were Delta and Sunday able to control, as their mother advised them, what to remember and forget, or do you think they felt adrift and out of control because of the lack of information about their father? How did the few facts that they did have affect their lives? What happens when they learn the truth about their father and that the "story" they memorized and internalized turns out to be fiction? How does Delta's statement, "Well, no one can run, can they? We're carrying the whole mess around, whether we want to or not, underneath the daily stuff," reflect and refract the sisters' lives?

16. Discuss the role of Clement Woods in revealing the novel's themes. What do Delta and Sunday recover through their visit to Clement? Now that they have found part of Mercury's story, will they be able to release him? If so, how and why? Is it their destination or the journey they have made that is more important?

17. Explore the idea of whether or not Mercury had the right to take another man's name and the past it carried. What is the significance of the name he took? Discuss the idea of whether you think a person owns the facts of his own life or whether the survivors do. How do Delta and Sunday make the story they need. How do you?

Browse our complete list of guides
and download them for free at
www.SimonSays.com/reading_guides.html